ALL

THE

KING'S

HORSES

Faith R. Mathewson

To my parents—Thank you for keeping my eyes on things above and for never letting me give up. You kept me afloat when the waves were intent on pulling me under.

A Note to My Readers
A Cautionary Warning

For those who struggle or who have struggled with mental health —this story is not a light read. It deals very heavily with mental health struggles, namely anxiety and depression and has mention of suicide and suicidal ideation—though nothing is graphic, the depiction of depression and anxiety can be intense.

But I also want to make it known that it's not a hopeless book. Hope and light are weaved through this story.

My intent with All the King's Horses and Eloise's story has always been to shine a light on certain stigmas surrounding mental health and to bring hope to those who struggle. To show God's heart towards the broken and hurting. Not to set people back in their progress.

So I would encourage you to pray over it if you are uncertain before taking the time to read it.

For those who do read it—I pray God brings you comfort and reminds you that you are seen and known and loved. You are enough.

Prologue

It is an awful thing for a child to learn that the monsters do not live under their bed but in the hearts of others. It is an even harder lesson to learn that the scariest of all resides in your own mind. Those were two things Eloise learned quickly in life. The truth was the world does not take kindly to things they do not understand, and she herself had been a mystery from the beginning, as no one quite knew what was wrong with her.

Some simply said she was slower than the rest. Others said she had been coddled too much as a baby, and too much coddling leads to a troublesome child. One aunt simply thought Eloise was what she called an 'impertinent snob.' Only her parents—her mother, especially—could see that it was something more than slowness. Or any of those things, for that matter.

The truth was, not even Eloise knew what it was that made her feel the way she did. All she knew was that she was overwhelmed by it. Overwhelmed with an anxiety she felt deep into her very bones, down into the very heart of who she was. Sometimes she felt as though that was the entirety of her existence: an ocean of anxiety, waiting for the next wave to drag her deeper beneath its dark surfaces.

The ocean was her mind, and she was drowning in it.

To slip beneath the water's surface had not been in her thoughts as she'd readied her bath. Not even as she slipped her aching body into the steaming tub. Hand to her heart, she had wanted nothing more than to soak her muscles that were sore from the ever-present tension anxiety left her with. But, as was its custom, her mind slipped into darker places. Perhaps it was

1

for that reason she chose to go the way she did—to slip beneath the water's surface with no intention of resurfacing

Eighteen, her mind screamed. *Eighteen years old and already so war-worn.*

Eloise couldn't say what it was that made her do it that day, though it was certainly not the first time her mind had dreamed up such awful things. So many times, she had pondered the idea of ending her own life. So often, when the pain was high, when the voices telling her she would never be enough raised their ugly heads, the thoughts would come, and she would wonder: Would it be easy? Could it take away all the awfulness she was feeling?

She felt those thoughts poke at her weak mind, and the temptation they brought was near impossible to beat. But, raised in a Bible-reading, church-going family, she knew the truth: to give in to such temptation would not relieve Eloise of her pain. That one simple truth was enough to hold her back each time, giving her the push she needed to move away.

Until it didn't.

Whether she no longer believed or simply didn't care, Eloise wasn't sure. All she knew, in that moment, was that she wanted to feel nothing at all.

One

July 1867

Eloise Riley buried her head into her pillow until she could scarcely breathe. Pulling down the ends so they covered her ears, she tried to block the screams coming from the room beside hers. Her lungs began to ache, but she didn't move. Maybe she would suffocate, she thought miserably.

A dark voice within her laughed. Unlikely. Even death didn't want her. Death would be too easy. She deserved this pain.

Fighting tears, Eloise pressed the pillow more forcefully into her ears, but she could still hear them fighting. They were always fighting. Her mother, crying. Her father, swearing.

Growing up, she had become used to listening to her parents argue over her, but never had it been like this. What they had done before was minor. They had been nothing more than whispered arguments that always resolved themselves before the day was through. It was normal. What she listened to now wasn't normal. This was screaming. This was hateful.

This was her fault. Her father had always hated her, and now she'd only made it worse. She would tear them apart with her mother's defending her.

"No," she whispered. "He doesn't hate me." But she had seen her father's face when she regained consciousness. That had been the last time he looked at her. Her father would never love her. Not when even work didn't provide a refuge away from her. Not when the whispers of what she had done followed him there.

Eloise's counter was weak, still painful, but she clung to it anyway. Her father had never been able to get away from her. She was certain even before "the incident," as her parents referred to it, the men at the mill talked. She could just imagine the words they had to say about her.

Stupid. Childish. Mental. The possibilities were endless, and Eloise knew her father joined in.

"No," she whispered again. No matter what, no matter the anger, no matter the way his eyes grazed over her now, she knew her father loved her. He wouldn't talk about her like that. Would he?

Eloise bit down on her lip until she tasted blood. Of course her father would. She'd heard how he talked with her mother.

Her mother, she knew, was different. But if the man had made known his thoughts with his wife, what was to stop him from sharing them with others?

Nothing, her mind taunted. When had he ever shown compassion? Patience?

Never. At least not often.

Never.

Sometimes.

Once.

Once. It was the one thought Eloise knew she couldn't fight. Her father had never been one to understand her ways. Not in the way her mother did.

Deep within the darkest crevices of her mind, that voice within her whispered that her mother thought it too. "No," Eloise hissed, shoving the thought from her mind. Her mother was one of two people who truly loved and understood her.

When the sound of her parents' fighting grew louder, Eloise eased the pillow away from her ears before tossing her blankets aside.

"What do you expect me to do, Lily?" her father was shouting. "Uproot our lives? Quit my job? Trek us across the country? For what?" he demanded. "For the vain hope that somewhere might be better than here?"

Tiptoeing across the room, she eased the door open and stepped into the hall, carefully avoiding the creaking step.

"It won't change anything, Lily. Eloise will still be Eloise. She can't get away from the things in her head. No matter how far we go, trouble will follow her."

Trouble will follow her. Of course it would. It would be better if she was gone. Even her father knew it.

Slipping past her parents' room, Eloise tried to block out the voices from within.

"But maybe she could get better, Morgan," Lily was crying. "Maybe if we found some place more accepting. If we found good people, maybe she could change."

"She will never change, Lily. There is something in her that is twisted. You can't fix that. No amount of kindness or good people can fix that."

Unwilling to hear more, Eloise quickened her steps. Quiet or not, they wouldn't hear her now.

Stepping outside, Eloise hurried toward the outhouse, indifferent to the mud that squished between her toes. If she wasn't drowning, she would have laughed at the thought of what her mother would say. Lily hated mud.

Closing the door behind her, Eloise slid her back against the rough wood before wrapping her arms around her knees.

She will never change. She's twisted. Can't be fixed.

The waves in her mind were getting stronger, and the harder she fought, the quicker she sank.

Twisted. Can't be fixed. Another wave dragged her under, knocking the breath from her lungs. *Selfish. Childish. Grow up, Eloise.* She couldn't breathe. She was running out of air.

"God, please," she whispered. "Give me peace."

Peace. The Lord would never give her peace. She didn't deserve peace. Not before and most certainly not now.

"Please, God." Eloise rocked slightly, her mind searching frantically for the scriptures she'd given herself to cling to. The ones she'd read before bed. Settling on one, she repeated it to herself a dozen times. "For the mountains shall depart, and the hills be removed; but my kindness shall not depart from thee, neither shall the covenant of my peace be removed."

Amidst the peace the scripture begged to offer, that voice penetrated through, a shadow snuffing out the light. The Lord was never there. When had His kindness ever been with her? When had He ever given her peace?

The word left her lips of its own accord. "Never."

Eloise sucked in a hard breath, as though she could breathe the word back in. But did she even want to? Was it not true?

The next words that crossed her mind were cold and only too inviting. *Never. Give up.*

Give up. Wasn't that what had led her to where she was now? Rocking next to a putrid toilet while her parents screamed their grievances at one another?

The Rileys had tried to pass it off as an accident. Eloise had fallen asleep in the tub. She hadn't meant to do it. But even still, word spread. The town knew what she was, and her mistake was all they needed to turn their already bitter view into something spiteful.

Lily came home crying. Morgan came home angry. Eloise fell asleep to her parents' screams like a dark and bitter lullaby, certain each night that when she woke, her father would be gone.

And all because of her.

"Lord, where are you?" she whispered. "I need you." In the following silence, she felt something break within her, and the tears that burned her eyes spilled over.

When Eloise was younger, her grandmother had told her that the Lord heard the prayers of her heart through her tears. But that was a truth she couldn't quite grasp. She'd cried enough tears in her life to flood all of Huxley, and the only thing she'd ever gained was a hollow ache that grew deeper with age.

Believing is more than feeling, EllieAnne, Nanny had told her. *That's the good in who He is. His love doesn't change with your feelings.*

A sharp knock at the door made Eloise jump, jerking her from her thoughts and the memory of Nanny Anne. If only for a moment, her mother's soft voice pulled her head above the waves. "Ellie?"

Removing the lock, Eloise let her mother pull the door open. Seeing her spot on the floor, Lily kneeled beside her. "Eloise." She tucked the girl's dark hair behind her ear. "I'm sorry," she said quietly. She couldn't blame the girl for hiding. Lily wanted to hide from the words she and her husband screamed at each other.

Pulling Eloise to her feet, Lily led her back toward the house, stopping at the door. "Wait there." Taking off her shoes, Lily stepped inside and filled a basin with water.

Doing as she was told, Eloise took the seat her mother offered and watched her kneel at her feet. Mud. Her mother hated mud. "I can wash my own feet, Mama."

"I've got it, Ellie." Lily met her eyes, smiling an almost believable smile. "It's just mud."

Eloise kept quiet as her mother ran the rag over her feet.

When Lily finished, she tossed the water before washing the basin and refilling it with fresh water. While Lily went to work scrubbing the mud off her hands, Eloise turned her attention to her parents' door and the sound of Morgan's pacing.

The sound of her mother pitching the water brought Eloise's attention back to her. With everything put away, Lily turned to face her daughter. "Why don't I sleep with you again tonight?" Her smile trembled, and Eloise felt another crack run through her, threatening to break her.

In Eloise's room, rather than going to bed, Lily moved about. Taking up the shirtwaist and calico skirt Eloise had discarded, she folded it and put it back before grabbing the blanket off the floor. Shaking it out, she hesitated before wrapping it around her daughter's shoulders. "I'm sorry, Ellie," she said again. "You shouldn't have to hear your father and I fight like that."

Eloise shrugged. "It's my fault," she said. "It's always my fault."

"None of this is your fault, Eloise." Lily sighed at the girl's shrug. "Ellie, you cannot take the blame for everything. Your father and I are not going to agree on every little thing. We never have."

"You only ever fight about me, Mama. I make him angry."

"Your father and I fight about plenty, Eloise. Just wait until you have a husband. You'll understand. As for your father, he just struggles to understand what goes on in your head. But he loves you, Ellie. More than anything."

That, Eloise knew, was a lie. She could list a dozen things her father loved more than her.

"So why is he so hard on me?" she asked. "Everything I do makes him angry."

"For the same reason he's hard on me." Lily looked about her daughter's room. It wasn't much, but it was something. A bed cloaked in the quilt Lily's mother had made her. A box of embroidering supplies atop the dresser. "Baby, you know he never learned anything but anger growing up." Lily waved a hand around the room. "He didn't even have this. But you have no idea how much softer he is. He used to scare me in the beginning with his temper. With the way he handled my own emotions. But I had to remind myself that it wasn't by his doing. His mother taught him anger and cruelty, and it was my job to teach him compassion." Lily tucked her hair behind her ear. "We've all got a road ahead of us, LuLu, and we need to offer as much compassion as we can."

When Eloise said nothing, Lily slipped her hand into hers. "Do you want to pray?"

Eloise nodded, ignoring that taunting voice as her mother took her hands. She wasn't sure why, but her mother's prayers held more power than her own. While they never rid her of that voice, they gave her the hint of peace she needed to stay above water.

Forcing her mind on her mother's words, Eloise felt that small bit of peace trickle over her. When she finished, Lily held Eloise closer. "I wish you could have Poppy pray for you. He was a warrior in prayer."

9

"Nanny was good too," Eloise said softly. She missed Nanny Anne's prayers. Of all prayers, her nanny's had given her peace.

"She was good," Lily agreed. "She and my daddy could move mountains together when they prayed."

"My prayers couldn't move a pebble."

"You don't believe in what you pray for, Ellie. You have to believe God is listening to you, or you won't be ready or even willing to accept the peace He is trying to offer."

"I'm trying, Mama."

"I know you are, Eloise, and you'll get there if you keep trying."

Eloise sighed. She was tired of trying. Every second of her life was spent trying, and all of it had led her to that tub with no strength to get out.

Why was she fighting? that voice had whispered. It wouldn't get better. It wouldn't get easier.

"I can't remember ever truly being happy, Mama," Eloise said softly, the words bitter on her tongue. It was true that she had happy memories. She had happy days. But those memories were few, and all it took was that dark voice whispering in her ear that the happiness she felt wouldn't last for it to end. "And no matter how hard I try, no matter how much I pray, no matter how hard I try to hold onto faith, I can't see it ever changing."

I can't remember ever truly being happy. Lily felt the ache in her chest deepen as fresh tears filled her daughter's chocolate eyes—the eyes of Lily's father. Eloise reminded her so much of him in ways beyond the looks she carried. It was a thought that broke her heart and yet gave her hope. Lily's father had managed, and Lily was certain Eloise could too if she only had someone to open her eyes to a truth she was unable to instill in her daughter.

Pushing Eloise's hair behind her ear, Lily kissed her forehead. "You have to start seeing yourself better than you do, Ellie. I know it's hard to believe, coming from your mama. But you are so much more than your mind is telling you."

Eloise let the words settle over her. "I don't understand God," she said quietly. "Or the Bible. Sometimes they seem to contradict themselves." Eloise had a million and one ideas in her head, and she had no idea what was right. She couldn't be more than what she saw. Not when she knew that the Lord looked upon her and hated what He saw. A child of His, gone to darkness. Cloaked in a fear and sadness she couldn't rid herself of no matter how hard she tried.

"People contradict the Bible, Ellie," Lily said, pulling the blankets tighter around Eloise's shoulders. "Not the other way around. You have read the Bible. You know what it says."

"I know what people say, Mama, and that's what I see when I read it—confirmation."

"Confirmation of what, baby?" Lily encouraged.

Eloise knew she couldn't say the words aloud, but they were there. To read the Bible led to one conclusion: the unbearable pain of knowing she contained nothing worth carrying on for. She wasn't what the Lord wanted.

"I want to believe what He says, Mama. But I can't see anything of worth in me." Anger still filled Eloise at the knowledge she had failed. That she had a life ahead of her that looked no different than the one before. "I want to die, Mama," Eloise said softly.

"I know," Lily whispered. "But you have to stop viewing yourself through the lies others have put on you. You are enough for Him, Ellie. We'll never be worthy of His forgiveness. We'll never be able to do enough to repay Him for His sacrifice. But we ourselves, coming to Him in our sin and our brokenness and laying them at His feet, are enough." Lily set her forehead to Eloise's. "You are enough, Eloise Anne, even in your struggle. And I pray God brings someone into your life who will show you just how lovable you are, baby girl. Someone who will teach you how to love yourself as you deserve to be loved."

Two

Brooks Harper had been in Huxley no more than five minutes and already knew he had no place in it. *What am I doing here, Papa?* Huxley had been ten miles west of where'd he planned, and still, when he felt the pull to turn westward, he did so reluctantly. The Lord would have good reason.

Upon seeing the mud-ridden town, Brooks couldn't imagine what that reason might be. The moment he'd ridden in, a heaviness had settled over him. Surely there was nothing here. This couldn't be where God wanted him to stay. But even still, he guided his wagon forward, eyes searching for the nearest stable. Maybe he could at least find a church. It had been two months since he'd had more than himself on a Sunday morning, and he ached for the fellowship. Even if it wasn't the sort he was used to.

A dark voice tempted him to leave. He was better on his own, and he'd never stepped foot in a church a day in his life. Why start now?

The thought was tempting, and it was for that reason Brooks set his mind to going.

Finding the stable, he hopped down and guided the horses in, hesitating when the stablehand reached for the reins. "Can I ask how long you've worked with horses?" Brooks asked. "And the sort you work with?"

The man looked back at him through bloodshot eyes. "What?"

Brooks cleared his throat. "I'd like to know who's taking care of my horses." He had known there was a risk in bringing the

13

two with the darkest history, and he was facing that decision now. But he had an attachment to Era in particular; one he knew she returned.

"Been workin' with horses since I was a boy," the man grunted. "A lot longer than you've been alive." Taking the reins, he led the horses into the stable. Era looked back at Brooks as though he was abandoning her.

"You wouldn't happen to know where I can find the church?" Brooks called.

The man swore. "Walk out that door and turn left. Walk about fifty yards and turn right. You can't miss it."

"Thank you." Tipping his hat, Brooks started out with the very real impression the man was happy to see the back of him—to see him gone. *This can't be where you want me, God.*

His mind was on his horses. It had taken him years to earn their trust, and he knew one bad experience could send them spiraling back to the broken creatures they'd been when they came to him.

In the silence, a small voice bid him to trust.

Trust. Holding onto that word, Brooks stumbled his way to the church, stopping now and again to pull his feet free from where they sank into the mud. He was going to make quite the impression walking into church looking as he did—mud at his feet and road dust on his face. But then he supposed he wouldn't be the only one covered in mud; the town was full of it and judging by the sky, it would only be worse by the end of service.

The church wasn't large, but it was something compared to what he was used to. Back home, church was his family all gathered together in their living room. The summer Sundays might see the gathering of neighbors, but he'd never experienced a true Sunday service.

Taking an empty seat, he tipped his hat at the woman next to him before wondering if he was supposed to remove it. Doing so, he clutched it in his hands.

"Newcomer?" the woman asked. "No need to be nervous, hun. Better late than never."

Brooks felt a blush fill his cheeks. "Thank you, ma'am. But only new to the church. I come from a very small town that has yet to get itself a church building." Holding out his hand, he introduced himself. "Brooks Harper."

"Ida James," the woman responded. Despite the woman's sweet demeanor, Brooks felt his uncertainty deepen as she looked him over. "This here is my son, John, and you'll see my husband up at the pulpit in the next few minutes. He'll be honored to know he's your first real experience in the church."

Brooks nodded along to the woman's conversation, letting his eyes roam the rest of the room and trying to ignore the sick feeling rolling about in his stomach. It was nothing. He'd been away from people too long.

That darkness within him told him he didn't need people. Go back to his wagon. To his horses. Fighting the urge to leave, Brooks found his eyes drawn to a family in the back corner. Despite the packed pews, he noticed the seats around them were empty. Not only those beside them but up to three pews in front of them.

Her hand on his arm brought Brooks back to Ida. "Don't pay them any mind, dear. You don't want to get mixed up with the likes of that family."

The previously sweet tone took on a darker note, making Brooks' stomach turn. "Do you mind if I ask why?"

"The girl isn't right in the head," Ida stated. "Word is she tried to kill herself not two weeks ago. Right there in the bath." The woman tutted as she glared at the family. "The parents tried to pass it off as an accident, but we all know. That girl's been off since she left the womb, and it's no wonder with parents like that. The father's always been trouble and with a conception like that one ..."

Brooks rubbed at his eyes as the woman prattled. He knew he should walk away. But he felt the words slipping from his mouth as his eyes wandered back to the family. "Why? What's wrong with her?" He couldn't see anything physically wrong with her. In fact, he found her rather pretty.

"Her parents call her timid," Ida replied. "As though that's much better than the truth of it. Let them say what they want. It doesn't change the fact that she's on a path that doesn't lead upward. Ruled by fear. Doesn't say a word to others. Doesn't care at all how rude it is." She gave a small tsk. "My daughter went to school with her. Said she was known for having a fit of tears when made to do anything."

"Hmm," was all Brooks could think to say.

"And, of course, her parents are no help. They pulled her out of school before she was finished, claiming the teacher was mistreating their daughter. Her father made a big stink of it all. Tried to get the board to let the teacher go. Thank heavens the board saw nothing wrong with the woman's actions."

Brooks felt something uneasy settle in his stomach as the woman continued. "Please, stop," he said quietly, further regretting his choice of seating. Regretting opening his mouth. Regretting stepping foot in the building.

"I know it," Ida breathed. "It's a mess is what it is. I wish they would stay home. They make everyone uncomfortable, and they certainly aren't fooling the Lord with their Sunday worship." Seeing his eyes roam back to the girl, the woman sighed. "Don't let a pretty face mislead you, boy. That girl is far from the Lord."

"That seems like quite a judgment," Brooks said softly. "The way you describe her, she sounds quite a bit like my mother—and a godlier woman there's never been." Biting his tongue against saying more, Brooks tipped his head and made his way toward the family. If the rest of the church wanted to isolate them, they could do just that. It didn't mean he had to.

"Excuse me?" They all seemed to shrink at his approach. "Do you mind if I sit with you?"

The older woman's blue eyes widened a moment before she nodded. "Of course. I mean, no, we don't mind."

Taking the open seat, Brooks held out a hand and introduced himself for the third time in twenty minutes.

"Morgan Riley," the man offered, giving Brooks a firm shake. "My wife, Lily, and our daughter, Eloise." When his daughter gave a small smile, Morgan squeezed her shoulder. "You'll have to excuse Ellie. Bit timid." The younger woman blushed deeply at her father's words and ducked her head.

Offering his hand to Lily, Brooks merely nodded at Eloise. "It's nice to meet you all."

"And you," Lily said softly. "Are you new to Huxley or just passing through our *lovely* town?"

Brooks felt his lips quirk at her emphasis on the word lovely. "Passing through. Been on the road a couple of months and was in need of some church fellowship."

"Well, welcome, Brooks. I hope the church treats you well."

Though said with no malice, Brooks couldn't help but wonder if there was something to it. By the looks the family was receiving, and the distance kept between them, he couldn't blame her if there was.

Nodding, Brooks turned his attention to the front as the singing started. *Don't want to get mixed up with the likes of them,* Ida had said, and as the surrounding congregation continued their hymn of praise, he couldn't help but take in his new acquaintances. Lily had her eyes closed, having no need for the hymnal provided. She didn't sing aloud, but her lips moved silently as she held her hands to her chest, her face turned heavenward. Next to her, Morgan had one hand buried in his pocket while the other held the hymnal.

Beside Brooks, Eloise stood stiff, her arms crossed tight in front of her. Like her mother, she had her eyes closed, only her head was down, and her mouth was closed. But even still, by the way her lips twitched, Brooks wondered if she might be praying. As he watched, a few silent tears dripped down her cheeks.

Whatever else Ida James might have said over the family, Brooks felt certain she was wrong on their faith. Perhaps they didn't look like the rest of the church in their worship of the Lord, but he saw something in them—something that stood out from the other encounters he'd had in his short time at this church. And then again, he didn't look much like the rest of the congregation either.

Brooks could almost see his own family in the one beside him, and it made him ache for home. It had taken only a few days on the road to know he would find no land or town worth leaving his family for, but he'd stuck to his plans. The Lord had called him out, and he would see it through.

When the singing ended, Brooks took his seat beside Eloise and watched as she rested her head on her mother's shoulder, wrapping the end of her dark braid around her pinky.

"Just breathe, Ellie," Lily said quietly, wiping the remaining tears from her daughter's cheeks. "We're here for the Lord and no one else. Focus on Him, baby."

Brooks felt a pang in his chest; whether for his family or the one beside him, he wasn't entirely sure. Both seemed likely enough. Brooks had seen his father behave that way with his mother on many occasions. His words soft and his hands gentle as he wiped the tears from his wife's face.

Papa, I don't care if any of what that woman, Ida, said is true. I pray you give this family someone. Give Eloise someone.

When the service ended, Brooks watched as the men and women gathered separately while their children ran out the door. He supposed he should introduce himself to the pastor and thank the man for his sermon, but no sooner than the thought crossed his mind did he notice the eyes on him.

From where the women stood, he could see Ida eyeing him, her lips moving quickly. "Should have known," her voice drifted. "To even think of stepping foot in a church looking like that. Calls himself a God-loving man; he should know better."

Brooks felt his cheeks run hot as the other women nodded in agreement. The road was a rough place, and while his clothing might not have been in the best of shape before leaving home, it had become tattered in his weeks of travel. There was a hole at his knee. A tiny rip at his shoulder. It didn't bother him any; worn clothes were more comfortable, and he needn't worry about them getting dirty or tearing. But he wasn't thick enough to enter a church looking as he did if he'd had another choice.

"Ignore them," Lily said softly. "Presence is what matters."

Brooks let out a small laugh, ignoring the ache in his chest. Every moment in this town made him wish all the more for the comfort of Rose Haven—where, even when the town did meet for a service, the only real expectation was that you got dressed. Patched-up Linsey-Woolsey dresses and frayed suspenders were the norm in a farming town.

The woman squeezed his arm as the pastor dislodged himself from the other men and made his way toward them.

Putting a smile on his face, Brooks accepted the pastor's greeting. "My wife tells me this was your first time in church?"

"Yes, sir, I come from a small town. But we make do with what we have in Haven."

"Oh, I'm sure." The man smiled, his eyes looking Brooks up and down, making him feel more like a boy than a man in his twenties. "But nothing is quite sufficient enough as a real church. Real sermons. A pastor."

Brooks felt another dip in his stomach. "A church building is certainly nice, and we do hope to get one someday, but even if we don't, I think the Lord will be happy. No one in my family line has stepped foot in a church, but they follow the Lord all the same."

Pastor James *hmmed*. "I suppose." His eyes met the Rileys. "Perhaps it might be good to take a page from your new friend's book, Riley, and keep your family home on Sundays." The man put a smile on his face as he looked at Eloise. "For your girl, of course. I'm sure she'd be more comfortable there."

Eloise's skin flushed a deep red, and she ducked her head.

Morgan shrugged. "It's an idea. We just might find the Lord that way." Squeezing his wife's shoulder, he nodded toward the door. "It was nice meeting you, Brooks."

"And you," Brooks replied, his unease ebbing at the gentle squeeze Lily gave his hand as she moved past him.

When they were gone, Pastor James turned his eyes back to Brooks. "Bit of a difficult family. But we try to be as gracious as possible."

Brooks simply nodded. Whatever he'd seen in this church, it wasn't gracious.

"Been telling the parents they ought to get the girl to a specialist. For her sake, of course. I would hate to see the girl suffer more than she has."

The longer Brooks spoke with the man, the more time he spent in this building, the heavier his chest grew. This wasn't what he'd hoped for at church. He missed his family, and he wanted nothing more than to hold on to his mother, thinking of all the times she had dealt with the sort of treatment he'd witnessed toward Eloise. "It was a wonderful service," he said quietly. "But I really ought to be going." Thanking the pastor, Brooks hurried to the door.

Shaking out his crumpled hat, Brooks placed it on his head. *Papa, I know this place isn't for me. So why did you guide me here? I feel more sick than renewed.*

The answer was the same: trust.

He hadn't been wrong; rain was pouring on the town, thickening the already dense mud. Everywhere he looked, families struggled to get their wagons moving. Through the crowd, Brooks could just make out the Rileys struggling with one of their horses.

Making his way through the mud, Brooks started toward them. "Need a hand?"

As they did before, all three flinched. What sort of treatment were they used to here? They reminded him of a group of abused and easily startled horses.

"If you wouldn't mind it," Morgan huffed. "No matter their effort, my girls" —he eyed Lily and Eloise with a slight smile— "aren't much help."

"Wouldn't mind at all," Brooks replied. "I'll handle the horses."

"Maybe I ought to do that. Theo is always stubborn when the mud gets thick."

But Brooks was already moving toward them. "Which one is Theo?"

"The one on the left," Lily called. "He got an abscess one year due to the mud. Hasn't liked it since."

"Well, that's no fun, is it?" Brooks said softly, brushing the horse's neck. "But I think we can do this, can't we?" Moving slowly, he took hold of the horse's harness and gave it a slight tug. When the horse refused to move, Brooks gave a small click, urging it to lower its head. Keeping his eyes on the horse, he blew softly on its nose. "You've got this."

After a moment, the horse gave a small puff of air. "Atta boy." Keeping the horse's eyes on his, Brooks led him forward as Morgan cleared the mud packed around the wheels.

Clearing the worst of it, Morgan came and clapped Brooks on the shoulder. "Don't know how you managed that, but thank you."

"Why don't you join us for lunch, Brooks?" Lily offered. "It's the least we can offer you for your help."

Brooks took in the woman's sweet, pale face and found none of the unease he'd felt with Ida. "Well, if you don't mind, I'd love to," he said quietly. "Thank you, Mrs. Riley."

"Lily, sweetheart, and we don't mind one bit. Just hop up with Morgan there, and I'll take the back with Ellie."

Three

Eloise picked at the food on her plate, listening to the conversation next to her. She hadn't said a word since that morning, and though she felt the man's eyes on her now and again, he had yet to force her words. For that, she was grateful.

"Headed home or out, Harper?" Morgan asked around a mouthful of potatoes.

Next to Eloise, Brooks gave a small laugh. "Home, I'm glad to say. Been away two months."

"Have you been on your own that whole time?" Lily asked, painfully reminding Brooks of his mother when he'd told her he was leaving.

"Afraid so. I've been looking to start a ranch, and I spent the summer looking for good land."

Lily gave him a sympathetic smile. "Doesn't sound as though you had much luck."

"Afraid not, though I admit I'm a bit pickier than I should be."

"Nothing wrong with being picky," Morgan said. "You don't settle on dreams."

"No, you don't. My parents would have my head before I settled."

"Are you far from home?" Lily asked.

"Little over a month's drive," Brooks said quietly.

Eloise glanced upward at the emotion in the man's voice. She'd never known a man to show any emotion, and yet Brooks showed no shame in it.

When the man met her eyes, she dropped hers back to her lap, fighting the new panic building in her. How long before he realized what she was? Had Ida James told him what she'd done?

"A ranch?" Lily was saying. "Horses, I assume? I was wondering how you handled Theo so well. That horse is stubborn even without the mud. We have thought of selling him off, but Ellie's attached herself to him."

Eloise felt the man's eyes turn back to her. "Is that so?"

She nodded, taken aback by the magnitude of those dark eyes.

"Sometimes, the most difficult horse has the most to offer," he said softly. "It takes a special person to see that." He winked at her, and Eloise felt her lips turn upward.

Turning back to Lily, Brooks cleared his throat. "You're right, though. Been working with horses just about my whole life. Mostly rehabilitating." At the look Lily gave him, Brooks chuckled. "I, uh, I like the seemingly hopeless horses. The ones others give up on."

"You don't see that often," Lily said quietly. "It's a trait more people need." Shaking her head, she took up the plates. "Ellie, why don't you help me?"

Easing the door shut, Lily looked at her daughter. "Are you all right, Eloise?"

Eloise shrugged. "I'm not terrible." She'd imagined worse when her mother invited the stranger to lunch.

Lily considered her a moment before nodding. "Sweetheart, I was thinking of inviting Brooks to stay until the storm passes. He'll have no chance getting out of town now, and I wouldn't want him wasting coin on that inn." She brushed Eloise's hair back. "But I also don't want you uncomfortable. Your home should be where you feel safest."

"It wouldn't be right to send him out," Eloise said, her voice soft. "Least of all to a bug-infested inn." The next words burned as they left her mouth. "I'll be all right."

"Are you sure, Ellie?"

"Yes, Mama. You can go and invite him. I'll take care of the dishes."

Lily kissed the top of Eloise's head. "Bring the bucket inside. It's too cold to be out here long, and you're already soaked through."

Doing as she was told, Eloise dropped the dishes into a bucket and dragged it inside, careful not to get caught up in the bottom of her skirt. "You got that, Weasel?" her father asked.

"Yes, Daddy." Ignoring their eyes, Eloise focused on the task at hand as she listened to the quiet conversation.

"I don't think I could intrude," Brooks was saying. "I don't mind sleeping in my wagon."

"The nights are cold here, Harper," Morgan replied. "And the rain is likely to soak through the canvas at this rate."

"We have an old cot," Lily insisted. "It won't be much, but it's better than a wet wagon bed. Not to mention your horses will be more comfortable in a stable."

Glancing up, Eloise watched the man's fingers tap the wood of the table. Would he consider it? Was he only being kind when he sat beside them? Or perhaps it was all some cruel joke?

Shaking the thought loose, Eloise scrubbed at a plate as Brooks answered. "All right," he conceded. "I suppose I can intrude on you for a night or two. But I insist you let me pay you back." Before Lily could refuse, Brooks continued. "Let me spend time with Theo. See if I can't get through to him."

Morgan laughed. "If that's what you want, you do that."

***

Eloise stared at the wall opposite her. Despite the guest in their living room, she could hear her parents arguing. Hushed but still audible through the cracks in the walls. If the man hadn't thought them crazy before, he certainly did now. Couldn't her parents keep quiet just once?

Eloise ran a palm over her face as fresh guilt washed over her. What right did she have to be angry or embarrassed? She was the cause of this. She deserved this.

"I am not stepping foot in that church again, Lily," Morgan hissed. "The Lord is not in that church."

"I don't think the Lord is in this home either, Morgan." Even through the walls, Eloise could hear her mother's cries. "And I don't know where we're supposed to find Him. He's not at that church. He's not here. I don't even think He's in this town."

"We're back to that again?"

Eloise dug her fingers into her hair. How long before her father left? All it would take was one wrong fight, and Morgan would leave, and then what would the neighbors have to say?

Only that wasn't quite true. Her father wouldn't leave. He had a job. Friends. If he wanted to leave Huxley, he would do so now as her mother requested. No—instead, he would send Eloise and her mother away.

Eloise didn't want to think of what Lily would be without Morgan. Broken. A shell of her former self.

"I can't just up and quit my job, Lily," Morgan shouted. "That is our livelihood. You don't work. You have no idea the pressure of keeping a family fed and clothed."

"I don't?" Lily laughed. "Do not for a second tell me that your reasoning for leaving church is because of Eloise or God. If that were so, you would see this whole town is no better."

It was the first time Eloise had ever heard her mother swear, and she felt sick at the thought of it. Her father was one thing; he hadn't sworn often before, but he'd still been known to do so at times. Her mother, on the other hand … Eloise couldn't remember a time her mother had sworn. "I can't do this anymore, Morgan. If you want to go out in that godforsaken town, you do that. Listen to every cruel word spoken against your daughter. But I won't."

"And what is that supposed to mean?"

"You said it yourself, Morgan. I don't work. I have no real responsibilities. So I suppose you won't mind doing the shopping. Fetching our mail. Paying our debts. If church is off-limits now, too, I see no reason to face those people again. You can do it if it's so easy for you to listen to their words against your daughter."

Eloise held her breath as she waited for her father's response. She expected shouting. Anger. Instead, it was quiet save for the sound of her mother's sniffling.

"It isn't easy, Lily," Morgan said, his voice softer than it had been a moment before. "But I have no other choice."

"You could— "

"No, Lily. I don't want to uproot Eloise and trek her out into the middle of nowhere with no idea of where we're going. No idea of how I'm going to provide for the both of you. I can't, Lily."

"I understand that, Morgan. But, honey, I don't think Eloise can get much worse than she is now. She needs away from here. She needs … someone. We're not enough for her, Morgan. Least of all now."

In the silence, Eloise heard the soft creak of the bed beneath her mother's weight. "When was the last night she went to bed without the sound of us fighting like this? Even with a guest in the house, we can't control ourselves."

Rolling over, Eloise pulled her pillow over her head. She didn't want to hear more. She didn't want to hear her mother blaming herself. It wasn't her parents' fault. It was hers. It was always hers. "God," she whispered. "Lord, please. Say something. Anything."

***

Lily avoided Brooks' eyes as she dished his breakfast with a shaking hand. "Thank you, Lily," he said softly.

"You're welcome, sweetheart." Giving his shoulder a squeeze, Lily took a seat beside her husband. "I hope you slept well?"

"I slept perfectly," Brooks assured. "It's been months since I slept in a real bed. Fell asleep the moment my head hit the pillow."

Eloise glanced up then, and one look into his dark eyes told her the truth. Like herself, he had heard every word spoken between her parents.

Accepting the reassurance, Lily sighed as new color filled her cheeks. "I'm glad of it. From the looks of that storm, you've got at least one more night with us."

"And you're sure you don't mind my staying? I really don't mind renting a room."

"I couldn't think to let you stay in that rat-infested hole," Lily replied. "Stop fretting, Brooks. So long as you're comfortable, we are more than happy to house you."

Settling into the meal, the table was quiet. Nothing but the sound of forks on plates. Why was Brooks keeping quiet about what he had heard last night? Why pretend they weren't just what Ida had told him?

Maybe he plans to take it back to her. Then the whole town will know just how messed up you all truly are.

"Eloise?" Eloise started at the man's soft voice. When she met his eyes, he smiled. "I was hoping you might help me with Theo this morning. If you have an attachment to him, it's likely he has one with you."

"I don't think I'd be much help," she said quietly. It was the first time she'd spoken directly to the man, and she noticed the way his lips curved upward in the smallest hint of a smile. "I don't know what I'm doing."

"No. But I do. All I need from you is to be there. Sometimes it helps the horses to have a familiar face."

Eloise glanced toward Lily, who nodded. "All right."

Giving her another crooked smile, Brooks turned his attention back to his food.

"I hope the rain doesn't go on too long." Lily eyed the dark clouds and the rain beating against the glass pane. "Hate to think of you being away from home any longer."

Brooks sighed. "I suppose the Lord knows what He's doing. Even if we don't always like it." He smiled. "I'm ready to get home, but it's nice to have a few days with people after so long on my own. It just might tide me over until I get home."

"Where is home?" Morgan asked. "Is it in Oregon or a neighboring territory?"

"Montana," Brooks replied. "In a little town called Rose Haven."

"What is the community like?"

"It's small," Brooks said. "Only about thirty or so families in all. But it's a good community. Friendly, save for a few—and the ones who aren't tend to stick to their own land."

Morgan nodded. "Is there, uh …" —he cleared his throat— "is there good work there?"

Eloise's eyes snapped to her mother's, whose own were wide and uncertain. "Morgan," Lily whispered. "Please don't do this to me."

Hushing her, Morgan listened to Brooks. "There isn't much, no. The town is mostly full of farmers. But it's a growing town, and if you have a trade, I can almost guarantee we need it."

"Lumber?"

Brooks smiled. "In desperate need of. We had a man who started up a mill a few years back. It shut down when he passed away. The building has just been sitting there since—along with all the equipment. Just needs a man to run it."

"Does it have a living space?" Morgan asked. "Big enough for three?"

Brooks shook his head. "Afraid not. But—and I mean, it's been a few months—I know my father was looking to sell off a piece of his land. It's a good one, too. I'd be willing to talk to him if you're interested."

There was silence as the words settled over them. It was Lily who broke the silence with a broken whisper. "Morgan?"

"I-I suppose I could think on it," Morgan said quietly. "But I've never owned land before. I wouldn't know where to begin."

"You would learn, honey, and Eloise and I would be there every step of the way."

Morgan nodded, his fingers tapping the table. "I never imagined I'd be running a mill myself."

"You would do wonderfully, Daddy," Eloise said quietly, a blush filling her cheeks as three pairs of eyes found her. "You practically run the mill now."

"She's right," Lily said, echoing her daughter's sentiment. "You'd be perfect for it."

"My father, and just about everyone else in town, will be more than willing to help as well," Brooks encouraged. "We take care of each other in Rose Haven."

At that, the tears that had been in Lily's eyes spilled over, bringing a new look of guilt to Eloise's face. "I'm sorry," she laughed, taking the handkerchief Eloise gave her. "I'm sorry. We're just not used to that sort of thinking. Huxley is very self-minded. It isn't easy to find help when needed." Her eyes met Eloise, who ducked her head. "It isn't very kind at all," she whispered.

"Well, you'll find nothing of the sort back home," Brooks said. My parents raised three children there with no problems. I'll admit that a large part of my struggle the past few months is my reluctance to leave Rose Haven. It's like a little slice of heaven over there."

"It sounds wonderful," Lily said softly. "Huxley is ... well, I wouldn't call it heaven."

"I wouldn't either. Bit too busy for my taste."

"Exactly what Ellie has always said. She's wanted to leave for years."

"Well, if you like the quiet, Eloise, you'll love Rose Haven." Brooks smiled in her direction. "It doesn't get much noise."

Eloise gave another small smile, her eyes meeting Brooks for only a moment before dropping back to her hands.

Clearing his throat, Morgan stood. "I'll think on it." Grabbing his hat, he left before Lily could stop him.

Four

After breakfast, Eloise reluctantly stuffed her feet into her boots and led Brooks to their small barn. Across the street, passersby stopped and watched as she pulled at the barn door with a man at her side. Though inexperienced where men were concerned, she understood social etiquette well enough to know that even a walk alone with a man was enough to spark rumors in any town. Eloise didn't want to think of what this town could do with a man and woman alone in a barn.

When the door got stuck in the mud, Brooks stepped in and forced it open, drawing whispers. "After you." He smiled, careless of the fresh rumors being made. Leaving the door open, Brooks made his way to where Eloise stood with Theo. "How old is he?"

"Twenty-four."

"Have you had him that long?"

Eloise shook her head. "About twelve years. He was my nanny's before," she said, her voice taking on that soft quietness of hers Brooks had grown used to hearing, even in the short time he'd known her. "My grandmother's," she clarified.

Understanding, Brooks took the spot next to her. "Can I assume he's been different since he came to you?"

She nodded.

"Grief can do that," Brooks said quietly. "Most people don't realize how attached a horse can become—especially when they have good people looking after them. A lot of times they get more attached than even we can become to them." When Eloise said nothing, he continued. "It's a difficult thing to work them through—grief. Not impossible, though, and seeing as he's made it this long, I would say there's hope."

Eloise's eyes met his. "How?"

Brooks studied the horse for a moment. He wasn't sure it would work. But it could, God willing. "Do you have anything that belonged to your grandmother? Something he might recognize?"

"A shawl?"

"That's perfect—if you're willing to bring it out for him."

Nodding, Eloise fetched the shawl from her room, ignoring the scrutinous eyes of her neighbors. Returning, she held the shawl out to Brooks.

Seeing it, Theo let out a snort, his feet moving. "Put it on," Brooks said softly, his eyes on Theo. Eloise did as requested, holding the fabric tight at her shoulders. The shawl had been a blanket on her when it was first passed onto her, but now it was like a hug from the arms she wished were there to hold her now.

Eloise took an involuntary step back as Brooks eased the stall door open, guiding the horse out. "It's all right." His voice was still soft, his hand gentle on the beast's chest. But the words were for her. "I won't let you get hurt. Just let him smell it."

Eloise's heart pounded in her chest as the horse sniffed her neck. Theo had been unpredictable since her grandmother died. But after a moment, the horse nudged her cheek gently. "I think he recognizes it," Brooks said, keeping his voice quiet so as not to spook Theo.

"It was Nanny's favorite." Eloise couldn't remember a day when her grandmother hadn't worn that black shawl now faded grey with age. She stroked the horse's neck. "I've worn it since she died." And for every day she'd worn it, the horse had always grown agitated at the sight of her. "I always thought he just didn't like me."

Brooks chuckled as he watched the horse nuzzle the woman's neck. "I'd say he recognized the shawl and wondered where his owner was. Horses don't understand death; they just know someone they love is missing. They need a chance to grieve as much as we do."

Turning her face into the horse's neck, Eloise hoped to hide the tears that burned her eyes. "I miss her too," she whispered. Everything might have been different if Nanny hadn't died.

Giving Eloise privacy, Brooks took in the small space. It wasn't the sort of barn he was used to. The building only housed the two horses and the small family wagon. But he supposed much wasn't needed when living on the outskirts of Huxley, the town mercantile little more than a hundred yards from their front door. His family barn was nearly the size of their home, having a need for equipment and enough space to store their food supply. Over the years, he and his father had expanded the size of the barn as Brooks acquired more horses, refusing to sell them to just anyone. He hadn't spent that time helping poorly mistreated horses only to send them back to the sort of life that had led them to him in the first place.

Clearing his throat, Brooks looked back toward Eloise. "You wouldn't happen to know how that stable near the church treats their horses, would you?"

"I've never heard anything bad," she said. "The, um, the man who runs it is a drunk, but he seems to treat the horses well."

Brooks nodded. He could only hope so. The Riley barn was too small to be bringing in two more horses, and by the looks of the sky, he was no sooner to heading out than he was last night.

"I hope you don't mind my being here," he said. "I know it can throw off one's routine."

Eloise shrugged one shoulder. "Mama's right—sending you to that inn wouldn't be very Christian."

"That bad, huh?"

Brooks smiled as Eloise laughed softly. More a soft exhale than a real laugh, but it was beautiful nonetheless. "I've never been in it, but I've heard stories."

The woman had the softest voice he'd ever heard. Even in the silence of the barn, each word was only just audible. Feigning interest in Theo, Brooks took a step closer. "Well, then, thank the Lord He led me to you," he said, with a laugh.

Eloise watched him a moment. "I'm sorry about my parents," she said, her voice little more than a whisper as she remembered her parents' words. "They aren't normally like that. It's just been …" She shrugged again.

"There's nothing to apologize for, Eloise. Broken people do things they wouldn't ordinarily do," Brooks said softly. "Your folks don't strike me as the sort to fight in such a way if they weren't both hurting."

When her lip trembled, Eloise turned away until she could trust herself not to burst into tears. When she did look up, she found Brooks occupying himself with Theo. "Thank you for not embarrassing Mama."

Brooks smiled. "Nothing to be embarrassed about, Eloise. I've heard my own parents go at each other a time or two."

A time or two. Not every night. Not for the reasons hers did. Forcing her lips to turn upward, Eloise nodded.

***

It was the first night in weeks her parents didn't fight. The first night Lily didn't sleep with her. For once, their family wasn't drowning. Eloise wasn't drowning.

They might be getting out of Huxley. Eloise had been praying her father would get them out since she was eleven years old. To get her away from the constant eyes of their neighbors and the whispers that followed their family. Every year that prayer had grown more desperate. Just two nights prior, she'd begged God to open her father's mind, and He had done just that.

Deep within her, that voice reminded her that it wasn't God. It was her father. The man wasn't willing to lose his wife over her.

"No," she breathed. It was God. It had to be God. "Thank you, God. Just don't let him change his mind."

Eloise wasn't sure whether Rose Haven would be any different than life in Huxley or if anything could change for her. But she wanted to believe it could. A new town full of new people who knew nothing of what she'd done. But it didn't matter if they knew her past. Just like Huxley, the people there would see how twisted she was. Brooks already saw it.

It wasn't that bad, she reminded herself. In fact, it had been almost comfortable with him. Though she had said little, he hadn't seemed affronted or turned off. He didn't talk down to her or make her feel small when she stuttered or stumbled in her words.

But that meant nothing. There had been others who seemed kind. Understanding. She'd even had friends, like Edith and Grace. They always grew bored.

Ignoring that voice, Eloise allowed herself to feel that little spark of hope. *Keep it small. Don't let it grow. Don't let it take root.* But even as she thought it, she felt the spark grow. "God, please don't let me be disappointed. Please let this be something."

Five

Morgan's decision to leave came two days later when he stomped through the door, slamming it hard enough to make the weak wood splinter. "We leave in a week," he snarled. Ordering Lily to follow him, he stormed past Brooks and Eloise and into his room.

The waters didn't hit Eloise like a wave so much as let her sink slowly, possibility upon possibility dragging her deeper. What had happened? What had she done and caused now?

Eloise startled as a hand gripped hers. "Look at me, Eloise," Brooks urged. Obeying, she looked into his eyes, his irises the same color as the thick soil outside. "Breathe, Elle."

She hadn't realized she was gasping for air until then. Doing as she was told, she forced a deep breath into her lungs, inhaling the smell of freshly cut hay that lingered on Brooks' skin.

"Why don't we step outside?" he said softly. "I think the rain has finally stopped."

Nodding, Eloise followed after him, unwilling to hear whatever it was her father was shouting.

What was it Brooks heard? Would he still want them following him to Rose Haven? If he did, what would he tell his family of them?

First laying out his jacket to protect her skirts, Brooks lowered her onto a damp hay bale and leaned against the house.

"I'm sorry," she whispered.

"For?" he asked.

Having no answer, Eloise simply shrugged. After a moment, Brooks let out a small laugh. "We all have our moments, Eloise.

I'd be lying if I said I didn't have a few nights like that since leaving home—especially in the beginning."

Seeing her tears, Brooks removed a kerchief from his pocket and held it out to her. Seemingly unwilling to touch her now, he pulled his hand back as soon as her fingers clutched it. "Thank you," she whispered, knowing he wouldn't hear it.

The mental waters were pulling her back under as Brooks tucked his hands in his pockets. He didn't want to touch her. He knew what she was.

No. He was being polite. Respectful. But why wasn't he saying anything? Eloise sank back in her seat and closed her eyes, trying to shut out the thoughts growing louder in her head. How often did she wish people would leave her be, and there Brooks was—silent at her side, eyes forward—and she almost wished he would speak.

Eloise's fingers clenched and unclenched in her skirt. She could feel Brooks' eyes on her now.

Say something. Speak.

But she couldn't. Her lips wouldn't move, and anyway, what would she say?

"Elle?" Brooks' voice broke through the noise in her head, and for just a moment, she broke the surface. *Elle.* The name hadn't caught her attention the first time. She'd been too focused on treading water. But now it played itself over for her. No one had ever called her Elle.

"You look sick," he continued. "Do you want something? Tea?"

"No," she whispered. "No, I'm ok."

The moment the words left her lips, she blushed as the voice inside her head pressed in. The offer wasn't for her. He wanted an escape.

Selfish.

Selfish.

Selfish.

Grow up.

The thoughts were screaming now. She couldn't breathe.

"Eloise." Brooks' voice was gentle, the way one might approach a spooked animal. When she met his eyes, he smiled. "I, uh, saw you weaving that crown earlier. With the flowers. Is that something you do a lot?"

"I-yes," she breathed.

"Well, you'll love Rose Haven," he said. "It's beautiful. Surrounded by meadows with lots of wildflowers. You'll never be in short supply of material."

Eloise couldn't force her lips to do more than form a small smile.

"Is it just weaving, or is it creating in general?"

"No, I-it's all of it." She needed to offer more, but her mind was going blank. "Knitting. Weaving," she said quietly, grasping hold of each love before they could leave her entirely. "But embroidery is my favorite." She loved anything that kept her mind busy.

"I'll have to remind my mother to send the corn husks your way this year. Get some proper use of them." Brooks' smile turned to the sky as the sun broke through the clouds. "Well, look at that," he said, distracted for the moment.

Eloise watched him turn his face towards the sun, his eyes closed as he soaked in the unexpected warmth. It was the first decent light she'd seen him in. The hair that curled at his temples wasn't the dark brown she'd thought it to be but a deep auburn that didn't quite match the red hair on his chin. Freckles covered his sun-kissed skin. But, as always, it was his eyes that caught her attention as he turned them to her. They were as dark and rich as the soil at their feet. "So, embroidery." He smiled, picking up where they'd left off as if they'd never stopped. "What sort do you do?"

Eloise hesitated a moment. "Pictures," she said stupidly. "I mean, I like to paint with thread." Realizing that sounded no better, she sighed.

Brooks laughed softly. "I think I know what you mean. You put down with thread what others put down with paint. But can I ask what you do? Landscapes? Realism?"

"Landscapes mostly. I mostly copy paintings my grandfather did." She hadn't been anywhere but Huxley, and she had no desire to put those memories down with thread, but through the paintings her parents had stowed away in the barn after Nanny died, her grandfather offered a whole world for her to embroider.

"You'll have to show me sometime."

The waters calmed, if only some, as they spoke. Her heart still pounded. She still couldn't wait to be back with her mother, or better yet, alone. But she wasn't drowning.

No one had ever done this with Eloise. Like their time in the barn, Brooks didn't force her conversation as so many others had tried. He didn't expect her to carry it. He prompted her with patience rather than irritation or humor.

By the time Lily came looking for her, the thoughts were little more than a hum in the back of her head.

***

The moment Brooks stepped inside, Eloise went into Lily's arms. Lily needed no prompting to hold her tight. "Why don't we take a short walk? Enjoy the clear skies?" Taking Eloise's hand, she led her away from the house. "Do you want to talk about it?"

Eloise shook her head. The thoughts were growing louder again, the waves growing bigger. Only now, they attacked what had previously been her peace. How many times had she stuttered? Did he notice just how loud her breathing had been?

"Eloise. Talk to me."

"It was ok," Eloise said quietly. "He was kind." He was always kind—and that was what scared her.

"Was he?" Lily smiled. "That's good, Ellie. Did you two talk at all?"

Eloise nodded. "He probably thinks I'm a dolt. Or rude. All I talked about was myself." Tears bit at her eyes. "I wanted to ask about him, but I ... I couldn't ..."

"I know, sweetheart, and I doubt he thinks badly of you, Ellie. Your daddy and I were talking, and he said Brooks was telling him you remind him a lot of his mother. Said she doesn't say a whole lot when others are around. He said that, like you, she can speak if prompted but struggles to find her voice otherwise."

"Really?" Eloise had never heard of anyone who struggled the way she did. She had met quiet women before. Even Lily was a quiet woman who didn't feel the need to fill every silent moment with conversation, but she could if she wanted to. Fear didn't bind her lips as it did for Eloise.

"That's what he told your father. It's part of what made him consider leaving Huxley. Daddy thinks it might do you good to have someone like you to talk with. As well as a few more people who understand." Lily smiled. "You could have a friend, Ellie."

"I don't want friends, Mama." Eloise had had friends, and they'd lead her to that tub. A friend was nothing more than another wave crashing into her.

"Not everyone is like Edith and Grace, Eloise."

"It wasn't just them, Mama." It was everyone who had ever entered her life. "I'm not what people want in a friend."

Or more.

"Ellie, we just need to hold on. It is going to get better."

That dark voice within her laughed. It would never get better. School never got better. Church never got better. No one ever stayed.

"Nothing will ever get better, Mama. Not when—not so long as I'm …" *Me.* But Eloise could never admit that aloud. She knew what her mother would say.

"Eloise, you are not the problem. They are the ones in the wrong. If they don't want to take the time to know you, then that is their loss. Not yours."

"Is it?" Eloise whispered. What was the one thing that every situation had in common? Eloise. "It's always me, Mama, and I don't even know why." Though that wasn't entirely true; people had made it clear enough what they thought was wrong with her.

But *she* didn't know why they were problems, and she had no way of changing them.

Six

Eloise could still remember a time when she was almost normal. At least, she thought she was.

She had been six years old when she was made aware of the difference in her, and that was when everything changed for the worse. Until then, her differences were minor. Perhaps she was quieter than other children, but then it had been endearing. But to be quiet in a world that liked noise could only be tolerated so long.

The day Eloise learned she was different, the day she learned she was bad, came the same day her parents left her alone for the weekend. It wasn't the first time—they did so every year on their anniversary—but this year was different: this was the first time without Nanny.

Nanny Anne had died only three months before, leaving her to stay with Morgan's sister. It wasn't that Eloise didn't know Aunt Alma; she did. She had even stayed overnight with her. But leaving her mother was never easy, and to do so without Nanny, who knew how to distract her, was unthinkable.

Clinging to her mother, she begged her to stay. Lily had been patient. She held Eloise and let her pour out her tears into her chest until the very last moment. "You'll be all right, Lulu. Alma will take care of you. You'll have cousins to play with. Give it a few hours, and you won't even miss me."

Perhaps that was true once—with Nanny. But Eloise knew it wouldn't be so now. She could feel it. They had a tradition, Eloise and Nanny. Nanny distracted her with love— the surest of ways to get her to smile. She would take Eloise's face in her hands, and she would kiss her. Brushing back Eloise's dark hair, she would start with her forehead. Then her nose. Next, she moved to Eloise's pale cheeks before moving to her lips. *As perfect as a doll's,* she would tell her. Just like her Lily's.

Alma did nothing of the sort. She had never been one to give hugs and kisses. Tears were a nuisance. "Please don't leave me, Mommy." Tears spilled back over, and Lily dabbed them with her sleeve.

"It's two nights, Ellie," she said softly. "Two nights, and then I'll be home. Now, can you be brave for me?"

Knowing she wouldn't win, Eloise nodded. She let her parents give their goodbye kisses and watched them ride away, her heart sinking low into her chest.

"Well, come on then," Alma chirped. "Let's get your stuff in your room, and then you can play."

But Eloise didn't want to play. She couldn't explain then what she was feeling. She didn't understand it. She had lost no one. She suffered no loss. So why did she feel the way she had while watching them lower Nanny Anne into the ground? Like she would never be happy again? Like she couldn't breathe?

Eloise spent the rest of that night in her room, pleading a stomachache. It wasn't a lie. She did feel sick—sicker than she had ever felt. She missed her mother. She missed her father and Nanny Anne. All that night fears played in her head. What if her parents didn't come back? What if they left her for good? What if something happened to them?

That was the first night Eloise wondered at the length of life. As deep as she was in her sadness and aching for her mother, she couldn't fathom not feeling that ache inside her. She ceased to remember how it felt to breathe easy.

Eloise had been allowed that one night to wallow, as Alma referred to it. The next morning, Alma ordered her to get up, dress, and play with her cousins. Only she couldn't. Fear— crippling fear—had begun to run rampant in her mind. All she wanted was her mother.

When she could do nothing more than stare at the woman, Alma frowned. "You look at me right now, young lady. I have put up with this little stunt long enough." Eloise blinked back. What stunt? What had she done wrong? "It's selfish and childish, and it's right time you grew up," Alma continued. "Do you understand me?"

Selfish. Childish. Grow up. The words echoed in her head. *Selfish. Childish. Grow up.* Was that truly what she was? *Did you think you were normal? Did you think you were good?* a voice whispered in her ear. It made her shiver. It made her sick.

"Your parents should have taught you this a long time ago," Alma went on. "But seeing as they refuse, it falls on me. You are six years old, Eloise Riley. You are too old to be behaving the way you do. Now you are *going* to get up. You are *going* to get dressed, and you are *going* to eat. Then you are *going* to play. I'm not having any more excuses."

Too old. Grow up. Selfish. The words pounded in Eloise's head. She was bad.

"Do you understand me?" Alma repeated, no kindness in her voice, unaware of the war she was birthing in her niece's mind.

Tears bit at Eloise's eyes, and she beat them back. "Yes, ma'am," she whispered. She felt nothing as she readied herself— nothing but that bone-deep sadness that had settled over her as she watched her mother ride away.

Childish. Selfish. Grow up.

That night when Alma tucked her into bed, she beamed at Eloise. "You did a good job today. Doesn't it feel good to act like a big girl?"

Eloise nodded. She knew if she spoke, she would cry, and Alma hated tears. How badly she wanted her nanny's lap and the arms that held her close as she read stories from the Bible, bringing them to life in a way the pastor at church never did.

"All you needed was a firm hand, is all. You could be a good girl if your parents worked with you."

Could be. But she wasn't. She was selfish. Childish. She needed to grow up.

In the weeks that followed, Eloise barely spoke a word, even to her mother. She couldn't let her mother out of her sight. Not for baths. Not for trips to the outhouse. Eloise had a newfound fear that if she let her out of her sight, Lily would disappear and leave her for good.

It took two weeks for Lily to work out what had happened while she was gone, and by then, it was too late. The words were there, and they wouldn't be leaving, no matter how many times she told Eloise they weren't true.

She was bad.

***

From the day Alma spoke those words over her, Eloise knew she was different. Born wrong. But she didn't know how to change it. No matter how hard she tried, she couldn't rid herself of the fear she felt in the presence of others. Instead, she only found it getting worse.

Where she had once been simply quiet, she was now a near-mute. Where she had once been happy, she now spent most of her days picking out every bad thing there was about herself she needed to fix; and if she couldn't fix it, she would simply have to make up for it.

So that was what she did. If she was selfish in keeping to herself, in being unable to speak, then she would be extra good. She did what her parents told her without a second thought, and when she did mess up, the guilt was nearly overwhelming.

Eloise watched her father now as he and Brooks worked to lift the wagon high enough to procure the broken wagon wheel. She wanted to help, and yet she couldn't bring her feet to move. Couldn't bring herself to ask what she could do. This was her fault.

Morgan barely glanced up, his eyes meeting hers for only a moment. "We are going to be awhile. Why don't you find something to keep yourself busy?"

Keep herself busy. Like she was a child underfoot.

Eyes burning, Eloise nodded. "I'll gather sticks for the fire." Her legs wobbled precariously as she stood and turned to hide her tears. He blamed her, and he was right to. Had it not been for her choice, they would never have found themselves at that river to begin with.

Don't listen, she demanded. *Find another thought.* They were lies. Only lies. *Don't listen to them.* Closing her eyes, Eloise tried to listen to what was around her: the birds singing to one another, the wind in the trees. In the distance, she could hear the rushing water of the river they had crossed that morning.

The river that most of the food had been lost in.

Her eyes flew open. *No. No. Another thought. Find another thought.*

But try as she might, the thoughts came like the waves of a storm-tossed sea. She knew that her father would have been better off without her. Everyone would be.

"You can't listen to him, Eloise." The sound of her mother's voice broke the dam that had held her tears at bay. Turning Eloise to her, Lily brushed her hair behind her ear. "The enemy has no control over you, Ellie. What he whispers are lies and nothing more."

"They aren't, Mama. It's true." Her voice cracked, and the tears spilled faster.

"What's going on in there?" Mama asked, her thumb grazing Eloise's temple.

"Daddy is angry. He blames me. I know he does." They never should have left Huxley.

"Why do you think that, Eloise?"

"He won't look at me. He hasn't since …" Lily didn't make her finish, and for that, Eloise was grateful. Instead, she wrapped her arms around her and let her cry into her shoulder as more images played behind Eloise's eyelids. "I'm sorry."

"You have no reason to apologize, baby. You have nothing to be sorry for. Your father needs time. That's all." Kissing Eloise's nose, she moved behind her and began braiding her hair.

"Why won't they go, Mama? Why can't they just leave me alone?" Eloise's voice cracked. "What's wrong with me?"

Those waves within her grew taller. *Selfish. Childish. Grow up.*

"There is nothing wrong with you, Ellie." Lily pulled Eloise close, urging her to rest against her shoulder. "I love you, Ellie-

Lu, and there is nothing you can do to change that. Remember that. No matter what you think. No matter what the evil one tells you, your father and I love you more than you could begin to imagine."

Not her father. It was easy enough to believe her mother's love. But not her father's.

They are only thoughts. They aren't true. They are thoughts. Only thoughts.

That was exactly what they were—thoughts—and she was drowning in them.

***

Brooks watched the woman beside him, shoulders hunched, unwilling to meet his eyes. Not for the first time, she reminded him of the horses he worked with—abused, broken. Something was feeding on her mind, keeping her trapped within herself even in moments of joy.

As the horses struggled to pull the heavy-laden wagon through the mess, most days had found them walking beside the weary animals. One small step had them sinking to their ankles as water bubbled up around their boots. Much of their day was spent pulling one another out of the mud only to find themselves sinking back in, and much to Lily's dismay, Eloise followed the men's lead and removed her boots.

"It's unladylike, Eloise," Lily said, tossing a disgusted look at her daughter's naked feet.

"I believe it is also unladylike to tramp about in the mud, Mama," Eloise had replied. "It is also unladylike to go about in the same unwashed dress and undergarments, and yet here we are."

Lily kicked up her foot, sending fresh mud onto Eloise's dress. "I believe that was also unladylike, Mama," Eloise teased.

Ignoring her, Lily turned her nose up, trying hard to walk gracefully and failing. She had gone no more than a few steps before her booted feet slipped ankle-deep into the thick mud. When she tried to move, she fell hard on her backside.

A short burst of laughter broke through Eloise's lips before she seemed to catch herself. One hand went to her lips as red filled her cheeks. Even Morgan's ears seemed to perk up at the sound of it.

Smiling, Lily yanked her feet free and pulled at her boots. "Would you put these in the wagon for me, Lu?"

"You uncultured swine, Mama," Eloise crowed, narrowly avoiding her mother's hand as Lily took a swat at her backside. Laughing, she retraced her steps to the wagon.

Like her parents, Brooks had enjoyed seeing her step out of the sadness that seemed to cloak her. But it hadn't lasted long. Within minutes the smile had faded, and she seemed to be fighting an inward battle. What that was, Brooks didn't know, but Ida James' words were loud in his memory. *The girl tried to kill herself not two weeks ago.* When those words came to him, he thought of his mother, and his heart ached all the more for Eloise. If they truly fought the same battles, he could only imagine what was on her mind.

Was this why God sent him out? The thought had crossed his mind a dozen times. Rose Haven seemed the perfect place for a woman like Eloise, who truly did remind him so much of his mother: Quiet. Sensitive. Rejected in many places.

Brooks' mind went to the conversation he'd had with Morgan the first night he'd asked questions of Rose Haven.

It had been long after both women had gone to bed that Morgan came home. Seemingly unaware of Brooks' presence, the man sighed heavily as he hung his hat.

Brooks knew that sigh. It was the same one he had given as he relented to the nudge that drew him to Huxley. "Everything all right?"

Startling just slightly, Morgan planted himself at the table. "Tired is all. It's been a rough couple of weeks. Years, really."

"Well, maybe Rose Haven will work," Brooks said gently. "It really is a nice little town. Full of good, God-fearing folk."

"Maybe." Morgan's eyes went to Eloise's door. "She doesn't mean anything by who she is. But folks tend to take offense to it."

Offense to the quiet? "Didn't think anything of it," Brooks reassured. "She reminds me of my mother in that way. She doesn't say much either if she doesn't have a need to, and almost never around new people."

That caught the man's attention. "Is that right?" At Brooks' nod, Morgan seemed to hesitate. "And your-your community, they don't mind too much?"

"No." A soft laugh escaped Brooks' lips, quiet enough not to wake the women folk. "Mama might be a personal favorite to most folks in Rose Haven. She may not say a lot, but you won't find anyone kinder."

"That's our Ellie," Morgan said quietly. "Sweet as can be, but most don't give her the chance to show it. As my wife said, Huxley hasn't been the kindest place, and we're hoping to find a home that accepts our girl." Clearing his throat, the man looked away.

Brooks' heart ached for the man. For the whole lot of them. They all had a sadness to them that seemed to permeate the air, though none compared to Eloise. One look into the woman's dark eyes and he'd had the same sensation of looking into the eyes of a neglected foal—and with that sensation came the desire to bring light to them.

"I think Rose Haven just might be the perfect place for a woman like Eloise, Morgan," Brooks said softly. "I really do."

Seven

Huxley featured prominently in Eloise's dreams that night, and she woke covered in sweat. Her heart beat in her throat.

The sun was rising before she managed to break the surface of the waters she had sunk beneath. She wasn't in Huxley anymore, and if the Lord truly did have any kindness for her, she would never see Huxley again.

Heart still pounding too fast, she made her way down to the pond to wet her face.

Fear was often described as cold. But Eloise had never experienced such fear. Fear was hot. Fear was a heat that spread from her stomach to her face, the fiercest fire growing ever stronger in her chest. Fear was stifling.

Unsatisfied with merely wetting her face, she gathered her skirts and waded knee-deep. She had always loved water. It was familiar—water in her mind, water at her feet. Only, unlike the water she spent her days treading in her head, these waters were something she could control. She could swim beneath the surface of the pond's clear waters, and the moment she'd had enough, she could leave it behind.

Eloise knew her mother would go mad if she caught her here. Despite the fact that she refused to admit the truth of what Eloise had almost succeeded in doing—taking her own life—she wouldn't even hear of her bathing on her own. But Eloise couldn't drag herself out. The cold water calmed her nerves.

The sound of water moving made her sigh. "I'll be out in a moment, Mama."

When there was no reply, she turned to face her mother and instead found Brooks ten feet away, knee-deep as he washed his face.

Eloise felt her heart stutter a beat as he turned his eyes to hers. "Mornin'." He smiled.

"Good morning," she whispered.

Brooks smiled as he watched Eloise's lips move inaudibly. "I hope I didn't disturb you. I would have waited, but I was hoping to get on the road as soon as possible and, well ..." He waved around, indicating the little space the pond allowed them.

He had nearly abandoned the idea of washing his face, uncertain of what the Rileys would think of his being in such close proximity to their unchaperoned daughter. But his dreams had been full of uncertainty, and he had woken with a need to wash it away.

Eloise's lips moved inaudibly again. When she took a deep breath, he could see the effort she put into raising her voice. It still didn't reach him, and even from a distance, he could see the tears that threatened to spill over.

Moving a few feet closer, he tried again. "I'm sorry?"

"You didn't disturb me," she said breathlessly, a pale pink filling her cheeks.

Brooks nodded toward the wagons, hoping to draw her mind elsewhere. "Theo seems to be doing well on the journey. You've done well with him."

"I didn't do anything."

"You did, Elle. You have to give yourself some credit." The woman had a gift for it. If only she would see it. Like Brooks, she understood horses.

When Eloise shrugged, Brooks tried something new. "About two weeks until we reach Rose Haven. Are you excited?"

That brought a small smile to her lips, and she nodded. "I, um, I'm sure you must be."

"Very much so. I've been on a few extended trips but never for this long. Been missing my family." He cleared his throat. "But I'm sure I'll appreciate it all the more having been gone so long."

"Eloise." They both turned at the sound of Lily's voice. "Eloise, get up here, please."

Nodding at Brooks, Eloise stumbled back up the bank while he made his way back to his own wagon. Expecting a lecture from her mother, she startled at the smile on Lily's face. "Ellie, would you get Brooks for breakfast?"

"What?"

"Tell him breakfast is ready."

"That's all?" Eloise asked.

"Yes," Lily said, exasperated. "What's wrong with you?"

"I thought you … never mind."

Seeing her confusion, Lily softened. "I did see you, and I am trying to trust you, Eloise. I can't look after you forever." Kissing her daughter's cheek, she pushed her forward. "Now, please go fetch Brooks. And would you please put your shoes on?"

Doing as requested, Eloise forced her feet into her boots before making her way to Brooks' wagon.

My mother wanted to invite you to breakfast. Mama was hoping you would join us for breakfast. Her heart beat faster as she approached him, his back to her as he rifled through a crate.

Eloise took a deep breath. *Mama was hoping you would join us.* Only her lips didn't move. *My mother wanted to invite you to breakfast. Just say it, Eloise. Mama wanted to invite you. Mama wanted to invite you. Mama wanted to invite you.* Still, her lips remained tight as if glue held them in place.

Stupid. Childish. Grow up.

Beating back tears, she tried again and failed. Finally, she cleared her throat. But it wasn't until Brooks turned on his own accord that he noticed her.

Giving a small start, he tilted his hat, another smile on his lips. "Elle."

In spite of herself, she gave a tremulous smile. "My mother was hoping you would join us for breakfast again."

"I'd love to." He smiled crookedly. "Tell your mother I'll be over just as soon as—" Before he could finish, one of his horses tossed its head back and brayed. "Just as soon as I finish with Era." Turning his back to her, Brooks set his forehead to the space between the horse's chestnut eyes. "Don't you worry, girl. We'll get you taken care of, and the moment we get home, I'll let you rest a good long while. How's that?"

The horse nickered, rubbing its head against Brooks. Turning her back on the sight, Eloise started back toward her own wagon.

"Eloise?" When she turned back, Brooks nodded toward the horse. "I could use your help if you're willing. Era's got herself a rock in her shoe, and she's a bit dramatic. Would you be willing to keep her distracted while I work it out?"

Eloise's face washed white. "Distracted?"

59

"With carrots." Grabbing a crate of them, Brooks set it at her feet. "She'll do anything for them."

"I—" Eloise glanced back toward her site, where both Rileys were watching. "All right."

"Right then. Stay back," Brooks warned. "I don't want you getting hurt. Just toss 'em, and she'll catch 'em." Instructing her on where to stand, Brooks went to work on the shoe.

The moment he touched the thing, Era reared her head, letting out an ear-splitting screech. "Easy, girl," Brooks cooed. "Carrot, Elle."

At his command, Eloise tossed a carrot, smiling when the horse's screams cut off to catch the vegetable in midair.

It took ten minutes and as many carrots to get the rock out. Standing, Brooks patted the beast's rump. "Good girl, Era." Turning to Eloise, he tipped his hat. "Thank you, Elle. That would have taken a good deal longer if not for you."

"Will she be all right?"

"Oh, she'll be fine. Didn't even puncture the sole."

Clearly having had enough now, Morgan's voice reached them. "Food is getting cold. If you two want to eat, you better come get it."

Laughing, Brooks waved Eloise forward. "After you."

Sitting at the fire, Brooks added a handful of his own food supplies to the mix. The Rileys' supply had been low on goods even before they crossed the river, and with what they lost, they were looking scarce. Though he offered his own food at every meal, his supply was still too large. Elizabeth had sent her son with enough to keep a family of four fed for six months. "I've been living on this for nearly three months, and I still have too much. My mother will accuse me of going hungry."

"I'll bet she'll be excited to see you again." Lily smiled. "I couldn't begin to imagine Ellie being gone so long. I don't know what I would do with myself."

"I don't think she would either, if not for my sisters. But Mabel was in a family way when I left, which I am sure has kept my mother's attention. It'll be my parents' first grandchild."

"How old are your sisters? And you, for that matter? Might be good to know a bit about you all before we get there."

"Twenty-three, ma'am. Mabel is twenty-one. She married the owner of the hotel, Matthew, just two years ago. Then there's Maisie, who turned thirteen at the beginning of the year. Maisie." Brooks smiled. "She's, uh … she's her own sort. Let's put it that way." He nodded towards his wagon and horses. "I have her to thank for their odd names—Era and Chesire. She's named every horse I've got after characters from her favorite books."

Lily smiled at that. "You said you grew up in Rose Haven?"

"Yes, ma'am." A blush filled Brooks' cheeks. "My family was the first to settle there. My parents founded Rose Haven with my aunt and her late husband when the latter two set up the mercantile."

"Town founders." Morgan laughed. "Would have thought you'd spill that secret sooner. Town founders, hotels, mercantiles, and here you are setting up your own ranch."

Brooks laughed. "I suppose the town brings it out of you, and you yourself will fit right in once you start up that old mill. You just might be a favorite."

The moment breakfast was through, the men went to ready the horses while Lily and Eloise cleared the dishes.

Lily nudged her daughter as Brooks gave her another tip of his hat before following Morgan. "He's sweet, Eloise, and respectful."

"Yes." Eloise smiled. "He is." It wasn't often she found someone who didn't make her feel guilty for her silence.

"You seem comfortable with him."

"I wouldn't say comfortable," Eloise said quietly. "But I don't hate it." Which she supposed was as comfortable as it got for her. It was strange, though, that aside from trying to get his attention, it wasn't often she felt paralyzed in his presence. How could she when he was nothing but patient and spoke to her as though she were as normal as anyone else?

Lily smiled, her eyes bright with tears. "I know I shouldn't say it, Ellie. I don't want to embarrass you. But I'm proud of you, sweetheart. You've done well with him. I haven't seen you so comfortable with anyone but me since you were a girl."

It was a long moment before Eloise could find the nerve to speak the words, "Do you really think his town could be it?"

"I do, Eloise. If they're anything like him, I can't imagine it being wrong."

Eight

Five miles to go. Five miles and Brooks would be home. With his family. Sleeping in his own bed.

Merritt would be finishing up in the fields now. Elizabeth would be setting the table for supper, probably prying a book from Maisie's reluctant fingers.

Being a Wednesday, they would have no other company, which Brooks was thankful for when thinking of the woman beside him. If Eloise truly was like his mother, he didn't want to overwhelm her.

Watching the way she worked at the blanket wrapped around her shoulders, Brooks had an image of a horse pawing at the ground in agitation. Despite Lily's concern over proper handling, she'd relented to Eloise riding up with him. The wagon beds were too packed, and walking would have doubled the time.

The woman had said little over their eight hours, and what she did say had been coaxed out of her. Perhaps it was simply his experience with his mother, but nothing in her demeanor told him she meant offense. Though reluctant to offer conversation on her own, when prompted with questions, she was accommodating. Soft-spoken. Unsure. Not proud or arrogant.

But people had a habit of writing off those they didn't understand. He'd seen it enough times in the horses he handled. Those who required more time and patience were deemed too proud or wild and were often passed off to another to handle or otherwise neglected and abused.

Brooks didn't know what it was about this woman. Perhaps it was that she did remind him so much of his mother, and he heard the stories of the treatment she had been given. Or maybe it was that he had never seen such a bone-deep sadness in one person's eyes. All he knew was that he felt the same way he did when he brought in a new and difficult horse, and when that feeling entered his bones, there was no way to turn him from it.

***

In his excitement to be home, Brooks near forgot Eloise as his feet hit the ground. He was halfway to the door when he remembered he wasn't alone. "I am so sorry," he said, sure he'd done it now. "Lost my head a moment."

The woman simply laughed, her dark eyes losing a hint of that sorrow.

"You go on ahead," Lily assured, her arms going around Eloise's shoulders. "We don't want to disturb your reunion."

The familiar scent of lavender washed over Brooks as he stepped inside, the last bit of stress falling away.

Maisie was the first to notice him. Her squeal was piercing as she threw her book aside. "Brooks." Her carrot hair near smothered him, wild curls breaking loose from their braid as she threw her arms around Brooks' neck.

"Oh, I missed you, Lilybit." He laughed, using the nickname he penned for her when she was two years old—when her tongue was clumsy on her given name.

"You're here to stay, right?" Maisie croaked. "You're not going to leave again?"

Before Brooks could answer, their mother urged Maisie aside with a gentle pat on her backside. "Brooksie." Her fingers brushed his cheek. "She's right; I can't stand to lose you to someplace so far away."

Seeing the tears she failed to keep back, Brooks wrapped Elizabeth in his arms. "I missed you, Mama." He hadn't realized just how much until now. "I'm not going anywhere." Keeping an arm around her, he looked at his father. "I was hoping we could talk about that stretch of land you were looking to sell."

"I thought you weren't interested in it?" Merritt asked.

"It's not for me." He quickly explained the Rileys' situation. "They're waiting outside now."

Elizabeth smacked his chest. "Brooks. Why didn't you tell us sooner?" Muttering something about men, she fetched four more plates. "Go bring them inside; I'll set a few more places for supper."

Ushering them in, Brooks made the quick introductions. "My mother, Elizabeth, and my father, Merritt, and there's Maisie over there, already buried in her book."

"Mae Elizabeth." Merritt sighed, holding out his hand. "Book."

"Yes, Papa." Handing him the book, Maisie rested her chin in her palm. "I only have a few chapters left."

Elizabeth smiled. "If you stop your pouting and help with the dishes, maybe I'll let you stay up late to finish it. How's that sound?"

That brought a smile to Maisie's face. "I think I could live with that."

Making sure everyone found their seats, Elizabeth looked at her husband. "Why don't we talk business after supper?" she said quietly. "Let Brooks and the Rileys enjoy their meal."

After a quick prayer, Lily pulled Elizabeth into a conversation about the town, asking about its people and the feel of it. Remembering what she'd been told, Lily was patient and willing to guide the conversation when Elizabeth hesitated.

Next to them, Merritt was telling Morgan about the old sawmill. "The man didn't have a wife or family, so it was all left to us when he died just a year after starting it up. We've been praying a man would come along and start it up again. Our oldest daughter is due to have a baby in a month or so, and they're still living in one of the rooms in their hotel. But getting decent lumber now requires a few days' travel."

"Do you have a price in mind?" Morgan asked. "I'm afraid, with buying land, I just won't have what I need to go starting up a business."

"The business is yours, Riley. It's going to waste as is." Seeing Morgan meant to protest, Merritt clapped him on the shoulder. "How about you pay me in the form of giving my girl and her husband a good home?"

Morgan laughed. "Sounds good. It'll be the least I can do."

Beside Brooks, Eloise was quiet, though she seemed content listening to Maisie babble on. She seemed almost comfortable. It was hard not to be with Maisie, who could make a friend out of anyone.

"Take a breath, Lilybit." Brooks laughed. "Give Elle a chance to process."

"I don't mind," Eloise said quietly. She liked not having to worry about sharing. Maisie seemed content to do all the speaking herself.

It wasn't until Maisie started talking about the upcoming school year that Eloise felt the waters stirring. Even Morgan's mood dipped. "I've never been to a real school." Maisie sighed. "Mama's taught all three of us. I bet you've been to a real school. Is it wonderful?"

And there it was, the wave to drag her under. "I, um … it's …" Maisie watched her expectantly. "It was … all right." Eloise could feel the tears biting her eyes now.

"It had to have been more than all right. I can just imagine all that you got to learn—math, and science and English."

Cruelty, humiliation, how to breathe when you're drowning —those were the things Eloise learned at school. "You really don't learn more in school than at home, Maisie. I promise you."

"But—"

"Maisie," Brooks whispered. "Drop it."

"But—"

"Mae Elizabeth."

"Oh, all right," she muttered. "I was just curious."

Excusing herself, Eloise hurried outside before the tears could spill over. *Don't think about it. You aren't there anymore. You never have to go back. Don't think about it. Don't think about it.*

Gaining a small piece of control, Eloise made her way toward their wagon.

Resting her head against Theo's, she sighed. "God, please." *Please what? Please release me? Please let me die?* She wasn't entirely sure what she wanted anymore.

***

Brooks resisted the urge to catch his sister as she followed after the women. He could talk to her in the morning. Now he had to take care of the horses.

"Would you send Ellie in if you see her?" Lily asked. Her eyes had strayed to the door a dozen times since Eloise disappeared.

Giving his word, Brooks slipped outside. He could have shaken his sister. It had taken everything in him not to take her aside right there. Had she learned nothing from growing up with their mother? He had seen the way the color had drained from Eloise's face at the mere mention of school, and yet Maisie had barreled on, as unaware of others as she always was.

Keeping an eye out for Eloise, Brooks led his own horses in the barn first. He found her when he returned for the Rileys' wagon. "Your mother was worried," he said. "She asked me to send you in."

Nodding, she turned in that direction. The woman looked so miserable that he felt the words slip out of their own accord. "Elle." She looked back. "I'm sorry about Maisie. She's sweet, I promise you. But she's not always the most aware."

Eloise simply nodded before taking him in. "Are you putting our horses away?"

"My parents invited you all to stay for the night. Mama is getting ready to show your parents the soddy while you'll be staying with Maisie in her room. We still have Mabel's old bed in there, so you'll have your own place to sleep."

Eloise said nothing, so Brooks tried again. "It's not like what you're used to here, Eloise. There's a reason my mother chose to name the town what it is. Rose Haven tends to be … well, just what it sounds like: a haven. My mother found her happiness here, and I believe you can too."

"It's not that simple," Eloise said quietly.

"No. It'll take hard work. On everyone's part, I am sure."

"Everyone?" The way the word left her lips was almost foreign, as though she'd never heard anyone tell her otherwise.

"Well …" Brooks looked at the horses. "Have you ever had a pet?"

Eloise shook her head.

"Well, I've had a few, and I've been training horses for almost ten years. Most of them have come with a history of abuse and neglect. If there's one thing I've learned, it's that you can't expect the horse to grow on its own. You have to earn its trust. You have to help it see that not everyone is out to hurt it. If you left the horse to fend for itself, it would only grow wild. Turn aggressive or withdraw. Do you understand?"

"I … I think so."

Brooks smiled. "This isn't Huxley, Elle. You aren't alone here."

Eloise pursed her lips. Edith and Grace said the same thing before they grew bored. How long before Brooks realized she wasn't worth the effort?

"You still don't believe me, do you?"

Tears bit at Eloise's eyes, and she didn't bother beating them back. "I've heard words like that before, Brooks."

"But not from me, Eloise. I've never given up on a horse, no matter how hopeless they might have seemed, and I have no plans to give up on you." He gave another crooked smile. "I don't mind a good challenge."

Nine

I've never given up on a horse, and I have no plans to give up on you. Eloise wanted to believe it. She wanted to believe that she had finally found her place, found people that cared. But Brooks didn't know her. She was a new object he would soon grow bored of as soon as he realized how dull she was.

Taking a deep breath, Eloise tried to force the thoughts away. To keep her head above the surface. "Don't let me drown, God. Please."

Rose Haven was a second chance, and she had to believe it would lead her away from that tub.

Due in part to Maisie's wonderings, school was the setting of her dreams that night as it often was. Each one dark and bleak and hopeless, Eloise woke in a cold sweat, heart pounding in her throat. Rolling over, she stared at the orange-tinted sky. If she were still in school, Lily would be walking through the door at any moment, urging her to get up.

But she wasn't. She was eighteen. She was an adult now.

The sound of the knob turning sent all logical thought out the door. Pulling the blankets over her head, she fought to keep herself grounded.

"Mais." Brooks' whisper broke through the noise in her head, offering a lifeline, and she clung to it. "Lilybit, I'm going out to take a look at the land. Did you want to come?"

"I can go?" Maisie whispered, the adoration for her brother clear even in her voice.

70

"If you want. I already cleared it with Mama." When Maisie let out a small squeal, Brooks hushed her. "Just get dressed and meet me outside, you little rascal."

Eloise waited for the door to shut behind Maisie before moving. Wanting to turn her mind from the dream and the memories that accompanied it, she dressed before making her bed and then Maisie's for good measure.

Easing the door open, she listened for her mother's voice. "Ellie." Lily laughed as Eloise jumped, nearly crushing her fingers in the door. "Easy, Eloise. Come here." Opening the door, Eloise moved to the small sitting room across from Maisie's room.

"Good morning, Eloise," Elizabeth said, soft-spoken. "I hope my children didn't wake you."

Eloise shook her head and accepted the mug of tea Lily passed her. Eyes moving back to Elizabeth, her mother kept one hand on Eloise's leg, her thumb moving back and forth across her thigh.

Eloise couldn't help but watch Elizabeth Harper speak. She could see it—the pieces of herself that were in her. Though she appeared comfortable with Lily, she didn't say much, and what she did say was quiet. Though perhaps not as badly as Eloise, she relied on Lily to guide the conversation. Maybe it was only because she did it herself, but Eloise couldn't help noticing the way Elizabeth's eyes would close every time she finished speaking. As though she were questioning her choice of word or perhaps the way she said it.

But, despite it all, she still seemed happy. She enjoyed the conversation with Lily. She had even managed to find a man who loved her despite all the reasons he could have chosen not to.

Maybe Eloise did have a chance.

***

Maisie kept up a steady stream of chatter on the ride, most of which went in one of Brooks' ears and out the other. He loved his sister more than life itself, but the child never quit, and most of it went over his head. The girl was too smart for her own good.

It was only when she was quiet, as she was now, that Brooks knew she was thinking hard about something.

"Cat got your tongue, Mais?" Brooks teased.

It was another moment before she spoke. "Eloise is pretty," she said casually.

"Is she?"

Maisie smacked his arm. "Don't pretend you didn't notice. I know you noticed, Brooks. I saw you looking at her last night." Maisie's dark eyes were dreamy. "You couldn't keep your eyes off of her."

Brooks laughed quietly. "What's the latest book you've been reading, Lilybit? I think it's getting you all romantic."

"I'm rereading Alice in Wonderland, thank you very much, and it hasn't got me all romantic. I'm not a child anymore, Brooks. I see things, and you were looking at her."

Brooks eyed his sister. "Now you choose to be observant?" He sighed. "You got me, Lilybit. She's beautiful. But I don't want you going and getting ideas. I barely even know the woman."

He barely knew her, yet it didn't stop the strange shift in his stomach when he looked at her or when she smiled.

"She reminds me a bit of the way Papa says Mama was when they met," Maisie said softly.

"Yeah, she does," Brooks agreed, thankful for the excuse to bring up what he had been working himself toward all morning. "That means you need to be patient with her, Mae Elizabeth. You can't go pulling what you did last night, you understand me? Don't go treating her like she's different than anyone else, but make sure you back off when she needs it."

"Well, how do I know when she needs it?"

"Open your eyes, Maisie. I know it's hard, but try paying attention to the world around you sometimes rather than just the one in your head."

"Oh," she said quietly.

Seeing he upset her, Brooks tugged one of her braids. "I don't mean to hurt your feelings, Lilybit, and there's nothing wrong with living in your head sometimes. But there are times when you need to come out."

"I didn't mean to upset her," Maisie whispered. "I was just curious. I wish I'd had her schooling."

"I know, and I am sure she understands. But from the looks of it, I'd say she wishes she'd had your schooling."

Maisie gave him a look. "It isn't even school."

"School isn't a building, Maisie, and Mama is doing the best she can with what she has. It's time you start appreciating it. You said it yourself—you're not a little girl anymore. You have to stop complaining about what you've been given. You need to start paying attention." Brooks nudged her. "If you can notice me looking at Eloise, I think you can pay attention to other things. Like Mama's feelings. Like Elle's. You can't just take the fun bits of growing up."

"I think I'd rather go back to being a little girl," she muttered.

"Too late."

"All right," she sighed. "I'll be patient with her. I'll try to pay attention. I do feel bad, you know—about last night. And I did apologize."

"That's good, Mais," Brooks said. "You're growing up."

Maisie shrugged, her mood souring. "Did you really have to 'Mae Elizabeth' me?"

"It got your attention, did it not?"

She glared back at him. "Did you invite me just to lecture me?"

"Not entirely." Getting an arm around her, Brooks kissed the top of her head. "I missed you, Lilybit. Now hush."

Sticking her tongue out at him, Maisie leaned back and closed her eyes.

Grateful for the quiet, Brooks tried to turn his mind back to the problem of his land. The land wasn't his yet, and he wasn't entirely sure it ever would be. He'd never intended to buy so much. But the land was beautiful and left him room to grow, should the Lord will it.

He had always planned for the ranch to be small—a place to train and rehabilitate horses—but he could do so much more with land that size. Brooks knew he could push it back, take a few more years. Earn and save. But by then, who knew if that land would be available? He had worked his entire life for the savings he had now, and he didn't want to wait. Seventeen years had already come and gone, waiting for this moment.

He could take a loan, but the idea of going in with that much debt over his head made him sick. He didn't want to spend the rest of his life paying off land. He wanted security—especially if he was right about the strange feeling taking root in him.

Brooks sighed as his mind wandered to Eloise. The woman was messing with his mind. He'd never desired marriage. He was content on his own and would be content with nieces and nephews. But that contentment didn't stop a strange knowing from growing within him in the time he shared with Eloise. He had known the woman little more than a month, and he knew—if he was being honest, he knew from the moment he looked at her —that she was beautiful. That fact couldn't be denied, but there was something more to it—an ache in his chest at the mere thought of her, at the idea of her pain.

God, I never wanted this. I was content on my own.

That small voice bid him to trust.

Trust. Why do I have the feeling I'm going to be needing a lot of that?

***

Brooks spent the rest of the day pouring over the numbers. Counting his savings and trying to force an answer. Looking for any miscalculation that might make the land a possibility.

Impossible. It was impossible. Even if he did work and save for another year, he wouldn't have enough. His chest felt heavy. He'd been building the dream since he was six years old, and his father had put him on his first horse and walked him about the property. He'd saved every Christmas and birthday penny. Done chores and odd jobs. Every second of his life had been devoted to this dream.

Setting his book down, Merritt stood and made his way to his son. "Take a break, Brooks." Getting a hand under his elbow, Merritt pulled the boy to his feet. "Why don't you and I take a walk? Get you some fresh air."

Relenting, Brooks followed after him. "I've got some bit of news that might cheer you up," Merritt said. "The Rileys bought that piece of land off me, and Morgan plans to take a ride down there tomorrow to check out the mill."

"That's great, Dad. Mabel will be happy to be getting a house."

"That she will." Merritt laughed. "The girl's shed a good number of tears worrying over it." An uncommon habit for Mabel, but then Brooks assumed that was the pregnancy. "We already got it worked out. The Rileys will spend the winter in the soddy while Eloise stays in with Maisie."

At least five months of Eloise under his roof? Sitting next to him for three meals a day? Brooks felt something inside him rise —a ray of hope at the thought of her close proximity—and he squashed it down.

Mistaking his silence for worry, Merritt clapped his back. "Now don't go getting so discouraged yet, boy. Your mother and I have been talking, and we want to help you purchase the land. We got that extra money now from the Rileys, and Annabelle and Archer said they'll provide what they can as well. It won't be much, but it will save you some."

"Dad, I can't ask—"

"You aren't asking. We are offering. You know your mother, Annabelle, and I have always made sure to give to those who need it, and you are no different."

Rose Haven had been founded with the intent of helping others reach their own dreams. To find a safe haven where they could put down roots and raise families. And part of that involved Brooks' parents giving his sister-in-law and her late husband what they needed to build up the mercantile with the promise of repayment in the form of goods. Whatever it took, Brooks' parents never turned someone out of their town because of things like money.

"It's a loan, Brooks, that you can pay back in whatever form you can. Horses. Boarding." Merritt smiled. "Your mother would say by giving her a daughter-in-law and some grandbabies."

Brooks let out a small laugh. "Mabel and Maisie aren't enough?"

"They would be if she knew you would be happy on your own. Your mother worries about you, Brooks. You may think you'll be happy out there on your own or that you can live your life without a family, and you could if that was the Lord's will," Merritt clarified. "But, son, you always said the same thing about the need for friends, and look at the road it led you down." Merritt squeezed his shoulder. "You may not require much in terms of people, but you can't deny that you do need more than yourself."

Merritt watched the boy run a hand through his hair. Whether Brooks admitted it or not, there was a hole in his life. Perhaps it could be plugged for a time when with his family, but out on his property, with nothing but himself and the horses, Merritt feared what would become of him. The two letters they'd received in his travels were not the humorous, unworried man he was when home with his family; they'd expected to see Brooks coming home forlorn, with pieces of him they'd have to pick up and try to lovingly piece back together. Instead, though a bit discouraged, they'd found a new, almost uncertain light in his eyes when he looked at the Riley girl.

Brooks sighed. "I take it Maisie isn't the only one with ideas?"

"I know that look, Brooks. You think I didn't have that same look when I met your mother? I am not saying it means anything. What do I know of the Lord's plans? But I do know that you would be good for someone like her."

Brooks wasn't so sure about that. "I never accounted for marriage," he said, "or a family."

"But the Lord did. Brooks, you can't let your fear of getting hurt keep you from something the Lord is leading you towards. You'll only end up going down the path you did ten years ago."

Brooks chewed at his lip, his mind going back ten years to that hollow, empty ache and the sins that accompanied it. "I do believe there might be something," he admitted softly, unwilling to walk that path again. "Don't know what it is, but I've felt it since the first moment I spoke to her."

Merritt smiled. "Accept the loan, Brooks. We all want to see you achieve your dream, and if a family is anywhere in your near future, you need to be set. Not worrying over every penny."

The tears that Brooks had been fighting all morning—all summer—finally spilled over, and his father brought him into a tight hug. "Thank you, Pa."

"You're welcome, my boy. Now go get your land."

Ten

An only child, Eloise had never shared a room before, and what she had thought would be one night would now be five months. At least. It would all depend on when the snow melted and the ground thawed.

She didn't mean to be selfish. She didn't mean to be ungrateful. But privacy was not a simple desire; it was a need. In Huxley, her room had been her haven. The place she went when she needed to silence her thoughts or otherwise break in privacy. She had nearly gone mad on the road with nowhere to escape.

"It's only a few months." Lily sighed. "The Harpers are being very kind to let us stay here, Eloise. You know we could never afford to stay in a hotel that long."

Another wave crashed over her. Selfish. Ungrateful. Grow up.

"I don't mean to sound ungrateful, Mama. But …" Eloise could feel the panic settling over her. No privacy. Living in a home that wasn't hers, full of people she didn't know.

"I know. But sweetie" —Lily tucked her daughter's hair behind her ear before tilting her chin up— "I think this will be good for you—to get a little distance from your father and me in a place where you know they will be patient with you."

"We can't know that, Mama."

"Yes, Eloise. We can. This time I really do believe we can trust these people. Maisie seems very sweet, and Elizabeth already loves you. She believes a little distance will be good for you too. She says she grew a bit more independent after she was married and couldn't rely quite so closely on her sister." Lily wiped the tears that dripped down Eloise's cheeks. "It will be good, Ellie. Merritt understands, and Brooks—well, he's been the kindest of all. Hasn't he?"

It couldn't be denied that Brooks understood, that he cared to some degree—and that was what made her nervous: she knew that his leaving would be the most painful.

"Just try having faith, Eloise. Not everyone is terrible. Not everyone is going to leave you." Kissing Eloise's head, she encouraged her to go to bed. "We can talk in the morning."

The soft click of the door behind her mother ignited the voices in her mind.

What did her mother know? They would leave her. Grow tired of her.

Before she could sink any deeper, Maisie burst through the door. "Sorry." She blushed. "I forgot you were in here."

Eloise shrugged. "It's your room, Maisie."

"Well, our room," Maisie corrected. "It's a good thing we never got rid of Mabel's bed. We almost did, but Papa never had the time." She smiled her brother's same crooked grin. "I guess God knew what He was doing, huh?"

"Yes." Eloise supposed it could have been God. But coincidence seemed more likely.

Maisie watched Eloise prepare for bed. "Are you all right, Eloise?"

"I'm fine. Just tired." Crawling into bed, Eloise wished her goodnight before pulling the blankets up to her chin.

"Mama uses that excuse," Maisie said quietly. "When her mind is getting to her."

The seconds ticked by as Maisie waited for Eloise to say something. But Eloise's lips refused to move.

Finally, Maisie sighed. "Goodnight, Eloise."

Eloise knew she wouldn't hear it, but she said it anyway. "Night, Maisie."

***

Eloise woke the next morning to Maisie giving her a small shake. "Eloise," she hissed. "We're all going into town. Your mother said to get dressed."

Five minutes later, Eloise took what had become her seat at the table between Brooks and Maisie. "Mornin'." Brooks smiled, causing Eloise's heart to give a small skip. It was too early for that smile. "Hope Mais didn't wake you too roughly."

Unable to speak, Eloise shook her head. She forced a small smile before taking in his own. That dark voice within her wondered what he thought of her smile. Ducking her head, Eloise prayed he would turn his attention elsewhere.

Though he might have, Maisie had other ideas. "Mrs. Riley, would you mind if Eloise rode with Brooks and me?"

"Maybe ask if Eloise wants to first, Maisie," Merritt said.

"Well, I don't mind if she does." Lily smiled. "Ellie?"

As if she could say no with everyone's eyes on her. "I can do that," she said quietly. "If Brooks doesn't mind."

"Not at all." His smile was so sincere that Eloise almost believed it. But waves were crashing over her, pulling her under. He couldn't say no if he wanted to. He was too kind for that.

Shut up. Shut up. Shut up.

Excusing herself, Eloise hurried outside, shutting herself in the outhouse before the tears broke free. Sliding her back down the wall, she brought her knees to her chest. "God, please. I can't breathe."

Her mind was a storm, the waters rough, the waves high as the thoughts grew and multiplied. One after the other. He wasn't listening. Nothing would change.

The sob that broke free was guttural. "Please." Her mind was screaming for her to give up. Shaking her head, she searched her mind for the old scripture Nanny had taught her, fighting every voice that told her it was pointless. He wouldn't hear her.

Unable to recall the scripture, she clung to the first that came to her. "Isaiah," she whispered. "Fear not: for I have redeemed thee, I have called thee by thy name; thou art mine."

That voice within her reminded her she was nothing. "I am His. I am His. I am His." She let out a sharp sob, painful truth settling over her. She wasn't His. There was no purpose in her birth. In her still being here. What was she doing for Him? For anyone? "Just let me die, God."

***

Eloise avoided Brooks' eyes as she let him lift her into the wagon.

Brooks couldn't understand it. The moment she had disappeared, he had gone over everything that had been said, trying to piece together what could have caused what he was looking at now, but he couldn't see it.

His mother found him after breakfast, discouraging him from looking for Eloise. "It could be anything, Brooks," she said softly. "Give her a moment. Let her calm down, and then you can check on her."

"It doesn't seem right to leave her alone."

"That is exactly what she wants right now, Brooks. I know. Lily knows. Don't you think Lily would have gone after her own daughter if she didn't know better?"

How was he to leave her when Ida's words were fresh in his mind? "Do you have any idea what it could be?" Brooks asked. "Maybe I can avoid it next time."

"You can't avoid setting off that voice, Brooks. Kind or cruel, something you say will bring it to the surface. The most you can do is be patient with her when something does get to her."

Patient. It sounded simple enough.

***

Eloise stared down at her hands. If not for the gentle shake of her shoulders, Brooks might not have known that silent tears still poured down her cheeks. She even knew how to cry in silence.

Papa, what do I do? What can I say to her?

That voice bid him patience.

Sighing, Brooks forced his eyes on the road. Was he supposed to let her suffer? How was it God could let her suffer?

Checking first that Maisie was distracted, Brooks spoke softly. "Eloise." When her eyes met his, they were red-rimmed. "Eloise, if you want to talk, I'm here. I'll listen."

She let out a soft laugh before shaking her head, the tears spilling over. "You wouldn't understand."

"Do you want to try, maybe?"

Eloise was silent, chewing at her lip. "You don't get it, Brooks. I don't say that to pity myself. I say it because it's true."

"Ell—"

"I've talked to people before, Brooks. I told them what went on in my head, and they acted like they understood, and then they left."

"I'm not them, Eloise. I'm not … I'm not going to grow bored of you. Or leave because you aren't what I think you should be." Shaking his head, Brooks tried again. "I'm not going to push you, Elle. I am not going to make you tell me anything. I just want you to know that I'm here. That I'll listen."

Eloise watched him, her eyes skeptical. "Why?"

"Because I may have only known you a few weeks, but I have seen and heard enough to know that you don't deserve whatever it is that people have done to you. Because—because my mother used to be this way." He waved at her. "And it breaks my heart to think of someone letting her go on feeling that way. So why would I let you go on this way?"

"You don't know anything about me, Brooks."

The words were little more than a whisper, but she may as well have shouted for the impact they had. "No," Brooks said quietly. "I don't. But that doesn't change the fact that I am here —that I'll listen."

Eloise eyed him a long moment before sighing. "You really won't understand, Brooks. If I told you what I was feeling, you would tell me it wasn't true."

"Well, it isn't."

That earned him a small smile. "I know." Wiping the last of her tears, she looked back at her hands. "Can we talk about something else, please?"

Brooks nodded. "Of course. Anything specific in mind?" When Eloise froze, Brooks smiled. "Are you excited to see the town? It's your town too, now."

Eloise nodded, another shy smile on her lips. Encouraged, she continued. "Have, um, have you always lived here?"

"Born and raised. Though, of course, it wasn't an official town yet, and we were still known as Dakota territory. Rose Haven was penned when I was about three, while Montana was designated its own territory only three years ago." Brooks almost asked about her life in Huxley before thinking better of it.

"I was born in Huxley," she offered. "It's where my parents were born too."

Brooks watched the way her hands worried at her gingham dress, the cream-colored fabric faded from years of nervous fingering. "Do you truly have no happy memories there, Eloise?"

"I have some, but ... not for a very long time." She rubbed at her eyes. "That sounds like I'm wallowing, doesn't it?"

"No. It sounds honest." His mother spoke the same over her old life. "But I hope we can change that."

Her lips trembled as she smiled. "Me too."

"We will," Maisie piped in.

"Geez, Mais," Brooks breathed. "I forgot you were back there."

"You told me to start listening. So I did." Resting her arms on the back seat, Maisie looked at Eloise. "I think you'll like it here, Eloise. The only people we ever have trouble with are the Mitchells. And just wait until you meet Auntie!"

"Annabelle's a good one," Brooks agreed. "She'll be good to you, Elle. She practically raised Mama, and I think she just might whack anyone who mistreated her." Eloise smiled at that, and Brooks found himself smiling back. "Believe me, she'll do the same for you. She's very passionate about it."

Pulling up outside the mercantile, Brooks helped Eloise down before going to help Maisie. When he settled Maisie on her feet, he kept one arm around her shoulder.

Eloise stood back. Was she supposed to follow after them or wait for her mother? Looking back, Brooks smiled. "Come on, Elle."

Brooks waited with the door open. "That there is Annabelle," he said, nodding toward the woman at the counter. "I'll introduce you when she's free." Seeing her uncertainty, he put a hand on her shoulder. "I don't have to. But she's a good one, Eloise. She'd make you feel comfortable."

Eloise looked back toward the woman. Annabelle Crawley was where the Harper children got their red hair, though her gray-streaked chignon more closely resembled Maisie's carrot-red mane. When the woman spotted them, she smiled. "Brooks."

At the sound of his name, half the occupants of the mercantile turned. Many eyes found her at his side, his hand still at her shoulder. Blushing, Brooks stepped back and shoved his hands into his pockets as people converged around him.

The air was full of questions and greetings. When did he get back? Did he have any luck? Who was the pretty girl next to him?

Like an anchor at her feet, Eloise felt herself sink. Her heart pounded in her ears. All around her, people pressed in. Her vision blurred. A dozen people talked over one another until it became a buzz in her ears.

Grabbing Eloise's hand, Maisie pulled her through the crowd of people and back outside. "Sit," she ordered. Taking the seat next to her, Maisie looked back toward the door. "Sorry about that. Brooks is popular around here. A lot of people missed him."

When her heart had settled, and she could breathe, Eloise forced a laugh. "That doesn't bother him?"

"I wouldn't say he likes it. Brooks is very private, but he can handle it when he has to." Maisie shivered. "I don't understand it."

That made Eloise pause. The way Maisie acted, Eloise would have thought she loved that sort of attention. "You don't like attention?"

Maisie smiled. "Not like that, and especially not when they press in on you. When they start talking over each other, I feel like my head is about to burst." Now that Eloise looked at her, the girl was breathing as hard as she was, and though she didn't shake as Eloise did, her hands were trembling. "I can handle some attention. I'll have to, to some degree."

"Why is that?"

Maisie was quiet a moment. "I expect you can keep a secret?" The smile Maisie gave her told Eloise she knew her secret would never pass her lips. Leaning closer, she whispered, "I haven't told anyone yet, but just as soon as I can, I want to start a school up here. I want to be a teacher."

"A teacher?" The words almost slipped from Eloise's mouth that Maisie was too sweet to be a teacher. Teachers were cold and cruel. At least, the ones she had known were. But then, maybe that's what made Maisie's desire a good thing: she was neither cold nor cruel. "I think you would be a good teacher, Maisie."

"Really?"

Eloise nodded. "You would care for your students. You wouldn't … treat any of them differently."

Maisie smiled. "No, I suppose I wouldn't. Don't know why I would." She quirked her head, debating whether or not to ask. "Is that what yours did to you? Is that why you wish you had my schooling?"

Unable to speak, Eloise simply shrugged.

"Well, I wouldn't do that," Maisie said softly. "I just want to teach. That's all."

Conversation spent, they sat in silence until Lily and Elizabeth found them. Going straight to her mother, Maisie went into her arms. "Is it a little crazy in there?" Elizabeth asked. At Maisie's nod, Elizabeth's eyes locked on Eloise. "Are you all right, sweetheart?"

"Yes, ma'am."

"Well, why don't we come back later? We can go and see Mabel until it settles down." Elizabeth smiled. "Don't worry, it'll be quiet up there, and we'll take the backstairs."

"That's the way Mama always goes," Maisie teased. Clearly having her mother there settled the last of her jangled nerves.

Linking her arm through Eloise's, Lily followed behind them. "Are you all right? And I don't mean because of the crowd."

"Yes, Mama." And oddly, she was just that—all right. Both Brooks and Maisie had given her a strange sense of comfort.

So did Edith and Grace in the beginning.

Ignoring that thought, Eloise chose hope.

Leading them behind the hotel, Elizabeth ushered the group up a small flight of stairs and down a narrow hallway. Stopping at the last door, she knocked softly before letting herself in. "Mabel?"

"In the nursery, Mama."

The nursery was little more than a closet with a bassinet and a rocking chair. "Should have known you would be here." Elizabeth kissed her daughter's cheek. "Do you ever leave it?"

"Did you ever leave ours?" Mabel asked, a small smile curling her lips. She had her father's eyes, but aside from that, she was the spitting image of Elizabeth with her white-blonde hair and dimpled cheeks.

"Not for a second," Elizabeth conceded. "But I brought some guests, so why don't you join us in the living room?"

Settling Mabel in a chair, Elizabeth made introductions. "Lily's husband just bought the piece of land your papa was selling, and what's more, he's going to open up the old mill. He and Papa are looking at your property now to see about getting your house done."

"Really?" Her hand at her stomach, tears blurred the girl's blue eyes.

"It won't be done before the baby comes, but they're looking to get it built before winter sets in."

The tears spilled over as Mabel turned to Lily. "Tell him thank you for me?"

"Of course," Lily said softly. "It'll be the least we can do."

"You'll have to thank your brother, too. He's the one who brought the Rileys here."

"Brooks is home?" Before Elizabeth could answer, there was a small knock at the door, and then Brooks stepped inside.

When Mabel struggled to her feet, Brooks laughed. "Stay down, Mabel. I'll come to you."

"How long have you been home?"

"I got home late Wednesday night. I would have made it down here sooner, but I had a few things to sort out." Releasing his sister, Brooks took the open seat next to Eloise and pulled out a piece of paper. "I just sent in for that piece of land. I should know within the next month whether it's been approved. If so, I'll be setting up the ranch come spring."

When everyone had gotten their congratulations in, Mabel took her brother's hand. "You're staying in Haven? For real?"

"For real, Mabel. I couldn't miss watching my little niece or nephew grow up now, could I?"

Excusing herself, Elizabeth went to make lunch. "I'm going to help," Lily told Eloise. "You stay here; get to know everyone."

"But—"

"You'll be fine, Ellie. Breathe."

Obeying, Eloise settled back against the chair. *You're fine. Ignore it. You're fine. God, give me peace. Please.*

"Breathe, Eloise," Brooks said quietly.

Nodding, Eloise took a deep breath. "I'm sorry."

"For?"

"I … I don't know."

Because she was a burden. Childish. Selfish.

"You don't need to apologize for your struggles, Elle."

"Sorry." The word slipped from her lips, and for some inexplicable reason, it made her smile.

Brooks smiled back. "Did you just apologize for apologizing?"

"Sorry?" Eloise could feel the waters rising as they spoke, but she fought them back—and when Brooks laughed, the laugh she returned wasn't forced.

Eleven

The moment her laughter had settled, Eloise seemed to shrink. Her eyes went to her hands, which trembled as they picked at a hole in her dress.

Lord, what is in her head? If Brooks knew, maybe he could do something. *I don't know how to help her, Papa.*

Giving her space, he turned his attention to the conversation his sisters were carrying on. Maisie was insisting that she was getting a niece.

Mabel laughed, her hand moving up and down her belly. "I don't think so, Mais. I felt certain it was a boy from day one, and I've only grown more certain in the last few months."

Rolling her eyes, Maisie looked to Brooks. "What do you think, Brooks?"

"I think I'm inclined to trust the mother, Lilybit."

"You only say that because you want a boy. What do you think, Eloise?"

The woman looked caught. "What?"

"The baby," Brooks explained. "Maisie insists Mabel is having a girl. Everyone else is inclined to believe it'll be a boy."

"Oh, um." Eloise swallowed hard. "Mama says a mother always knows."

"I'm afraid we have you beat, Maisie." Mabel laughed. "But you will love having a nephew if that is the Lord's plan."

"Have you got any names picked out?" Brooks asked.

"We have one for a boy, but we've never been able to agree on a girl's name. Though funnily enough, Eloise, your name was the closest we came to agreeing on."

Eloise blushed, though she didn't seem ready to bolt.

Watching her brother, Mabel raised an eyebrow. "So, Eloise —how are you enjoying Rose Haven? Have you gotten to look around much?"

"She's only been here since Wednesday night, Mabel. Today is her first time in town."

"Well then, you should show her around, Brooks. A girl needs to know her town."

"Mabel."

Smiling, Maisie piped in. "I agree. Eloise needs to see the town."

Forcing back a sigh he instinctively knew Eloise would take wrong, Brooks turned to her. "It's up to you, Eloise. I'd be more than willing to show you around. If your mother is ok with it?"

"Ok with what?" Lily asked, a platter of sandwiches in her hands.

"With Brooks showing Eloise around town," Maisie explained.

"Oh well, I don't know if ..." Lily trailed off as she looked at her daughter. "You know? I think that sounds like a wonderful idea. Ellie needs to know her way around, and I trust you will look after her, Brooks."

Brooks didn't know what it was that changed her mind. He had felt certain a mother would readily be against her daughter spending so much time alone with a man, and yet the disapproval she had shown in the beginning seemed to melt off of her as she looked at Eloise. "Elle?"

"All right." Leaving the group behind, the tension in Eloise's body seemed to ease.

"I hope they didn't make you feel too upset," Brooks said quietly. "I think they have their ideas about us."

To his surprise, Eloise smiled. "My mother is the same way. But you're very lucky, Brooks. I'd always wished I'd had someone. I might have been ..." Stopping, she shook her head. "But I suppose in some ways, it's better this way; Mama and I have always been very close."

"It looks that way." The two almost acted more like a pair of friends than a mother and daughter. The few times Brooks had seen a real, comfortable smile on Eloise's face was when she talked to Lily. "It's something special."

"I think so," she said softly. "But I often wonder what it would have been like to have a sibling. Maybe ..." She sighed. "It doesn't matter."

"Was it never a possibility for more?"

She shook her head. "My parents came to have me easily— too easily, really—but they could never have more."

"Well, I'm sure that makes them all the more grateful for you," Brooks said.

Eloise shrugged. "Maybe." That veil seemed to be settling back over her, and Brooks searched desperately for anything to pull it back.

"There really isn't much to see," he admitted. "Rose Haven still has quite a bit of growing to do. The last census had us at about a hundred and twelve residents."

"I think it's perfect," Eloise said softly. "It was never this quiet in Huxley."

"We'll just walk, then."

"It really—it really is beautiful."

"Now you see why I hated to leave it." Three months outside of Rose Haven, and Brooks hadn't found anything that compared to it. It had everything from mountains to wildflower meadows to forests, all within miles. The town itself was filled with flowers, something Brooks thought caught Eloise's attention most. "Huxley was always so bare," she said. "It must be so beautiful here when it snows or when the trees change."

"Just about the prettiest thing you'll see," Brooks agreed.

"We never had much snow before. Do you get a lot?"

"We get a fair amount. The ground is covered most of the winter. Your family will have to learn to stock up for the winters. Some years, the snow makes it impossible to get to town for weeks or months at a time." Though he knew he should leave it be, he couldn't resist asking. "Surely there must have been some good in Huxley? Even little things?" Brooks couldn't imagine hating the place he'd been raised.

"There were good things," she admitted. "It rained quite a bit, which most people hated. But I loved it."

"You love the rain?"

"And storms." When she stopped and blushed, Brooks encouraged her to continue. "I—I love the sound of the rain falling on the roof. I love the smell. I love the thunder and lightning." Her skin flushed a deeper pink. "My father thinks I'm mad, but I never found much beauty in blue skies. I suppose it can be beautiful after a long winter, but I love when the sky is gray and cloudy. I love when it gets cold."

"That's certainly different," Brooks agreed. "I'll have to pay attention next time it rains."

Blushing even deeper, Eloise dropped her head.

94

"Don't be embarrassed, Elle. You see beauty in things most people look at as a burden. It's a good thing." In the distance, they could see the sawmill, where Morgan and Merritt were looking over the machines. "Why don't we go and see how your father is making out with the mill?"

Eloise shook her head, her eyes wide. "I don't think he'll want me to bother him."

"You wouldn't be bothering him, Eloise."

Before she could respond, Merritt caught sight of the two and called them over. "Where is your mother?"

"Visiting with Mabel. I thought I'd show Elle around."

Merritt smiled at the girl. "How're you liking our town so far, Ellie?"

"It's beautiful, Mr. Harper."

"Merritt, sweetheart. No need for such formalities around here."

Eloise nodded before letting her eyes roam to her father. "Hey, Wheezy," he said softly. "How're you doing?"

Eloise blushed at the name. "I'm fine, Daddy."

After a moment of silence, Brooks cleared his throat. "What do you think of the equipment, Morgan?" he asked. "Up to your standards?"

"Better. Everything is newer than what I worked with back in Huxley. Better shape, too."

"Will it be safer then?" Eloise asked.

"I would say so, and you can tell your mother that, Weasel. The woman never liked me working out there," he explained. "A couple of men have been injured in the last few years. Most lost a finger or two."

"Well, here's to hoping her mind will be eased," Merritt said.

95

Leading Eloise away, Brooks leaned in. "Need I say it again?" When her eyes narrowed, he laughed. "God was looking after all of you when He guided you here."

Eloise sighed. "You have no idea what led us here, Brooks. But it wasn't God."

***

The voice was relentless in its pursuit to pick apart everything she had said and done that day. Why had she shared so much? What had come over her to make her talk to Brooks as she had?

Because he's kind. He didn't think badly of you. He encouraged it.

Or was that just what she thought? Was he just being nice? What if he hadn't actually wanted her to share? What if he was lying on the other side of the wall in his own bed, thinking through their conversation as she was?

Of course he was thinking of it—about how painfully annoying she was. Who was she to think he could like her? No one would ever look at her like that. But why? She knew she shouldn't ask it; the water she was barely treading was slowly rising above her head, and as the question entered her mind, she found herself sinking deeper with every word. Every reason.

Stupid. Childish. Grow up.

Did she really think she would make a good wife? A good mother? She could barely cope without her own mother. She couldn't even speak.

Heart pounding, Eloise turned her eyes upward. "God?" In the silence, she bit down on her lip.

Don't focus on the silence, EllieAnne, Nanny's voice whispered. *Focus on who He is. A moment of silence can be a moment to listen. To trust.*

Twelve

It had been a week since Maisie and Brooks left for Idaho to retrieve a horse from a man Brooks had met in his travels. Maisie had been allowed to go at the promise she would get her studies done on the road, and Eloise was given the privacy she'd been craving since they'd first left Huxley.

Only now that she had it, she felt lonely. Eloise had grown used to Maisie's presence. She had grown used to falling asleep to the girl's constant chatter. She liked Maisie. She was comfortable with Maisie.

Though the first night spent by herself had been a luxury she hadn't expected, she found herself counting down the days until they returned.

Maisie. That was why she was excited. No other reason. Only, her mind went to Brooks, a habit that was becoming much too frequent for her liking. She didn't have it in her to go and catch feelings for him. Not when she knew where those feelings would lead her.

I think they have their ideas about us. The smile he'd given her in that moment sent a feeling of warmth through her when she thought of it. A feeling that was quickly squashed by the knowledge that, though their families had ideas, it didn't mean he did. She knew he didn't.

He could, she countered that voice. *And if he doesn't, it doesn't matter. It doesn't mean anything.* Except Eloise knew, even if no one ever knew what she felt, when nothing came of the situation, she would feel the embarrassment as though everyone did know her feelings. As though there was a window into her thoughts.

Though maybe they didn't need a window; it was probably written all over her face when she looked at him.

Before unwelcome heat could wash over her, Eloise murmured a small prayer and, to her relief, felt a trickle of peace come over her. Breathing in the gentle peace, she turned her mind back to the canvas in front of her.

In the absence of the two she'd come to spend most of her time with since coming to Rose Haven, Eloise took to embroidering the sights she'd seen since leaving Huxley. The sunset over the river. The pond and its reflection of the rising sun. Trying her hand at more than landscapes, she sketched out the shape of two horses pulling a wagon. It wasn't easy, but it kept her mind busy—and when she had the sketch just right, she felt a sense of accomplishment washing away the previous doubt.

"Finally got it?" Lily asked, watching Eloise pull the cotton taut in the hoop.

"I think so," Eloise said softly. "But I don't know yet what stitches will work best." Grabbing her box of supplies, she carefully selected the threads she would need.

Though the Rileys had never had much in terms of money, Eloise's parents had spoiled her with the one thing that was sure to bring her peace, and she was never in short supply of threads and needles, canvases and hoops. Her father had even made her a box to store all her supplies in. It had been her gift when she turned ten and was the most beautiful thing she'd ever owned, with intricate designs engraved into the wood and her name on top.

"You'll figure it out," Lily reassured. "You always do." Setting her hands on Eloise's shoulders, she leaned down. "Don't neglect this when they get back, Ellie."

Not like you did with Edith and Grace. Lily didn't say it, but Eloise knew she was thinking it. She'd denied herself completely to stay in their good graces, and they'd still walked away.

"I won't, Mama," Eloise promised. She'd learned her lesson.

***

Before she opened her eyes, Eloise knew how today would play out. She felt the same way she had that morning when she was ready to slip beneath the waves and cease to breathe.

That voice cooed for her to do it. No one would miss her. She would feel better. In the end, she would feel nothing.

Only that wasn't true. She may have had her qualms with the Lord, but she knew the truth. Death would not ease her pain. Even if it somehow accomplished that feat, deep down in her soul, Eloise knew she didn't want to be set free in that way … not by ending her own life.

Forcing herself out of bed, she dressed quickly and hurried downstairs, unwilling to even make the bed. She didn't want to be alone. She didn't want to face those thoughts and temptations by herself.

In her hurry, she didn't stop to think about who would be downstairs. Or worse, who wouldn't be. Lily wasn't there, and neither was anyone else, it seemed.

Eloise's heart beat harder in her throat, the silent emptiness of the house pressing in on her. She couldn't be alone. *God, please.*

"Eloise?" Eloise near jumped out of her skin at Elizabeth's soft voice. "Are you all right, sweetie?" The woman sat in the chair nearest to the stairs, tucked into the corner, hidden from sight in Eloise's panic.

Moving to Eloise now, Elizabeth set a hand to her cheek. "You slept late. Are you feeling sick?"

"No," Eloise whispered. "No, I'm ok. Where's Mama?"

"Your parents went to look over your land. Come sit down." Leading Eloise to her seat, Elizabeth settled her into it. "Ellie, you look very pale. Do you maybe want a bath? I can bring the water in if—"

"No," Eloise said, none too calmly.

Elizabeth startled and then seemed to feel the need to check for fever again. "Are you sure you're all right, sweetheart?"

"Yes. I just ... I don't need a bath just yet." She didn't have the strength. Feeling as she did now, she would sink. She wanted it. She needed it. "I don't need a bath."

Elizabeth watched her for a long moment, a strange, knowing look coming over her face. "All right," she said gently. "How about a hot cup of tea?"

"Yes. That would be nice, thank you."

Eloise could feel Elizabeth's eyes on her as the woman prepared their tea. Pulling the other chair up next to hers, she watched Eloise a moment. "Ellie," she said softly. "Is there anything you want to talk about?"

Yes. "No."

"I am sure you've noticed, Eloise, that we have a few similarities. I also know that Brooks has told you about me and what I struggle with. So I know, darling, what goes on in your head. The horrible and sometimes scary thoughts."

"Do you?" Eloise whispered.

"I do," Elizabeth said. "Which means you can't tell me that I wouldn't understand. So, why don't you talk to me?"

Eloise could feel the words bubbling up in her. The desire to share it. The desire to rid herself of the guilt. She couldn't talk about it with her mother. She couldn't talk to her father about anything. But could she tell Elizabeth the very secret that had made such a mess of not only her life but her parents' marriage?

"I can't."

"Eloise, please. I am asking you to trust me." Seeing Eloise refuse, Elizabeth sighed. "Sweetheart, I think you know that I already know what just happened. I have had those moments."

"You have?"

"More times than I would care to admit."

There it was again—the urge to confess what was bubbling up her throat. She knew she shouldn't, and that voice was screaming every reason why. Elizabeth wouldn't look at her again. She'd be disgusted. Even if Eloise could make Brooks love her, Elizabeth would never approve. He deserved better.

When Elizabeth took Eloise's hand in hers, giving it the gentlest of squeezes, Eloise felt the words spill out of her. "I ... I tried to kill myself." The words poured out of her like a sickness. "In Huxley. It's why we left."

Now she'd done it. But rather than look horrified as Eloise had expected, the woman didn't even look surprised. "I wondered if that might have been it."

"Please don't tell Brooks," Eloise pleaded.

"Ellie, I would never tell anyone." Moving closer, she sat on the armrest of Eloise's chair. "That isn't my secret to share."

Elizabeth stroked her cheek, wiping away the tears on her face. "Ellie, were those thoughts there today?"

Everything in her told her to keep quiet. *Don't tell her. She would tell Mama.* "Yes." The tears broke then. Loud and hard and painful. "I don't want to. I don't want to."

Finally seating herself fully in Eloise's seat, Elizabeth pulled the girl to her. "Of course you don't. But that voice is tempting, isn't it?"

Eloise nodded. "I-I-I'm afraid to be alone. I'm afraid I—" But she couldn't bring herself to say it.

"I know." Brushing back Eloise's hair, she pressed her lips to her forehead. "I won't let you be alone. I'll stay right here until you feel comfortable, and tonight you should have Maisie back."

"Why?" Eloise breathed. "Why aren't you disgusted? Everyone in Huxley only assumed what I had done, and they still hated me for it."

"Because they are blinded by their own hypocrisies, Eloise. I know what you are feeling. I know how hard it is to stay strong when it comes to that."

"Do you still struggle?"

"No," Elizabeth said softly. "Not like that … not for a very long time. I hope that gives you even a little bit of hope."

***

True to her word, Elizabeth didn't leave Eloise's side until Lily came home.

Taking up her own needle, Elizabeth worked at stitching a pair of Brooks' pants while Eloise finished the horse and wagon she'd been embroidering. As they talked, Eloise felt any residual anxiety in the woman's presence leave her. She found herself sharing with her the thoughts she had never even shared with her mother. Thoughts so dark, she knew they would kill Lily if she heard them. But Elizabeth understood. She had felt them too, once. Some, she said, she still felt.

"I don't say that to discourage you, Ellie. I am so much happier than I was when I was your age. But I do still have my days. But the good news is that I haven't felt what you are feeling now since I was your age."

"How? I mean, how did you change?"

"It was a combination of things. I had Merritt. My sister. By your age, I had Brooks and Mabel. They all helped." Getting up, she retrieved something from her knitting drawer. "But this," she said, "is what helped the most."

A Bible. Of course it was a Bible. "I believe in God, Elizabeth. I read the Bible."

"I believed in God too, Eloise. But that doesn't mean I believed what God said. The Bible told me that God loved everyone unconditionally and wished for none to suffer, but that was not what I had seen. God didn't love me. How could He? I was nothing, and according to so many people, I was without God because of my struggles." Elizabeth laughed softly. "I was once accused of being possessed by a hoard of demons. That was why I was fearful. Depressed. I couldn't talk because they held my tongue. It wasn't until I chose to believe in His Word that I started to change. It was a constant battle to better my thoughts. To tell the evil one where he could go. But I made it."

Before Eloise could object, Elizabeth set the Bible in her lap. "This is the Bible I used during that time. I want you to take it."

"Why?"

"Because it just might help you," Elizabeth told her. "Take it, Eloise. Read it. Write in it. It's yours now."

That night, Eloise sat with Elizabeth's Bible in her lap, willing herself to open it. "God?" she whispered. "Please. I'll open it. Just speak to me. Please." The tears spilled slowly, splashing onto the worn cover and soaking into the cracks.

Thirteen

As promised, the next time it rained, Brooks paid attention. Opening his window, he watched the dark clouds roll in, overtaking the previously blue sky. He listened to the sound of raindrops on the roof, on the windowpane. And the smell of it— he'd thought her mad on that one. But she wasn't wrong: it smelled incredible.

Going in search of Eloise, he found her in his mother's sitting room, wrapped in the blanket from her bed. As he watched, she took a deep breath before her lips curled into a smile.

The woman might have been a little mad. The room was freezing, and she had her bare feet poking out beneath the blanket, seemingly unfazed. Taking a seat next to her, Brooks nudged her bare foot with his knee. "How are your feet not cold?"

Eloise shrugged, her face going red. "I love this. I feel … peaceful when it gets cold." Looking at him, she smiled. "Do you smell it? It's one of my favorite parts."

"I smell it. It's crisp. Clean."

She nodded. "It's wonderful." She truly was at home there. With the window open, the cool air blowing the stray hairs at her face, Brooks had never seen her look so content. Her dark eyes, lovely in their own right, seemed brighter. Happier. She was beautiful.

Catching his stare, she blushed deeper. Burrowing deeper into the blanket, she turned her attention back to the sheets of rain. As Brooks had grown used to in her presence, they sat in silence, listening to the sound of the rain against wood and glass.

Now and then, Eloise would close her eyes, her breaths deepening as though she was fighting off something in her head. But a moment later, she would open her eyes and turn her focus back to the rain pelting the window.

In the short months he had known her, Brooks had grown used to that look on her face, and it took everything in him not to ask what it was that bothered her. What thoughts were taking her mind captive?

"What makes you love this so much?" Brooks asked. "It is beautiful, but it seems to mean something more to you."

"I don't know," she said quietly. "I've always loved it. When I was little, Mama used to let me stay up late so we could watch the lightning. She would make us hot chocolate and popcorn, and we would bundle up in the doorway." She considered it a moment. "You saw it. In Huxley, it rained so hard that the streets were covered in thick, sticky mud within minutes. It made it impossible to get anywhere, and so the school would close."

"So, to you, it means quiet days at home."

Eloise shrugged. "I guess. But really, everything about it is comforting. The cold. The sound. The smell. I know it sounds mad, but the heat is oppressive. It makes me feel like I'm being smothered. Like ... like I can't breathe."

"Well then, I think you'll love it here," Brooks said softly. "Even in the summer, it's rarely hot."

"Rose Haven really is perfect, isn't it?"

"Well, I wouldn't say it's perfect but—" Brooks stopped when he saw her teasing smile. "Right, sorry."

"I do love it, though." She smiled. "It's as close to perfect as any place can be."

"You sound mistrustful."

"It's hard to explain, Brooks." Seeing he wouldn't relent, Eloise sighed. "Rose Haven seems perfect. Everyone here seems perfect. So what happens when—" She shook her head. "*If* it all falls apart? If people like your family in a place like this can walk away, I have no hope of finding anyone who will stay."

Brooks watched her swipe at her blush-filled cheeks. "Eloise, what makes you think we'll leave?"

"Because they always do. I've always had trouble making friends." Her cheeks went a shade redder. "But there have always been those who saw me and seemed like they wanted to know me. But, in the end, I was nothing more than a shiny new object. A project they could take on and fix—and the moment they realized they couldn't, they would leave."

"That's their loss, Elle. I am not leaving, and neither is anyone else here."

Eloise looked skeptical. "Even if I never change?"

Brooks felt his own eyes burn as tears glistened in Eloise's. "Eloise, I don't want you to get better or happier for my sake … I want to see you achieve all those things for yours. What I said before—about liking a challenge? I didn't mean that I saw it as my personal goal to change you." Brooks chewed his lip, trying to think of the best way to phrase his thoughts. "Do you want to go out to the barn? I have something I want to show you."

Five minutes later, he guided her into the barn and to a large horse. He patted the beast's chest. "This guy is Charlie," he said, beaming at the chestnut stallion. "He was the first horse I trained. Got him for my fourteenth birthday. He was young and healthy, and my parents thought he would be easy to train. But he had a stubborn streak." Traveling further into the barn, he pointed to another horse. "Era was my second horse. She came from an abusive home. She was aggressive. Distrustful. Then there's Hatter. I found her a few miles outside of town. She had been attacked by an animal, and once she got back up, she was scared. Jittery. It made her hard to train." And on he went, sharing how he had come to acquire each horse and the struggles that came with them.

"And you've never given up on one?" she asked.

"Not a single one, and I never will." The man's eyes were bright as he looked them all over. "See, Elle, I don't train them for my sake. I train them because I can't stand to think of a horse out there that's scared and alone and in pain. I don't believe in putting them down for anything less than sickness or injury that can't be helped." Nodding for her to follow him, Brooks led her to the last stall—to the horse he had brought home not two days ago.

This one he didn't touch but maintained a fair distance from, urging Eloise to do the same. "She's a Clydesdale," he said softly. "They're a rarity in the States. The man I bought her off has been in the States for about three years and brought this one's parents with him in the hopes of breeding them. Only this one was a bit frightful, and he didn't know why. He didn't know how to handle it, and he wanted to hand her off before he could make it worse." Brooks had respected the man. He knew many who would refuse to admit their methods didn't work. "It's not often I get a horse before they've been damaged by human hands."

Eloise looked up at the horse. It was larger than the others, though she looked to still be young. The horse was pacing the small space allowed to it, pawing at the ground every few moments. "Will you still take ones like her when you start the ranch?"

"Course. I couldn't live knowing there were horses out there I could help but chose not to. Animals like her have always been my favorite to work with." He smiled at the mare. "It hurts to see their struggle. To know what they've faced. But that's what makes seeing their growth so incredible—watching them go from hopeless, broken, and bruised to whole and trusting." Brooks turned back to Eloise. "I'll breed them, of course. Raise 'em. But my focus has—and always will be—on bettering animals like her. They deserve better."

"What if you can't?" Eloise whispered. "What if there's no reason? What if she's just ... scared?"

"Then we still handle her the same way we do any others," Brooks said softly. "It helps to know what's causing it, but it's not necessary. We just have to be patient. Give her attention. Love. Time. I believe that if we do that, we can get her to a good place."

"We?"

Brooks turned that smile on her. "I want you to help, Elle—if you're willing."

She shook her head. "I don't know what I'm doing. I would just mess it all up."

"No, you wouldn't, Eloise. You did well with Theo, and just like then, you don't need to know what you're doing. I know, and I'll be there every step of the way."

Eloise watched him uncertainly, the voice within her picking his words apart. "You really want my help? Why?"

"Because it looks to me as though you understand her. That's important, Eloise. With every other horse I've trained, I knew what the root of the problem was. But with this one, I think you're right: I think she's just skittish."

"All right," she conceded. "Though I don't know how much help I'll be."

"Perfect. Let's start with a name."

Eloise's eyes snapped to his. "Me?"

"Seems about right, seeing as she's going to be yours, Elle."

"Mine? As in ..."

Brooks laughed. "As in, she's yours, Elle. All yours."

"But if she's rare, won't she be worth a lot?"

Brooks gave her a look that asked if she'd listened to a word he said. "That's not why I do any of this, Eloise. Selling a horse to someone who's only getting it because it's a rarity is how you end up with horses like Era. They aren't loved and cared for; they're used and abused. Even if it loses me money, I send my horses where I know they'll be treated well."

"And you trust me?" Eloise asked.

Brooks nodded.

Smiling uncertainly, Eloise looked back toward the horse. A black and white Sabino, the animal truly was beautiful. Her dark eyes stood out against her bald face. "Juniper?"

Always a question. Never certain. "Juniper is perfect."

"And she really is mine?"

"She really is yours, Elle. I'm simply assisting in getting her where she needs to be."

Eloise smiled. A real, happy smile. "Thank you, Brooks."

Fourteen

Every night Eloise stared down at Elizabeth's Bible, willing herself to open it. To read it. Elizabeth had felt the same way as Eloise, and this Bible had helped her. *Open it.*

But Eloise had been reading the Bible her whole life, and it had never done much for her. Sometimes she read it, and she felt peace in His presence. Other times, she read it and only felt lonelier as she found herself confused and frustrated. Everywhere she looked, the Bible said not to worry, but that was all she did—worry.

But she couldn't stay away from the thing. Even if she couldn't read it, she gained a strange comfort in simply holding it. In sleeping with it beside her. She held it tight as she prayed every night, hoping one day she'd have the courage to open it.

"God, I want to." She wanted to know Him the way Elizabeth and Brooks knew Him. The way Nanny had known Him. But every time she got a finger under the cover, a dozen voices pressed in on her. She didn't deserve to know Him. Her faith was weak, and it always would be.

But Elizabeth was the same way, wasn't she? Even still, she was like Eloise, and she had faith. And Maisie and even Mama, whether she realized it or not. But as that voice within reminded her, the difference between them and her was this: they coped with their struggles. They had never found themselves at the bottom of a tub, ready to give up.

Tucking the Bible under her pillow, Eloise let her mind wander to Brooks and Juniper. Despite Brooks' hope, she had no idea how to cure Juniper. How would she? She didn't even know how to cure herself.

"But you know what not to do," Brooks had explained. "That's just as important, if not more, as knowing what to do."

Eloise supposed that was true. She had no idea how to help Juniper, but she knew how to keep her fears from getting worse.

The next morning, Brooks met her in the kitchen, a mug in each hand. One coffee, one tea—his usual greeting for her. Taking the latter, she followed him out to the barn.

"Any plans today?" he asked before taking a cautious sip from his mug of black coffee.

"We'll see," she said quietly. "It all depends on if she wants to."

Brooks laughed softly. "Will she ever want to, Elle? She's looking pretty stubborn."

Did he not trust her? Was he regretting letting her take charge?

No, Eloise countered. *This will work.* "She'll come out, Brooks. I know she will. She just needs to feel comfortable. It needs to be her choice."

"All right. I trust you."

I trust you. Eloise clung to those words, warmth spreading through her as she made her way to Juniper's stall. She would come out when she was ready. Eloise, of all people, knew that. If they gave her time, if they were patient with her, Eloise knew Juniper would grow to trust them—and that's when she would leave her stall.

"She does seem to be liking you more," Brooks conceded as Juniper let out a small, happy noise at the sight of Eloise.

It was true. Though Eloise had yet to try approaching her, Juniper no longer seemed to shrink at the sight of the two of them.

Helping Eloise onto the stall railing, Brooks leaned against the wall. "It's certainly a different method."

"But you still trust me?"

"I believe you know what you're doing. You seem to know the way her mind works." He considered her a moment, his dark eyes soft on hers. "That's a rare thing, Elle. To connect so completely with an animal. To understand them the way you understand her."

For a moment they sat in silence, listening to the soft patter of rain on the barn roof. "She will come out," Eloise said quietly, as much to herself as Brooks. "When she's ready. When she sees that we can be trusted."

"And you believe she will start to trust us if we leave her be?"

"In a way." Eloise tried to think of a way to explain it. A way to make him see how it might work. "We will have to push her some. Encourage her. But it's like me—I don't do well when forced to do something. My father used to think that if I just faced it and went to school, it would get better. Easier. But it never did; it just got worse. But when you compare it to things like now, where I was given a choice, when I was given a reason to trust, it's easier."

Brooks nodded. "I suppose it makes sense. But can I ask you about this? Why do you think that simply sitting with her and talking as we have been will help gain her trust?"

"Because we're with her. We haven't abandoned her. We ..." Eloise felt herself blush as she thought about it. She was stupid.

She should just admit it wouldn't work and let him train her before she ruined the horse beyond repair.

"We what, Elle?"

"We include her," Eloise said. "We aren't simply leaving her alone, expecting her to decide she wants us. We're letting her know we're here." Taking an apple, she tossed it to Juniper to prove her point. "We're letting her know she's wanted. For more than what she might have to offer."

Again, that voice pressed in on her, and she squashed it down. Maybe Brooks would think it sounded stupid. But she knew the truth of it. Wasn't that how she had always wished to be treated? Why should an animal be any different?

"It makes sense," Brooks agreed. "And it does seem to be working."

That voice crooned in the back of her head. It was only a matter of time before Brooks took Juniper back.

"Do you really think I can do this?" Eloise whispered. "Please, just be honest, Brooks."

Brooks was quiet, careful in his wording. "They are different methods, Eloise. But I believe you know what you are doing. Whatever you have been made to believe, different isn't always wrong. I don't train the way many others do, but I trust my methods more than theirs. I know what has worked for me, and this is working, Elle. Look at her."

Eloise did as she was told. Juniper was closer, and though the horse didn't approach her, she was within reach. If Eloise reached out, she would just be able to graze her muzzle with her fingertips. It was the closest she had come so far. In the beginning, Juniper had kept herself tucked in the corner of her stall, braying loudly when Eloise dared to even look at her.

"Hi there, girl," Eloise said softly. "It's ok. You can come closer if you want."

Juniper brayed, shaking her head wildly.

Behind her, Brooks laughed. "There's no forcing that girl to do anything."

She was close, though. Eloise could feel it.

***

Morgan dragged his fork across his plate, his eyes on his daughter. She'd been locked in that barn with Brooks all morning. His daughter had always slept long after the sun, and now she was rising with it. What else would she do if Brooks wanted it?

He knew he should keep quiet about it just then—peaceful family lunches in the soddy were important to Lily—but even so, his concerns had to be addressed. "I don't like it," Morgan grumbled. "A girl shouldn't be alone with a man."

Eloise startled and looked to her mother. "Ma-Mama said it was ok. Brooks said he asked."

"I thought it would be a day or two," Morgan said. "Not every day, every hour, spent locked away in that barn." And he would have said no to even that had Lily not twisted his arm.

"It's not every hour," Eloise said quietly. "It's only an hour or two in the morning and then after lunch."

"Has he tried anything with you?"

"No." Even Eloise was shocked by her outburst. "It isn't like that," she said, softer now. "He isn't like that. He doesn't touch me at all. He keeps his distance." Except to lift her onto the stall, but that was innocent. "The barn door is open, Daddy. Because he respects me. Because he respects you."

"A boy who respects a girl doesn't spend so much time alone with her without having married her." He shook his head. "I want you to ask Maisie to assist you. Keep an eye on her brother."

"What?" Eloise asked. She loved Maisie, but she didn't want the girl there in those few precious hours she had with Brooks. They would be changed. Too different from what they were now.

"Morgan," Lily said quietly. "Brooks is a good man. He's been nothing but kind and respectful."

"I don't like it," Morgan repeated. "I want Maisie in there."

"Maisie has schoolwork. She has friends. You can't expect her to give that time up to spend it playing chaperone, Morgan."

Eloise watched her mother, uncertain of the conversation taking place. She'd thought her mother would be the problem. Her father never paid any attention to her, so why start now?

"Then I'll go in there," Morgan said.

"No," Eloise hissed. Both her parents turned to look at her, and she flushed red. But she wouldn't take it back. Her father had barely looked at her in months, and now he wanted to intrude on her privacy?

"Why, Eloise?" he demanded. "What are you doing that you don't want us putting an end to?"

"Nothing. We just talk—that's all. I sit on the stall, and he stands six feet away from me." He never stepped across that invisible boundary of propriety. Not even when her voice refused to travel far enough for him to hear every word she said.

"Then what difference will it make to you if someone else joins you?"

"I—" Eloise looked to Lily for assistance.

117

"Because she's comfortable with him, Morgan," Lily said. "If you are in there, she will lose that. Ellie needs this, honey."

Morgan turned his glare on Lily, and Eloise shook her head. She shouldn't have looked to her mother. She shouldn't have let her defend her. She was just leading them back to what they were in Huxley: a couple who spent most of their time together fighting.

"You're on her side in this?" Morgan spit. "She's a girl, Lily. It isn't right she spends so much time alone with a man. I thought you, of all people, would understand that." Hadn't they lived with the rumors of a pre-maritally conceived child? They hadn't spent a second alone before their wedding night, but it didn't stop the rumors from spreading when Eloise came so quickly, and now Lily wanted to pin those rumors on their daughter?

"I trust both of them, Morgan. And as for rumors—who's going to know about the two of them working together except our two families?"

Morgan stared, incredulous. "And if she comes up pregnant?"

Eloise flushed deeper and sank lower into her seat.

"I would hope you know your daughter better than that." Lily sighed.

Unwilling to see the fight go further, Eloise forced herself to speak. "Please, Daddy," she said softly, inwardly praying God would open her father's eyes. "I need this. Please don't take this from me."

Morgan looked at his daughter, his dark eyes softening at the obvious way she fought her tears. "It isn't proper. Mistakes can be made, Eloise."

"Not by me. Not like that," she told him. "He's just a friend."

Morgan scoffed. "I've seen you two together, Eloise."

Eloise's lip quivered, and she bit down to hide it. "Please, Daddy. I know you can't trust me anymore. But you can trust Brooks."

Morgan's eyes softened. "It isn't that I don't trust you, Weasel. It's that you don't know how easy it is to make mistakes. That's why there are rules." But after a moment, he sighed. "But we can keep trying it. For a time. But if I tell you I want it to stop, I don't want a fight from either of you. Is that understood?"

Eloise nodded.

Sighing, Morgan sank back into his seat. "You're a good girl, Ellie. I just want you to be careful."

"I will, Daddy. I promise."

Fifteen

The waves roared in her ears, knocking her down and dragging her under. She couldn't breathe. She couldn't hear anything but the sound of rushing water and her heart in her ears, and no matter how hard she kicked, she only sank deeper. When she tried to scream, water rushed down her throat, choking her.

Waking with a gasp, Eloise sat up and tried to breathe through the panic threatening to undo her. The thoughts in her head were nothing but a jumble, buzzing like wasps in her ear.

Breathe, she told herself. *There's nothing wrong. Nothing upset you.*

It was almost worse that way—worrying over nothing, unable to tell herself that they were lies planted by the enemy. Nothing worried her, and yet she felt it, and so her mind tried to think of every possible reason.

How long before Rose Haven fell apart? How long before Elizabeth told everyone the secrets Eloise had entrusted to her? How long before Brooks grew tired of her?

None were the thoughts that had started her panic, and bringing them to the surface now did nothing but serve to make the anxiety worse. They pulled her deeper, giving her more reasons to worry as she searched for the one reason that caused her to spiral in her sleep.

A sharp roll of thunder made her jump, bringing her attention to the rain hammering against the window. Needing the cool air on her damp skin, Eloise eased the window open enough to let in the cool breeze.

Setting her head against the cold glass, Eloise watched the rain pour. "Lord, I need you." Ignoring the voice telling her to give up, that He wasn't listening, Eloise searched her mind for another scripture. *Come unto me, all ye that labour and are heavy laden, and I will give you rest.*

All, that voice laughed. *All but her.*

That isn't true. He's good. He loves me.

But why would He love her? What purpose did she serve? "God, tell me it isn't true. I know you're there. I know you're listening. So why do you leave me alone?"

Have faith, that voice mocked. If she had faith, it would go away.

"Faith," she whispered. "Right."

Eloise startled at a light knock at the door. "Elle?"

Easing the window shut, Eloise hurried to the door before Maisie could wake. Outside, Brooks stood in his boots and jacket, drenched from head to toe. "What's wrong?"

"It's Juniper. The storm sent her into a bit of a frenzy. I can't calm her.

Understanding, Eloise followed after him. Stuffing her feet into her boots, she accepted Brooks' help into her coat. "Take this," he said, placing his hat on her head. "It's pouring hard out there."

The wind was almost worse than the rain. Eloise couldn't walk two steps without being knocked into Brooks. It took his strong arm around her waist to keep her upright.

Ushering her into the barn, Brooks put his weight into the door, forcing it closed.

Turning back, he found Eloise making her way to Juniper. "Easy, Elle. I don't want you getting hurt."

Nodding, Eloise stopped a few feet from the stall. "It's all right, Junie," she cooed. "I'm here now. It's all right."

When Juniper reared, Brooks pulled Eloise away from the stall, her back slamming into his chest. "Don't get too close." The words came out harsher than he meant them to. All it would take was one kick from the rearing animal to end it all.

"I don't know what to do," Eloise moaned. "I can't touch her. I can't … I don't know. Look at me—I don't know how to handle fear. I don't know how to—"

"Eloise, breathe," Brooks whispered. "What do you want—when you're scared?"

"I don't know," she snapped.

"Patience?" Brooks prodded. "Compassion?"

Eloise nodded, her eyes going back to Juniper. "Just do what we always do?" she whispered. "Let her see us? So she knows she's not alone?"

"That sounds good, Elle." Pulling up a hay bale, he grabbed a blanket from the wagon. "Sit. It could be a long night." As he said it, another crack of thunder sounded, sending Juniper into another fit.

"It's ok," Eloise said quietly. "Is it normal to storm like this now?"

"Not normally, no." Brooks took in Eloise's hands and the way she trembled. "Are you all right, Elle? I heard you moving around in there. It's the only reason I came for you."

Eloise shrugged. "Just couldn't sleep."

"Is your mind getting to you? Mama has nights like that too. Sometimes she'll be up all night, too afraid to sleep."

"I don't know." Eloise closed her eyes. "Sometimes I just wake up feeling like I can't breathe, and I don't even know why."

"Did you have a dream?"

She shook her head. "Just woke up with it."

Brooks watched the woman curl in on herself, her forehead pressing into her knees. "I'm sorry, Elle."

"It is what it is."

"But it shouldn't be. It isn't what the Lord wants for you."

That made Eloise laugh. "Can we please not with that?"

"Do you not believe?" Brooks asked. He knew it was a personal question, but it slipped out before he could stop it.

"I believe in God," Eloise said softly. Her eyes went to Juniper, who had calmed now as she listened to Eloise speak. "I love God, I do, and I believe He died for the world. But … some things make me question."

"Do you mind if I ask what makes you question?"

"What you just quoted at me. That, along with a dozen others that have never meant a thing. Not when applied to me."

Brooks waited a moment before speaking. "The Lord doesn't have favorites, Elle. Least of all, least favorites. If the Word applies to one, it applies to all. If it doesn't apply to one, it applies to none."

"It doesn't seem that way sometimes." Eloise let out a trembling breath. "Do you really believe He can love everyone? No matter who they are? No matter how insignificant they are?" She swallowed. "No matter what they have done?"

Brooks was silent for a moment, his eyes watching her. "I do," he said softly. "But I don't believe anyone is insignificant in the eyes of the Lord."

Then where is He? she wanted to cry. *Where has He been all my life?* "I just don't know."

Forgetting his own rules, Brooks took the seat next to her. "I'm sorry. I shouldn't have said it that way. I don't mean that you aren't going to suffer or that the Lord won't allow suffering. You will, and He does. I just mean to say that He doesn't want you to do it alone, Elle."

"I know," Eloise whispered. "I do. But the thing is, Brooks? You can know that something is true and still not believe it."

Sixteen

Brooks woke to his mother patting his back. "Sweetheart, wake up."

Groaning, he turned over. "What time is it?"

"Late for you," she said softly. "I take it you and Eloise were up late?"

"Until about one, I would say." The only thing that had calmed Juniper was the sound of Eloise's soft voice, which she demanded to hear until long after the thunder had stopped. "Do you need me for something?" He yawned.

"No, I brought something for you." Pulling Brooks into a sitting position, Elizabeth handed him an envelope with shaking hands. "Annabelle just brought it by. I think it's about the land."

Brooks' own hands shook as he turned the envelope over. What if it was denied? What if someone else had already purchased it?

Brushing back his sleep-mussed hair, Elizabeth smiled. "Whatever happens, Brooks, it's the Lord's plan. If you don't get it, then there will be something better."

"I can't imagine anything better than that land, Mama." It had everything. Space. Water. It was secluded enough to keep the horses protected but not so much so that he couldn't be found. It was perfect. "Papa," he prayed aloud, "I need that land."

"And I'm sure you've got it, sweetheart. Now open it." She gave him a shake. "I've been wanting this for you for seventeen years."

Brooks watched her a moment. It was true that she supported him through all of it. From the moment he had decided

125

what he wanted, Elizabeth had found every way and reason to help, whether it was simply encouraging him in times of doubt or finding any odd job she could give him. "You open it, Mama."

Smiling, Elizabeth took the letter back and tore it open. Her eyes scanned the page before growing wet. "Brooks," she whispered.

I didn't get it. Of course I didn't get it. Oh, God, give me peace.

"You got it, Brooks."

The tears were unexpected. "I got it?"

"You got it, baby. It's yours." She pressed the letter into Brooks' hands before wiping at her cheeks. "What do you say we have one last picnic in celebration? We can all drive down and have it on your land."

His land. He nodded, unable to find his voice.

"I'll go get everything ready." She kissed the top of his head as she stood. "You deserve this, baby. Enjoy it."

Enjoy it. Brooks could hardly wrap his head around it. He was a landowner. Come spring, he would be breaking ground. Building up the dream he'd had since he was six years old. Seventeen years of working and saving, and it was six months away from becoming a reality.

Dressing quickly, Brooks made his way downstairs and endured the round of congratulations before he could reach the door. Of all people, he wanted to see Eloise.

Why, he couldn't fully understand. He hardly knew her, yet she was the one his mind had wandered to first.

Brooks found Eloise with Juniper, talking softly. Seeing him enter, she smiled. "I think she might let me touch her soon. She nudged my hand a few times but backed away as though changing her mind."

"That's good, Elle. I told you you could do it."

Eloise flushed a shade of pink that made his stomach take a hard dive. "What is that?" she asked, eyeing the paper in his hand, and then she was smiling that soft, timid smile. "Is that about your land? Did you get it?"

"I-I, uh." Brooks shook his head. "Yes. I mean, yeah, I got it. Mama's planning a picnic down there tonight."

Eloise smiled. "That's wonderful, Brooks. Congratulations."

"You seem in better sorts today," Brooks said.

She shrugged. "I think it's a good day." They were known to happen now and again. When the thoughts weren't so loud, the waters calmer. "I just hope it stays that way."

"It will. We'll make sure of it."

Until he was distracted by something better. Once they got to that picnic, he'd forget all about her.

Seeing the shift in Eloise, Brooks nudged her. "Don't let them ruin it, Elle. It's a good day."

"Right," she whispered. Turning back to Juniper, she draped a hand over the stall, letting the horse sniff at it. "Will she be ok if we leave her?"

"It will only be for a few hours, Elle, and we can leave early if you want."

"We?" She shook her head. "I don't think that will be allowed." Morgan didn't even want her in the barn. "Besides, the picnic is for you. You can't leave early."

Seeing a new unease settle over her, Brooks resisted the urge to take the hand that rested on the stall. He settled for leaning against the stall beside her. "You'll be all right, Elle," he said. "You won't be alone there."

Maybe not at first. But others always got distracted.

"Why don't we go and help get everything ready?" Brooks suggested. "Keep your mind distracted? Then maybe you and I can head out early? Let you see it without a bunch of other eyes?"

Eloise nodded. "All right."

***

Brooks hadn't exaggerated the beauty of what was now his land. Eloise couldn't take her eyes off of it. Set right at the foot of a mountain, the land was surrounded by dense trees. Farther along, she could see a small, bubbling brook.

"There's a trail there that leads to a meadow," Brooks said, pointing toward the trees. "It's got a small lake and everything. I already promised Maisie a camping trip first chance I can. Haven't had the chance to venture further, but I'm sure that same trail leads to a good view." He smiled sheepishly. "Can't decide if I'll turn it into a trail for customers or keep it my own little secret."

"I say keep it your own," Eloise said. "At least for a while." Shutting out the voice in her head, she forced herself to speak. "What all do you plan to do?"

Smiling, Brooks brought the wagon to a stop. "I'll show you." Helping her down, he led her to a spot fifty yards over. "This here will be the boarding house for my workers. Not too big, but room enough for them to be comfortable. Over there, closer to the brook, will be the stables." Moving her along, he pointed out where he wanted the pastures. "Then up there, nestled up against the mountain, will be the house. I want it as separate from the rest as possible for my wife and children in the future. Give my wife a garden. Give the children space to run and play without getting in the way or feeling restricted."

Eloise felt a pang of jealousy at the thought of this fictional wife. "You really have thought of everything," she said quietly.

"That's not even the half of it." Brooks forced his mind from the unexpected turn of the conversation. He had never once thought about where a wife and family would go in his plans. "I want a lot of things, Elle. Things I never even thought of until I saw this land. Not only will I be able to rehabilitate the horses that need it, but I'll have the room to keep them with me after."

He could breed horses to sell in Rose Haven. Though he'd require a personal history of their experience with horses, as well as asking them to take a few free lessons on training, he could offer a few classes for those wishing to learn training and riding. Brooks smiled. "I've been building this dream since I was six. It's just about all I've thought of since." Brooks nudged her. "Surely you have something you've been dreaming about all your life?"

Eloise felt pink heat fill her cheeks. It wasn't a dream she would ever see come to light. Even if a man were willing to look past everything she carried, there would always be that voice within her. *Selfish. He deserved better. Her children deserved better.* Worst of all, what if her children were like her? She couldn't bear the thought of passing her pain onto her child.

For once, she agreed with that miserable voice.

Eloise was sinking again, and Brooks could think of no way to stop it. No matter what he said, that voice within her knew how to twist his words and drag her under when all he ever wanted was to lift her up. "Why don't you set up the blankets?" he asked. "I'll get a fire going."

The ground and wood, still damp from the storm, were nothing a few blankets couldn't fix. As for the fire, Merritt had sent Brooks ahead with some of the firewood they had stored in the barn. By the time the others arrived, the fire was blazing, and the blankets had been laid out. While Eloise took on setting up the food, Brooks gave a second tour of his land.

"Any idea what you're going to call it?" Morgan asked.

"Not yet," Brooks replied. "Thought I would keep it simple with 'Harper' or 'Brooks,' but Maisie told me it was too boring."

"You can still use your name." Maisie smiled. "I have the perfect one."

"I am not calling it 'Down by the Brooks,' Mae Elizabeth."

At that, Morgan laughed. "I think 'Down by the Brooks' is perfect, Mais." He clapped the girl on the shoulder. "You aren't really going to deny the girl, are you, Brooks?"

"Morgan," Lily admonished, but even she was smiling. "Leave him be."

"No, no." Merritt laughed. "I think Morgan and Maisie are right. 'Down by the Brooks' sounds right to me."

Elizabeth shook her head. "You three are awful. You'll find the perfect name, sweetheart." Ruffling his hair, she went to help Eloise.

With the women gone, Morgan tossed an arm around Maisie's shoulder. "We'll get him, Mais. Just have to wear him down."

Eloise watched her father with Maisie. It had been years since her father had joked so easily with her. Months since he had joked at all. But he had a special connection with Maisie. The sort Eloise had always wished she'd had with him.

Tearing her eyes off of them, she tried to keep up with the conversation between Lily and Elizabeth. Of course, they were talking about children. Grandchildren. Finally, she gave up and turned her attention to worrying at her skirts.

Plopping down next to her, Brooks took up a sandwich. "What do you think, Elle? About a name for this place? It's the one thing I don't have figured out."

Eloise's eyes went back to Maisie and her father. "I think they're right. Everyone uses their name, but they don't all get to be creative with it. I think it would be a missed opportunity not to use what you have."

Brooks laughed. "You'll all be the death of me. But I suppose I'm outnumbered."

As Brooks promised, he didn't let Eloise fade into the background. As though he could see her mind slipping, he would pull her back to him with a question or prod her with a mention of Juniper.

Brooks had a way of both easing and increasing the thoughts that dragged her under, and she wasn't sure which would win in the end.

Seventeen

October

"You've got to eat, Maisie Girl." Merritt squeezed the girl's hand. "Your mama will be back soon."

"I know," Maisie mumbled. She speared a piece of broccoli on her fork. "Just as soon as Mabel doesn't need her anymore." The girl had steadily declined since Elizabeth left for Mabel's with no plans to return until the baby was born. The baby was now over a week late, extending the woman's absence and Maisie's sour mood.

When supper was finished, Maisie stalked back to her room while Eloise and Lily managed the dishes.

"Is she always like this when Elizabeth is gone?" Eloise had asked Brooks.

"No." He sighed. "But my father said Maisie has been a bit moodier lately, and Mama knows how to handle her. They think Maisie's showing a few signs of taking after my mother."

Eloise felt something in her twist at the thought of it. Not Maisie. Not like this. "Taking after Elizabeth?" she asked, her voice little more than a whisper as she remembered her old fears: that her children would carry on her pain.

Seeing her concern, Brooks smiled. "Don't you start worrying, Elle. Some of these things seem to be passed down, but that doesn't mean it always is. Your mother has blue eyes, but she didn't give you those, did she?"

"I suppose not. But I could pass this on to my children."

"But you might not, and on the off chance that you do—you'll learn how to go about, just as my parents have."

"Just have faith?" Eloise muttered.

"Faith helps, Eloise. It doesn't take it away, but it makes it easier to endure."

"You sound like you speak from experience." The idea was ludicrous; Brooks couldn't struggle the way she did. But there was something in his voice that planted the tiniest seed of doubt in Eloise's mind that he could.

Brooks shrugged. "I'm not perfect, Elle."

That night, Eloise watched Maisie prepare her bed. "Maisie," she said softly. "What do you say we move our beds together tonight?" Maisie often spoke of the nights she and Mabel would move their beds together, talking until their father ordered them to sleep.

"Really?" she whispered.

Eloise nodded. "Would you help me?" Getting a grip on the footboard of Maisie's bed, they pulled it away from the wall before turning it and sliding it in next to Eloise's.

Getting into her bed, Maisie watched Eloise through dark, sad eyes. "Thank you, Ellie."

"Of course, Maisie. It's no fun sleeping alone when you're feeling the way you do." It made you want to not sleep at all. "If you want, I'll stay awake until you fall asleep."

Maisie smiled. "That's what Papa does with Mama when she has her bad days."

Eloise smiled. Lily had always done it for her, as did Nanny when she'd stayed with her. If she lay in bed alone, her mind would be too free to wander.

"I'm not like you and Mama," Maisie said quietly. "I'm not."

"I know you're not, Mais. Everyone has their moments." Eloise tucked a strand of Maisie's hair behind her ear. "But even if you are, there's nothing to be ashamed of."

"You're ashamed," Maisie called out.

"I'm different, Maisie. I'm not good like you are."

"You don't seem bad to me."

Eloise shrugged. "There are a lot of things you don't know about me, Maisie. I don't know how to fight like you do."

"That doesn't make you bad, Eloise," Maisie said. "Brooks didn't always know how to fight, either. He had to learn."

"Brooks?" Eloise asked.

"I know he seems perfect and unbothered, Ellie, but he's not. His mind gets to him far worse than mine ever has."

Eloise thought about that long after Maisie had fallen asleep. She couldn't believe that Brooks struggled more than even Maisie did. Brooks had always been nothing more than a pillar of peace. His relationship with the Lord was like nothing she had seen before, with Brooks referring to Him as his papa.

Brooks couldn't struggle … but if he did, what did that mean for her?

***

Eloise stared down at Elizabeth's Bible again. Brooks had never seen her open the thing; she simply stared at it, her fingers sometimes tracing the lettering on the cover or picking at the cracks in the leather.

"That's a testament to my mother's love for you," Brooks said softly. "I don't remember a day in my life when that Bible wasn't in her hands. Some days, she would spend every waking hour in it, writing like mad." Looking back now, Brooks wondered if his mother had been writing all those notes in the margins for a girl she didn't know would need it as desperately as she had until now: Eloise.

"She shouldn't have given it to me," Eloise said softly. "I don't deserve it."

"Why do you think that?"

She shrugged. "God doesn't want anything to do with me. He made that clear years ago."

"Elle, that isn't how God works."

Eloise laughed humorlessly. "Maybe not with you. You have no idea what He's like with me."

Sighing, Brooks sat next to her. The woman could be exhausting.

"I'm sorry," she whispered. "But it's true. God has never been there for me. Not like He is for others. I'm not good enough."

Brooks felt the urge to reach out and touch her. To wipe away her tears and hold her. This was not self-pity; the woman genuinely believed she was insignificant to the Lord. *God, what's been done to this woman to make her so certain of your indifference?* "Eloise, can I ask why you seem so certain that it wasn't the Lord's will that you came to Rose Haven? Despite all the signs, you refuse to see it. Why?"

"Because I know why we left Huxley, Brooks. Even if you think you know, you don't. It wasn't God, and if you knew, you would agree. It wasn't God."

"Do you want to tell me why?" *Admit it,* he thought. He already knew, but he wanted her to tell him. To trust him.

"No," she said quietly.

"All right. What about this, Elle? Maybe God didn't guide you out of Huxley. But He most certainly guided me there, and I believe you and your family are the reason. Can you believe that?"

Eloise shook her head, chewing her lip.

"Why?"

"Because He wouldn't do that for me." Eloise glared back at him. "I don't deserve any of this. I don't deserve y—" She clamped her eyes and mouth shut, tears afresh on her cheeks.

Brooks felt as though a hole had been punched through him. Uncaring of rules now, he reached out hesitantly and wiped the tears from her cheeks. "We aren't our mistakes, Elle. Repentance and the blood of Christ free us from that burden."

Eloise nodded. "I have repented, Brooks—a hundred times. But I'm afraid I'll do it again."

Something told Brooks she was still paying penance—every day. "So, then you get back up, dust yourself off, and you try again." He knew it wasn't so simple. But he couldn't let her hold to guilt that wasn't hers to carry. "I've had sins that I stumbled in and repented of a dozen times, Elle, but God forgave me every time, and eventually, I beat them." Brooks set his hand over hers, resisting the urge to lace his fingers through her own. "You're stronger than you think, Elle, and I … I'll help you in any way I can."

Eloise studied him before quietly saying, "You wouldn't understand, Brooks."

"You know, I really wish you would stop saying that," Brooks snapped. Eloise startled, and fresh tears filled her eyes. "Elle, I'm sorry." He squeezed her hand. "I'm sorry. But I do wish there was a way to make you see that you can trust me."

"I can't tell you, Brooks."

"Because I wouldn't understand." Brooks sighed. "I know."

"You wouldn't, Brooks."

"I suppose I'll just have to make you see."

Eloise watched after Brooks, her heart aching to call him back. To tell him everything. But she couldn't. No matter what Maisie might have said, he wouldn't understand what brought her here or what she needed.

No one, not even Lily, understood that she didn't need advice. She didn't need lectures or to be told to let it go. They couldn't see that what she needed was an understanding heart and a shoulder to cry on. She needed them to wrap her in their arms and say nothing at all.

Getting up, she followed after Brooks. The house was in chaos when she stepped inside. Rather than find platefuls of lunch, Annabelle Crawley was sitting at the table.

"Is everything all right?" Brooks asked.

"More than all right, sweetheart," Annabelle cried. "Your mama sent me. Mabel had the baby this morning—a little boy. Henry Matthew Woods."

Eloise watched Brooks' dark eyes light up. "A boy," he cried. "Well, it's about time, isn't it?" Taking a seat, Brooks was silent for a moment, tears on his cheeks. "And Mabel? She's all right?"

"She's perfect, Brooksie. You couldn't ask for a more perfect labor. Aside from your parents, she's taking a few days with just her and Matthew, but she wants you all to come on Saturday. Your father is on his way down now, and your mama's gonna stay down until Saturday."

Brooks looked to Maisie. "You want me to drive you down to see Mama for a bit, Mais?"

"Maisie's going to stay with Archer and me until then," Annabelle explained, patting the girl's leg. "And we should be heading out soon, Maisie girl. Let's get you packed."

When they had gone, Brooks sat back. "A nephew," he breathed.

"Congratulations," Lily told him. "You'll be a wonderful uncle."

He smiled. "Thank you. Truth be told, I was starting to doubt we'd ever get a boy. Don't get me wrong, a little girl would have been perfect—I wouldn't trade having sisters for the world—but I think we're all ready for a boy. I've been the only one for twenty-three years."

"Does Annabelle have no boys?"

"My aunt only had one child—a baby girl. She died about a month or two before I was born. Fever."

"Oh." Lily sighed. "Annabelle's first husband died, didn't he? Was it fever, too?"

"No." Brooks pursed his lips. "He was a drunk. After they lost Opal, he couldn't cope. He wound up killed in a tavern brawl just two years later."

Lily shook her head. "That poor woman. How long has she been married to Archer?"

"Little more than four years. Though, she had known him long before Luke died. Annabelle can be very stubborn. She refused to admit, even to herself, that she was in love with him. Only took her near twenty years."

"Well, I can imagine it would be hard." Lily squeezed her husband's hand. "I don't think I could ever remarry if I lost Morgan."

Brooks shook his head. "No, I don't think I could either. If I were to lose … whoever God might have planned for me. But Annabelle is a strong one, and she found ways to cope. She often says it was those losses that led her to strengthen her relationship with the Lord. Never had much of one before, but she had to, after everything she went through."

Another person calling on the Lord. He answered their call. Why did He ignore her while so readily jumping to answer others? Ignoring that voice, Eloise focused on the conversation at hand.

"Is that how the name Mama Belle came about?" Lily was asking. "I've heard Maisie refer to her as such a few times."

"I believe so. She's always looked at my sisters and me as her own, and she near raised my mother. It just seemed fitting, and I think it helped her some, to be a mother of sorts."

Eloise's mind went back to the conversation she had with Brooks in the barn. All those emotions crashed over her, drowning her in a sea of unworthiness—to live, to dream of being married someday and becoming a mother, to think God truly loved her and wanted her.

"Ellie?" Lily asked. "Are you all right?"

"I'm fine," Eloise lied. "Excuse me."

Hurrying up the stairs and into her room, she took Elizabeth's Bible from her pocket. She stared at it. *Open it.*

Easing a finger under the leather, she lifted the cover. That simple action caused a surge of waves to crash down on her. It wasn't going to help, they said. She wouldn't understand it. She didn't deserve to understand it.

Was she worthy of anything? If even the Lord looked down on her for her struggles, what hope did she have of anyone else understanding?

Letting the cover fall closed, she set it aside.

Faithless. Weak.

Eloise let out a mix between a sob and a laugh. Was there anything that voice wouldn't pick at? Too worthless to read it. Faithless if she didn't.

Nothing she did would ever be right.

Eighteen

Eloise had had that thought reiterated a dozen times over in her life: she would never be enough. That her abnormalities made her something unworthy, and though she knew the truth, it became an all too easy thing to believe that she was a disappointment, unworthy of God's time and energy.

Eloise had been ten when she began questioning what the Bible said of an all-loving God.

As with her aunt Alma, there was a time when the church looked past her quiet nature. They didn't see anything out of the ordinary—just a shy little girl who clung to her mother's hand. But there came a day when she was deemed too old to still be so withdrawn, so afraid, so timid—all the things that the good Lord deemed ill-fitting to find in one of His children.

When Eloise found herself unable to participate in group activities or perform in church pageants or plays, she dreaded hearing the inevitable words that followed when her parents tried to explain their daughter's predicament.

"God didn't give you a spirit of fear, young lady," they'd said. *"You'd best take a good look at your heart and figure out why you feel so much fear."*

Her faith began to crumble with every recitation of that verse. But the words that took the most from her, the words that made her question, came from a woman who had just moved to Huxley. On her very first day in church, she had found her way to Eloise and her parents.

The woman had been kind. She had smiled warmly at Eloise and introduced herself as Rosemary. "And you are?"

"This is our daughter, Eloise," Morgan had said for her, giving Eloise's shoulder a small, comforting squeeze.

Eloise had smiled and said hello, but the woman didn't hear her. They never did.

"You'll have to excuse her." Lily smiled. "She's a little quiet."

The woman had turned her attention back to Eloise. "Well, you'll have to get control of that, won't you?" she said. "The Lord doesn't like timidity."

Eloise stared back, speechless. *The Lord doesn't like timidity.* Why was she so shocked? Hadn't she been hearing it for years? But it was the wording. The insinuation behind it. "The Lord doesn't like timidity."

Alma may have destroyed Eloise's self-worth, but until that day, she had continued to believe that the Lord loved her. The Bible said it. Her parents said it. Nanny had sung her to sleep with words of Jesus's love for her. God loved her in spite of her sins. All she needed was faith.

But it had been impressed upon Eloise that she didn't have faith. If she had faith, she would be normal—happy. She would be able to speak. And over time, the words 'The Lord doesn't like timidity' became 'The Lord doesn't like you.'

***

Brooks watched the stairs, hoping Eloise would reappear. Again, he tried to think what it was that caused her abrupt departure. But, as was always the case, she had been fine, and then she wasn't.

A sigh belonging to Morgan jolted Brooks from his thoughts. The man shook his head as he left the room, heading for the front door. The relationship between Eloise and her father was one Brooks couldn't figure out. It couldn't be denied the man loved his daughter. That much was clear in the way he watched her when she wasn't looking. But the moment the two were made to interact, they each held themselves uncomfortably, unable to meet the others' eyes.

"Don't pay him any mind." Lily sighed. "He'll be all right."

Brooks couldn't help but notice the hint of anger in her voice. The entire family left him confused. It was clear they loved one another, but Morgan and Eloise could barely stand to be in the same room, and it became common to find Lily and Morgan in whispered arguments that were far more heated than the ones he seldom found his parents in. More than once, he'd made a late-night trip to the barn and heard them shouting from the soddy. The only two who truly seemed to enjoy one another's presence were Lily and Eloise.

Brooks knew he couldn't ask over Lily and Morgan, but perhaps some insight into Eloise's relationship with her father could help him understand her. "I don't mean to pry," he started. "But is everything all right between them? They always seem rather agitated when the other is around."

"They weren't always like that, but as Eloise got older and her troubles became more evident, neither of them knew how to handle the other. Morgan, I think, blames himself for—" Lily stopped short. "Well, a lot of things, really."

Something in the way she spoke told Brooks that Lily blamed her husband as well. "Lily, I know about Eloise."

Lily's eyes flashed to his. "You do? How … Ida," she hissed. "She told you that? Just right there at church?"

"I noticed you were alone." He laughed humorlessly. "I noticed Elle. Ida wanted to discourage me from introducing myself."

"And you didn't let it?" Lily whispered, her voice cracking. "You still care?"

"Of course I care, Lily. I know what pain can do to you, and I can only imagine the sort of pain one has to be in to try and commit such a thing. Though, I admit, I was hoping Ida was wrong." To know he was right only made it all the harder to leave Eloise where she was—alone. His mind painted images he didn't want to see.

"I know it. I never wanted to admit it—I didn't. Not until she broke down and told me the truth of it." Lily sighed. "Morgan was the one to find her. I think it's why he struggles more. But he does love her, Brooks—more than anything. He was the one who wanted a little girl, and he's the one who wanted to name her Eloise. They were close when she was young. But … Ellie is a difficult one to understand, and I think somewhere along the way, he just stopped trying." Slowly, tears dripped down her cheeks. "She's difficult. But she's worth it."

"I know she is." Brooks only wished he knew how to understand. He wanted to know what it was that upset her, what it was that triggered that voice in her head.

"You can't avoid upsetting her, Brooks," Lily said softly, reading his thoughts as clearly as words on a page. "Sometimes, it takes nothing at all. She'll be happy—laughing, even—and then in that same moment, something switches in her, and she's fighting tears."

"And there's nothing we can do for her?"

"Nothing but give her time. She'll come back down when she's ready. If I went up there now, it would only make it worse."

"That's what she says about Juniper," Brooks said. "She believes if we simply leave her be until she's ready, then she'll let us know when she wants to leave the stall."

Lily smiled. "How is that working?"

"Surprisingly well. She hasn't left the stall of her own accord, but you can see that she's beginning to trust us—Elle, especially."

"And does Eloise seem happy there? I mean, does she talk at all?"

"She seems happy enough," Brooks admitted. "And she does talk. Not a lot, but she does talk."

"I wondered if she might. She does better one-on-one." Lily chewed her lip for a moment. "You really do enjoy your time with her? I mean, you care about her?"

"I do, Lily."

She nodded, fresh tears spilling. "Keep taking her out there, Brooks. I don't care about what's proper now, I just want to see her happy. I want to see her trust again."

"And you trust me?" Brooks asked. "Why? You don't even know me."

Lily laughed. "I don't know. It's just a peace I feel, and I know my daughter. She'll never talk to you if I am around. If anyone is around, it's too easy for her to let others speak for her or let others speak over her. It's easier for her to go unnoticed." Sighing, she rested her head in her hands. "It's always been easy for her to go unnoticed, at least in the ways she should be noticed."

"I notice her, Lily."

"I know you do, and that's why I have to put aside what might be proper and disregard what others might say. If there's no one else to talk for her or over her, she'll speak for herself. She needs that time with you in the barn."

"I'll keep taking her out, Lily," Brooks promised. "Whatever Elle's head might be telling her, I really do enjoy her presence."

Lily watched Brooks for a moment. "Elle," she repeated. "Brooks, I just have to ask … What is it for you? I know what she's worth, but no one else has given her the time to see it. So I can't help but wonder if it's just …" She trailed off.

Seeing where she was going, Brooks felt his cheeks flush red. "She is beautiful, Lily, and maybe that might have been what drew me to her at first. But it isn't what holds me to her."

Lily's lip quivered. "You see it," she whispered. "What I see in her."

"I do, Lily, and I am not going to give up on her."

Nineteen

After nearly three weeks, Juniper was opening up. Eloise could touch her now, so long as she asked permission first. She learned the horse loved to have her muzzle rubbed. Starting at the spot between her eyes, Eloise would run her middle finger down to her nose. It was more a graze than anything else, but Juniper loved it, and after a few days, she was nudging at Eloise's hand, demanding it.

Brooks laughed as the horse's eyes closed at Eloise's touch. "I believe she's beginning to love you, Elle. Before too long, she'll follow you right out of this stall."

"But not too soon," Eloise reminded him. "I don't want to rush her."

"But not too soon," he agreed. "We'll give her all the time she needs."

Eloise's eyes went back to Juniper. "I don't think I can leave her. She'll think we forgot about her."

"She'll think nothing of the sort, Elle, and we'll see her the moment we get back."

"Are you sure?"

"I'm sure, Elle, and if your parents agree, I'll be more than willing to drive you back up early."

"I think I should stay with her," Eloise said quietly. She didn't want to go into town anyhow.

"Why do I feel like your mother will never agree to that?" he asked. "Come on, Elle. Let's go." Setting a hand at Eloise's back, he ushered her toward the door. "And I don't believe this is entirely about the horse, either."

Giving Juniper one last goodbye brush between her eyes, Eloise let him lead her outside.

"I saw the way you held Henry last week," he continued. "Your time will come, Elle."

But would it? Who would ever choose to have a child with her? Who would ever see her as fit?

But Brooks had it wrong; at least, he didn't have it all right. It wasn't only seeing Mabel with a child of her own that caused a bone-deep ache inside of Eloise. It was the fact that Eloise had spent most of her life feeling left behind. While others got married, left home, and had children, she was the one who lived with her parents, incapable of taking care of herself. Eloise had made her peace with knowing that was the life she would lead.

At least, she had tried. Only now, she couldn't. Not when she watched Mabel with her little boy. Not when she watched Elizabeth and Merritt gush over him. Not when she herself held him. But when Brooks held his nephew ... Eloise hadn't expected to feel that pain stab her heart.

When he had first seen the child, he'd held him for the longest time, just looking at him until Mabel begged to have him back. He wanted children—and something in her broke, knowing someday he would have them. With someone else, someone better, and then those sweet, private moments in the barn would be gone. He would be gone. Just like everyone else who had come through her life.

It could be you, a tentative voice whispered, offering her hope. *It could.*

But it wouldn't be.

It amazed even Eloise how much louder that voice was. Hope was a life preserver; that voice was a wave always ready to knock her back under, tearing it from her grasp. Yet she kept reaching for it, knowing it was only an illusion. Knowing it would only end in disappointment.

Offering a hand, Brooks lifted Eloise onto the wagon seat. "Do you never feel anything?" she asked. "I saw how you looked at Henry. You want children."

"Now," Brooks said quietly. "But I didn't always. My mind was always on the ranch."

"What made you change your mind?"

Eloise watched a deep red fill Brooks' cheeks. "A couple of things," he said simply. "And I suppose now that I want it, it can be difficult. But I trust that the Lord has the perfect woman for me, and it will all happen in His perfect time."

"Perfect? I thought no one was perfect?" It was a poor attempt at teasing, and he saw right through it.

"I don't mean that she'll be perfect or that our relationship will be perfect." Brooks smiled lightly. "I know that it will be anything but, to which I'm grateful for. Perfect would be boring. What I mean is that she'll be perfect for me and I for her." He glanced at Eloise. "Do you believe in soulmates, Elle?"

"Yes."

He smiled. "I do too. I believe that when the good Lord created you, He had a very specific man in mind, and He gave you the qualities He knew they would need. The same goes for the man and what he will bring to you."

"I don't have anything to offer, Brooks," Eloise said quietly. "I don't know what special qualities any man could need from me."

"I can think of a few. Would you like me to name them?"

Eloise blushed red. "No."

"Too late." Brooks flashed another crooked smile. "For one thing, you know how to listen, and it doesn't matter that you don't always know what to say. It's nice to simply be heard. You're sensitive." When Eloise opened her mouth, Brooks cut her off. "Don't say that's a bad thing, Eloise. I've seen you handle Maisie. Juniper. It's almost like you feel their pain. You feel *with* them. I can think of about a dozen more. Need I go on?"

"No," she whispered.

Brooks was quiet for a moment, and when he continued, there was a hint of frustration in his voice. "You don't see yourself clearly, Eloise. It's like you're looking at yourself through murky water—what you see isn't you. It's what the world has put on you."

"Water?"

Brooks blushed. "Maybe that's a stupid analogy. But it doesn't make it wrong." It took Eloise a moment to realize Brooks was actually embarrassed.

"It's not a stupid analogy," she said quietly. "Brooks, I live in water. That's what it feels like—like I'm drowning in my own thoughts." Eloise had never admitted that aloud, and it was strangely freeing.

Brooks' lips quirked bleakly. "You ought to learn how to swim."

For some inexplicable reason, that made Eloise laugh. Not a half-hearted or humorless laugh but a real laugh. "I should."

Brooks looked at her like she was mad. "Is that funny?"

Sobered, Eloise sighed. "I don't know. Maybe not. But sometimes it's easier to laugh at how ridiculous all of it is."

Sticking with the water analogy, Brooks said, "You know all you have to do is tell me when you're drowning. I'll toss you a preserver. I'll ... swim through the waves myself if need be."

"I won't let you go down with me, Brooks. I'm not worth it."

"You are worth it, Eloise," Brooks snapped. It was the first bit of anger she had seen in him. Seeing he had startled her, he sighed. "You are worth it, Elle. You are more than worth it, and I would willingly swim those waters with you. I ... I would drown with you."

"You say that now, Brooks. But you would realize I wasn't worth it. The moment you saw what lurked beneath the surface, you would see you'd made a mistake." And then it would be too late.

The moment you saw what lurked beneath the surface, you would see you'd made a mistake.

Brooks had all but admitted his feelings for her, and that was the response he got?

The woman was infuriating. With every piece of encouragement he tried to give her, she had a reason to contradict it. Maybe it wasn't her fault—he knew it wasn't her fault—but that didn't make her any less maddening.

Papa, how am I supposed to reach her when her mind is trapped? She's drowning, God, and I don't know how to save her.

Brooks felt that small reminder that he couldn't. He wasn't her savior.

Well, then can you do your job? Where have you been for eighteen years?

Brooks sighed as he felt another reminder, heavier than the one before it.

I know. You were always there. But it doesn't look like it.

"I'm sorry," Eloise said quietly, pulling him from the silent conversation.

"Elle, you don't need to apologize. I know you can't help it. Don't apologize, just let me in."

"Brooks—"

"Don't tell me I'll regret it, Eloise." Brooks sighed. "Shouldn't that be my decision? If I suffer or not?"

"Not if it means I'm left with the guilt of it." Her fingers wrung her skirt into a tight knot. "I don't want to be the reason you get hurt."

"Elle, look at me." When she obeyed, there were tears on her cheeks. "I'm not giving up on you."

"Then I guess we'll both end up getting hurt."

"Eloise."

"Fine," she snapped. "I'll come to you. I'll let you try and help. But don't blame me when it becomes too much."

"I won't, Elle. I promise you."

She nodded, unhappy and entirely unconvinced.

***

By the time they reached town, neither was speaking. Helping her from the wagon, Brooks let Eloise go without a word.

Elizabeth watched him as he carried in the supplies. "You two all right?"

"She's maddening," Brooks muttered. Slamming down the crate, he went to retrieve the last one.

"You have to be patient with her," Elizabeth said gently. When Brooks opened his mouth, she set a hand to his. "I know you are, Brooks. I'm just reminding you. It's hard—I know it's hard. I know exactly what she's feeling. I was far worse than Maisie, and I still struggle to remain patient with her at times. I lost my patience many times with you."

Brooks ran a hand through his hair. "How do you do it? How did Dad do it with you?"

Elizabeth considered that for a moment. "I remind myself of what I told your father when it came to understanding and handling me. You are allowed to be frustrated, Brooks. You are allowed to be angry. You're even allowed to snap on occasion. We understand that we are a frustrating kind. But know that no matter how angry and frustrated you are with her, I can guarantee you that she is infinitely more frustrated with herself."

Brooks sighed. "It really doesn't make it any easier."

"I know." Stretching on her tiptoes, she kissed his cheek. "But I know you'll find a way. You always do."

Leaving him alone, Elizabeth made her way to Lily and Eloise. Aside from her own mother, his seemed to have a special hold on Eloise.

Will she ever be that comfortable with me, Papa? Will she ever trust me like that?

***

Eloise knew it would happen. She knew he'd give up. She knew he'd walk away.

He didn't walk away. He's busy.

The man hadn't stopped moving since they had arrived, and neither had she. It was busyness, not anything the voices in her head tried to tell her it was, that kept him from her. On top of putting the finishing touches on Mabel and Matthew's home, the men were helping them move in. None of them had sat in three hours.

While the men hiked up and down the hotel stairs to lug out furniture and crates, Lily, Maisie, and Annabelle hung curtains and arranged furniture. Elizabeth and Eloise used the hotel kitchen to prepare the meal for supper after the work was finished.

The first snow of the year was expected to come later that night, and the Harpers wanted one last night with their daughter and grandchild before being separated for one only knew how long.

"We don't always know how long it will be," Elizabeth said quietly. "For all we know, we could go all winter without a break. Henry could be months old before we see him again."

"It won't be so long, Mama," Mabel assured. "Papa will never allow you to go so long." Standing, she passed the baby to her mother. "Let me help with dinner while you soak up all you need from him."

Though Eloise preferred Elizabeth, who she could speak with almost as easily as Lily, she didn't mind Mabel. Like Merritt, she had a serene way about her. She didn't say much, not because she couldn't, not because she was afraid, but because she didn't feel the need to. In the few moments they spent in each other's presence, they had said little more than a handful of words to one another. But her silence, unlike so many others, didn't feel personal. It felt intentional, as though she sensed Eloise needed it —and when she did speak, her words held the strange near sense of comfort as Brooks speaking with her.

"Are you excited for the snow?" Mabel asked after a few silent moments. "Matthew moved from a city near Huxley. He said it was rare to get much snow." She smiled. "He was like a child on Christmas morning the first time the snow stuck."

That made Eloise smile. "I can't picture Matthew behaving in such a way." Despite the man's boyish face, he was much like his wife from what Eloise had seen: quiet and collected.

"Oh, the man is much more like a child when it's the two of us." Mabel laughed. "I'm sure you can understand that—acting differently when with those you're comfortable with."

"I suppose." At least, she used to. Things between Eloise and her mother had changed in the past few months. Their midnight conversations were few and far between, and when they did have them, they didn't hold the same light as they once had—not when Lily held her just a little too tightly.

"I am sure Maisie will insist you partake in every snow tradition. She did the same with Matthew." She gave Eloise a small smile. "You've been warned: though Brooks might be more inclined to save you from Maisie than he was Matthew, he loved to watch the man squirm."

"He did?"

Mabel nodded. "Matthew was the first man I ever took an interest in. Made Brooks nervous. I pity the man who goes after Maisie. She's had Brooks wrapped around her finger since the moment he looked at her."

That, Eloise could see. Brooks was the only one who called her Lilybit, a story Eloise was itching to ask about.

By dinner time, the supper table was set with onion soup, roasted chicken, and vegetables fresh from the Harpers' farm. With eleven people, the table was full and loud, but with Brooks sitting beside her, it didn't bother her. Not the way it would have if she were alone. Settling in, she listened to the conversations around her. Annabelle and Elizabeth were discussing the few last-minute goods Merritt had ordered. Mabel was speaking in hushed tones to Archer, the town doctor, about a rash on Henry that she wasn't sure what to do about. Lily and Morgan were actually laughing, though about what, Eloise wasn't sure.

The atmosphere was light and happy, but that voice was always lurking, ready to pull her under. Brooks wasn't talking to her. No one was talking to her. Why would they? Why would he? *They're busy. They're giving me space. Brooks is giving me space. Maybe he thinks I want it.* She had snapped at him ... maybe he was being patient with her?

Keeping her head down to hide her trembling lip, she blinked back tears. She wouldn't give in.

Brooks set a gentle hand on her shoulder. "Elle." He smiled that smile that left her breathless. "Do you want to go for a walk?"

"A walk?" she whispered.

"A walk. Just you and me." His eyes softened. "You look like you're drowning."

Eloise nodded. Taking his offered hand, she let him drape her shawl over her shoulders. The cold air outside helped her resurface a little as they stepped out the door.

"I think Dad might be right about the snow," Brooks said. "It feels like snow."

When Eloise shivered, Brooks didn't hesitate to take off his jacket and hold it out for her. Slipping her arms through the sleeves, she pulled it closed. It smelled like him, and she took comfort in that. It was almost like being wrapped in his arms.

"What is it, Elle? You said you would come to me. That you would let me help. So let me."

"I can't."

"Why?" He sighed. "Because you still don't trust me? Because you still think I'll leave?"

"No. It's … I can't tell you everything, Brooks. It's humiliating."

Understanding, Brooks smiled. "You aren't alone in what you're feeling—if I'm right in what you feel. My mother says I am, but I question it sometimes." Brooks went quiet as a couple walked past them. Nodding his head in a gesture of greeting, he waited until they were out of earshot. "You know," he said quietly. "I get it—the difficulty in trusting others. It's why I've always preferred animals. It's why I never thought about marriage until I met you. I don't know why, but I have always preferred to be alone. I was never comfortable with most people."

Leading Eloise to the mercantile steps, he pulled her down next to him. While Brooks tossed a bit of the dinner roll he'd brought with him to a hungry squirrel, Eloise toyed with a tear in his jacket. "Everyone loves you, Brooks."

"And everyone here loves you. But it doesn't make it easier, does it?"

"No," she said quietly. "I guess not."

"I have one good friend, and he doesn't even live in Haven. He visits now and again, and that's always been enough for me. I've never felt the need for more." Brooks shrugged one shoulder. "I prefer to spend my time with horses because I know what to expect. I understand them. I trust them." Brooks laughed humorlessly. "Never told anyone but my mother that."

Eloise studied Brooks now, looking for all the world like that pillar of peace he was. "You don't seem like you struggle."

"Some of us hide it better." Brooks gave her a teasing smile. "But there's always this voice that likes to get in there when I meet new people. One that tells me I'll only be hurt in the end. It makes it difficult." He chewed his lip for a moment. "That day in church? When those women started talking about me and the pastor looked me over in agreement? I felt like a boy again, scared and hurt."

"Like it was confirmation of your own worst fears," Eloise said quietly. "Is all of that why you never wanted to marry?"

Brooks nodded.

"And you trust me, even when I tell you you shouldn't? You still think I won't hurt you?"

"No," Brooks told her. "No, I knew from day one I'd be hurt. But it wouldn't be by you. It would be the struggle of loving you and watching you suffer that would hurt."

Loving? "You shouldn't—"

"Can you please stop that, Eloise?" Brooks dropped his head into his hands, willing himself patience. "Stop telling me what I shouldn't do."

"You don't know anything, Brooks. If you did—"

"I would still love you, Elle. But I'm not asking you to tell me what you think is so awful. I'm not asking anything right now."

"I don't have anything to give, Brooks. Not like this." The tears started slowly. "I'm not good enough."

"Elle, come here." Eloise went to him easily—too easily. Resting her head against his chest, he wrapped her in his arms.

"What if I feel this way the rest of my life?" she whispered. "I don't think I can do it. I'm not strong enough. I'm not."

"You are stronger than you give yourself credit for, Elle."

"I'm not." *You don't know what I have done.*

"I won't let you do it alone, Elle. You will never be alone again." Eloise shifted so she could see Brooks' face in the moonlight.

"You'll realize the trouble I am, Brooks, and then you'll leave."

"Elle." Brooks set his forehead to hers. "I couldn't leave you if I tried." His lips brushed hers before he pulled away with a small sigh. "I want to do this right."

"Right?" Eloise breathed.

"Your parents trust me. The least I can do is get your father's permission to court you before I start kissing his daughter."

"You want to court?" she asked. "As in …"

Brooks laughed softly. "What is it going to take to make you see I'm here for the long run, Elle?"

Twenty

Brooks' hands shook as he paced a trail through the fresh snow. He wasn't ready for this. Though he and Morgan got on well enough, he wasn't sure what the man would say to Brooks' wanting to get to know his daughter as more than the friends they had become. Brooks still didn't understand the strained relationship between Morgan and Eloise, and he had no way of knowing whether it would make him more or lesser inclined to give his permission.

Brooks had spent the night tossing over the decision, caught in the feel of Eloise in his arms. Every time he was with her, he noticed new things about her. Like the way she embroidered a handful of flowers poking out from the pockets of her calico skirts like a permanent bouquet. Or the way she would release her hair from its braid the moment Lily had her back turned, preferring to tie a portion back with ribbon.

Whether he'd planned for this life or not, the woman had gone and worked her way into his heart, and if she would have him, he was there to stay.

But that didn't stop that old fear or uncertainty from making itself known. There was a reason he'd never planned for a family. People left. People died. He'd grown up watching Annabelle grieve her husband and watched the painful, guilt-filled way she'd given in to her feelings for Archer—afraid to betray what she'd had with her first husband.

Maybe Eloise wouldn't leave him. But she was lost, and what if one day she took herself from him as Luke Crawley had taken himself from Annabelle? It was a pain Brooks wasn't sure he could take.

He'd spent the night in prayer, and though he still didn't feel ready, he knew where God was leading him. Pushing through the terror in his mind, Brooks trudged through the snow until he was outside the Rileys' soddy.

Lily smiled when she saw him. There was no doubt she knew why he was here, and for some reason, that made it all worse.

Where Lily knew, Morgan was oblivious as he clapped Brooks on the shoulder. "What can I do for you, Brooks?"

If Brooks hadn't already spoken with Eloise, he was certain he'd turn back as his heart began to pound in his throat. "I was actually hoping we could talk?" he breathed. "About Elle?"

The older man stiffened. "Why would you want to do that?" he asked.

"Well, as you know, we've been talking some and spending a bit of time together, and I was hoping I could get your blessing to make it something more official?"

"Eloise isn't in a place to be doing anything like that." Morgan shook his head. "If she gave you her heart and she ended up hurt—"

"I would never hurt her, Morgan. Please know that."

"You would, Brooks. People always do."

"Morgan," Lily whispered. "Let him talk."

"She's difficult, Brooks, and she's infuriating," Morgan told him. "There will come a time when you realize it's too much, and then Ellie will be hurt."

Brooks bit down the need to defend Eloise. Rebuking Morgan now would gain him no favor. "Morgan, I understand your fear. I understand Elle has been hurt in the past. But I promise you, I have no intention of hurting her. No intention of leaving her." Brooks felt the uncertainty leave him as he spoke. "I have loved getting to know her, Morgan. Even the harder parts. Even the parts that infuriate me."

Morgan watched him a moment. "I don't want to see her hurt."

"Neither do I."

Morgan looked to his wife. "Do you think she's ready, Lily? For this? For marriage, if it does come to that? Children?"

"I think it's what she needs to be ready for it all, Morgan," Lily said softly. "How else can she prepare if denied the right to?"

Morgan sighed. "Can you give me a few days? To think about it?"

"Of course, sir. As long as you need. I just ..." Brooks gnawed at his lip, trying to find the right words. "I just hope you know that I do care about her, and I am not at all blind to the frustrations she can bring. I see it. I feel it at times. But I believe she's worth it." Moving toward the door, he reconsidered. "Talk to my dad if you're concerned. He knows what it is to love someone like Elle. Maybe it will ease your mind to know how he fought for my mother."

Morgan nodded. "I'll do that, Brooks. Thank you."

***

Unable to face Eloise, Brooks avoided the barn. He started for the house before remembering Elizabeth would be waiting, and he thanked the Lord his mother was the only one he'd shared his plans with.

Preferring to face Eloise, Brooks turned back toward the barn. Leaning against the stall, he watched the woman talk to Juniper, her fingers grazing the horse's skin.

She's difficult, Brooks, and she's infuriating. There will come a time when you realize it's too much.

Looking at her now, Brooks couldn't imagine it. She looked almost at peace there. What had always been his refuge had quickly become her own, and rather than find himself resenting the thought, it only made him feel closer to her. As he watched, Juniper nudged Eloise's hand, bringing the sort of rare smile that he knew wasn't forced or timid.

Morgan was wrong. A stubborn horse always made him more empathic. More determined to bring them through it. And the same was proving to be true with Eloise. Even in the moments where she frustrated him, rather than make him want to give up, it made him want to try harder. Find new tactics to reach her. To comfort her. He could never walk away from an animal in pain, so how could he walk away from a woman who had already weaved her way so deeply into his heart that it was almost painful?

Though he had so far been denied getting to know the woman as more than a friend, he hadn't been denied these moments, and he thought he had a way to help rather than discourage her.

"You're not scared of heights, are you?" Brooks smiled as Eloise startled, her hand jolting back from Juniper.

"You scared me," she mumbled. "How long have you been standing there?"

"Just a minute. But I was hoping to show you something. So, are you afraid of heights?"

She shook her head.

"Good." Brooks grabbed a blanket. "Come here." Resisting the urge to take her hand, he led her up the ladder into the hay loft. Pushing open the window, he looked back to find her lingering by the ladder. "I thought you weren't afraid of heights?"

"I'm not," she scowled.

"All right, then come here." Wrapping the blanket around her, he held her steady as she seated herself next to him, tossing her feet over the side.

Eloise let out a small gasp as she took in the view. It was the first time she was seeing all the Harper property, beautiful in its own right. But coated in white layers of snow, it was breathtaking. The trees blowing in the soft breeze. The rolling hills. The mountains in the distance. Even the fog, which he knew she would love.

Resting her head against the wall, Eloise watched the fog roll in.

"I come here when I feel distant," Brooks said. "When I need to feel closer to God. I thought maybe it might help you to see Him—in the rain, snow, and fog."

"I do see Him in it," Eloise said softly. "I told you I believe in Him, Brooks. I do. I see Him in this, and it's why I love it so much. I just ..."

"Don't see Him in your life."

She shook her head. "I try, and it's not entirely that I don't see Him." Eloise was quiet a moment, choosing her words carefully. "I know I have so much good in my life. So I don't know why—" Her voice choked with emotion. "I don't know why I feel like this. I look at my family and yours, and you and views like this, and I see Him. But ... I don't know how to explain it in a way that makes sense, Brooks. But it's like, I know that what the Bible says is true, but ... I don't believe it. Does that make sense?"

Brooks considered her a moment. "I think so. I felt the same way once."

"You did?"

Brooks smiled. "I've tried to tell you I might understand what you're feeling, Elle."

"Maybe some of it," Eloise said quietly. "But you wouldn't understand all of it."

"And I'm not asking you to tell me any of it. At least not yet. Maybe someday you'll trust me enough to share more of you."

Eloise laughed softly. "Maybe."

***

Morgan slipped from the house before Lily could wake. The woman's accusations were still fresh in his mind, and he couldn't take another fight now. He couldn't see the look of disappointment in her eyes.

You don't want to see her happy. Whether you admit it to yourself or not, you are still punishing her for what happened.

And perhaps it might be true. No matter how wrong it might have been, he couldn't look at his daughter without anger. Anger that she was what she was. Anger that she could hurt herself. Anger at himself that he had let her slip so far. Yes, he was angry. But Lily was wrong about him punishing her, not wanting to see her happy. Happiness was all he'd wanted to see in her since he'd picked her up from Alma's. His girl had been happy. Quiet. Anxious at times. But happy.

The night before they'd left her, he had tucked her into bed. She'd been happy and making jokes with a smile on her face as she always had. When he'd finished with her prayers, she had held onto his hand, reluctant to let him leave. The girl had always been closer to her mother, but she did still rely on Morgan in those days. "What's on your mind, Ella-weasel?"

"Will you stay a little longer?" At six, her young voice had still been high and almost musical.

"Of course, Wheezy." Laying back down with her, he let her curl into his side, her little fingers twirling a button on his shirt. "You'll be all right, Ellie Girl. Once you've got your cousins to play with, you'll feel better."

Eloise shrugged. "I miss Nanny."

"Me too, Weasel. She was a good one. But Alma will take good care of you." Seeing she wasn't convinced, Morgan tickled her side, making her squeal. "There's my Wheezy smile."

"That doesn't count," she wheezed. But she was still smiling when he got an arm around her shoulder, urging her to settle back down. "Do you promise it will be ok?"

"I promise, Ellie. You'll be having so much fun you won't have the chance to be homesick."

Morgan sighed now as he made his way through the snow. Eloise hadn't needed him since that night. She clung to her mother as though Lily was the air she breathed. He had tried for a time—to regain that relationship they'd had before—but somewhere along the line, as Eloise slipped further into her mind, Morgan had ceased trying.

Knocking twice at the Harpers' door, Morgan let himself in. Elizabeth looked up as he came in. Wishing him good morning, she offered him a mug of coffee. "I was actually hoping I could speak with Merritt?" he said.

"He should be down any minute," Elizabeth said softly. "You might as well eat while you wait." Placing a plate of eggs and bacon in front of him, she went back to the stove.

It amazed Morgan still how much the woman reminded him of his own daughter. In his two months in their home, the woman had spoken only a few words to him. When they were all gathered together, she hardly said a word at all.

Merritt clapped Morgan's shoulder as he sat down. "Mornin', Riley. Everything all right? You look troubled."

"Maybe we can talk after breakfast?"

Merritt nodded. "You can help me shovel out a path to the barn. I was about to wake Brooks, but if you don't mind helping, I'll let him sleep in a little while longer."

After breakfast, Morgan followed Merritt out to the barn, wondering just how to start the conversation. Unsure, he went to work on the snow.

"You wanted to talk?" Merritt pressed.

"Right." Morgan sighed. "Your boy came asking after my daughter."

"Did he?"

"I told him I needed to think it over."

Merritt nodded. "I can understand that, but he's a good kid, Morgan. Real good."

"I don't doubt that he is, Merritt. It's not Brooks that's the problem. It's Eloise. Brooks doesn't know her like I do. She's … difficult, and I don't want to see her getting hurt. Not again."

"Brooks couldn't hurt her, Morgan. That boy is something special, and he cares about her."

"You don't know Eloise, Merritt, and even if I could trust that he wouldn't hurt her, I can't say that Ellie is ready for something like that. She still relies on her mother too much, and after everything that happened in Huxley—" he stopped short. "I don't think she's ready."

Merritt considered him a moment, his arms resting on the handle. "You're right that I don't know Eloise. But I know someone like her. I may not know anything about Eloise's situation, but I have my theories, and from what I do know, she doesn't seem any worse off than Libby was when we met."

"She doesn't?" Morgan asked.

"In some ways, maybe. But in others, she's better. Elizabeth didn't talk at all when I met her. Not to anyone but Annabelle and Ruby Crawley, the woman that helped raise her. It took two months for her to speak to me."

"Really?" Morgan whispered. He'd never imagined someone being worse off than Eloise. "You said you had your theories?"

"Theories that, in the end, are none of my business. But I know how a mind like that works, Morgan. I've loved one for over twenty years. I know they can be dark, and I know that she can't help it."

"You're a better man than I am." Morgan shook his head, swearing under his breath. "I can barely stand to look at her, Merritt. Knowing she could do something like that to herself. To her mother." To him. "I could have killed her right there." Looking away, Morgan drove his shovel into the snow.

"I don't think those like Libby and Ellie think quite like we do, Morgan," Merritt said gently. "We can rationalize. They can't always do that, from what Elizabeth has told me. The more they rationalize, the worse it gets. That voice in there is loud, and it's convincing. In Eloise's mind, she was doing you a favor."

"A favor?" Morgan snapped. "A favor letting her mother or I find her dead? I count both of us lucky it wasn't Lily that found her that day. It would have killed her on the spot."

Merritt frowned. "Morgan, have you ever listened to your daughter? Let her tell you what it's like to be in her head?"

"Eloise has barely spoken to me since she was a girl. It's always been about her mother." Clearing his throat, Morgan turned back. "She tried to kill herself, Merritt. I don't think knowing what's in her head would do anything." Not when he looked at her and didn't know how to forgive her.

"You'll continue to struggle with that forgiveness, Morgan, until you listen to her."

Ignoring him, Morgan focused his attention on his work. "Tell Brooks he has my blessing if he wants it. He can't break her any more than she already is."

Twenty-One

Two days had passed since Brooks spoke about the courtship, and he hadn't mentioned it since. Eloise wanted to believe she had expected nothing less, but she had allowed a small flicker of hope to take root in her.

Maybe he forgot, or he changed his mind. Like Edith and Grace.

Brooks is different. Even if he did change his mind, it's not like them. That, she had to believe. Unlike others who had passed through her life, it was Brooks who sought her out rather than leave that job to her. He pursued her and encouraged her voice.

Focusing on that thought, Eloise dressed and made the bed before starting downstairs. "You're up early," Lily said, patting the seat next to her. "Juniper can wait long enough for you to eat breakfast. Sit."

"Where is everyone?"

"The men are shoveling pathways, and Elizabeth and Maisie are taking advantage of some alone time together. I think Maisie needed some time with her mama." Lily nudged her. "It gives the two of us a little time. I hardly see you with all that time you spend in the barn."

"That's a bit dramatic." Eloise smiled. "I still see you more than Brooks."

"Maybe. But we went from spending our days together to my having to share you." Lily touched Eloise's cheek. "I'm happy about it, knowing you have a friend. But I do miss you."

Eloise smiled. "Do you want to come and see Juniper? You haven't even met her." Hurrying through her breakfast, Eloise led her mother through the freshly shoveled snow.

"That horse is spoiled with your attention, Elle," Brooks shouted.

Blushing, Eloise quickened her step. Could that be true? Was her attention only creating another problem?

"Don't listen to him, Ellie," Merritt shouted next. "That boy's been known to sleep in the barn when caring for a new horse."

At that, Brooks flung a ball of snow in his father's direction, hitting him hard in the cheek. "Watch it!" Merritt shouted, sending another back in Brooks' direction.

"I don't think so." Ducking her head, Lily took hold of Eloise's elbow and dragged her toward the barn. "I have thus far avoided Maisie's plea for such a fight. I am not getting into it now."

Laughing, Eloise helped her mother get the barn door closed just before a snowball flew in their direction, hitting the wood with a rough smack. "I don't think we'll be able to avoid it forever, Mama."

"Well, I can avoid it for the moment." Dusting herself off, Lily looked around. "Where is this horse of yours?"

"At the end. The black and white one." Going ahead of her, Eloise approached the horse slowly, gaining approval before moving close enough to touch her. "Don't touch her," she warned. "She lets Brooks and me, but she doesn't know you."

"She's beautiful, Ellie." Seating herself on a bale, Lily watched her daughter stoke the horse's muzzle. "And she's yours —completely?"

"Completely," Eloise beamed. "Brooks said he'll keep her at the ranch for me, but she'll be mine." She looked back at her. "He said when she's ready and trained, he'll teach me to ride."

Lily smiled. "You always did want to." The girl had always loved the idea of learning to ride, but with Morgan busy and Eloise too timid to take lessons with the local stables, she'd been unable. "It will be better here. More sights to see."

"And Brooks will be good. Patient." Shaking her head, Eloise turned her attention back to Juniper. "I might see if she'll leave the stall tomorrow so we can clean it, but I want her to come willingly. Brooks thinks she might be ready to let me in with her at the least."

Lily felt tears bite at her eyes as she watched her daughter. She couldn't call the girl happy yet, but she was something more than the shattered thing she had grown up to be. It was something she wanted to take comfort in, but fear ate at her. She had seemed to be healing with Edith and Grace before they decided she wasn't worth their time.

She had to shake that memory loose. The Harpers were different than any she had known, and she knew that the way Brooks looked at her daughter was far more than infatuation. The man already loved her in a way Eloise had never been loved. Not because Eloise wasn't worthy but because no one else was. Not when they refused to see past the most visible parts of her mind. Lily couldn't understand how, but Brooks had seen beneath it all from day one. He understood her. She could see it even in the simple gift of a horse.

"She gives you a sense of purpose, doesn't she?" Lily asked.

"She makes me feel less alone," Eloise said softly. "Like … I have a reason to fight now."

"You've always had reason to fight, Ellie. You just didn't see it."

Eloise shook her head. "It's not the same. You and daddy have each other in the end. But Juniper—she doesn't trust many people, but she trusts me. She needs me."

"Your father and I need you, Eloise. But I do understand. There's a reason the Lord gave Elijah a job in his loneliness." The story of the prophet Elijah had always been a favorite of Lily's father, and she'd had it memorized since she was a girl. It was the story that brought her the most hope with Eloise. "You were what I clung to after both Poppy and Nanny Anne died," she said softly. "I knew I couldn't fall too deeply into my grief when I had you to care for. As much as I love your father, it was you that kept me going. You needed me."

Eloise was quiet a moment, her own lips trembling. "Do you think Nanny would have been angry if she was here? Do you think she would have … would have treated us like the others?"

"Ellie, I don't think you would have found yourself in that tub if Nanny was here."

"So, you admit it now?" Eloise whispered. "That it wasn't an accident?"

Lily shook her head. "It was an accident, Eloise. No matter what happened, it was an accident."

Eloise nodded. "I think you're wrong, though," she said. "I think I still would have ended up there. It would have started regardless of whether I went to Alma's or not. It took nothing for her to undo me, Mama." Eloise chewed her lip, forcing back tears. "This is just me, Mama."

"Well, we're going to change it," Lily said firmly. "Elizabeth found her happiness, Eloise. Hold to that."

***

By the time they made their way back inside, all three men were coated in white, their hair and clothes wet with melting snow.

Throwing another log on the fire, Brooks looked over the wet floor. "Mama's not going to be too happy about that."

"Already on it." Taking a towel, Merritt wiped up the footprints. "Why don't you go let the ladies know it's safe to come in?"

"I'll come," Morgan said. "I might have to drag Lily out." Judging by the look on his face, Brooks felt that was exactly what the man planned. Right into a snowbank.

"My father told me about you giving your blessing?" Brooks said. "I wanted to thank you and reassure you again that I'll take care of her, Morgan, and I won't rush into anything she isn't ready for. Right now, I just want to know her more."

Morgan nodded. "I know, Brooks. But it really doesn't make it any easier. She's been hurt before a dozen times over. People come in, make her think they want to know her, and then decide she's too something—too much work, too boring. Then they would up and leave her, leaving her feeling worse off than she was before."

"These were all friends?" Brooks asked. "Not courtships or the possibility of such?"

"No. She never had those. It was all girls."

Brooks turned that over in his head. "So maybe what she needs is more? Friends may have always led to pain, but in this area, she's never been hurt."

"You think if she sees you seeking more, she'll trust it more?"

"It's a possibility. Friends leave, but with a courtship, there is every intent of staying, of wanting more, and if you don't mind my saying, sir—my end is marriage, if she wants it."

Morgan sighed. "And I think you could be good for her, Brooks. But if you don't mind my saying it, you are going to have to earn my trust as much as hers. Maybe even more so." Leaving him behind, Morgan forced the barn door open.

Following after him, Brooks could see Eloise leaning over the stall as she talked to Juniper. Even from a distance, he could see the stiff way she held herself as Morgan came closer.

"That thing towers over you, Wheeze," Morgan said. "Surprised you aren't scared of the thing."

Eloise blushed deeply as she tossed the man a look. "I'm not scared of everything," she mumbled. Her lips moved silently as she muttered something under her breath.

"Just leave her be, Morgan." Taking her husband's arm, Lily pulled him out of the barn.

Avoiding Brooks' eyes, Eloise wiped at the tears on her cheeks.

Maybe she was dramatic. She knew her father meant no offense to it. But that didn't stop the pain or embarrassment every time he demeaned her. *Surprised you aren't scared of the thing. The girl is scared of life.*

"I don't think he meant anything by it, Elle," Brooks said softly. "I don't mean to say he should have said it—he shouldn't have—but you can't let it cripple you."

"He says stuff like that all the time, Brooks."

"But is it true?"

She shook her head.

"Then why let it cripple you?"

175

"It doesn't," she muttered. "It … never mind."

Brooks watched the girl a moment, understanding dawning. "It makes you angry?" he prodded. It would explain the look of resentment she had given her father. "It's ok to admit that. Whether his intent is malicious or not, it's not right to mock you."

Blinking back tears, she went back to Juniper. "It doesn't matter. I'll get over it."

"It does matter, Elle. If it hurts you, it matters, and you don't have to get over it."

Eloise seemed to startle at that. "I don't?"

"No, darlin'." Moving closer, he tucked a stray lock of hair behind her ear. "Not letting it ruin your day is not the same as getting over it. It matters, Elle, and it's ok that it hurts."

Eloise's eyes met his. "I hate it," she whispered. "I feel like that's all he sees in me."

"It isn't, Elle. He loves you. Believe me."

"What do you know, Brooks? I don't mean to be rude, but you don't know us."

"I know because I was just talking to him, Elle—about you."

Her eyes widened. "About—you mean …"

Brooks smiled at the look of surprise on her face. "Yes, about that, and just so you know how much he loves you, he was hesitant. He's scared to see you hurt again."

"That isn't wh—"

"Yes, it is, Eloise. He made it clear I have to earn his trust as much as yours. Now." Taking her hands, Brooks smiled. "Will you allow me the honor of asking you officially?"

"You really want—"

"Elle?"

Blushing, Eloise nodded.

"Well then, Eloise Riley, would you do me the honor of entering into a courtship with me?"

Eloise simply nodded, her eyes still wide.

Chucking her chin, Brooks turned her eyes to his. "I'm not going anywhere, Elle."

"And you really think I'm worth it?"

"Would I be asking you if I didn't?"

Eloise shrugged. "People have pretended they wanted to be my friend before."

"I'm not them, Elle." Brooks sighed. "Please."

"I'm sorry," she whispered. "I do want this, I just … it's hard to believe you could actually like … me." She looked down at her hands. "I don't like me."

"I know, Elle," Brooks said gently. "But maybe we can change that."

Eloise came into his arms of her own accord this time, her ear against his chest. "I'm drowning."

Brooks pressed his lip to the side of her forehead. "Then hold on to me. I've got you."

Twenty-Two

Eloise watched the snow fall outside the window, glowing in the moonlight. In the room beside hers, she could hear Brooks pacing. She should feel happy now. Hopeful. Instead, her chest felt heavier as she sank deeper beneath the waves in her mind.

Brooks had asked. He had made it clear he desired more than friendship. Something she had always hoped and believed would be reassuring to her. A friend could leave, but if a man desired more, surely he would stay?

But it wasn't even a real promise of marriage. Brooks could still leave. That thought had plagued her since the moment the words had left Brooks' lips. Instead of relief, she had found herself feeling more uncertain, more afraid, and unable to stop the tears that came with it. She had avoided real tears in his presence for months, and she'd chosen the perfect time to break —in the middle of his courtship proposal.

The moment she had settled enough to speak, Eloise had stepped away from him, eyes on her hands. She didn't have to look to know the front of his shirt was soaked through. "I'm sorry."

Brooks had said nothing but simply looked at her.

"Sorry," she mumbled. "I know. Don't apologize."

Rather than let her pull away, Brooks took hold of her hand, bringing her back to him. Eloise hated the way she went so easily, craving the comfort of his touch. It was a lie. Or at least, it could be.

"Why do you think you need to apologize, Elle?"

"Because this isn't how it should be. I should be happy. You shouldn't have to comfort me all the time."

"I don't, and I don't mind comforting you when it's needed. Elle, I expected nothing less than this reaction from you." Seating her next to him, he wiped the tears on her cheeks. "You've been hurt, darlin'. I know it's going to take time for you to be comfortable with this—with *us*. To trust."

"Is it hard for you?" she whispered. "To trust me?"

Brooks laughed softly. "No. You don't strike me as the type to fear."

Throughout the day, she had felt herself beginning to feel the uncertainty slip away. Brooks was kind. He understood her. He wanted her. She could believe it. But bedtime had always been when the voice was at its loudest, its strongest, and when he had left her that night, she felt the peace Brooks had instilled in her washing away as the waters rose around her.

He wanted her for now. That didn't mean he would want her forever. Edith and Grace had wanted to know her for a time, too. Eloise's stomach rolled as she remembered every friend she'd had that eventually walked away. What started out as a friendship where she was always invited and included changed over time into one where she was excluded and left behind.

Sitting up, Eloise wrapped her arms around her knees, fighting the panic in her chest. "He'll stay," she whispered. "He'll stay. Someone has to stay." She bit down on her lip to keep from crying. "Somebody has to stay."

The sound of Maisie's bed creaking made her freeze, and she held her breath to keep quiet. "Ellie?" Dragging her blanket with her, Maisie seated herself at the foot of Eloise's bed. "You cry a lot at night."

Unsure of what to say to that, Eloise shrugged.

"We will stay, you know. All of us." She shrugged. "We want to know you, Eloise. I ... I want to be your friend."

For now. Maisie could do so much better, and Eloise feared the day the girl would realize that.

"You know, I don't have many friends either," Maisie said quietly. "I have a couple that I see sometimes. I have one good one. Sort of."

"Sort of?"

"His name is Jeremy." Despite her tone, Maisie couldn't disguise the light blush that filled her cheeks. "He's all right, I suppose. But it's why I always wished I could go to school. Maybe I could meet new people."

"School doesn't get you proper friends, Maisie," Eloise told her. "It gets you school friends who want nothing to do with you once the bell rings."

"Oh."

Feeling guilty, Eloise tried again. "I don't mean that to discourage you. I promise. Anyone would be lucky to have a friend like you, Mais. But I just don't want you to think that that's the only way you could meet someone who cares about you. Find someone who wants you for you. Not convenience."

Maisie considered her a moment. "I could say the same for you. But you won't believe it, will you?"

"We're different, Maisie. I lived in a town full of people. Once Rose Haven grows more, you'll make friends."

Maisie frowned. "What is it going to take to make you see that we all like you? That we're staying?" Tears filled her dark eyes. "Why don't you want to be my friend?"

"I want to be your friend, Maisie," Eloise said softly. "I do. But it's ... it's hard." It was terrifying. She was already opening herself to Brooks in a way that would destroy her when he left. She wasn't sure she could take more.

If he left, that small voice corrected. *If. Not when.*

"We won't leave, Ellie, but you'll never believe it if you don't choose to."

"It's not that simple, Maisie."

"But it doesn't make it any less true," Maisie replied. "Everything is a choice. You can choose to trust us and be happy, or you can choose to be miserable."

When Maisie had gone back to bed, Eloise chewed on her words. *Choice.* It wasn't that simple. She couldn't choose to trust when everything in her screamed that she would be hurt.

But what if you aren't hurt?

But she would be. She always was.

You'll never know if you don't try. If you can't make the choice to trust, make the choice to try.

"God, if I do this," Eloise said softly, "don't let me be hurt again."

***

Eloise delayed going to breakfast as long as she could. Supper had been near unbearable simply knowing what others knew, and though they'd been respectful in keeping quiet, she was sure they would only do so for so long.

It was Brooks' knock at the door that lured her downstairs. "No one will pay any attention to it, Elle," he reminded her. "My parents especially. You know, my parents never even courted.

They went straight from friendship to marriage, and my mother still talks about the attention taking away from the moment." He set his forehead to hers. "Neither would take these moments from you, darlin'."

Dropping her hand as they neared the bottom steps, Brooks ushered her into the kitchen.

As promised, no one said a word as they took their seats next to each other. No one paid them any mind at all but to wish them good morning before going back to previous conversations. How they had managed to keep Maisie quiet, Eloise wasn't quite sure, but the girl had yet to say a word.

"It will have to be acknowledged at some point," Brooks teased. "I hope you don't plan to hide it forever."

"I'm not hiding it," she whispered back. "They know it's happening."

"Yes, but there are some things I would like to do. This, for example." He took her hand beneath the table and squeezed it. "Will this be allowed?"

Blushing, she nodded. "I just don't want anyone to make an ordeal out of it." That voice in her head made it difficult enough to enjoy it, but it would be something entirely different to have others watching and commenting.

Brooks smiled. "Neither do I, but I don't think it's something we need to worry about."

It was true, the only person who seemed to be paying attention at all was her father, and likely at her mother's command, he was staying quiet.

"Morgan and I were planning to roll out a path into town," Merritt said. "You wouldn't mind if we borrowed a few of your horses, would you?"

"Not at all," Brooks reassured. "Take Charlie and Posey; they handle the snow best and need to be worked."

After breakfast, Brooks went ahead to ready the horses. Both horses began to move about in their stalls as Merritt uncovered the weighted roller. "You know what that is, don't you?" Brooks asked, patting Charlie's back. "You feeling neglected?"

Charlie blew out a small puff of air on his face. Smiling, Brooks kissed his muzzle before slipping him into his halter. "Are you sure you don't want any help?"

"We've got it, Brooks," Merritt replied. "Enjoy your time with Ellie."

Brooks waited until they were gone before going back for Eloise. "Give me one more moment," he told her. "I'll meet you in the barn." From his room, he retrieved his Bible. He'd prayed the night before, pacing his floor until his father ordered him to bed. He wanted to do right by Eloise. For her. For him. But above all, for God. He knew the risks of spending so much time secluded in the barn, and he feared that temptation. He feared leaving her in the state she was, distant from the God he loved. He feared her drawing himself from Him.

He'd poured out his fear to the Lord until one simple solution had come to him.

Eloise watched Brooks pace the barn before turning to her. He hesitated before starting. "I know this is what you need," he said quietly. "Being alone, and I am not going to say that I would have it another way. Having spent this time just the two of us, I wouldn't change it." Brooks felt his nerves rise as Eloise watched him. He was rambling, and as she watched, he felt his tongue dry.

"But?" she encouraged.

"But," he choked, "this is all different than what I always expected when it came to courting. I didn't expect to have a real moment alone with you until we were married. But seeing as being alone is what you need, there are a few things I want to do to ensure we keep the Lord present and from making any mistakes.

"Like what?" Eloise whispered.

"Like praying together. Praying that He keeps our eyes on Him rather than ... other things."

Eloise felt her own cheeks burn as the man blushed. "What else?"

"Studying His Word. I know you struggle with that, Elle. I thought maybe it would help. It would get you into the Word, and I'll be there to help you understand where you struggle to."

Eloise nodded. "All right."

"Are you comfortable with that?" Brooks asked. "This isn't a condition. At least, not now. I do want a godly, Bible-reading wife, Eloise. I can't deny that, and I won't back down on it. But I understand that you have questions. Frustrations. That's why I don't want to force you into it. Following God needs to be a choice."

"It's not that I don't want to follow Him, Brooks, or that I don't want to read the Bible. I do." Eloise chewed her lip. "I do. It's just ... every time I do, I just ..."

"Just what, Elle?"

"Just end up hating myself more," she said quietly. "I don't feel loved when I read His Word, Brooks. I don't feel closer. I feel farther."

"Maybe we can change that."

Eloise let out a hurt laugh. "Do you intend to change everything?"

"Everything that hinders you? Everything that makes you think life isn't worth living? Yes, Elle, I plan to change those things."

Eloise nodded. "I want that—all of those things—but do you have a Bible?" No matter what, she knew she wasn't ready to open Elizabeth's Bible.

Brooks smiled. "Yes, Elle. I have my own Bible. You don't have to use hers. That's yours, and you'll use it when you're ready."

New tears blurred her eyes, her lips quivering. "Do I have to pray aloud?"

"No. I'll pray." Bringing her to him, Brooks pressed his lips lightly to her forehead. "You don't have to do anything you aren't comfortable with."

"Even that?" Her voice cracked miserably.

"God never said you had to pray aloud, Elle. In fact, He said the very opposite. 'But thou, when thou prayest, enter into thy closet, and when thou hast shut thy door, pray to thy Father which is in secret.'"

"I can do that," Eloise said quietly, a small smile pulling at her lips.

"I am sure." Brooks laughed. "And our Papa loves it just as much as the prayers we pray aloud."

She shook her head. "I always thought He expected us to pray aloud. The women in Mama's church group always said I would have to learn."

"They were wrong, Elle. It isn't a requirement, and should the Lord ever call you to do so, He would give you the words you need whether you were practiced or not." Seeing the confusion on her face, Brooks sighed. "This here is why I think we need to study the Word together, and you need to open your ears on Sundays. Something tells me you've been given wrong ideas of God and what He wants of us."

She nodded, fresh tears spilling over.

"So let's change that." Brooks smiled as her own lips turned up tremulously.

Everything is a choice. Make the choice to try. Eloise held out a hand. "Let's change it."

***

Make the choice to try. Easier said than done. The moment she had agreed, that small voice that had encouraged her faded, and the darker, haunting voice seeped back in, dragging her under.

It wouldn't end any differently. She'd tried a hundred times over to change and have faith, and it always amounted to nothing.

But it could. And she clung to that thought. It could.

Eloise forced her mind to stay present when the voice pecked at her through Brooks' prayers or when she failed to understand what he read from the Bible. Again and again, she beat back the voice. But everyone she knew was wrong: It didn't get easier. The harder she fought, the quicker she sank.

"Take it one day at a time," Elizabeth encouraged one night. "It's going to get harder before it gets easier. But it will get easier."

"It doesn't feel like it," Eloise whispered.

"But what you're feeling doesn't matter in the end, Eloise. Though it feels true, in the end, all those thoughts, all those fears? They are lies. I know it doesn't make it easier, but it also doesn't make it untrue."

Eloise watched Elizabeth, wondering how she had gone from where Eloise was now to the woman before her. "Do you really not feel it anymore?" she asked. "How?"

"I feel it, Eloise. Every day. But I no longer let it control me. Some days are harder. Some days it does control me no matter how hard I fight it. But those days are fewer now, and they get fewer and fewer as time goes on." Elizabeth set a hand to Eloise's knee. "It takes time, Ellie. A lot of it. It takes practice. But if you keep trying—if you keep fighting those thoughts—their grip on you will get weaker."

"It's different, Elizabeth," Eloise said quietly. "You had God."

"You have God, Ellie. You are simply too deep in your pain to hear Him. To feel Him. But He is there, Eloise, and He is trying to lift you out of the water."

Eloise tried to hold to that. To believe it.

"Darling, you have to choose to believe He is for you. If you don't, you will always feel lost."

"I want to believe it, Elizabeth. I've tried—I *am* trying—but reading the Bible … it doesn't help. I pray every day, and I only feel more alone."

"Because you are trying too hard. You're looking for loud replies when the Lord's voice is small. He speaks in ways you have to look for. He speaks through those who love you. He replies by *giving* you those who love you. Do you really think your family came here, found an entire community that can understand your ways, and even someone who can understand what you are feeling, on your own? By mere chance?"

"Why would He give me those things, Elizabeth?"

"Because He loves you, Ellie. He wants to see you happy. Healed."

"I'll never be healed."

Elizabeth sighed. "No, maybe you won't be healed of the thoughts and fears. Those might always be there. But I told you they will get easier, and He will heal you of the hurt if you let Him. He never intended for you to walk around with so much pain, Eloise."

"Then why didn't He stop it?" Eloise demanded. "I prayed every day that it would change. That my friends would treat me better. That they would stay. It seems to me He wants me in pain. That, or He simply doesn't care."

The Lord didn't like timidity. The Lord didn't like her. Why would He? Timid, faithless, weak—the voice went on and on until Eloise wanted to scream.

"You can't listen to what your mind is telling you, Ellie. Your thoughts? Your feelings? They are liars. The evil one wants you to be miserable."

"This is not my fault," Eloise hissed. "I can't help it."

"You're right," Elizabeth replied calmly. "You can't help the thoughts that come into your head, but you can control how you respond to them, Eloise, and how you let them control you. I know that is hard to see now. It took me years to believe I could change the way I responded. It was so automatic, I didn't even think when it happened. I simply panicked."

"How did you change it?"

"One thought at a time. When they come, your instinct is to panic. To shove the thought away. But that will only make it worse. When a thought comes, take a deep breath and counter it with truth. It will take practice. It won't happen right away, but eventually, you will notice a difference."

"But they feel like truth," Eloise whispered. "I try to tell myself they aren't, but ..."

"But they are convincing," Elizabeth finished. "I know, Eloise. That's why you need to actually look at what you see. Look at how much your mother loves you. She may not know what it's like to live in your head, but she still understands. She has supported you through everything. Do you truly think she would do all of that if she didn't love you?"

"I know Mama loves me." Lily was the only one she never doubted.

"Then focus on that when the voices get loud. The rest will come over time, so long as you keep trying. If you want to, then go out with Maisie when she asks. Don't let fear keep you from it. Keep spending time with Brooks. Focus on what they say, what they do with you. If you do that, it will get easier, Eloise." Elizabeth hesitated a moment before continuing. "I know you don't want to hear it, Ellie, believe me. But spending time in the Lord's presence will help. It won't cure you, not if He doesn't will it, but it helps to be able to counter those lies with His truths. "But," she continued, "I also know that it's hard to see those things as truth when you don't see yourself in the best light."

Because there was nothing good to see. She wasn't enough for Him.

"Keep reading the Bible with Brooks, Ellie. Keep letting him pray over you. Maybe sitting with him and learning with him will help you understand more, and then maybe someday you'll be ready to open that Bible for yourself."

"Do you want your Bible back?" Eloise asked.

"It's not my Bible anymore, darling. I gave it to you."

"I'm not even using it, Elizabeth. I haven't even opened it."

"Not yet," said Elizabeth softly. "But you will. When you're ready."

Eloise rolled her eyes. "How can you know that?"

"Because I can see that you do love the Lord. You're curious, and you desire that relationship. But circumstance has warped your mind, and if you had no intention of ever opening it, I don't believe the Lord would have laid it on my heart to pass that Bible onto you."

Twenty-Three

Everything in Eloise screamed to put the Bible down. It wouldn't help. It would only hurt.

But it could. It helped Elizabeth.

She wanted to open it. She wanted to read it. She wanted to feel His presence the way she did when she was listening to Brooks read from the Bible.

It's an illusion. What she felt was for Brooks. Not her. *It will never be for you. Give up.*

"No." She had given up before and found herself at the bottom of a tub. She didn't want to give up again. Eyes closed, hands shaking, Eloise slid a finger under the cover and lifted it.

What good will reading it be if you don't understand it? You won't understand. You never have.

"God, please. I want to know you." Tears dripped down her cheeks. "Please." Opening her eyes, Eloise found a note inscribed on the inside cover.

When my heart is overwhelmed: Lead me to the rock that is higher than I. - Psalm 61:2 - It doesn't take the pain away, Ellie. But it makes it easier to bear.

Eloise's eyes settled on the name. Ellie? Had Elizabeth planned to give the Bible to Eloise before that morning? But that didn't sound right, and as she thought on it, the handwriting didn't match that on the list of supplies Elizabeth had passed Merritt just yesterday. Ellie—she supposed it could have been a

191

nickname for Elizabeth as well. Hadn't she heard Annabelle call Elizabeth 'Ellie' once?

The oddity of it made her uneasy. It felt almost as though that inscription was written for her.

It's a coincidence. Lots of people could be called Ellie.

Coincidence—of course it was coincidence. The idea that God would be looking out for her years ago before she was born or even a child at most was ridiculous. Even more ridiculous was to create such a connection between her and Elizabeth. The Lord didn't care for her like that. If He did, He wouldn't have let her feel like this for so long. He would have stopped every awful thing from happening to her.

I marked a few verses throughout that helped me, the letter continued, *as well as a few that I think should help you. Read it. Write in it. Do whatever it takes. I love you and I believe in you, Ellie. You can best this.*

Everything screamed for her to put the Bible down.

Take a deep breath and counter it with truth.

Eloise wasn't sure where to start, but the beginning seemed a good enough place. Opening to Genesis, she stared down at the words. *Write in it.* She wasn't sure she would be able to. She'd thought Brooks' Bible was full, but Elizabeth had filled almost every bit of open space in her small writing.

Discouragement pressed in on her, thick and suffocating.

Shut the book and move on. It was better to accept defeat now than get her hopes up. *Unless you want to end up at the bottom of a tub again.*

It was precisely that thought that urged Eloise forward. She didn't want to end up in that position again. No matter what she felt, she didn't want to give up. She didn't want to give in.

You can best this, Ellie. Maybe the words weren't written for her, but they resonated nonetheless. She could best this. She would.

Do you really think this will earn you favor? It will do nothing for you in His eyes. Not when you're too stupid to understand a word of it.

But she didn't have to understand on her own, did she? That was why Elizabeth gave her this Bible rather than a new, unblemished one. *Counter it with truth, Ellie.*

Doing her best to block out the voice, she started reading.

It won't last. Even if you manage to scrape anything out of this, you'll fail in time. When you realize how useless it is. How little you mean to Him. The Lord doesn't like timidity.

He loves Elizabeth. Elizabeth is timid.

Elizabeth is better than you. Clearly, she has something you don't.

Like what? What could Brooks and Elizabeth have that she didn't? What was it about Eloise that made the Lord look down on her?

Counter it with truth, Eloise.

She was countering it with truth. But that voice wasn't wrong: no prayer she had ever uttered, screamed, or pleaded had been answered with a *yes.*

"What did I do to deserve this?"

The Lord doesn't like timidity. You have nothing He cares for.

Eloise shook her head. "No."

She couldn't breathe. She was slipping so far beneath the waters of her mind that she couldn't see the surface. Tossing the Bible away, Eloise wrapped her arms around her knees. "Please, God. Tell me I'm wrong. Let me see that I'm wrong." She couldn't breathe—not around the deep ache in her chest or the lump in her throat.

"Please."

Why did He despise her so much? Why love and heal others, like Elizabeth, but not her? What was she doing wrong?

Having drawn her mind from seeking the Lord, the voice shifted. *Weak. How do you expect Him to love you when you don't read His Word? Elizabeth read it herself. Look at it, and you couldn't make it for even half a page. Grow up. Pick it up. Read it. It would help if you would just read it.*

Eloise shook her head. She knew better than to fall for that. The desire to pick it up. To read and understand it. The belief that it would help would all fall away the moment she opened the book. No matter what she did, that voice was loud and unrelenting.

Her chest ached with effort to keep her tears at bay. *Childish*, that voice hissed. *Grow up, Eloise.*

"God, please. Please."

***

Where he had hoped getting into the Word would help Eloise, Brooks found her slipping further. She sat silently while he read from his Bible, and when it was over, she stood and made her way to Juniper.

Giving her space, Brooks put his Bible away before approaching her. "Do you still want to do this?"

Her eyes flashed to his, and he realized his mistake before Eloise even spoke. "Do what?"

"Read the Bible. Pray together."

"Oh," she whispered. "Yes."

She's doing it for you, that dark voice cooed. *The woman is hopeless.*

Brooks shook his head. No one was hopeless. Least of all, Eloise. He saw the curiosity in her, the desire to know and understand. But something in her head was holding her back. "All right then," he said quietly. "Let me know if you need a break. Putting too much pressure on yourself isn't going to make it any easier."

Eloise shook her head. "What if I never understand? What if I never reach where you and Elizabeth are?"

"You will, Elle." Bringing her to him, Brooks kissed the temples at which she massaged. "You're expecting too much of yourself. A relationship with Him isn't an instantaneous thing; it takes time and work."

Eloise turned her face into his chest. "Did you ever struggle, Brooks?" she whispered. "You don't seem as though you have."

"Darlin', I have struggled far more than you realize. It took me years to reach where I am now. I've only just in the past few years started to truly feel the relationship I wanted with Him, and I still struggle."

She shook her head. "That's what everyone says, but then they judge me for struggling."

"I'm not judging, Elle. How long will it take you to see that I understand and that what I don't understand, I am trying to understand?"

When Eloise said nothing, Brooks felt himself deflate. He wasn't good enough for this. He wasn't a preacher. He wasn't a teacher.

Perhaps you are exactly what she needs, a small voice countered. *Not a teacher. Not a preacher. But someone who loves her as she is, not what she could be.*

What good could Brooks be? He was a rancher. What did that have to do with her struggles?

Brooks found his eyes drawn from Hatter and Era to Posey and Cheshire. Perhaps there was a reason for what he did. "Is that true, Papa?" Was there a reason for his lifelong passion for healing wounded creatures?

Eloise glanced up at him. "Why do you call him Papa?" she asked.

Brooks considered that question for a moment. "Because it's who He is, and to see Him as such makes Him feel closer." He played with her fingers. "I told you it took me years to get here, Elle, and I meant that. I haven't always been close to Him. I really didn't even know Him until I was about fourteen."

"I imagined you had always followed Him."

Brooks shook his head. "I tried. I wanted to. He was the foundation my parents raised me on—Bible reading every morning, church every Sunday. But I could never wrap my head around any of it. I told you I had a certain level of distrust. Don't know why or how it started, but by the time I was about thirteen, it had gotten bad. I found myself spending more and more time on my own." He shrugged. "I wasn't happy, Elle, and it made me vulnerable to many things."

Leading her to the haybale, Brooks pulled her down beside him, keeping her hands in his. "I told you I only ever had one friend. He's still a friend—a good one—but there was a time when he wasn't the best friend I could have had. He had his own struggles—real struggles—and we got into some things together.

Drinking, mostly." Seeing the shock on Eloise's face, Brooks laughed softly. "I'm not perfect, darlin'. Never have been, never will be, and I especially wasn't back then."

"So what changed?" Eloise asked.

"Annabelle," Brooks said simply. "She caught Wiley and me drinking one day. Never seen her angrier than she was then. She told me how stupid and selfish I was being. Her husband and her father both had been lost to alcohol, and I had the nerve to go following in their footsteps." But it wasn't the anger that had caught his attention that day. It was the way she had looked at him, as though she could see his own life coming to an end at the bottom of a bottle. She hadn't just been angry; she had been terrified.

"After she had finished her yelling, she let me stay with her so I could sober up before sending me home. That night we stayed up late talking. She got me to tell her everything I'd been struggling with." Brooks let out a trembling breath, and the hand he held gripped his back. "She told me she understood. She'd never understood God either. To her, God felt distant. Unapproachable. But when she looked at Him as a friend, He felt warmer. So, she suggested I look at Him in a different light: still God above all things, but to make Him more approachable. If anyone was like Jesus, it was my parents. Always loving, kind, and forgiving, that's who they've always been. I could see God in them in a way I couldn't see Him anywhere else. So that's how I started trying to see God—as a Father. It helped, but I still felt distant towards Him. I still felt ashamed approaching Him after everything I'd done. It was my mother who suggested I call Him *Papa*. He's our Father, after all."

"And that helped?" Eloise asked, one eyebrow raised skeptically.

Brooks smiled. "It did. It removed a barrier between He and I. Like with my parents, I felt no shame in going to Him. I slowly began to trust Him."

Eloise was quiet for a moment. "Doesn't it feel weird?"

"It did at first, but now it's as natural as breathing. I don't think about calling Him Papa any more than calling my mother Mama. It's who He is to me."

Eloise shook her head. "I couldn't do that."

"You could," Brooks told her. "If you wanted."

"No. I don't see Him as a Father. He doesn't love me like that."

"Elle, He loves you the way He loves me. If He doesn't love you, then He doesn't love me."

"The Bible says that God loves in a way that we, as humans, could never understand. That the love we have for others is nothing compared to the love He has for us." Eloise shook her head. "And that isn't true. Why can I, a simple-minded human who can't even begin to understand what it means to love unconditionally, not even imagine letting anyone, but *especially* my child, cry out every night for some sign of love? Some sign of hope? I could never imagine letting my child or anyone else live their lives feeling like a worthless, unlovable piece of nothing while I sit back and watch. That's what God does, Brooks."

"Then He doesn't love me," Brooks repeated. "If one piece of the Bible is a lie, then it's all a lie. Do you believe the Bible is a lie?"

New tears filled her eyes. "No."

"Then how can you believe that the Bible applies to all but you?"

"I don't know." She let out a harsh sob. "But it doesn't."

"Elle," Brooks whispered. "What have you been taught?"

"God didn't give me a spirit of fear," she said quietly. "He doesn't like timidity, and that's all I'm made of."

Brooks let out a humorless laugh. "I hate when they use that. Elle, if people are using that scripture to shame you, they are the ones in the wrong. That isn't what it means."

"How do you know?"

"Because it doesn't work in that context. No, the Lord doesn't give a spirit of fear or timidity or anything other than what is good. But He also doesn't give a child cancer. The Lord doesn't wish for any of His children to suffer, which means that all the brokenness, sadness, and pain—none of it comes from Him. All of that is the result of living in a sinful, fallen world. We can't control it."

"But if I just had faith—"

"It would make it easier. But having faith doesn't mean that the Lord would take your problems away any more than He would take the child's cancer because she had faith. I don't know why, Elle, but He doesn't heal everyone of their physical impairments, and I believe it's the same with whatever goes on in your head. In my mother's. In Maisie's. It doesn't mean any of you are unworthy of His healing. It doesn't mean you don't have enough faith." Brooks took her face in his hands. "The Lord is not punishing you, Elle."

"He doesn't like timidity."

"Timidity is not a sin. Timidity itself is not cowardice. The scripture they are referring to is taken from a passage in which they are speaking of sharing the Lord." Taking his Bible, Brooks found and read the scripture. "For God hath not given us the spirit of fear; but of power, and of love, and of a sound mind. Be not thou therefore ashamed of the testimony of our Lord." Finishing, he set the book aside and met her eyes. "Do you hear that, Elle? Whatever people might like to think, He is not calling out timidity or even fear itself. He is calling out those afraid to speak about the Lord. Those embarrassed. Those who are ashamed."

When Eloise said nothing, Brooks sighed. "Are you ashamed of God?"

"No," she whispered.

"Are you ashamed of me or my family for the way we follow Him?"

"No. I—" She swallowed. "I admire it. But—"

"Eloise."

"But my faith isn't strong, and the pastor at our church said it's my timidity. You can't be timid and trust in Him. To have timidity means to lack in trust."

"Well then, I guess my mother is the worst sinner of them all, isn't she?" Brooks countered. "Do you think so?"

Eloise shook her head.

"Well, she must be if having a timid sort of spirit is a sign of lacking trust in God.

"Are you making fun of me?" Eloise whispered.

"No, Elle," Brooks said softly. "I am trying to help you see the truth. Timidity is not a sin. Not when it has nothing to do with sharing God's Word. If God asked you to share His Word and you refused, then yes, that is sinful. But I also don't believe it is an unforgivable sin, and I don't believe you would refuse.

Because He doesn't give a spirit of fear but of power. If you built and had that solid relationship with Him that you long for, then I believe if He asked you to, you could, and would, share. Perhaps in your own timid way, but I don't believe the Lord would see fault in that. Your timid nature is who you are, Elle, and His strength is made perfect in our weakness."

Eloise's lips trembled. "But Brooks, you're not a pastor."

"Neither were most of the people telling you that your timidity was a sin," Brooks replied. "But you're right, I am not a pastor, and I don't pretend to understand everything that I read. However, even pastors do not understand everything, Elle, and a good one will admit that."

"I want to believe you. But that doesn't seem right. God has never cared about me. That has to be why."

"He does care. But you are too caught up in the belief that He doesn't to see the good He does for you. To hear Him. Maybe now, with a few fresh ideas in your head, you'll be able to look at it differently?"

Eloise chewed her lip. "Do you promise that's not what it means?"

"I can promise you, to the best of my knowledge, that the Lord does not see sin in your timidity, Elle."

Twenty-Four

There was no sin in timidity. Why was that truth so much harder to convince herself of than the lie that it was? One had embedded itself in her soul on impact while the other merely tapped the window. The latter drew her attention for a moment before the destruction of the former stole it back.

The Lord doesn't like timidity. What does Brooks know?

He knows God. She knew and trusted that much. *And he's smart.* When he had spoken to her, he didn't speak with an air of pride as everyone else always had with her. He spoke with a gentle sort of certainty, and when she looked at Elizabeth, she couldn't help but believe him.

But Eloise wasn't Elizabeth. Elizabeth had read and understood and loved God's Word. Eloise loved it when it came from Brooks' lips. She understood bits and pieces when she read Elizabeth's words written along the margins of her Bible. But she understood nothing on her own, and it hindered the love she desired to have for the Word.

"But you are trying, Ellie," Lily said softly. "If you keep at it, eventually you will get there. Do you think Elizabeth or Brooks understood what they read in the beginning? I read the Bible for years before I felt confident enough in what I read to take notes. My Bible looked untouched for years, though I read it daily."

"Really?"

Lily nodded. "It was your poppy who helped me understand, and after a time of studying it with his help, I began to understand on my own."

Poppy. Her grandfather had pastored Huxley before he died when Eloise was only two. "What would Poppy have said about me?"

"Ellie, Poppy saw the signs in you from day one. I believe, and he believed, that he is where you get these things. My daddy wasn't much for people, either. He didn't like being up in front of the congregation, and you could see it sometimes. I used to find him pacing his room Sunday mornings, praying for peace. But he loved the Lord, and he loved sharing Him."

"Did he struggle with anything else?"

"He did. He was known to be a worrier, oftentimes over nothing, and he struggled with sadness too." Lily touched her daughter's hair. "He was a wonderful pastor, but he struggled and got a lot of criticism for it. He was told that if he truly believed what he preached, he wouldn't struggle. After his heart attack, people told Mama and me that God was punishing Daddy for his lack of faith. For his hypocrisy."

Eloise bit her lip. "Why are God's people so cruel? Doesn't it make them hypocrites?" She didn't know or understand the Bible well, but she knew God's children were supposed to be loving.

"Yes, there is certainly hypocrisy there. But they don't see it. They believe they are right. They believe they are doing God's work."

"Then the Bible must tell them to be that way. It must speak against us."

"Eloise Anne, would you listen to me?" Lily sighed. "Listen to Brooks. Listen to your poppy. People interpret the Bible in many ways. Some right. Some wrong. Some see fear as sinful, but I don't believe they are right. God gave us those feelings for a reason. It can save your life. Your poppy said that your struggle doesn't make you lesser in God's eyes. It's when you decide that how you feel will never change and you'll never get better, so you live in that fear. You let it rule you."

"But I do let it rule me, Mama," Eloise whispered.

"At times, Ellie. But only at times. The fact that you are still here, that you are fighting, that you are trying to know Him is proof that you haven't given in. That you aren't giving up. That you're fighting your fears, not letting them rule over you."

Remembering an old sermon of her father's, Lily continued. "Daddy spoke on fear once—on being ruled by it. He said that to be ruled and allowing something to rule over you are two very different things. He said the Lord doesn't turn His back on a kingdom ruled by a malevolent king simply because of that king and His power over them. He doesn't ignore a battered wife when her husband hits her. No, He sees the way the people of that kingdom call on God's name and fight for freedom. He sees the wife, who tries to run and is dragged back by her husband. Both are ruled, but neither is complacent. Both are ruled but always fighting. It's the same with fear and sadness. You may be ruled by your mind now, but you are fighting, Eloise, and like that kingdom, like that wife, you will be freed."

Eloise chewed on that. "Poppy said that?"

Lily nodded. "He was always trying to soften people's hearts. Make them see the truth. Once he died, any progress he might have made with them was lost with Pastor Warren. He'd known your father since they were children, and they'd never seen eye to eye on those things. It just got worse after Pastor James took over."

"How did Poppy stay faithful?"

"He stayed in the Word. He studied the original translation. He struggled at times in his youth, but when he was your age, the Lord spoke peace over him by leading him to the story of Elijah. Do you remember that one?"

Eloise shook her head. "Just that he was a prophet."

"He was a prophet," Lily confirmed. "One who dealt with a period of fear and depression. When Jezebel threatened Elijah's life, he ran and hid in the wilderness. Overcome with loneliness, he became depressed. He saw no good in himself and begged God to take his life."

"He begged God to take his life?" How often had Eloise done that?

"But rather than condemn him," Lily continued, "the Lord sent him an angel to comfort him. When your poppy read that, he knew the Lord was telling him his struggles were no sin. In fact, what He told him was that He saw his pain, and He met him there in the midst of it. Your poppy made it his mission from then on to help others see God's heart toward the pain of the mind and heart."

"But he failed," Eloise said quietly. "No one in Huxley cared."

"Maybe. But he made me and Nanny see the truth so that when I had you, we knew it wasn't your fault."

Eloise felt a rush of anger. "Why does He talk to everyone but me, Mama? He's never led me to anything like that."

"He has, Ellie. But you don't see it. You think of God's voice as one way. But He speaks to us in many ways." Lily sighed. "Eloise, do you think your father showing up that day in school was a coincidence? Do you think leading Brooks to church that day was?" When Eloise said nothing, Lily took her hand. "Do you remember the conversation we had the night before church? That I would always believe for you? After you went to sleep, I prayed He would send someone to us. Someone to love you as you are. Ellie, the Lord led Poppy to scripture because He knew he would understand it. He knew you wouldn't understand such a way, so He gave you the Harpers. To show you, rather than tell you, what He thinks of you."

"I want to believe that," Eloise said quietly.

"Then just keep trying, Ellie. That's all any of us are looking for now."

Just keep trying. Make the choice to try.

"Will that really get me anywhere?" Eloise asked. "Just trying?"

"I believe it will," Lily replied. "It's better than not trying."

Eloise nodded. "I am trying."

"I know, Ellie. I can see it; and whether you see it or not, I see little changes in you."

"I don't see anything." That voice was as loud as ever.

"No. I think you're too close, Ellie. This is one area I just might know you more than you know yourself."

***

Her mother was crazy. There was no change in her.

What was it she could have possibly been seeing? Nothing was changing. Eloise wasn't capable of changing.

Elijah, she reminded herself. *The Lord comforted him. David suffered, and God loved him.* At Maisie's recommendation, she had taken to reading the Psalms, which the girl had said helped her when she felt distant from the Lord. When sadness kept its hold on her.

I am His. She was His. Again and again, she reminded herself of that truth. Screaming it in her head to block out that voice. *I am His.* And that was everything.

Until she failed. She always did. She always would.

The water rushed up as she imagined sliding beneath the surface of the tub. *No. I am His. I am His.*

Sometimes it worked. Sometimes she could say the words and feel the slightest piece of relief—that inch closer to the surface. That voice in her head was still there, still pecking at her mind, but it didn't break her. Other days, most days, the voice crippled her.

Today was not one of those days. As she spoke the words over herself, she felt the slightest relief in her chest, her head breaking the surface. "Thank you, God," she whispered. She had tried to call Him Papa, as Brooks encouraged, but she couldn't get past the discomfort.

Because you know He doesn't love and accept you like that.

Clenching her teeth, Eloise spat the word out. "Papa." If only to prove that voice wrong, she would get used to it. She would choose to see Him as the Heavenly Papa He was.

Finishing her reading, Eloise tucked the Bible back into its spot under her pillow just as Brooks knocked at her door. Ignoring the jolt of panic that shot through her, she countered it with truth.

Brooks greeted her with a tip of his head. "Mornin'."

Taking his offered hand, Eloise focused on the feel of it, ignoring the eyes she knew weren't truly on her.

Eloise squeezed Brooks' hand, and without a second beat, he squeezed back. *I've got you,* it said. Her preserver among the waves.

When they'd been seated, and prayers said, Brooks leaned in. "Are you drowning?"

She shook her head. "Not yet." *I am His. I am His.*

"Well then, let's keep it that way."

Until it pulls you back. He can't keep you afloat forever. But he can help. And she intended to let him.

Brooks smiled. "I was thinking we might include Maisie in our ventures with Juniper today? We need to get her used to more people."

"I think Maisie will be perfect," Eloise said quietly.

"I was thinking maybe she's ready to have you lead her out yourself."

"By myself?"

"Do you think she's ready?" Brooks countered.

Eloise considered that a moment. Did she think Juniper was ready? They had been taking her out daily now, and she was doing well, but it was always with Brooks' help.

"I think she's ready," Brooks said softly. "Are you ready? Do you remember how to put her halter on?"

"I think so."

Brooks pursed his lips at her uncertainty. "Why don't we try that tomorrow? Let me watch as you ready her on your own, and we can go from there." Afraid he had upset her, he continued. "It's not that I think you are incapable, Elle. But horses can be unpredictable. Especially one who is easily spooked, and I don't want to see you hurt."

Eloise nodded. "Tomorrow?"

"Tomorrow. And I'll only be observing today. You're in charge."

Eloise felt relief wash over her. Though she wanted to take charge and handle Juniper, she couldn't help fearing it. What if she messed it up? What if she or someone else was hurt because of it?

"Tomorrow, Elle," Brooks repeated. "I know you can do it, but I want *you* to know that you can."

Until tomorrow. You'll mess everything up today. You always do.

No. No. She had been doing well. The last few days, he had only instructed her once or twice on how to handle the halter.

But now she was nervous, and her hands were fumbling. Taking her hands in his, Brooks pulled them back. "Easy, darlin'. Take a deep breath and then try again."

"I'm going to mess it up," she whispered. "I'm too stupid for this."

"You are not stupid, Elle. You have been doing well, but you are overthinking."

Eloise shook her head.

"Eloise, look at me." When she did, Brooks brushed the tears from her cheeks. "You have to stop and breathe. Elle, your fear of messing up is what's causing you to. Do you see that?"

"Can you show me one more time?" she asked.

"I'll show you on Posey, and then you can try again on Juniper. How's that?"

Eloise nodded.

Wiping away her remaining tears, Brooks kissed her cheek. "Breathe, Elle. You know what you're doing."

Seeing the war brewing in her mind, Brooks sighed. "Let's do this later, Elle."

"I can do it," she whispered.

"I know you can. But you've worked yourself up."

The waves were pulling her under. She was too old to be so worked up. Childish. Grow up. "I'm sorry." Eloise pressed her palms to her eyes. Why could the voice never leave her alone? Why could she never have one easy day where no tears were shed? Where her heart didn't race? She just wanted one day where her head stayed above water.

"Darlin'." Bringing her to him, Brooks felt the woman's tears soak through his shirt, too quickly for the simple tears he was used to watching her cry. "Don't apologize. We all have those moments. It doesn't make you stupid." When she shuddered, Brooks sighed. "Elle, what's wrong?"

Eloise shrugged.

"You don't know, or you don't want to tell me?" When she shrugged again, Brooks set his head to hers. "You can, Elle. If you want to."

Eloise shook her head. "I don't know how. I just feel like I can't breathe." After a moment, she let out a small sob. "I'm such a child."

"You're not a child, Elle. Everyone gets overwhelmed."

"I shouldn't get so worked up."

"No," Brooks agreed. "But it's understandable that you do. You have a lot going on in your head. I remember what that felt like. I may not have broken down like you do, but I was almost worse."

"How?" Eloise whispered.

"I used to lash out. I was so on edge all of the time that the slightest thing made me snap. It only got worse once Wiley and I started drinking."

"I can't see you getting angry," Eloise said quietly. "Especially enough to lash out."

Brooks laughed. "I don't anymore. I slowly learned how to handle it when I get that agitated. But it was hard, and I used to ask the same questions that you ask yourself." Taking her chin, he brought her eyes to his. "I know it's not quite the same. I know you struggle more. I know it's going to be harder and take a little longer. But it doesn't make you childish, Elle. Even my mother still breaks down like that at times. And don't get me started on Maisie. If she can't do anything perfectly the first time, she's certain she must be the stupidest woman alive."

"I don't think it's the same, Brooks. I feel like this every day. I've never seen Maisie or Elizabeth act like I do."

"Maisie doesn't struggle quite like you or my mother, Elle, but she does struggle. As for my mother, she's older. She's had more time to work on it. But she used to be just like you. I remember it." It hadn't been often when his mother would break down with him, but there had been times as a child when he'd witnessed her break. "As a child, I had grown used to hearing my father trying to calm her for one thing or another, and her tears could be much worse than what I've witnessed this far from you." It was a thought that got to him when he witnessed even the simplest of tears from Eloise. Even days like this were hard to watch, and by the way Eloise watched him now, her dark eyes blurred by tearful pain, Brooks was reminded that he'd witnessed nothing near the full potential of Eloise's tears. He dreaded the moment he would.

Twenty-Five

Eloise spoke softly as she led Juniper out of the barn and into the paddock. Behind her, Brooks stood ready to pull her back should the horse get spooked. It had happened once or twice when one of the men working in the fields shouted or one of the dogs barked, and Brooks had narrowly pulled Eloise aside to avoid injury.

Today, Juniper made it safely into the paddock. Satisfied, Brooks stepped in and gripped the lead rope. "We'll let her run again before messing with her."

Nodding, Eloise watched the way Brooks held the rope as Juniper ran circles around the entrapment. Over the past week, they'd been working on addressing Juniper's many fears, hoping to help her see there was nothing to be afraid of so that when someone shouted or a dog barked, Juniper wouldn't hurt Eloise.

Eloise had been uncertain at first. "We aren't throwing her out with the dogs and expecting her to get over her fears," he'd said, attempting to reassure her. "We take it step by step, so she slowly sees there's nothing to fear." And when she'd frowned at that, Brooks smiled. "It's necessary, Elle. The way she reacts now makes her a threat to both those around her and herself. I've trained every other horse this way, and they've all come through it unscathed."

Choosing to trust Brooks, she had simply watched the first day as he did nothing more than work on touch. Applying light pressure to her head, ears, and legs. Juniper had fought at first, and when she did, Brooks backed off, talking to her in hushed, soothing tones.

Eloise had never seen anyone as patient as Brooks. Each time the horse fought him, rather than get angry, Brooks would grip the lead and poll tighter and bring her eyes to his, his voice soft. He didn't give her her way, but he let her know she was safe.

"I still don't like it," Eloise said quietly, watching Brooks gain control of Juniper. "I know it's necessary, but …"

"But it's hard knowing she's scared," Brooks replied. "I understand, Elle. But when she faces real moments of danger and responds how she does now, not only would you get hurt, but she would, too." He nodded to the horse. "Do you want to know why I'm doing this?"

When Eloise nodded, Brooks waved her closer. "Do you see where I'm holding her?" He nodded toward his hold on the poll and lead rope. "By doing this—gripping the poll at her ears and the lead up near the buckle—I can apply a light pressure to both and lower her head." He did so, and this time, Juniper let him without complaint. "This simulates a situation in which she might get stuck." Releasing the horse, Brooks looked to Eloise. "I lost a horse because he got his head stuck between two fence poles and panicked. I started doing this with the rest in the hopes that if it ever happened again, they might stay calm." Seeing her uncertainty, Brooks sighed. "We aren't trying to desensitize her, Elle. Just teach her to remain calm."

"You promise she's ok?" Eloise asked.

"Does she look upset at all?" Brooks nodded to Juniper, who was now trotting around the paddock again.

"No." Eloise sighed.

Nodding for Eloise to follow him, Brooks leaned against the paddock fence. "We're taking it slow, Elle. We aren't pushing her."

"I just hate thinking of her scared," Eloise whispered.

"That's why we're trying to help her face her fears, darlin'. In safe and controlled ways." He nudged her. "Kind of like you and I in the barn, right? It was hard for you at first. But even you have said it was easier because it felt safer than school or church. That's what we're doing with Juniper."

"I know."

When tears spilled over, Brooks took hold of her hand. "I think this is about more than Junie, Elle."

Eloise shrugged. "It just brings back a lot."

"Do you want to talk about it?"

"It's stupid, Brooks. I just ..." She shook her head. "Where is Wiley?"

Brooks blanched at the strange turn. "Somewhere in California," he said. "Rose Haven didn't have what he was looking for." Brothels. Saloons. Women willing to give themselves over without a ring.

"Was it Wiley who convinced you to drink?"

"Yes. I mean, I didn't fight him on it. But it was his idea."

Eloise considered that a moment. "Did he ever try to convince you to do other things?"

A hundred other things. All of which Brooks was thankful that he had been too scared to go after. "Yes," he admitted. "More than once, he tried to convince me to go two towns over, where they had a brothel."

When she stiffened at that, Brooks laughed softly. "I said no, darlin'. I won't say I wasn't tempted. I was lost. But I was also terrified and aware enough to know I wasn't ready for anything near that."

"But Wiley was still a good friend?" Eloise asked. "He still cared about you? Even when you said no? Even when you stopped drinking?"

"Even then, Elle. He's lost, but he's a good man. We're brothers, he and I."

Eloise nodded. "I never had that," she said quietly. "I thought I did a couple of times. But no one ever stayed." After a moment, she continued. "I had a friend until I was about twelve. Kate. She was a good friend—a really good friend. But eventually, she and another girl I had become friends with became closer, and the two of them spent all their time together without me." Eloise laughed humorlessly. "After that, I didn't have anyone until I was seventeen."

Eloise chewed at her lip as she forced down emotion. "Edith and Grace," she said quietly. "They had just moved to Huxley, and on their first day of church, they introduced themselves and asked me to show them around. After that, they sought me out after church every week. They invited me over to their home." She shrugged. "I felt safe with them. So, when they asked, I told them things about myself. Things I struggled with. But after a while, I started to notice things. They didn't treat me very well. They talked to me like I was a child. Constantly pushed me to do things I wasn't completely comfortable doing and made me feel guilty when I didn't. The more I started to push back, the less they sought me out until it finally stopped altogether." Three weeks later, she had found herself in that tub. Lonelier and more full of self-loathing than she'd ever felt before.

Eloise jumped when Brooks set a hand to her cheek, catching the tears that had leaked over. "I'm sorry, Elle."

"For?" she asked, smiling half-heartedly. "I know that it's stupid," she said quietly. "I know that it shouldn't have hurt the way it did and still does. But I felt something in me break when I realized they didn't really want me. That I had shared so much with them. That I had let them control so much of me." And even still, she had blamed herself for the outcome. If she had tried harder, maybe they would have stayed.

"It's not stupid, Eloise," Brooks said sternly. "You trusted, and you were hurt."

"After that, I told myself I didn't need anyone. That I could be happy on my own."

"I told myself the same thing. It led me to drink."

Eloise bit her lip. She wasn't going to tell him where that lie had led her.

Turning her to him, Brooks cupped her cheek. "Thank you for sharing that with me. It makes me understand your hesitancy with us a little more."

"I'm still so afraid you'll realize I'm not worth the hassle."

Brooks chucked her chin. "You are worth every bit of hassle, Elle."

***

"Ellie." Eloise neared jumped out of her skin at the sound of Elizabeth's voice in the darkness. There was a hint of a smile in the woman's voice when she spoke again. "I'm sorry, sweetie. But I was hoping I could give you something?" Turning the kerosene lamp up, Elizabeth patted the seat beside her.

Abandoning her need for the outhouse, Eloise took the open seat. "I won't keep you long," Elizabeth reassured her. "I noticed you have been reading the Bible more and remembered you probably don't have room to write in it yourself. So I had Merritt pick this up for me."

Eloise looked at the small pocket diary Elizabeth handed her. "Why?"

"Because writing has always been a source of relief for me. Whether it's my prayers. My thoughts. Whatever the Lord places on my heart while reading. Not only is it beneficial in the moment, but it's nice to look back on in the future and see how far God has brought you." Elizabeth smiled. "It's come in quite handy a few times when I've found myself sinking."

"Elizabeth." Eloise fingered the pages, unsure what she wanted to say. "I can't accept this." The Bible had been a free gift. Elizabeth hadn't spent hard-earned money on her.

"I can't accept your refusal," Elizabeth countered. "You need it, Ellie." Seeing Eloise still wanted to refuse, Elizabeth continued. "I didn't spend a dime on it, Eloise. When my sister and her late husband started up the mercantile, Merritt loaned them what they needed. In return, they promised to supply the simple needs we might have here and there." It wasn't something the Harpers took advantage of often, but it was necessary at times.

"I don't think I'll have anything to say in it, Elizabeth. I'm still not understanding much of what I read. Not without reading what you've written."

"So write your prayers for now. Your goals. It helps, Eloise. I promise you. I've had my children doing the same since they were old enough to write. I even got Merritt doing it." Now that Elizabeth said it, Eloise had seen Maisie pouring over a diary near every night.

"It didn't cost you a penny?" Eloise asked.

"Not a one," Elizabeth said.

Eloise nodded. "Well then, thank you, Elizabeth." Perhaps it would be nice to write her prayers, where she could focus on her words rather than lose them.

"You're welcome, love. I hope it helps you like it's helped my family."

When Elizabeth brushed a lock of hair out of her face, Eloise felt a rush of emotion, her earlier conversation with Brooks coming back to her. Despite the age gap between them, Eloise had come to think of Elizabeth as a friend. One she trusted and who understood her. "Thank you, Elizabeth," she whispered, trusting the woman to understand.

Elizabeth smiled, tears in her own dark eyes. "It's my pleasure, Ellie."

Twenty-Six

December

Eloise pushed the needle through the canvas, forcing her mind to focus on the movement. The steady rhythm of it. Embroidery kept her head above water as she watched the image come to life before her, like a preserver keeping her afloat.

Beside her, Maisie watched her untangle a new piece of thread. "Wouldn't it be easier to paint?" she asked. "Or draw?"

"Never interested me much," Eloise replied. "This is more peaceful to me." It had become as simple as breathing—to paint pictures with thread rather than oils as Poppy had. Nanny Anne had been the one to notice Eloise's gift with a needle and had encouraged her to go beyond the simple sayings and outlines she had started with.

"You may not have Poppy's gift with paints," she had said, "but you have his eye, EllieAnne, and you need something to get yourself out of here" —she tapped Eloise's head— "just like he did."

Despite her mother's reassurances, Eloise couldn't help but wonder what Nanny would have to say about what had led them to Rose Haven.

She would have been disgusted. Like everyone else.

Shutting the voice out, Eloise focused on the work in front of her—a chestnut horse against a rising sun. Nanny would have loved her still.

Desperate to rid herself of the voice, Eloise jammed the needle through the canvas and into her skin by mistake. Sucking in a sharp breath, she set the hoop aside, accepting the rag Maisie passed her.

"Are you all right?"

"It happens," Eloise replied. Though the worst she'd ever done was prick herself, not jam a needle into her finger as she did now. Her forefinger throbbed, and she thanked the Lord her mother wasn't there to see the blood. "Just keep it between you and me, Mais. My mother will worry about infection if she sees it."

Maisie raised an eyebrow at the small drop of blood on the rag. "Over that?"

"She's always been nervous over things like that." Lily refused to leave their side if Eloise or Morgan took on so much as a cold. Eloise couldn't help but wonder at times if she wasn't more like her mother than they thought.

And yet she managed. Why couldn't Eloise manage?

Before she could say more, Lily walked in with Elizabeth, her face hidden behind a stack of bedding. Snatching the rag, Maisie stuffed it in the pocket of her skirts while Eloise tucked her hands into her sleeves.

"Do you need any help, Mama?"

"Not from you," Lily replied. "Maisie and I can take care of the beds. You can help Elizabeth get supper started."

With her mother gone, Eloise freed her hands. The throb had died away to a dull ache, and with luck, the redness would be gone before her mother came back down.

Settling into the comfortable silence that existed between her and Elizabeth, Eloise rinsed the potatoes before cutting them into squares for stew. Upstairs, she could hear Maisie chattering to

Lily. When Eloise heard her mother laugh, she felt a small pang in her chest, denting that bit of peace she had built up in herself.

Why was she so different? She could see it more and more in Maisie—the pieces of herself. But even still, the girl was vibrant. She loved life—and Eloise couldn't help but wonder if that might have been her had she not gone to Alma's house, school or church. In those places, she'd been hounded and unaided. How different would things have been if she'd been supported and encouraged?

Why did you let it happen, God? If it isn't your will, why let them do it?

Both of her parents had taken to Maisie in a way that made Eloise only more certain that they had been done a disservice by being given her. Maybe that's why Lily had chosen Maisie to make the beds with? Maybe she was beginning to prefer her presence over her own daughter's?

Setting the knife aside, Eloise dumped the potatoes into the boiling water, forcing her mind on preparing supper rather than the sound of her mother enjoying the child she should have been given.

By the time her mother found her, Eloise had beat down the pain in her chest until it was a dull ache that beat in time with the pain in her finger.

Lily ran a hand over her hair, taking in her red eyes. "Are you all right, Ellie?"

Distrustful of her voice, Eloise nodded before maneuvering out of her touch.

Taking the second stack of bowls, Lily followed after her. "You seemed fine when I came in. What happened since then?"

"Nothing," Eloise said quietly. "Nothing I want to talk about now, anyway." Not with the entire family taking their seats at the table.

"Later then."

Taking her seat beside Brooks, Eloise felt a sliver of peace creep over her at his touch. "Juniper misses you." He smiled.

"Does she?" she breathed. "And do I get to spend more time with her tomorrow, or am I still barred?" It had been almost a month since Eloise had spent more than a few moments in the barn with Brooks—though he still spent most of his days there, he was always ready with an excuse to send her out.

Brooks laughed at the hint of contempt that tinted her tone. "I suppose we could take the day. But if I don't finish on time, don't hold me accountable."

"Finish what?" But Brooks had already turned his attention to Maisie, and whether he didn't hear her or pretended not to, she wasn't sure.

What do you think it is? He's growing tired of you. Did you really think he wouldn't?

Ignoring that voice, Eloise focused on the truths: He still met her with a smile at her door every morning, mugs of tea and coffee in hand. He still spent the morning with her in the Lord's Word. Praying over her. And now, he was weaving his fingers through hers, squeezing to gain her attention.

"Are you drowning?" he asked.

She shook her head. "No," she whispered. "Not anymore."

For now. You can't fight it forever. Of course she couldn't. But she could try. She would try.

Leaning in, his lips brushed her ear, sending her heart racing. "Let me know, and I'll throw you a line." When he pulled back, he smiled at the blush that filled her cheeks. "No one is paying any attention, Elle."

Was that what he thought affected her? Did his own heart not race when he touched her? When she touched him? Did she not cause in him what he caused in her?

Blinking back tears, she dropped her eyes to her supper, ignoring the way Brooks nudged her. "Elle?" When she said nothing, he sighed and turned his attention back to his sister.

***

Eloise woke to Maisie shaking her. "Get up," she hissed. "Hurry."

"What?" Eloise whispered. "Are you all right?"

"Brooks just disappeared into the barn."

"So?" Eloise sat up, trying to breathe through the panic Maisie had stirred in her. "I thought you were hurt, Maisie." She had to bite her tongue to keep from calling her the given name she knew would earn her a harsh glare.

Uncaring, Maisie took Eloise's hand and dragged her out of bed. "Get dressed." She laughed. "We're going to get Brooks."

"What?"

Maisie nodded. "You're going to go and get him, say I'm hurt, and then we ambush him."

Eloise felt the anxiety in her rise. "Why?"

"Because you need to have a little fun in your life, Ellie. You're either worried sick or stuck up in that barn or both. Have fun."

"I enjoy my time with Juniper."

"Juniper," Maisie scoffed. "I'll be sure to tell Brooks that. Now," she said, tossing Eloise a dress while slipping into her own, "get dressed."

Huffing, Eloise pulled on her skirts and followed after Maisie, muttering under her breath. She didn't want to go out now. She didn't want to ambush Brooks, who seemed to value her time less and less. She wanted to sleep and forget it all.

Outside, Maisie began creating a pile of balled-up snow. "You go and get Brooks. Tell him I'm hurt bad and need his help."

"Maisie, maybe you should get him. I won't be able to—"

"Eloise." Maisie sighed. "Please? He won't buy it if I do it."

"All right, but he won't buy it with me either." She wasn't a very good liar with anyone, but Brooks could read her as well as her mother could. Better, even.

Picking up her skirts, Eloise stomped through the snow, muttering what she'd like to say to Maisie if she could.

Shoving the barn door open, she watched Brooks jump before hiding something behind his back. "Elle?" Covering up whatever it was he hid, he moved toward her. "Are you all right?"

"Maisie," she whispered. "She, um …"

Brooks smiled. "She's planning an ambush. Isn't she?" When Eloise nodded, Brooks laughed. "Come here." When she listened, he put an arm around her shoulder, sending an unwelcome warmth running through her. "What should I do, Elle? Let her fulfill her plans? Or …" He smiled wickedly. "Do I plan a counter-attack?"

"Well, it would be pointless to let her attack you now, wouldn't it?" Eloise asked. "And really, she ought to have listened to me and gotten you herself." She knew it wasn't kind of her. But she had warned Maisie, and fair or not, she hadn't forgiven the girl for waking her. "Get her," she whispered.

At that, Brooks laughed. "And are you switching sides, or do I need to take you hostage?"

Eloise sighed as he toyed with a piece of her hair. Even the most innocent of touches made her heart race, and did she do nothing to him? If she did, he didn't show it. "Traitor or hostage?" she breathed. Stepping back, she held out a hand. "Allies?"

"Allies." Placing his hat on Eloise's head in solidarity, he started toward the door. "I'll go get her. You just come when you're called."

"You're not going to send me back out there?"

"Are you kidding me, woman?" he asked. "You betrayed Maisie quicker than a cat on a mouse. Forgive my trepidations, my lady, but your loyalties are questionable." Winking, he left her alone.

Taking the lamp Brooks had left burning, Eloise moved closer to Juniper. Within touching distance, she let Juniper close the remaining space, setting her forehead to the spot between the horse's eyes when she did.

When Eloise sighed, the horse let out a small whinny. "I'm ok," she whispered. "I'm just stupid." At that, Juniper let out a small puff of air. "He doesn't have to spend every second with me." She didn't need it. No matter how much she loved her time with Brooks, she still valued the moments she had with herself.

With her mother and Maisie. She had loved the extra time with Elizabeth, working tirelessly to finish the blanket she intended to give Brooks only hours from now. But in the last month, he'd shut her out of the barn almost entirely, and that old nagging doubt was beginning to drag her back under. That was how it had started with Edith and Grace. With Kate, who had promised herself to be a forever friend. What had started as regular meetings had slowly dwindled into nothing, and she was steadily watching the same thing become of her time with Brooks.

Before she could sink any deeper, Eloise removed the hat and turned it over in her hands, her mind returning to the conversation she'd had with Elizabeth as they finished Brooks' gift.

"My son is mad about you, Eloise Riley. No time spent apart is going to change that." Elizabeth smiled. "The way he puts his hat on your head? That's a real good sign of how much he loves you. He trusts you."

"What does that have to do with anything?" Eloise asked.

"It matters because, aside from his Bible, that hat is his most prized possession," Elizabeth told her. "It was Merritt's. He gave it to Brooks when he was struggling. Brooks has held that thing close to him since. Doesn't leave the house without it."

"Was it important to Merritt?"

Elizabeth nodded. "It was his pa's. He died when Merritt was young, and it's Merritt's only real piece of his father. Brooks took that sacrifice of his to heart."

Eloise considered that now. She had known Brooks was attached to the hat, but she had never thought to ask the significance of it.

Before she could sink deeper, Brooks whispered at the door. "Elle."

The sun was beginning to rise when she stepped out, and she could just make out the landscape. "Brooks?" She didn't see the snowball, but she heard it hit the barn wall behind her. Eloise felt a small smile tug at her lips as she realized she'd been played. Stepping back into the barn, she heard another ball hit the wood.

Peeking around the corner, she searched for Brooks. "My loyalties are questionable?" she hissed. "What about you?"

Brooks' laugh drifted from somewhere to the left of her, hidden in the shadows. "I didn't let it hit you."

"No." Eloise sighed, kneeling slowly to grab a handful of snow, ducking back in just before another ball could hit her. "I suppose you didn't."

"Maisie's right, darlin'. You needed a little fun."

Eloise *hmmed*, her eyes trying to find him in the dark. Perhaps if she kept him talking, she could pinpoint where he was. "And where is Maisie now?"

"Hiding." Eloise still couldn't see him, but she had a vague idea now. Flinging the ball in his direction, she heard his sharp intake of breath as it connected with some part of him.

Laughing, Eloise turned and ran for the house. She made it only halfway before a ball hit her in the back. She stumbled over her feet and hit the ground.

Brooks laughed as he kneeled next to Eloise, offering a hand. Taking it, she pulled herself into a sitting position. "Are you all right?" He hadn't intended for her to fall. He'd thrown the ball only enough to know she hadn't won. But she didn't seem upset. She was laughing, pushing back the hat that had fallen over her eyes, and Brooks felt something inside him shift as it always did when he looked at her. It wasn't often he heard her laugh like that. As though, for a moment, the troubles of her mind were a figment of both their imaginations.

She was beautiful—and with the sun just beginning to rise, her dark eyes glittered like gold in the soft light. Bright, happy, and for the moment, entirely untroubled.

Brooks didn't stop to think about what he was doing. Didn't stop to think that maybe this wasn't what she wanted now or later or ever. Without a thought, he brought her to him, his eyes meeting hers for the briefest moment, seeking approval before pressing his lips to hers as though they held the air he needed. He heard her gasp against his lips, but rather than pull back as he had feared she would, he felt her press closer, her fingers curling into the front of his shirt.

It was the sound of Maisie calling for them that brought their senses back, and Eloise felt Brooks pull back too soon.

"I'm sorry," he whispered, his breath washing over her. "I shouldn't have done that. Not like that." Sitting back, he dropped his head into his hands.

"It's ok," Eloise whispered, unnerved by the way he seemed to shake. "It's ok," she repeated. What did he think she wanted? Permission? The idea almost made her laugh. She had thought of this moment almost every night for weeks, and amidst the desire for it, she felt certain the actual moment would not meet her expectations. Not if he hesitated. Not if she had time to question and doubt and worry over whether she would mess it up.

Taking his chin between her thumb and index finger, she felt a thrill run through her at the way his breath hitched at her touch. The way his eyes betrayed the sort of desire she was never sure truly lived in him. She'd never seen him show much weakness or desire when he touched her, but now his defenses were down, and she felt a slight irritation at the doubts he'd planted in her. "Why haven't you wanted me in the barn?" she whispered. "I mean if you—if you still want me then—"

Brooks laughed softly. "You thought it was because I didn't want you anymore? Eloise Riley, what is it going to take to make you see I'm yours for as long as you'll have me?"

"Well then, why?"

"Have you not bothered to pay attention to the month, Elle?" Taking her hand, he pulled her to her feet, ordering Maisie inside as he did so.

"What does the month have to do with it?" Eloise demanded.

Laughing again, Brooks pulled her into the barn and to the back wall. He patted the object he'd been covering when she found him working on it. "I only just finished it when you came in. I was planning on giving it to you in the morning, but maybe now is better." Seeing the look of confusion on her face, he sighed. "Christmas, Elle."

Eloise felt her face flush. "Christmas," she breathed. "You've been making me something?"

"Yes. Would you like it now or later? If you say later, we can still come out here. Just the two of us."

Eloise blinked back tears. How could she have been so stupid? She'd spent the month working with Elizabeth to prepare Brooks' gift. Why was it so easy to doubt he could be doing the same?

Eloise nodded toward the gift. "Do you want yours?"

"No," Brooks said softly. "I can wait. But if you don't mind, I'd like you to open yours now."

"Why?"

"Because you aren't the only one who doubts themselves, Elle." He patted the covering again. "I've never done this before. It's not perfect by any means, and I think I'd like to get it over with."

Eloise laughed quietly. "That's a way to get a girl excited." Stepping forward, she curled her fingers around the rough canvas covering, knowing whatever it was, she would love it regardless.

When the cover snagged, Brooks helped her free it, revealing a rough-looking saddle. "Your father helped to get the shape of it right," he said quietly. "Like I said, I've never done anything like this before. But you needed a saddle, and seeing as buying a new one is too much money right now, I thought this seemed like a fun challenge."

"And you do love a challenge," Eloise said softly, her fingers grazing the rough material. It wasn't perfect. The leather was old and worn, the stitching crooked. But a lump was forming in her throat. He had spent weeks in this barn. For her.

Seeing her tears, he brushed her cheek. "I hope it fits. I was able to measure Juniper, but I had to guess on yours."

Taking his hand in hers, Eloise held it to her chest. "It's beautiful, Brooks. Thank you."

Twenty-Seven

Maisie's birthday was coming, and with a small reprieve from the snow, Brooks wanted to make a trip into town. With the Rileys' permission, he had Eloise up and in the wagon seat with him before sunrise.

Curling into the blanket she had made him, she rested her head against his shoulder. "Did we have to go so early?" she groaned.

"I have a few things I need to do that might take time," Brooks replied. "And afterward, I'd like to take you to lunch." Smiling, he kissed the top of her head. "We've got an hour to go. Just sleep awhile."

Not needing to be told twice, Eloise tucked her arm through his, her breaths turning rhythmic.

At the comfort in her, Brooks felt something in him stir. She might still have her doubts about him. He knew that, and he prayed daily that the Lord would grant her peace in knowing that he was hers. That everyone around her now loved her. It was moments like this when he knew, whether of conscious thought or not, some deeper part of her did trust him. She found comfort in him that she didn't find in others.

As she grew in that comfort, Brooks began to notice the little things about her that weren't so obvious before. In moments when she let her guard down and did something unexpected. Something that made Brooks see the lighter, sillier side of her. The more time she spent with Maisie, the more resemblance she bore to her, and he didn't think it was merely Maisie rubbing off on her. But rather than find himself truly enjoying those little pieces of her, he couldn't help the pang he felt in his chest with each new revelation.

She had slowly begun to share the painful pieces of her past, and every time she revealed the carefree, amusing parts of herself, he wondered who she might have been if not for that needling voice in her head. If not for the countless people who belittled her and turned her thoughts against her.

Nearing town, Brooks nudged Eloise. "Feel any better?" He felt her yawn against his shoulder. "I suppose we should have set out later."

"No." She yawned. "I don't mind." But rather than move away as he'd expected, she stayed curled into his side.

After a moment's hesitation, he put an arm around her waist. He wasn't sure he'd ever get used to the lines they were slowly crossing. Hours in the barn. Their closeness. The kiss. He hadn't kissed her since that morning. To do so could too easily lead to a line he didn't dare cross. But the little area in which they lay now, a place of boundaries that were their very own, felt righter than he would have first imagined. He'd never once felt guilt or condemnation; rather, he felt the Lord leading him in every step. Eloise needed that time between the two of them, and as the weeks passed, it became clearer how much peace she gained even from his touch, and if he could give her the slightest comfort, he would do it.

Holding her closer, he urged the horses to slow, unwilling to see the moment end.

After a time, he felt Eloise readjust, turning to face him. "I'm glad we came early," she said quietly.

"Even if you slept the whole ride?" he teased.

"But I was still with you, and that's what matters, isn't it?" Her cheeks flushed red, and she ducked her head.

"Don't be embarrassed, Elle. It's nice to have time outside of that barn."

Eloise laughed quietly. "I never thought we'd have that much. Mama's always been so fussy about following rules and worrying over being proper. Daddy quite honestly looks ready to commit murder every time I so much as look at you." She met his eyes. "I don't know how you managed the barn or this. Not if you asked my father."

"He didn't look happy to say yes," Brooks conceded. "But your mother convinced him. I almost decided against it, but your mother insisted."

"My mother?" She laughed. "I think she's lost it."

"She knows you, Elle, and she trusts you."

"Maybe, but ..." Eloise sighed. "I don't know. She's always been ... odd about certain things. We couldn't miss a single Sunday of church because it disrupted routine. Getting her to change her mind or go against any sense of what she felt was right has always been impossible." She shook her head. "I don't know, I just thought it would be her that gave us trouble, but she's not, and I ..."

Eloise was beginning to work herself up. Pulling the wagon to a stop, Brooks took hold of her arms. "You what, Elle?"

"I just...I know that it's hard for her," she said, her eyes moving to the town in the distance " So why is it that she can face things—things that are hard and scary for her—and yet I can't?"

"Darlin', sometimes simply facing the day is enough."

"It doesn't feel like it sometimes. It never does."

"Because the world has made you feel as though you should be doing more?" Brooks asked.

Eloise shrugged. "I just want to be different."

Brooks nodded. "Well then, maybe it's time we take a little step?" Urging the horses forward, he nodded to the mercantile in the distance. "I have a few things I need to do, so why don't you go into the mercantile and get whatever you need while I do that?"

"By myself?" she whispered.

Brooks shrugged. "If you're up to it."

Eloise chewed her lip as they came to a stop at the mercantile steps. "Ok," she breathed. "Will you be gone long?"

"Thirty minutes, Elle." She let him lift her down from the wagon. "You've got this, darlin'. It isn't Huxley, and I know you may not know her well, but Annabelle is there. She'll keep an eye on you."

Eloise's heart pounded in her throat, and for a moment, she feared she would be sick right there. Resisting the urge to call Brooks back, she made her way up the mercantile steps with shaky legs.

Eloise cringed as the bell above the door dinged. Why did they always have to have those wretched bells? It was like they wanted to draw every eye in the store.

No one is paying any attention, she told herself. *No one cares.*

No one paid her any mind as she eased the door shut, ringing that wretched bell again. Eloise found herself looking for

Annabelle, a familiar face amongst a sea of strangers. Finding her, she forced down the memories pressing in on her. No one was looking at her. No one was whispering about her.

Focus on what you need.

Eloise had been in the store only a handful of times, always with someone and never for herself. She didn't know where to find what she needed. For a moment, she considered asking Annabelle. But while the woman might have been familiar enough to keep her mind present, she didn't know her enough to go up to her. She'd almost rather face a stranger than a woman she'd see again.

Deciding against help, Eloise glanced around, taking in the store. Ahead of her stood the counter at which Annabelle stood, too busy with a customer to have noticed her yet. Turning before she could, Eloise found a wall of household goods: washtubs, washboards, pots and pans. To the left of the goods hung bolts of fabric. There were blankets, clocks, and candles all stacked on tables. Moving forward, she searched for yarn and embroidery goods.

"Eloise?" Eloise felt a mix of relief and anxiety at the sound of Annabelle's voice. "Can I help you, sweetheart?"

"Embroidery supplies?" Her voice was nothing more than a whisper, but Annabelle nodded.

"Just up to your right." Setting a hand to Eloise's back, Annabelle led her forward. "All you could ask for right there."

Thanking her, Eloise looked over the shelves, relieved when another customer grabbed Annabelle's attention. Drawing to mind the images she wanted, Eloise carefully selected a mixture of blues, reds, and yellows before grabbing green for good measure. Selecting a new set of needles, she quickly made her way to the counter.

"Have you got a big project?" Annabelle smiled. "Elizabeth says you have quite a talent."

"It's for Maisie's birthday." Again, Annabelle seemed unfazed by Eloise's volume. "Elizabeth is making her some new dresses, and she wanted me to embroider a few things along them." She felt herself blush as Annabelle took in the flowers embroidered in the pocket of her skirts. "Maisie isn't very happy about becoming a woman. Elizabeth wants her to know it doesn't mean she has to lose her spirit."

Annabelle rolled her eyes. "I don't know where that child's spirit came from." Suddenly, the woman sighed. "Well, that isn't entirely true. My mother was a bit like Maisie. Always dramatic. Always looking for the next adventure."

"Is that a bad thing?"

"No." Annabelle smiled. "Maisie's always been a light in this family. A very bright light."

Eloise smiled. "She is special, isn't she?" She'd been the best friend to her that Eloise could ask for.

And she got stuck with me.

Eloise jolted from her thoughts as she felt a hand on her shoulder. Lips to her ear, she felt Brooks smile. "You did it."

Eloise *hmmed*. "Was there ever any doubt?" she teased, breathing against the sharp ache in her chest. She had done it.

"Not for a second." Pulling her aside, he brushed her coins back into her bag. "And I'm paying," he added before stacking two books onto the counter. "Maisie's been hinting at these for months."

Annabelle smiled. "I have books coming in for her as well. Everyone has gone and ordered in books for her. Archie's plain spoiling her with schoolbooks he thinks she'll find interesting."

"I think I'm going to wait outside," Eloise whispered. "Excuse me."

Climbing onto the wagon seat, Eloise closed her eyes against the few families that walked the streets. She could feel the water rising, pulling her beneath the waves of the weak pride that had welled up in her for just a moment. *God, don't let it be ruined. Give me peace, Papa. Don't let it take from the moment.*

She wished she had the diary Elizabeth had given her. She had scriptures in there. Prayers she liked to reread when the voices grew loud.

She jumped as Brooks joined her on the seat, tossing their spoils between them. "Auntie's invited us to supper if you want to go." When she hesitated, Brooks tucked a stray strand of hair behind her ear. "We don't have to. We can still go to lunch and head home after. But if it makes you feel better, she likes you, Elle."

"Would we still go to lunch?"

"Of course. I already reserved a seat in the hotel diner." He smiled. "You still have to try Mabel's cooking."

"Then I suppose we can go," Eloise said quietly. Anything to extend her time with him.

Leading the horses toward the hotel, Brooks took her hand. "Thank you, Elle. I know it's not easy. But it'll be nice to see her and Archer, and I want them to get to know you."

"It's not that I don't want to get to know them. I just don't know how."

Brooks nodded. "You see, Elle. That's the good thing about the people in my family: we know how to get to know you." He winked at her. "All you have to do is let us, and the rest will fall into place."

The hotel diner felt more like a home than Eloise expected. The hotel in Huxley had been run down and infested by so many vermin it should have been condemned. But walking into the room felt like stepping into her own home. "Mabel dreamed of opening up the diner from the day she and Matthew started courting," Brooks informed her. "She's always had a talent in the kitchen."

He ushered her to a window seat that overlooked the mountains in the distance. After a moment, Mabel appeared, carrying two plates of roast turkey and potatoes. At her chest, Henry slept peacefully in his sling.

Mabel smirked at Brooks as she poured them each a mug of tea. "I didn't get this kind of time with Matthew before we were married."

Brooks laughed. "No, but you still got more than what most would. I seem to remember you taking quite a few walks."

Blushing, Mabel looked at Eloise. "It's good to see you again, Ellie. I hope you enjoy your day with Brooks."

Sharing a few more words with her brother, Mabel disappeared to help another customer.

Off and on throughout their meal, different patrons came and spoke to Brooks. Asking his plans for the ranch. Offering assistance when the time came. Most seemed pleased for him when he introduced her, though a few women seemed disgruntled.

Though Eloise had been in town a few times and heard the many stories the Harpers had about the people of Rose Haven, the kindness and patience she received from all of them still felt alien. A few people of Huxley had been understanding, but she had yet to find a member of Rose Haven who looked at her the way those in Huxley had.

"Are you sure no one is going to assume anything?" Eloise asked, her mind on the conversation with her parents—her father's fears. "With the two of us alone?"

"I am sure, Elle. It is a bit unusual, and I am sure there are several who disapprove, but most people around here allow at least a few moments between a couple."

With their meal finished, they walked the town until Annabelle called them to supper. People milled about the street —a few doors down from where Eloise and Brooks walked, a storekeeper swept their porch, covering the group of children that played out front in a cloud of snow. The children squealed and ran in the direction of Eloise and Brooks—their laughter trailing behind them.

"Were there a lot of children around here when you were that age?" Eloise asked.

"Not many." Brooks laughed, his eyes following the children. "Rose Haven has really grown in the last three years. We had four families aside from our own when Mabel and I were young, but only two had children." At the sound of Annabelle calling, Brooks turned Eloise back in the direction of the mercantile.

"It's a bit early," Annabelle said, setting dishes on the table. "But you'll be wanting to get back before dark."

Throughout the supper, Eloise listened to Brooks and Annabelle talk back and forth, bringing both she and Archer into the conversation when they needed differing opinions. Eloise decided she liked Archer. He was a man of very few words and, like herself, seemed content listening to the conversation. The way he watched Annabelle told her he could have listened to her speak for the rest of time and died happy.

When the meal had finished, Eloise offered to take care of the dishes, letting Brooks get the last few minutes with his aunt.

Brooks watched Eloise disappear around the corner, Archer at her heels. She had shown the slightest uncertainty at the man's offer to help, but rather than deny him, she had thanked him quietly.

She was trying, he thought, to beat those voices in her head.

Across from him, Annabelle smiled. "I never thought I'd see that look in your eyes." Despite the many girls who'd expressed their interest, the boy had never returned it. She'd begun to think he was slated to spend his life alone on that ranch. "You seem happy."

Brooks laughed. "I am."

"I don't suppose there will be wedding bells soon? The way you two look at each other, I'm surprised we haven't heard them already."

"Just waiting, Auntie. I want to make sure the time is right. That I can give her a home."

"Of course. How old is she again? She looks young, but I assume her to be about Mabel's age?"

"A few years younger. She'll be nineteen in March."

Annabelle nodded, her fingers going to the chain at her neck. Brooks knew she was thinking of her late daughter and husband.

She'd lost Opal at nineteen. After a moment, his aunt met his eyes. "Do you have a ring?" she asked.

"Not yet. I was hoping you'd have a catalog I could look through."

Annabelle nodded. "I have one. But I also have this." Removing the chain from her neck, she held the ring that hung from it between her fingers. "You could give her this."

"The ring Uncle Luke gave you?" Brooks shook his head. "I can't take that, Auntie." He'd never seen her a day in his life without that ring. The moment she married Archer, the ring had gone from her finger to a chain at her neck. "That's your piece of him."

Annabelle laughed tearfully, the ring to her lips. "Yes, it is," she said softly. "But it doesn't bring him closer to me than he already is, Brooks." Holding the ring a moment longer, she pulled the chain over his head and tucked it into his shirt before giving it a small pat. "I want you to take it, Brooks." She smiled tremulously. "The symbol of that ring brought me so much joy, and I'd like that to carry on to you. I may not know her well just yet, but I can see how much you love her, Brooks. I know to see that look in your eyes, she must be something special."

"She is, Auntie," Brooks breathed. "And I know she'll take care of this."

"Just let me know when you plan to ask?"

"The moment I decide," he promised.

Twenty-Eight

Elizabeth was beginning to wonder about the strenuous relationship between Eloise and her father. Morgan didn't talk about her as Merritt spoke of their children. Merritt couldn't resist speaking of his children when the opportunity presented itself. But Morgan always cleared his throat and changed the subject when the topic of Eloise came up, as though his daughter was the last thing he wished to hear about.

It had tainted him to her in the beginning, witnessing how he handled his own daughter. To listen to the hate-fueled screams that came from the soddy every other night. The way Morgan and his wife fought took her back to her childhood and how she would fall asleep to her parents' screams. But it was in those moments she saw Morgan's own brokenness, and she couldn't find herself angry when their screams echoed late into the night. They were two broken people handling their daughter's actions in their own flawed ways.

Listening to the faint sound of their screams now, Elizabeth watched Eloise. Her eyes were intent on the pattern she was embroidering for Maisie, but she kept fumbling with the needle, dropping and rethreading it a dozen times.

Standing, Elizabeth removed the hoop and set it aside. "Come here." Taking the girl's hand, she led her upstairs and into her room. "Sit."

Eloise looked uncertain as she seated herself at the edge of Elizabeth's bed. "I'm sorry," she whispered.

"There's no need to apologize for your parents, Eloise."

"It's my fault. It's me they're fighting over."

"I don't think it is, Ellie. Darling, there is so much more to your parents' struggles than you."

"But it started with me." Tears dripped lazily down her cheeks. "My father hates me."

"No," Elizabeth whispered. "Sweetheart, I'll admit, I did wonder at first what your father thought of you. But it's become obvious that he loves you."

"I'm not what he wanted. He wanted a Maisie or Mabel. Instead, he got me."

"And he loves you, Eloise." When Eloise said nothing, Elizabeth sighed. "I know it's hard to see. I know that he has been hurtful, and I am not condoning the way he has treated you, Ellie. But he is trying to understand you better."

Eloise studied her for a moment. "Did your parents understand?"

Elizabeth hesitated. "No," she admitted. "My papa was a good man. He didn't see anything wrong with the way I was, but he didn't defend me quite like your mama does." Sitting next to her, Elizabeth bit her lip. "My mother was what you think your father is to you, and I'm not saying you aren't allowed those feelings. I just don't want you to think your father doesn't care. Flawed as he may be, he doesn't deserve to be seen as all bad."

"I don't see him as bad," Eloise defended. "I just think he wanted better."

"No parent wants their child to be us, Eloise. Would you want your children to be like you?" When Eloise shook her head, Elizabeth continued. "He handles you wrong. But he still cares."

"Your mother didn't care?"

"My mother …" Elizabeth was quiet a moment. "My mother was very much like Maisie in that she was very excitable.

Dramatic. Everything was an ordeal. But where Maisie was gifted with kindness and compassion, those things seemed to skip over my mother. She was angry and bitter and drunk. Both my parents were drunks. Most nights, Anna and I were left alone while they went and drank saloons dry." Elizabeth laughed humorlessly. "I loved the nights she was gone and would sleep all the next day. To me, Anna was Mama. My papa was always good to me when he was home. Drunk or sober, he loved his girls. But Mama? She tolerated Anna, but I was something else."

"Because you were quiet?" Eloise asked.

"Because I was quiet. Because I was sensitive. Annabelle could fake being what my mother wanted, but I couldn't."

Tears dripped slowly down Elizabeth's cheeks. "You don't have to share any more," Eloise whispered.

"It's all right, Ellie. It's good, you know. Because I know you don't believe me when I say I know what you are feeling. But I do." She was quiet another moment before continuing. "It wasn't often my mother hit me. Anna kept me out of her way the best she could. But when I was eight, my mother snapped when I couldn't answer a question she'd asked. She was drunk and had just finished fighting with my father, which only made her angrier."

Eloise's stomach rolled miserably at the image of a young Elizabeth at the hands of her mother. The words spoken over her were not far from what Alma had spoken to Eloise. "She beat you?"

"It was the only time she went that far," Elizabeth said simply. "But that was the first night I begged God to let me die— and not because of the pain in my body. It was the first time I ever hated myself."

"I know that feeling," Eloise said quietly, and she found herself sharing Alma's words with her. She hadn't even shared that moment with Brooks yet. "It's when I realized I was different."

"And you can't help but wonder what you might have been if not for those words?" she asked. When Eloise nodded, Elizabeth continued. "I didn't say a word to anyone again for years. Not to anyone but Anna, and even then, it took three days of pleading on her part."

"Was Merritt the first you spoke to?"

Elizabeth smiled. "The second. My mother left a year after that, and a neighbor started looking after Anna and me. The mother of Annabelle's late husband. She was the first one I spoke to. I was eleven, and she had just taken us in after my father had died."

"Your mother left?" Eloise chewed at her lip. How often had she feared her father doing the same? "Did-did you blame yourself?"

"For a time. But I quickly learned after having Brooks that it couldn't have been because of me. My children can drive me mad at times, but I could never leave them."

"Did you ever blame yourself for their struggles? Do…" At Elizabeth's encouragement, Eloise continued quietly. "Do you ever feel unworthy of Merritt?"

"I used to," Elizabeth said softly. "After every breakdown I had in the beginning, I would wonder if I had ruined his life by marrying him. When Brooks started to show signs of struggling, I took all the blame on myself. I should have known not to have children. I should have known they would be like me. I can still feel that way at times, watching Maisie struggle. But I have to remind myself that Merritt chose me, and no matter how infuriating I know I can be, he never seems put out dealing with me." Elizabeth smiled. "As for my children's struggles, they are just that—their struggles—whether passed on genetically or not."

"We're all a little messed up, I think," she said softly. "Whether through blood or circumstance, we all have something that hinders us."

Eloise chewed at her lip. "So you don't regret it—getting married and having children?"

"No, Eloise, and you won't either. Not if you fight the lie that you aren't enough." Elizabeth touched Eloise's cheek. "Don't be afraid to love Brooks, Ellie. Do not be afraid of having children. You will get better, and your children will have an army of support behind them."

"You don't think Brooks deserves better?"

"Eloise, I don't think Brooks could do better. Not because he's undeserving, but because I know him. It was no surprise when, after all these years, it was you he opened his heart up to."

"Brooks has always been drawn to … broken things." Elizabeth smiled. "He was always bringing creatures into this house as a child. Dogs. Cats. Even squirrels and rabbits. He would find them injured and nurse them back to health, or he'd find a litter of puppies that didn't have a mama, and he would raise them up until they were ready for new homes. I see now it was all in preparation. The Lord knew you needed someone like Brooks."

"And the Lord knew Brooks would need my brokenness?"

Elizabeth laughed. "I wouldn't say it like that. I think he knew Brooks needed someone he would have to work for. Someone he would have to fight for. I know it seems odd to say, but I don't think he would have trusted someone who was so easily acquired. To him, something worth keeping is something worth fighting for. As he always likes to say, the most difficult horse has the most love to give."

***

Morgan's fingers tapped against the table as he watched his daughter with Brooks. She'd grown more comfortable with him; so much so that Morgan was beginning to question the morality of letting them spend so much time alone. How his wife saw it fit, he couldn't understand. The woman had always been so strict about propriety, it was almost a sickness. The idea of her daughter going around barefoot or with her hair down near put the woman in hysterics, and yet she let their daughter stroll into that barn every morning with no one to keep the two accountable.

"I don't like it either, Morgan." Lily sighed. "But she isn't us. She never would have been able to get to know Brooks and grow comfortable with him if she wasn't able to have that time with him. I don't like it. Every time they go in there, I know what other people would say, and I feel sick. I want to drag her out by the hair. But Morgan, we have to trust her. We have to trust Brooks."

"I don't know Brooks."

"You don't know your daughter well, either." The moment those words left her mouth, Lily's head dropped. "I'm sorry, Morgan." Tears pooled on her cheeks. "I know you love her, honey. I know you worry. But Brooks is a God-fearing man. Eloise needs the privacy to let herself be herself with him; and she's a good girl, Morgan. She talks to me. Nothing goes on between the two of them that I don't hear about from her."

Morgan tried to keep that in mind as Eloise moved closer to Brooks, setting her forehead against his shoulder. Lily would have keeled over from so much as handholding in their courtship. The fear of making a mistake on Lily's part had been enough to keep herself a foot apart from Morgan until their wedding night.

"Are you all right?" Though no more than a whisper meant for Eloise, Brooks' voice jolted Morgan's thoughts back to the party as his daughter eyed the stairs. "Do you need a moment?"

When she nodded, Brooks started to turn her toward the door. "I'm just going to go upstairs," Eloise said quietly. "It's Maisie's birthday. You shouldn't leave her."

Brooks was quiet a moment as he considered her. "All right. Come find me when you're doing better." Kissing her hair, he went in search of Maisie.

As Morgan watched her disappear upstairs, he fought the urge to call her back down. To make her face her fear as frustration fired in him. The girl wasn't to be trusted alone; he didn't need to know her thoughts to understand that.

Swearing softly, Morgan followed after her. She didn't need to stay downstairs, but he wasn't leaving her alone. Not when the memories of finding her were nearly drowning him. Nearing the top of the stairs, he heard her sniffle, and for a moment, the anger left him. Turning the corner, he found her curled onto the seat of Elizabeth's sitting room, her forehead against the glass.

"Please, Papa," she was whispering. "I don't want to hide."

Morgan sighed. No matter his anger, her tears had always been enough to break him. "Hey, beautiful," he said quietly, hesitant to startle her.

Glancing up, her eyes widened in surprise before her cheeks flushed red. "Hi, Daddy."

Sitting across from her, Morgan watched the way she curled in on herself. It was moments like this that made him see past the anger and brought him back to when Eloise was a little girl who toddled after him every morning, wanting to be part of everything he did. He could remember it so clearly—how she'd beg her mother to take her by his work when he was on his lunch break and how she'd run to him with that toothless grin of hers. He hadn't seen it in too many years. The happiest parts of Eloise had disappeared the night he and Lily sent her to stay with Alma.

Why had he left her with his sister? He should have known she couldn't handle Eloise. But he had ignored that gnawing uncertainty, and not only did he pay the price for that mistake, but his daughter had paid for it every day since. He shouldn't have sent her to Alma's. He shouldn't have sent her to school.

Morgan's head ached. *School.* Lily had told him a dozen times over of the things Eloise told her about school, but like everything else, he had brushed it off. The girl was exaggerating. But he'd been wrong, and he felt almost certain it was a punishment on his part to see first-hand just what his daughter had experienced in that school.

Eloise had forgotten her lunch that day, and with the school only two buildings away from the mill, Morgan offered to save Lily the extra burden of taking it herself.

An uneasy feeling had overcome him as he made his way into town. A feeling that only grew stronger as he grew nearer.

School in sight, he picked up his step, eager to rid himself of the awful cloud hovering above him. From the door, he could hear a student reading aloud. Stepping inside, he kept to the shadows of the far corner. He could see Eloise near the front, her head down. She had looked so small, so alone, as the rest of the class whispered to their desk mates.

Taking a step forward, he faltered as a small voice told him to wait. A moment later, the teacher ordered the student to sit, and as though expecting what was next, Eloise sank lower into her seat.

"Eloise Riley," Miss Garrett called, ignoring the snickering that echoed around the room.

Ten feet away, tucked into a corner, Morgan could see the violent way his daughter shook. "Come on," he whispered. "You've got this, baby." She was smart. He knew she could read better and quicker than he and Lily combined.

If it hadn't been for another student speaking up, he wouldn't have known she'd already begun to read aloud. At the student's complaint, other students started in. "We can't hear her," they echoed.

"Speak up, Duncy!" one shouted.

Morgan could see the panic building in his daughter. Her shaking had worsened, and she was wiping at her cheeks. "Speak up, Miss Riley," the teacher ordered. When Eloise tried and failed, and Morgan knew she was trying, the woman's mouth set angrily, her fingers tightening on the desk. "Come up here, Miss Riley. Now." Doing as she was told, Morgan watched his daughter move further from him, her head down as the children laughed. "Turn and face the class and try again," the teacher ordered.

Eloise's eyes traveled the length of the classroom, somehow finding him in the noon shadows. Even though tears cascaded down her pale cheeks, he knew Eloise was trying to keep it together and not fall apart entirely.

The teacher's hand slapping against the desk behind her had brought Eloise's attention away from him. "I don't care if we're here all day, Eloise Riley. You *will* finish your reading."

He had seen enough. Stepping forward, Morgan ordered Eloise to his side. "Now," he snapped. She tripped over her feet as she hastened to obey. Grabbing her book bag, Morgan took her arm and pulled her outside. He knew he was hurting her. He was scaring her. But words were building on his tongue, and he knew if he didn't get out of the building, he'd only get her into more trouble.

He waited until the school was out of sight before slowing. The moment he let her go, she scrambled back, her feet tangling, causing her to fall backward.

"Ellie," he whispered. She looked too broken for only twelve.

"I'm sorry," she cried.

"Eloise." Kneeling next to her, he took hold of her chin, hurt at the way she flinched. When had he ever hurt her? "Baby girl, you are not in trouble."

"I'm not?" When he shook his head, she let out a harsh sob and went into his arms. "Please don't make me go back." Her tears soaked quickly through the front of his shirt, and she shook so violently he was sure her bones were rattling beneath her skin.

Morgan watched his daughter now, arms around her knees, her eyes glued to something outside. How far removed was she from that little girl? He wanted to believe something in her was changing. That Brooks was changing her. Sometimes he could almost see it, and then he looked at her now, tears staining her cheeks.

"Did you want something?" Eloise asked quietly.

"No. I suppose not." Standing, Morgan made his way toward the stairs.

"I'm not going to hurt myself." The words were spoken so quietly he wasn't sure she'd really spoken. Turning back, he found her picking at her nail. "At least, I don't want to."

When she met his eyes, they were wet. *She isn't right in the head. Rotten. Twisted. Unfaithful.* The list of words used to describe his daughter had only grown longer and more dangerous as she grew older. The one doctor they'd dared to take her to had suggested they institutionalize her, and the people of Huxley— many of which they'd called friends—had been of little help. He might have listened to their prodding if not for Lily's threat to leave if he ever did try. *If God can't forgive me for it, I don't care,* she had sobbed. *I won't lose her.* But words ate at him day after day as he worked with men who belittled his family. His daughter wasn't normal. She wasn't right. She was a hundred things to the people of Huxley.

But what is she to you?

Looking back at her now, he could think of only one thing: his Ellie.

Sitting next to her, he took her hand. "You know you have a whole army behind you, Weasel."

Her eyes met his. "Even you?" she croaked.

"Even me, baby." He didn't have to understand her to stand with her. He gave her a small nudge. "Though I don't suppose anyone else matters much when you have Brooks, huh?" As he'd hoped, her lips turned up as a pretty pink filled her cheeks. "You love that boy, don't you?" When she nodded, Morgan felt something uncomfortable stir in him. He'd never thought about Eloise leaving them. "And does he treat you well when you're alone? He isn't taking advantage of that fact?"

The way her hand went to her lips told him enough. The way her lips curled told him even more. "Does he do that a lot?" he asked.

"No," she said quietly. "It was just the one time. He's respectful, Daddy. I promise."

"Good. I'll have you know I don't like you two spending so much time alone." He knew too well the temptations that lay in a simple touch, and he didn't want his daughter making those same mistakes.

Unaware of the worries in his mind, Eloise met his eyes, her lips turned upward. "I know. But thank you for understanding."

Twenty-Nine

Eloise's tongue poked between her lips as she scribbled in the pocket diary his mother had given her. "What are you writing?" Brooks asked, expecting her to refuse him.

"A prayer," she said softly. "For Maisie."

"Ahh." Brooks rested an arm on one knee, his other leg hanging out the hayloft window. "I've written a few for her as well lately." His sister had been far from the bright, imaginative little girl he had watched grow up. As of late, she was sullen, and he was beginning to worry she was heading down the same road he and Eloise had found themselves on. "She'll find her way out of it," he said. "Though it would happen a lot quicker if the girl would just admit her feelings."

Eloise laughed softly. "Why is she so reluctant to admit her feelings?"

"A few reasons, I think. For one, Maisie has never liked change. She struggled after Mabel was married, trying to adjust to not having her. For another, Jeremy Tuft was always a bit of a pest to her growing up. He teased her relentlessly, though it was only because he liked her. The other reason, probably the biggest, is I think she's afraid that any sort of relationship will hinder a few dreams of hers. I think she's forgotten Annabelle and Mabel both achieved dreams of theirs after they got married."

Eloise glanced up at him. "Do you know? What she wants?"

"She admitted it to me when we went to pick up Juniper. She was wondering if our parents would pay for correspondence lessons."

"Well, I wish she would come out of this," Eloise said quietly. It hurt too much to watch Maisie struggle, especially when she herself wasn't. It wasn't right.

The months hadn't been easy. She still struggled daily. But there had been something stirring in her since Christmas. After returning from the barn, she and Brooks had found the rest of the family up and waiting for them, candles in the tree lit, a bucket of water ready to extinguish any accidents.

The morning had been full of swapping gifts, playing games on the living room floor and doing puzzles on the kitchen table, and laughs that had eased away so much of the ache in Eloise's soul. She loved these people, and it was in moments like this one, Brooks' arm around her shoulder and their families gathered together, that she truly believed they loved her too.

After much encouragement, Brooks and Elizabeth had taken a place at the piano to sing carols. She hadn't known either could sing or that Brooks could play. But it was the song that captivated her the most as Brooks' deeper voice harmonized so perfectly with his mother's soft one: *O Come O Come Emmanuel.* She'd never heard the song before, and something in the lyrics sent warmth coursing through her. That the same God who mourned the lonely and closed paths to misery had given her a room full of people she loved.

Eloise clung to that truth for Maisie now as she watched the girl and Merritt settle on the porch swing, Maisie's head on her father's shoulder.

Following Eloise's gaze, Brooks took hold of her hand. "She'll move past it, Elle."

"I'm sure she will," Eloise said. "But it doesn't make me feel less … guilty."

"Guilty?" Brooks asked, concern shadowing his face. "Why?"

"Because as much as I hate seeing her struggle, I can't help but feel grateful that I'm not. I should be the one—"

Taking her chin, Brooks turned her eyes to his. "Eloise, it is not your fault that Maisie is having a hard time. She's human like the rest of us. She isn't going to be happy all the time, and she doesn't have to be."

"I know, but it's like with you," Eloise said quietly. "When you have a bad day, it doesn't feel right for it to be you. I feel like it should be me. I deserve it more."

"Elle, you do not deserve to be in pain. You do not deserve to hate yourself." Brooks wiped the tears from Eloise's cheeks. "And you do not need to feel guilty because you're grateful to be happy for once. We all have days, darlin'. Sometimes those days last a little longer. For some, those days are most days. But they are not a result of poor faith."

Eloise chewed at her lip. "I'm sorry. I shouldn't make this about me."

"You didn't, Elle. I brought it up, and I've done the same thing when talking to my parents. It's natural to want to take the pain of those you love. It's also normal to be glad you aren't the one hurting."

"You do think she'll come out of it, though, don't you?" Eloise breathed. "She won't end up like us?"

"No. I don't think she'll end like us. Lilybit knows how to fight."

Eloise laughed softly, thankful for a change of topic. "You never told me why you call her Lilybit."

Brooks smiled. "When Mais was about two, she went through a stage where she no longer wanted to be called Maisie," he explained. "She would introduce herself to everyone as Mae Elizabeth. Only she couldn't quite say it, so it sounded more like My Lilybit. I guess it just stuck."

"It's sweet." Eloise had always loved when her father called her his little Ella-weasel. When he used it, she felt not only seen but loved in his eyes. "I'm sure she loves it."

Brooks groaned as he watched his family leave the house. He'd nearly forgotten their plans to go to town. "You know you can still come with us?"

Eloise shook her head. "Spend time with your family, Brooks."

Brooks pulled her to her feet before wrapping his arms around her waist. "You're part of the family now, Elle. Maybe not officially just yet. But one of us all the same."

"I know." Removing a stray strand of straw from Brooks' shirt, Eloise twirled it around her finger. "But I think Maisie needs a little time with you."

At the sound of his parents' voices nearing the barn door, calling for him to come down, Brooks set his forehead to hers. "Just come, Elle." When she shook her head, Brooks sighed dramatically. "What will I ever do without my Eloise?"

Though she knew he was teasing her, Eloise felt a rush of warmth run through her. He wanted her, he would miss her, and she was choosing to believe and trust in that. "I think you'll survive," she breathed.

When he was gone, Eloise turned her attention back to the words she'd been writing, ignoring the regret she could feel settling in as the sound of the wagon grew more distant.

Beside her, Juniper nudged her arm. "I can't take you out," Eloise told her. "Not without Brooks." Swinging her feet over the stall, she allowed the horse to rest her head on her shoulder, her eyes closing at Eloise's touch. "Don't act as though you haven't been out already."

Juniper had been out daily from dawn to dusk as Brooks worked with her, teaching Eloise how to train and handle her. The difference between the horse she had met months ago to the one with her now was night and day. Though less skittish than she had been and well accustomed to the halter and lead rope, the horse still wasn't fit to be ridden. Brooks refused to hear of it until the horse had proven herself, and even then, he wouldn't trust Eloise on her until Juniper was practiced.

"One kick," he told her. "One fall from that height is all it would take, Elle. I am not taking that risk."

Kissing Juniper's muzzle, Eloise left the barn. The place was lonely without Brooks.

Finding her mother cleaning in the soddy, Eloise rested her arms against the table. "Sweeping seems kind of pointless," she teased, her eyes looking over the earthen walls—at the prairie grass that peeked through the cracks. Her mother would be happy to have a home—one with real walls and rooms and a floor that wasn't made of dirt.

"It gives a sense of normalcy." Lily sighed, the hand that held the broom going slack. "I take it where I can get it."

"Well, are you willing to take a break?"

"For you?" Lily smiled. "Always. Are you wanting to take a walk?" At Eloise's nod, Lily stored the broom in a corner.

"Are you regretting not going with Brooks?"

Eloise shrugged. "Some. It's only getting harder not to be with him."

"I can tell," Lily said. "We've barely seen you two apart in months." When Eloise blushed, Lily continued. "I am happy for you, Ellie, and I do believe the Lord has led you two together. But, sweetheart, I want to make sure you aren't putting too much on Brooks."

"What do you mean?"

"I mean that Brooks isn't your savior, Eloise."

"I know he's not," Eloise said, fingering the leather wristband Brooks had made her for her birthday. "It is easier with him, though—to stay above water. I try to read the Bible and pray and have faith, but nothing helps like Brooks does."

"You're walking a dangerous line, Eloise. I just want you to be aware. Brooks can't replace God."

"I know he can't," Eloise assured. "I don't want him to, and I'm still trying with God. I'm just being honest in what I'm feeling now." Focusing again on those lyrics, Eloise told her what she felt on Christmas. "I'm trying to believe it all, Mama— that He gave me all of this because He loves me—but it's getting harder as the weeks pass."

Seeing her distress, Lily turned her back toward the house. "Why don't you go get your Bible? You and I can spend a little time in it together."

Conceding, Eloise hurried upstairs and retrieved the book from beneath her pillow. Taking a moment, she held it against her chest. "Don't let me sink, Papa." She'd been doing well. She was learning to keep herself afloat. But she didn't know how to pull herself back up after she'd already sunk. Her fingers dug into the worn leather. "God, I'm sinking."

Eloise bit down on her lip, fighting inward panic as she felt herself slip further. "No," she whispered. "I can do this. I can fight. Papa, please."

Straightening up, she stood, pressing the Bible tighter to her chest. She could do this. She would stay afloat. She kept a prayer on her lips as she made her way across the lawn. Nearing the soddy, she slowed as she heard her parents' hushed voices.

"Could you not just do it for her?" Lily asked. "Eloise needs our help."

Eloise heard her father swear. "I can't, Lily. Where was God when Eloise was in that tub?"

"Do not use Eloise as an excuse, Morgan. You gave up on the Lord long before Eloise tried to hurt herself. You can't keep blaming her for all of it."

"No, you're right," Morgan snapped. "I am not blaming her. I blame Him. Where was He? Where was He with Alma and that school and that godforsaken church, Lily?"

"He was trying to keep us home, Morgan. Eloise begged us to stay. *We* made her go to school. *We* stayed in that church." Lily uttered half a swear word before biting it back. "It is not God's fault. It is not Eloise's fault. It's ours." Lily was quiet for a long moment. "Morgan, do you even know what she thinks of herself? What she thinks you think of her?" When Morgan said nothing, Lily let out a small sob. "Of course you don't. Because you have never sat and listened. Never let her explain it. Nineteen years you have pushed her. Pushed her away. Pushed her to try harder until she stretched herself thin."

"And look what happened," Morgan growled. "She tried to kill herself, Lily. I made her stay in that godforsaken school, and look what happened to her." He was quiet a moment. "If I had known just what that woman was doing to her, I wouldn't have made her go."

Lily was quiet for a long while. "Morgan, I didn't mean to say that it was your fault. We both are to blame. We both pushed her but—"

"But I pushed her more," Morgan spit. Taking up his jacket, he left, slamming the door hard enough to make the house shutter.

Eloise's stomach churned as she watched her father move across the yard, oblivious to her. *You can't keep blaming her.* Urging her feet to move, she eased the soddy door open.

Lily sat with her back to her, her shoulders shaking as she silently wept.

"Mama?"

"Please, not now, Eloise."

Heart in her throat, she stepped outside to find her father entering the barn. Running to catch up, she found him readying the horses.

"Daddy?"

The saddle slammed on the table. "Not now, Eloise."

"Ok." Eloise walked slowly, each step as though bricks weighed down her feet. *Please, not now, Eloise.* Even Mama— dearest Mama—could no longer bear her problems.

Reaching the field, she dropped the Bible and broke into a run, desperate to put distance between her and everything.

She ran until the barn was far behind her. Ran until her legs could no longer carry her. Ran until she found herself at the edge of the small pond.

Heart pounding, she took a step back. Eloise shook her head. She needed to go back. To find her mother. Her father. Anyone.

They didn't want you.

Eloise closed her eyes. "I'm not going to do it. I'm not. I won't." But the storm inside her was growing. The waves of everything she'd held at bay crashed down on her, one after the other.

Even her mother didn't want her.

Heart in her throat, her mind a blur, Eloise waded into the water, not stopping until it came waist-deep. Slipping to her knees, the tears began to fall. She didn't try to stop them. She couldn't.

How easily, how quickly, that newfound peace had crumbled. "God, please," she cried. "I don't want to do it."

But all the strength was seeping out of her with each tear that fell. She leaned back until only her face remained above the water.

It would be easy.

It will hurt them.

But for how long? They wouldn't miss her. She would be doing them a favor, ridding them of her and the problems she brought.

It isn't like that. They love me. Mama loves me. "Brooks," she whispered.

Brooks loved her … but he would grow tired of her.

Eloise shook her head, letting the water fill her nose. They would move on, and it would be so easy.

"No." She sat up, disturbing the peaceful water. "No. It isn't true."

They wouldn't miss her. Her parents probably didn't even realize she hadn't come home.

Falling back, Eloise let the water rush over her and screamed.

***

Annabelle's eyes found Brooks as she placed the tea before her sister. The boy had his arm tossed over Maisie's shoulder as he spoke, drawing a smile to her face.

"What's Maisie gonna do when Brooks moves onto his land?" she asked. "No one knows how to get her out of her head like he does."

Elizabeth laughed. "Oh, she and Eloise have gotten close. She'll be finding any excuse she can to find her way over there."

Annabelle raised an eyebrow. "So you think Eloise will be moving up there with him? From the beginning?"

"I think so," Elizabeth said quietly. "He's certainly talked about marriage a lot more the closer he gets to moving, and I don't think he's ready to lose time with her. But I think he's afraid of bringing her into the mess of starting his business."

"Did he never listen at all to you and Merritt?" Annabelle laughed. "You married into far more stressful circumstances, Ellie, and you and Eloise are just about one and the same." When Elizabeth smiled, Annabelle frowned. "What?"

"You know everyone calls Eloise by Ellie."

"Everyone can call you two whatever they want. You'll always be Ellie to me, and I stand by it. If the only reason he's waiting is because he thinks she deserves better, he's underestimating her. He's underestimating how hard it will be on his own. The Lord gave Adam Eve for a reason." Annabelle's eyes found Brooks once more. "He's good for a girl like her, Elizabeth. But it can't be denied that she's good for him too." Whatever the boy might have presented, there had always been something just beneath the surface. "He's finally attracted someone good for him."

"I don't think it's that he attracts what isn't good for him," Elizabeth said. "I think he gravitates to them; and it's not that Wiley was all bad for him, Anna. It was that he met him at the wrong time. Even Ellie might have been bad for him if they had met then. Maybe not in the ways Wiley was, but she wouldn't have turned his eyes to the Lord any more than Wiley did either."

Annabelle sighed. "No, I suppose not. I still can't say I like the boy being in his life. I know it's not fair, but to me, he's still the boy who led Brooks onto that road."

"Encouraged, Anna. Not led. Brooks is stubborn. Wiley couldn't have gotten him to drink if it wasn't already in his head." Elizabeth watched her a moment. "I know it's harder for you, Annabelle. But Wiley was a child as much as Brooks. He may still be living that life, but I don't think he would ever try to lead Brooks back. He respects him."

"But can a person who drinks ever be trusted, Elizabeth?" Annabelle hated drink. Her father had been lost to drink. As a child, she'd taken care of him as he died, his body bloated and his skin yellow. Her husband might as well have been lost to drink, his addiction to alcohol leading him back to that saloon in the first place, too drunk to even protect himself when the other guy started throwing punches. To think her nephew could find the end of his life at the bottom of a bottle had been too much to bear upon finding him in a drunken stupor.

Annabelle could have killed him right there and Wiley with him if it hadn't been for the pain so evident on his young face. His dark eyes wet and scared as he looked back at her. When her anger had turned to sympathy, the boy had broken, going into her arms and clinging to her like a child.

"I'm sorry." Sorry. Not for fear of trouble but because he knew what it was to her, what it would mean to his parents. Drink was something every Harper child knew was never to be touched.

"Why?" she'd hissed, unable to rid herself of that anger entirely. Not when she saw her husband, her father, and even her mother in the drunken boy before her.

She'd expected excuses and instead found the boy falling apart entirely, pouring out every deep dark thought he carried. The way he viewed himself. The hatred he felt toward the God he was taught to love and the way the alcohol numbed it all. He shared the guilt he felt when the numbness faded, and he was left to face what he knew his parents would hate.

"I don't know why we were so surprised," Annabelle said softly now. "That he took after you." The boy had shown signs from the beginning. Even as an infant, he clung to his mother when others came near. When more families joined the town, bringing with them their own small children, the boy kept his distance as they played, preferring the company of animals or otherwise sticking to his mother's side, always watching the other children with a sort of distrustful air. "Or that he took to Wiley in the end."

"Especially now, looking at him with Eloise," Elizabeth agreed. "Wiley didn't want to be a friend simply because Brooks was there. He loved Brooks for who he was. That means something to Brooks."

"Do you regret it all? Letting him befriend Wiley?"

Elizabeth considered that a moment, her eyes finding Brooks. "No," she said quietly. "I think Brooks needed him. Sometimes we have to break in order for God to shape us into what He always meant us to be."

Annabelle followed Elizabeth's eyes, smiling when Brooks caught her gaze. After that night, she had watched him grow. Slowly. But even behind his smile, she had seen pain. That old loneliness that had simmered beneath the surface. But that loneliness was gone. When she looked at him now, she saw a man in love. A man certain of where his path was leading because he was allowing the Lord to guide him.

Thirty

Lily met their wagon a mile out from the house. "Eloise?" She ran toward the back of the wagon. "Have you seen Eloise?"

At their denial, the woman began to scream for her daughter, moving away before Brooks took hold of her. "Lily, what's going on?" Brooks resisted the urge to shake her as his own emotion got to him. "What happened?"

"We can't find Eloise," Lily sobbed. "We haven't seen her for hours."

Needing no more, Brooks unhitched one of the horses from the wagon. "Dad?" he called.

But his father was already unhitching the second horse. "I'll take the east. The women can search on foot."

Not waiting for another word, Brooks turned the horse south. "Elle," he shouted. "Eloise." Fighting the rising panic, he searched the trees. "Elle."

She tried to kill herself, Ida's voice whispered.

"Eloise!" Brooks screamed, all calm forgotten. "God, where is she? Please, Papa, lead me."

Not two weeks ago. Right there in the bath.

The bath.

Turning the horse back in the direction of the creek, Brooks ordered her into a run. "Don't let me be too late."

Nearing the creek, he pushed the horse harder than he'd ever pushed one before. He'd make up for it later. When he knew Eloise was safe. Not finding her, he followed the creek. She wasn't under that water. She wasn't. But that didn't stop the mental images that came nor the bile that came up his throat.

The sun was gone by the time he reached the outskirts of his land. "Elle."

It was several minutes before he spotted her walking through the creek, just visible in the moonlight. "Elle." At the choked sound of his voice, she turned, her feet slipping from beneath her. "What are you doing?" he demanded. "It's freezing." Hopping down, he removed his jacket, anger replacing the relief in finding her. "Get out. Now."

Doing as she was told, she picked her way out of the water and slipped her arms into his jacket. Seeing the blue tint to her lips, Brooks snatched the blanket off the horse and tossed it around her shoulders. "We need to get you home," he said quietly. "You'll catch your death out here."

But then, maybe that was what she wanted.

"I don't want to go home," Eloise whispered.

"I don't care what you want right now, Eloise." Brooks watched her flinch at the name, but he didn't care. "Your parents are worried sick. Your mother is in hysterics." He was beginning to shake with anger.

Brooks felt that small voice bid him patience.

Patience. He could shake her now. What was wrong with her?

"What were you thinking?" he growled. "Do you know what I've been going through? Looking for you?" When her blue lips quivered, he felt his anger waver slightly. But he was still angry. "What happened?" he demanded.

She shook her head. "You'll just get angrier," she whispered.

"Maybe I have a right to be angry, Eloise. You have no idea what I have been through tonight. I thought you were dead." The look of guilt in her eyes told him the truth of where her mind had been. *Admit it,* he begged silently. *Tell me.* But she said nothing.

"I know, Elle. About what happened in Huxley." Her eyes snapped to his, her blue lips trembling. "Ida James told me that first day."

Without a word, Eloise kneeled to the ground. Her teeth chattered miserably, and Brooks felt the last of his anger fade. Kneeling beside her, he waited for her to speak. "I wanted to die, Brooks."

"And today? I thought you were doing better?" he said quietly. "You were happier. This morning you were happy."

Wasn't she? Had he only seen what he wanted to see?

"I was happier," she said, hugging her knees to her chest. "But that's how it always works: I surface, then I sink."

"What—" Brooks cleared his throat. "What made you sink this time?"

Eloise chewed at her lip. "It started with Maisie. She shouldn't be the one suffering."

"I know that isn't all of it, Eloise. You were fine when I left, and after tonight, I am not letting you shut me out."

"Mama and I talked," she continued. "We were going to read the Bible. She and Daddy ended up fighting over it. About me." She met his eyes. "They hate each other, Brooks. Because of me. My father is losing his faith because of me. He blames himself for what I did." She let out a small sob. "It's always me, Brooks. No matter what I do, it's wrong. No matter what I do, I just make it worse."

"You don't make things worse, Elle."

Eloise shook her head. "You'd be better off without me. All of you would be."

"What do we have to do to make you see the truth?" Brooks shook his head, his anger returning. "Do you have any idea what you have put all of us through? Eloise, your mother is losing her mind right now. My father didn't hesitate to get on that horse for you, leaving his wife and daughter horseless a mile out from home. The Lord only knows what your father is feeling now."

"I know," she whispered. "I know. Why can't I do anything right? I try, but I always sink."

Brooks took in her wet hair and blue lips and the sharp chatter of her teeth. "But you got up," he said quietly.

Eloise shrugged. "I don't want to die, Brooks." Her eyes met his. "But I scare myself."

Unsure of what to say, Brooks moved closer and pulled her to him. Words would do nothing for her now, so he simply let her rest against him. Her wet hair soaked through the front of his shirt, mixing with the tears that wet her cheeks.

Eloise's fingers curled into the fabric of Brooks' shirt. Despite the heaviness in her stomach, her heart slowed at the feel of her body pressed against his. His touch seemed to make her warmer somehow, her future within its walls seeming a little less bleak.

It's all a lie. He can't keep you afloat.

No, she thought. She knew he couldn't. But he wasn't all she had.

Curling closer to Brooks, she focused on his scent. Why couldn't she believe that he was hers? Not her savior but a tool. A lifeline.

Because you know the truth. Sooner or later, they all leave.

A small voice bid her to trust. Reminding her of that Christmas song. Of the words on Brooks' tongue.

God, I want to trust you. Help me.

"I am not going anywhere, Elle." When she met Brooks' eyes, they were blurred by his own tears. His thumb stroked her cheek. "I love you."

"Even knowing what I've done?"

"I always knew it, Elle. It never changed anything." His hand cuffed her chin tenderly and brought his lips to hers. She moaned against his lips as she felt warmth rush through her, thawing the icy cold in her bones. When he pulled away, he set his forehead to hers. "We need to get you home, darlin'."

Lifting her onto the horse, Brooks swung himself up behind her without a word. A small part of his own nerves eased as she rested against him, comfortable in his arms.

***

Eloise lay awake long after her mother had fallen asleep. Even in sleep, the woman's breath still hitched, and there were tears dried onto her cheeks.

Because of her.

In the room beside hers, she could still make out the muffled sound of Brooks' tears and his father comforting him.

So many tears all because of her, and she couldn't bring herself to shed a single tear now. She felt almost numb.

"Papa," she whispered. "I don't want to stay here. I don't want to keep hurting people. I—" Tears pricked at her eyes now. "I don't want to keep hurting myself. Please. Help me." Sitting up, she reached under her pillow for the Bible and found the spot empty and cold. The field—she'd left it there.

Easing away from her mother, Eloise tiptoed across the room and into the hall. She knocked at Brooks' door quietly enough that it wouldn't be heard by the others. Merritt answered the door, no surprise showing on his face at finding her.

Nodding, he stepped aside, squeezing her shoulder gently as he did so. "I'll be out in the hall."

Eloise looked around the room. She hadn't so much as seen Brooks' room from the stairway until now. The room had a cluttered sort of state to it: a pair of dungarees were slung over the chair, and a shirt lay rumpled in the corner, a pair of suspenders on top of it. Above his bed, he had a horseshoe nailed to the wall. "My mother would murder me if my room ever looked like this," she said quietly, hoping to bring a smile to his lips. "She might go mad seeing this."

Brooks smiled wryly but said nothing.

"Are you still mad?"

"Yes," Brooks breathed. "We all have a right to be a little angry, Eloise. I know you can't help whatever is going on in your head right now. But it doesn't change the fact that it hurts. That I live in fear of losing you. That you could willingly take yourself from me."

His voice cracked, and Eloise felt sick with guilt. Knowing she was breaking every rule, Eloise glanced back at Merritt before stepping inside, taking a seat beside Brooks. "I'm sorry."

"You've already apologized, Elle."

Eloise's fingers toyed with a loose thread in the sleeve of her nightgown, unable to meet his eyes. "Then can you forgive me?"

"Of course I can. Being angry doesn't mean I don't forgive you." He stroked her cheek with his thumb. "I am trying to understand, Elle."

When Eloise said nothing, Brooks closed his eyes and took a deep breath. "I don't want any more secrets," he ground out. "So explain it to me. Let me inside your mind."

Her eyes turned back to his. "Are you sure?" When he nodded, Eloise's lip trembled. "I hate myself," she whispered. "No matter what I do, I can't seem to do it right. I can't walk or talk or breathe or even blink without overthinking it. It's like there is this voice in my head, screaming at me that I'm doing it wrong." She bit her tongue against a curse. "As if you could blink wrong. I know that, yet somehow, in those moments, I can't convince myself of it. All I hear is that voice telling me how stupid I am. How worthless I am. How I don't matter."

Eloise dissolved into tears then. It was not the sort of tears Brooks had grown used to from her but the sort of tears that only someone deprived of any hope could shed. She pitched forward, her arms tight around her middle as though trying to hold herself together.

She is used to this, he thought miserably. His father had spoken of his mother's attacks. The way she cried as though her world had fallen around her, desperate sobs wracking her body.

Brooks felt himself shaking as he slipped his arms around her, bringing her into his lap as he pressed his lips to her hair.

Don't say anything, his father had warned. *Words will do no good. Let it pass.*

"I don't want to feel this way anymore." The words came out stilted and broken as she fought to breathe. "I ... I—"

"Shh." He kissed her wet cheek, tasting her tears on his lips. "Just let it out, darlin'."

Thirty-One

Lily didn't let Eloise out of her sight in the days that followed, limiting Brooks' time with her to meals and the small space between supper and bed. Every night his mind took him back to finding her in that creek. Lips, blue. Hair, wet.

In his sleep, he was haunted by images of finding her too late, and he woke in a cold sweat, unable to keep his tears back.

I don't want to die, Brooks, she had said. *But I scare myself.* Any anger he felt faded when he remembered those words. Spoken so quietly, they were little more than a breath. He couldn't blame her that her mind led her to a different release than his own had. In his family, to drink was no less selfish than to willingly take his life. Yet his family had never viewed his actions as anything less than that of a broken spirit. Not selfish but defeated.

During the day, Brooks distracted himself with the plans for the ranch. With the weather warming, they would begin the work on his land in a matter of weeks. Just as soon as they finished the Rileys' home.

The closer the time came, the louder that old voice in Brooks' head was becoming. In two months' time, he would be moving onto his own land. Into his own home. In time, he would have to hire men and trust them to care for the horses he brought through. Would he be able to trust them to implement his methods and get a horse to obey them out of respect and not fear? Would he have to fight them? Would they damage the ones that needed more time and patience?

Brooks shook his head. Hiring men was years away. But once he got his mind off the ranch and all the future problems he may run into, his mind went to Eloise. They'd been courting near six months now, and he knew with unwavering certainty that he wanted to marry her. Soon. Now. He'd known since the beginning. But one dark thought kept him from going to Morgan to ask for his daughter's hand in marriage: Was he even good enough for someone like Eloise?

Brooks didn't know how to keep her afloat, and he feared his ability for patience. It was too easy to get frustrated. To grow angry when she insisted on staying inside her broken mind. Perhaps she couldn't help it, but even now, he couldn't help but wonder sometimes if she wasn't reluctant to let go. To step forward and see the good that was in her and her life.

"God, I am not capable of this. She deserves more." Only, Brooks wasn't sure he was selfless enough to let her go. Not when he thought about that night in his room. She had stayed in his arms for over an hour, no words spoken, but both gained peace by nothing more than the others' presence. Fighting fresh emotion, Brooks threw his blankets aside and knocked on his parents' door.

Needing no explanation, Merritt nodded and eased the door shut behind him. Pouring them each a mug of coffee, he passed one to Brooks and waited for him to speak.

"I want to marry her, Pa. More than anything, I want to marry her."

"But?" Merritt encouraged.

"Did you ever question whether you were enough for Mama?"

"Every moment since the day I met her, Brooks. It's what kept me from going after her as more than a friend all those months, even when it killed me. It's why she had to defeat her own fears and confess her love first."

Brooks smiled, recalling the words his mother had near shouted at his father after finding out he was leaving the state. He'd heard that story and the words that followed a dozen times, but it never ceased to make him smile. "I love you, you idiot," she'd said.

Merritt laughed. "Your mother's and my relationship was different. I didn't get to know her as anything more than a friend before I married her. We had one short week between friendship and marriage, and I spent every second of that week hating myself. Thinking she needed someone better than me. Someone more patient. Someone who could offer her more security than I could. But I learned she was having the same thoughts about herself." Merritt watched Brooks nod as he sipped his coffee. "I think if we're being honest, we all feel that way, Brooks."

"I've never seen you lose your patience with Mama," Brooks said quietly.

"You're looking at over twenty years of marriage and practice, boy. Your mother and I fought horribly in the beginning. There wasn't a day I didn't lose my patience with her over something." When Brooks raised an eyebrow, Merritt laughed. "You don't have much of a temper either, Brooks. But they bring it out of you sometimes, and that's ok. Your mother understood my frustration. People like her and Eloise don't expect perfect patience, Brooks. Do you think Lily is always patient with her daughter?"

Brooks sighed. "No."

"It's impossible to remain patient every moment with the easiest of people, Brooks." Merritt smiled. "Mabel's always been easy, but as much as you loved her, you two used to fight like cats and dogs. So do you really think you won't lose patience with someone like Ellie at times?"

"Dad, when I found her in the creek, I—" He shook his head. "I could have killed her myself. She can drive me mad at times but that? I have never felt that with her. I shouted at her. I practically screamed at her."

"Because you love her, Brooks," Merritt said quietly. "It's hard not to get angry when you think that the person you love could so easily take themselves from you. It's a reality you live with daily—that you could lose them in a hundred different ways that are all out of our control."

When the tears started, Brooks set his head on his arms. "I should have given her patience."

"You were scared, Brooks, and Eloise understands that." Merritt rubbed his son's back. "Even if it hurt her, she understands it. Son, you're going to lose your patience a dozen times over with that girl. But you would with any woman God placed in your life, and just like you would then, you'll learn how to handle the hardest moments. That's not to say you won't still have days when she drives you mad. Your mother, whether you see it or not, can still make me crazy at times with the things she gets into her head. But it's easier now."

"And the timing?" Brooks asked. "Is marrying her now, when I'm going to be busy with the ranch, the best time to do so?"

"Do you think waiting would be better?" Merritt countered. "For either of you? Do you think you have it in you to wait?"

Brooks laughed softly. "No. I don't think I could." He didn't want to. He struggled to leave her at her door every night to sleep alone, knowing she was only on the other side of his wall. He couldn't imagine leaving her every night to go home to an empty house, and though Eloise never so much as mentioned marriage without his prodding, he knew it was on her mind.

Leaving her was only becoming harder now, and though he understood Lily's possession of her, the time away was only making the wait harder. He wanted to be the one she went to without fear of boundaries being crossed. Without the temptations he knew she felt with him. "But is bringing her into the mess of this not cruel?" he asked. "I'll be traveling. I'll be busy building and—"

"And your mama and I were in the same boat when we got married, Brooks," Merritt interrupted. "You have to remember, we got married in a week with no real idea of where we were going, and it did put stress on the both of us. But I also know that neither one of us would change it. It brought us closer. We love looking back on those memories now." He smiled. "I loved starting my dream with Libby by my side. I loved watching her work beside me as we built this home. Our farm." When Brooks said nothing, Merritt continued. "If Eloise loves you, and I believe she does, she would rather face the stress of it all with you. And who's to say you can't take her with you when you travel? That's the joy of marriage, Brooks: you don't have to leave her."

"And if children happen early?" Brooks asked.

Merritt smiled. "Children make it all the better, Brooks. There's nothing like coming home to your children after a long, hard day. Or watching them toddle along beside you as you work." Squeezing his shoulder, Merritt smiled. "Having a family doesn't have to make it harder, Brooks. With the right attitude, it makes it better."

***

Eloise was beginning to grow cross at her mother's constant eye. She understood it. She didn't question it. But she didn't like it. She wanted her privacy. She wanted her time with Brooks that she knew was limited. The men would be finished with their home in a week, and then when would she see him?

Their land was five miles away from the Harpers, and before too long, Brooks would be on his own land. Another six miles away, and he'd be too busy with his new life to pay her any mind.

Eloise rubbed at her temples. The fears were there, but something in her was shifting. There was a newer desire to try. To not simply survive but to live. She wanted to believe the thoughts that plagued her were lies. She wanted to believe her father loved her. She wanted to believe Brooks spoke the truth when he mentioned marriage and children.

Marriage. Would her mother let her marry? If her mother had her way, Eloise would be chained to her hip, never to know a moment of solitude again. Whether it was Lily's watchful eye on her or someone else's keeping her company during her mother's absence, Eloise was never allowed a moment alone anymore.

"She means well, Ellie," Merritt said to her one afternoon, taking a seat next to her. "It's difficult to see your child hurting themselves."

Eloise's fingers stilled as she wrapped the thread around the needle. "Is this how it was with Brooks?"

Merritt nodded. "Didn't let him out of my sight for a month. He worked with me from sunup to sundown. It drove him mad, but it was for his own good. He admitted later that he would have gone looking for alcohol if he'd been left alone."

"It isn't that she doesn't want me alone," Eloise said quietly. "I don't want to be alone. But I'm not. There's Maisie at night, and the least she could do is let me see Brooks." Her voice cracked, and she hid her face in her knees. The ache was beginning to grow unbearable.

"And she will. It's only been a week, Eloise. She's grieving."

"And Brooks?"

"Brooks will recover, Ellie. But he needs some time to process it. He loves you, and I know what it's like to love someone who thinks the way you do."

Eloise pursed her lips. "I didn't mean to hurt anyone."

"But you think that everyone is better off without you," Merritt said quietly. "I heard the same thing a hundred times over from Elizabeth. No one is blaming you, Eloise. No one is punishing you. Everyone just needs time."

"Do you ever regret it? Do—" She took a shaky breath. "Do you ever wish you had never gotten into it?"

"Does it look like I do?" He smiled. "There hasn't been a day that I regret knowing my Libby. My marrying her. Even in our darker periods, she was my light." Merritt took Eloise's hand. "I know it won't be easy for you two. But I know that you will make it through. So long as you want to."

When Lily came back, she thanked Merritt, avoiding Eloise's eyes. When Merritt was gone, Eloise turned to her mother. "Mama," she said quietly. "Can you at least look at me?"

The moment her mother met her eyes, she felt something in her crack. "You have to let me go, Mama."

"Let you go?" Lily hissed. "Let you go? You have tried to kill yourself twice now, Eloise. I am not letting you go."

"I didn't," Eloise said. "The other night, I thought about it—I almost did it—but I decided on my own not to."

"But you considered it, Eloise." Lily looked back at her daughter. She had never lost her temper with her before. Never shouted. In a matter of days, she and her husband had traded places. Morgan was patient with their daughter. He blamed his actions for her ending up at that creek. But all Lily could see was that her daughter had tried not once but twice to take herself from this world. "You considered it, Eloise, and that is enough."

"I know. But I also fought it." Eloise chewed her lip. "Isn't that enough too? I wanted to do it, but I didn't."

Lily met her daughter's eyes at the small crack in her voice. "And now?"

"I'm not going to do anything, Mama."

Lily shook her head. Something in the way Eloise held herself was different. It wasn't like the last time when she was angry to have failed. She looked determined rather than despondent.

"Can I show you something, Mama?" Reaching into her pocket, Eloise held out her pocket diary. "The last page."

Taking the book, Lily flipped to the last page marked by a ribbon. The handwriting wasn't her daughter's usual, dainty scrawl but messy and rushed and tear-streaked.

"I wrote this that night," Eloise said softly. "After I came back from Brooks' room."

Lily looked back to the poem.

My mind is an ocean—
An ocean of thoughts, of fears, of sorrow.
'Hold on,' they say, 'for help is sure to come.'
But iron bars wrap my ankles, a rope and three thick bricks tied
at the end. My anchor, dragging me under.
I'm losing sight of the shore.
But still, they shout, 'Keep faith. Keep faith. Don't let them drag
you down.'
I tread these waters of my mind, the shore a distant memory now.
My mind is an ocean.
And I am drowning in it.

"What is this supposed to mean, Eloise?" Lily asked. "Is this supposed to make me feel better?"

Eloise's face flushed red. "I suppose not. But I've been rereading it since then, and I started thinking." She tapped the page. "Right there—'keep faith, don't let them drag you down'?" Thick tears rolled down Eloise's cheeks. "Mama, what does it mean to have faith? Because I don't think I know anymore."

Lily countered her question. "What do you think faith is?"

"Healing," Eloise said quietly. "Pastor James said that faith was always the answer. If you had faith, then you should have no pain. Sorrow. Worry. A lack of faith is the root of all misfortune."

"Ellie." Lily sighed. "Your father and I failed you, keeping you in that church."

"But is he wrong?" Eloise asked. "Isn't faith supposed to move mountains?"

"Yes, but it takes more than faith alone. The Lord has to will the mountain to move. Ellie, a lack of faith isn't keeping you where you are. It's what you expect from your faith." It was Lily's turn to tap the page. "You said it right there—hold on. That is faith, Eloise. Faith gives you the strength to keep going. It doesn't heal; God heals. And if you believe that it only takes faith to be healed, you are not only putting yourself above God, but you are calling God a vindictive God who punishes those of imperfect faith."

"Doesn't He?" Eloise asked.

"Did the Lord punish Moses when he feared speaking to the people of Israel?" Lily countered. "Did He punish Elijah when he ran and hid and begged to die? Did he punish Thomas who doubted or Sarah who laughed when the Lord promised her a child?" Lily wiped the tears from her daughter's cheeks. "He didn't, Ellie. He gave Moses a helper. He fed Elijah and then gave him a purpose and a friend. Even through her laughter and continued doubt, He blessed Sarah and Abraham with a son."

"Their faith was still better than mine, Mama."

"Eloise, our God is a loving God. He is not going to withhold healing because you struggle in faith or because you doubt sometimes. You may think your faith is weak, but Ellie, no one else here is thinking that. We all see the way you cling to Christ. You may have moments where you forget who He is, but you never stay there." Lily's lip quivered. "Baby, you got back up. That means something."

"It was God, Mama."

"I know it," Lily whispered. Pulling her daughter to her, Lily kissed her hair. "He's put an entire army behind you, and we've all been praying."

Eloise laughed softly. "I know. Can I go see Brooks, though, Mama?" She hesitated. "It's not that I don't need you, but I need him."

"I know, baby." Lily touched Eloise's cheeks. "You're supposed to want him more. Go."

Kissing her mother's cheek, Eloise hurried out to the barn. She caught Brooks as he was leaving, his arms full. Seeing her come toward him, he set the boxes aside and met her halfway. "Does your mother know you've escaped?" he whispered.

Ignoring his question, Eloise looked at the boxes. "Are you headed back to the house?"

"Your house is almost done, Elle," he said. "We have a few finishing touches, but by the weekend, you guys should be home."

"Home," she whispered. No matter how she tried, she couldn't see it as home. Brooks was her home.

Seeing where her mind had gone, the ring against his neck felt heavy. Now wasn't the time. "I should go, Elle. But we'll spend some time with Juniper tonight. I was thinking she might be ready to start training to ride."

Eloise nodded. "All right. Tonight." Letting him kiss her cheek, she started back toward the house.

"Elle." Turning back, she found Brooks removing something from his jacket. "Dad found it in the field last night. You're lucky it hasn't rained." He pressed Elizabeth's Bible in her hands. "Don't lose it again, huh?" Winking, Brooks lugged the boxes toward the wagon.

Back inside, Eloise hurried upstairs and closed the door behind her. Leaning against it, she slid to the floor, the Bible to her chest. She had thought it was gone forever. "Thank you, Papa." Opening back to the original inscription, she read it again.

Thirty-Two

April

Eloise wasn't ready. Silly though it might have been, knowing Brooks had promised to visit in every spare moment, she couldn't help but fear what felt to her an inevitable abandonment.

No. Fighting back the voice, she focused on the feel of Brooks' arms around her as he lifted her from the wagon and settled her feet on the ground. Having arrived a few moments before the others, he took advantage of the solitude and kept his arm around her waist. "Quit your worrying. Don't you know we still share a horse?"

"Share?" Eloise asked. "What happened to her being mine?"

Brooks smiled and raised his hands. "I've grown a bit attached to her. But yes, she is yours, and I stand by it. Nothing is changing, Elle."

Forcing her lips to turn, she met his dark eyes. "That isn't exactly true. It won't be the same not waking up to you at my door, mugs in hand." She reached up and flicked his hat. "You placing that on my head."

Laughing, Brooks did just that, tipping it up so he could see her face. "If you're willing, I can meet you here bright and early tomorrow, and we can spend the day with Juniper."

Eloise would love that, but she knew it wouldn't work. "You're starting on your house tomorrow."

"Monday," he corrected. "So, if your father is all right with it, I'll come for you tomorrow, and then we'll still have Sunday service at my parents' as well." He kissed her cheek softly. "Maybe time will be limited for now, but it's not changing the way I love you, Elle. I couldn't forget you if I tried."

At the sound of approaching wagons, Brooks stepped away and opened the back of the wagon. "Let's get you and your family unloaded. It's been a long time coming." Seeing her raise an eyebrow, he smiled. "Well, for your parents at least."

Grabbing what she could manage, Eloise followed Brooks inside as the rest of the families piled out of their wagons and began to unload their own haul. While Brooks headed out for another crate, Eloise set her box at the table and let her eyes wander. Though smaller than their home in Huxley, it was a great deal larger than the one-room soddy her parents had been staying in. The cream-colored walls were new and crack-free, unlike the aged walls of her childhood home. It looked like a home, and with all the old things from Huxley that had been stored away for nearly nine months, it would be their home. So why did she miss the Harpers' land?

Unfolding and shaking out the curtains, Eloise kept her mind busy hanging them until Elizabeth came and set a hand to her waist. "Your mother, Maisie, and Anna are going to handle getting everything in order. Why don't you help Mabel and me get supper fixed up?"

Following the women outside, Eloise set to work. "We'll cook over a fire to keep out of everyone's way," Elizabeth told her.

"I hope you like chili," Mabel told her, tossing ingredients into her Dutch oven. "It's Brooks' favorite, and it will be easy to make on the road when you're traveling."

Eloise felt something thaw in her at the words. Brooks hadn't even asked, yet they already saw her as a part of him. She wasn't a piece unwanted but accepted.

Eloise was quiet while Mabel and Elizabeth talked, bringing her in often enough to know she wasn't forgotten. She hadn't found it within her to join without invitation, but then maybe she never would. Even Elizabeth was quiet at the table until someone caught her attention.

You will never be Elizabeth, that voice taunted. Sighing, Eloise turned her face skyward. How she wished she could block herself out the way she could block out others' voices.

Eloise startled at a gentle hand on her shoulder. "What's true, Ellie?" Elizabeth whispered.

"It will get easier," Eloise whispered. "I can reach where you are."

"And you will." Squeezing her arm, Elizabeth went back to her conversation with Mabel, all the more intent on bringing Eloise into it.

The men had finished unloading the wagons, and the women had found a home for most of the crates' belongings by the time the chili was finished.

Dishing up Brooks' bowl, Eloise watched him toy with something at his chest, as he had throughout most of the night. Whatever it was, and she told herself it wasn't what she hoped, she'd caught him handling it often in the last weeks, but now it was a constant. She didn't want to hope. Hope had always been an anchor at her feet. But despite it all, it was growing.

"Thank you, darlin." Kissing her cheek, Brooks promised to save her a seat. As he took his seat, Eloise could see him pawing at his chest, holding tight to what rested there.

A war was beginning to rage within her. A battle between her old desire to shut out hope and the new desire to hold onto that hope in faith.

Battle still raging, she took her place next to him and kept her mind on the present and the promise that whether the question was tonight or a year from now, Brooks was hers.

***

Brooks continued to toy with the front of his shirt throughout the next day. Through the breakfast Lily demanded he sit for. Through the five-mile drive to the Harper property. Leaving Eloise in charge of preparing Juniper, he sat back and watched, his fingers at his chest. Each time she caught his eye, a strange red would fill his cheeks, and he'd turn, his fingers still toying at his chest.

She wanted to demand he tell her what was on his mind. His nerves were getting to hers, and his fidgeting only made hers worse. But she bit her tongue. Whatever it was, he'd get to it when he was ready.

"Any chance I'll be riding her soon?" she asked as she set Juniper loose in the paddock.

"Not a chance," Brooks told her. "I want you starting out on one of mine first. Older. Smaller. Less touchy."

"And then?"

"And then we'll go from there," Brooks answered. "It all depends on how she rides with me, Elle." Hand going back to his chest, he smiled at her. "I'd like to keep you around."

"Well, you do think she'll get there, don't you?" Eloise asked, her eyes on his hand. Despite the smile, there was something else in his tone. Something was eating at him.

"Without a doubt, Elle. So long as we don't give up."

The slight catch to his voice didn't go unnoticed. Was that what kept him from moving forward? Moving toward him, she set her arms around his neck. "I'm not giving up, Brooks."

"Neither am I," Brooks whispered. His head dropped to hers. "I need you to fight for me, Elle."

Unsure of herself, she took his face in her hands, her thumbs caressing his rough cheek. "I'm sorry," she said softly, "that I've caused this in you."

New tears filled his eyes. "Don't be sorry, Elle. Just fight."

"I'm fighting, Brooks." Setting her forehead to his chest, Eloise felt the shape of the ring that rested there. "I'm afraid you're stuck with me."

Thirty-Three

Brooks felt the empty spot next to him as they settled into dinner. Their first without the Rileys in over six months. Maybe this itself was normal. It was certainly what his relationship with Eloise would have looked like under different circumstances, but he'd been spoiled having her so close for so long and having her gone now left something in him feeling incomplete.

The dinner was quiet as everyone felt that hole. They'd become used to a table that was loud as everyone talked over the other. Merritt and Morgan trading jokes, not all of which were appropriate. Lily admonishing her husband with red cheeks, and Maisie asking what they meant.

He missed Eloise's fingers gripping his when she began to grow overwhelmed at the noise. Her silent plea for his distraction.

When dinner had finished, Brooks avoided the barn. It felt empty without her.

"It's only temporary, Brooks," Elizabeth said quietly. "It only has to be as long as you make it now."

"I know it," Brooks said. "I'm just giving her a bit more time. She's been more vulnerable lately, and I want to make sure she feels up to it."

Elizabeth raised an eyebrow. "Brooks, your father did the same thing to me, and it left me to have to take the step. We're not as vulnerable as you like to think, and if you try to wait until you think she's ready, that time might never come." When Brooks said nothing, Elizabeth continued. "Has she ever mentioned the desire for marriage? Without you bringing it up first?

"A few times," he admitted. "I think she's embarrassed."

"Probably, but she has brought it up around Lily and me, Brooks. She wants it. She's ready. But it's up to you to take that step." Elizabeth smiled. "You are enough for her, Brooks. Everyone but you can see that. Morgan said just last night he was waiting for you to ask. He's never seen her happier than she is when she's with you."

When Brooks went to his room that night, he paced his room until Merritt banged on his door for the third time, yelling at him to get some rest.

"You're keeping the whole house awake," he had said, softening at the sight of Brooks. "You know what you're going to do, Brooks. There's no need to make it so difficult." Mussing the boy's hair, Merritt warned him once more to get into bed before he sent him to sleep in the barn.

Settling into bed, Brooks watched the light rain that fell outside and wondered if Eloise was doing the same. He'd found her almost nightly sitting in his mother's sitting room long after the rest of the house slept. Watching the snow fall. Embroidering with the window cracked open.

The thought of her now, window open despite the rain, made him smile. He knew she would be reading the Bible if she was awake. It had become all she did in the short week since he'd given it back to her. He couldn't say she seemed happier. She still remained deep in her head. But there was a new determination in her eyes. He'd seen it settling in her as they spoke that night. *I don't want to die. But I scare myself.*

I don't want to drink. He'd spoken those words to his mother weeks after Annabelle had found him. *But I'm tired of feeling.*

Like Eloise, he'd been reading the Bible. He'd been praying, and he knew the Bible spoke truth. He didn't simply know it anymore, but he believed it. So why was he still struggling? Why was the loathing he felt for himself still so strong?

"Because whatever some might say, Brooks," Elizabeth had said, "it takes more than faith to battle those thoughts. I have faith. I know the Lord is good. I know He's with me and loves me. Those things give me what I need to keep going. They give me hope. But they don't rid me of the very things that make me need them."

"So what does?" Brooks asked.

"Not giving them what they want," she said simply. "The enemy wants you to sin. He wants your misery. So he will use those broken parts of your mind to lead you to it. See, that's where the sin comes in, baby. Not because you struggle. Not because you desire to rely on other things to numb it. It's when you accept that your struggle is your struggle, so what can you do but let it win? When you let it win, you let it lead you to sin."

Standing now, Brooks eased the window open, allowing fresh air and the smell of petrichor to drift in as he remembered his mother's final words that night.

"I don't know why, Brooks, but there is something broken in you and me. Something that doesn't work quite right. It might always be a bit harder for us to keep going. To trust. But that doesn't make us any less worthy of Him. Any less faithful. I am confident that my faith is just as strong as your father's. It just takes a bit more work."

Was Eloise where he was that night? Dependent on the Lord, but still blaming herself for what was out of her control? If she was, where did he want to be for her? Five miles away, unknowing of when and how she struggled or did he want to be beside her?

"But, Papa, it's up to you," Brooks said softly. "What do you want me to do?"

In the following silence, he felt peace wash over him as a life with Eloise flashed before him. No more goodbyes. Holding her at night when those thoughts attacked her hardest.

"All right, God," he said softly. "I understand."

***

The next morning Brooks wasted no time getting ready and heading toward the Rileys' land. Eloise was a late riser most days and, if he made it early, he would have plenty of time with Morgan before she woke.

It wasn't until he'd reached their land that he remembered it was Sunday. They'd be up, headed to his parents' in a few hours —them along with half a dozen other families from town, all ready to hear Merritt speak. There wouldn't be a moment in the day for him to get Eloise alone, let alone Morgan, and Brooks knew the enemy would place doubts about what the Lord had promised. He had tried all night until finally, Brooks gave up on the idea of sleep and spent time in the Word. Every time he doubted, he found himself facing another image: Eloise with him on the long trips that had nearly done him in on his own. Children to come home to and teach to work the land and train and ride horses.

Morgan clapped him on the shoulder as he welcomed him inside. "Hoping to drive Ellie to your place? I'm afraid she's still sleeping." He offered Brooks a seat at the table, where Lily set a plate in front of him.

"I actually wasn't here for Elle. Not like that anyway." Brooks tried to sound sure of himself and cringed at the way his voice cracked. *You've already got his blessing,* he reminded himself. *You just have to ask.*

Eyes widening, Lily excused herself.

"We've been expecting you to come for a while." Morgan laughed. "Lily's been a bit of a mess over it." He patted Brooks' shoulder. "Breathe easy, boy. You've already got my blessing, and Lily's too if that means something to you."

When Brooks blanched, Morgan laughed again. "I know I put up a fight in the beginning. But you've gone and proven me wrong. You've been good to her, Brooks. Sometimes I don't even recognize her." After a moment, he shook his head. "That's not true. I've begun to see more of who she was before."

Brooks smiled. "Good. I've loved seeing her step out more."

"Just you wait till she's real comfortable. That girl can be something else."

"Thank you, Morgan. For giving me the chance to."

Morgan nodded. "You're just what Lily and I have been praying God would give Eloise. I'm just sorry it took me so long to see it."

"She's your daughter, Morgan," Brooks said. "I never questioned you. Only prayed I'd be able to calm your nerves."

"No, but I could have handled it better. I think I was twisting it all up with what we've dealt with in the past."

Brooks watched the man play with his food. "She's been hurt," he said. "It's understandable that you might be hesitant."

Morgan shook his head. "It's not just that, Brooks. I pushed her to do so much in her life, thinking if she just kept going, it would get easier for her. She'd come out of her shell and be happier for it. Only that didn't happen." He ran a hand over his face, putting pressure to his eyes. "She got worse. Sank in deeper. Hated herself more. I encouraged her to keep seeing those so-called friends even when she expressed something didn't feel right."

"And you didn't want to push her again," Brooks said quietly.

"I couldn't." Morgan sighed. "I know you have seen darkness from her, Brooks, and I can imagine what it must have been for you to find her in that creek. But whatever you might think, you haven't seen her at her darkest. Not like Lily and I have. There have been moments in her life where she terrified us." Though Brooks could see the effort to keep them back, tears blurred Morgan's eyes. "I had to breathe life back into that girl, Brooks. My girl. All because a couple of girls decided she wasn't worth the effort. Because I had pushed her one too many times." He let out a small sob.

Brooks squeezed the man's shoulder in comfort. "That isn't your fault, Morgan. It had to have been more than a few girls. I think these last few weeks have shown that anything can pull her under."

When he had gained control, Morgan shook his head. "I knew I wouldn't be pushing her with you. It was obvious there was something between the two of you. But you have to understand

I've seen her hurt a dozen times over, and I knew that this sort of relationship would push her in ways she hadn't been."

"But she was pushed on her own terms," Brooks said softly. "In areas that gave her something."

"And I should've known." Morgan had faced his own problems before Lily, and it was her loving him that had changed him. "She needs you, Brooks. You know how to push her gently. I never could do that."

***

Eloise had never seen Brooks so nervous. His knee bounced restlessly, and when he smiled at her, it wasn't his usual, crooked smile.

She had woken to her mother's hand on her cheek, telling her they were going to have Sunday service on Brooks' land, and he wanted to drive her.

Though she tried her best, Lily's lips had quivered, and her hands shook as she'd helped Eloise get ready, insisting she wear her nicest dress. Why? Eloise had ideas, and she didn't want to indulge them.

Because you know it isn't what you think, that voice taunted.

Of course it wasn't. Brooks would be busy building his ranch. He wouldn't have time to invite her into that. Would he?

God, take this hope from me. If that is his plan, let it be a surprise, but I can't be disappointed. Not like that. Please, Papa.

When they reached the land, Brooks hopped to the ground and helped her down with clammy hands. "Are you all right?" she asked.

Brooks nodded before pointing west. "We'll be building in the next few days, and I need to figure out the layout of the house."

Hand in his, Eloise followed after him. "You're wanting it here?"

"Do you like it here?" he asked.

She nodded. It was perfect, nestled at the base of the mountain. "It would be beautiful," she said quietly. "And you said you wanted a garden over there?"

Brooks nodded. "I think so. I was hoping to get your opinion on all of it."

"My opinion?" She watched him fiddle with the ring at his neck. "Now?"

"Now's as good a time as any. We have some time before the others get here."

The man was beginning to sweat. Stepping around him, she looked over the space. "Do you know how big you're wanting?" she asked. "A cabin? A house?"

"Nothing too big," Brooks said. "Most of what I have needs to go toward the barn and horses. But I was thinking one-story, two bedrooms? Children can always share, and if need be, we can add on in the future."

Eloise felt a flutter in her stomach at the mention of children, and that hope built within her. Squashing it down, she nodded. "The door there," she said quietly. "You can see everything from here, so a nice porch would be a good idea. You'll be able to see your workers from home. Your children when you're working." Emotion was building in her now. Hope was cruel, and yet she wanted nothing more than to lean into it as she pictured their children running across the yard. "Over here, you could put the bedroom."

As she spoke, Brooks heard her voice crack. "I-I would want the children's room next door," she whispered. "So we could hear them."

We. It was the first time she'd admitted to seeing them together.

"Elle," he breathed. She turned to face him, tears blurring her dark eyes. "Come here." When she obeyed, he pressed his forehead to hers. "Why are you crying, Elle? Do you truly think I'm simply teasing you?"

She laughed. "No." Her hands went to his chest, pinching the ring between her fingers. "But you've had that for weeks. I haven't been oblivious to your messing with it."

"I wanted the time to be right."

Leaning back, Eloise smiled. "And is the time right now?" she whispered.

Brooks' lip quirked. "I don't know," he said softly. "I might need a few more days to think on it."

She smacked his chest lightly. "Brooks."

Laughing, Brooks kneeled. "Eloise Anne Riley, would you do me the incredible honor of becoming my wife?"

Unable to speak now, Eloise nodded.

Thirty-Four

The twenty-year-old fabric of Lily's dress was soft and supple as they pulled it from the chest. They'd searched all day, growing increasingly worried the dress might have been in one of the chests lost to the river.

The moment they'd found it, Eloise watched her mother sink to her knees, her fingers running over the yellowed chiffon. She'd grown increasingly miserable as their search yielded no results. After a moment, she buried her face in it, her shoulders shaking.

Kneeling beside her, Eloise rubbed circles on her back. "Are you sure you want me to wear it, Mama?"

"Yes," Lily croaked. "Of course I do. It just brings back memories."

It brought back more than memories, Eloise knew. Though her parents no longer fought, they seemed more cordial than in love. When one wasn't looking, she saw the other watching with so much pain she nearly hated herself for what she was feeling with Brooks.

Lily wiped at her tears, only to have more spill as she helped her daughter step into the dress, suddenly looking much too old for her liking. "Do you remember when you found this in my chest?" she whispered.

"A little," Eloise said softly. "It's a bit of a haze."

Of course it would be. Eloise had been four when she begged to put it on. Though she swam in the dress, the girl's young smile had never been brighter as Lily held up the small mirror. "Will I be able to wear it when I get married, Mama?" she had asked in that chipmunk voice that Lily longed to hear now. That little voice from a little girl who knew nothing of the harsh realities of life.

Buttoning up the dress, Lily reminded herself that from harsh realities would come deeper joy. She tucked that reminder in her heart. Both for her daughter and her own crumbling marriage.

Finishing with the buttons, Lily pinched at the small bit of fabric that would need to be cut away. Though a few years older than Lily had been, the dress was still half a size too big on Eloise. "You're so tiny. I was barely fifteen when Nanny made this for me."

"I've even put on weight." Eloise sighed. She'd noticed it in her skirt waist.

"Being happy will do that to you." Lily smiled. "Don't be so concerned, Ellie. It will take no time at all to take it in."

"I don't want you to have to alter it, Mama. Everyone is already doing too much." The men, including a dozen men from town, were working day and night to get their home built in time. The women were busying themselves with putting together blankets and anything else they might need. Then there was Brooks, who was spending more money than she was comfortable with to provide for their needs. He had placed a large order of goods through Annabelle to fill their home, including a stove he refused to hear she didn't need, no matter how much she insisted she had been used to cooking over a fire back in Huxley.

"I could see how much you enjoyed cooking over a stove, Elle," he had insisted. Setting his forehead to hers, he had sighed. "The moment we're married, it's my duty to provide for you and your needs. That means buying food goods and fabrics for clothing and thread for your embroidery—yes, that too." He had laughed when she opened her mouth, ready to object. "You'll have to stop seeing it as my money, darlin'. My providing for you includes a few simple pleasures in life."

Even still, the weight was growing steadily heavier as she watched everyone work so hard at her expense.

"It isn't all for you, Ellie. Neither you nor Brooks wanted to wait longer, and everyone is more than willing to work a little harder. We love you two. We're excited." Inserting the last pin, Lily eased the dress over Eloise's head. "You and I have been dreaming of you in this dress since you were just a girl. So stop your worrying and get dressed."

Doing as she was told, Eloise stepped into her newly let out skirts. She finished the last button on her shirt at the same moment a knock came at their door.

While her mother went to stir the stew, Eloise removed the bar from the door and let in her father. He ruffled her hair before stepping inside. "Got a surprise outside for you." He chuckled.

Glancing around her father, she saw Brooks tying his horse. When she met him, he smiled. "Your father invited me for dinner."

She *hmmed* as he pulled her to him, her arms going around his neck as he pressed his lips to her forehead. "Did you get a lot done today?"

"We got the framing up. I'll take you down after dinner to see the progress." Slipping his hand into hers, he led her toward the house. "Did your mother find her dress?"

"Yes. It'll have to be taken in a bit, but we should get it done in time."

They discussed the wedding further as they ate. It was going to be small with no one but their families. Archer would officiate the ceremony.

"Have you decided on where you'll go after?" Morgan asked. "Your father said there's a town about a two-day journey from here."

"Tuffin," Brooks said. "But Eloise and I agreed we'd stay home. We can't spend too much money with building up the ranch, and neither of us is willing to borrow. But I promised we'd take advantage of a trip I had planned for July, and it will be better than Tuffin."

"Well, you'll be just as happy at home," Lily said. "Morgan and I didn't get away either. The old man who ran the mill wouldn't give him the time."

"He gave us the wedding." Morgan laughed. "Still expected me bright and early the next morning. We made it up in the future." He nudged Lily. "Maybe you and I can plan a trip to Tuffin."

"Maybe," Lily whispered. Taking everyone's bowls, she turned quickly, her face hidden behind her hair.

Following after her, Eloise grabbed the soap and rag. With the door closed, Eloise spoke. "Mama, maybe a trip would be good for you two. You haven't been on a trip since I was six."

"For good reason." Lily sighed.

"Yes, but that reason is void now. Isn't it? I won't be here. You won't be leaving me behind. You won't be leaving me alone. You have no excuse now to—"

"Eloise, leave your father and me be," Lily snapped. Taking the rag and soap, Lily scrubbed the bowls. "None of that is your business."

Eloise glared back at her, eyes burning. "Fine," she breathed. "I just wanted to see the two of you happy. It seems to be a bit of my business when it was me who kept you from ever going away again." It was her actions that had further torn them. Feelings hurt, Eloise spoke the words she'd been too hesitant before. "And Daddy is trying. With both of us. You're one the pushing him away now." Turning on her heels, she started toward the house.

"Eloise." Expecting a reprimand, Eloise turned slowly. But rather than find her mother angry, fresh tears rolled down her cheeks. "I know he's trying, Ellie. But I am trying too, and it is not your fault that your father and I have found our marriage where it is now."

Eloise didn't believe that for a moment, but she kept quiet. If her mother wanted to deny it, then let her. "So go away with him, Mama," she said quietly. "My fault or not, maybe when I'm married, and it's just the two of you again, maybe things will get better between you."

"Maybe, Ellie." Standing, Lily kissed Eloise's cheek. "But don't you go worrying over all of it. I love your daddy, you understand? We're just in a rut. Now go enjoy your love."

Obeying, Eloise squeezed her mother's hand before going back inside. When Brooks pulled himself up behind her, he slipped an arm around her waist before urging the horse forward. "Your parents will be fine, Elle. You can't let their problems steal your joy."

"But it's my fault, Brooks. You've heard them fight. It's always about me."

"No, Eloise. It wasn't. We all heard plenty that wasn't about or caused by you. They are two very different people living life together. They are going to fight."

"It shouldn't be like that. I've never heard your parents fight at all, let alone like that." The most she'd heard from Elizabeth and Merritt were little arguments that were resolved quickly and easily. "I don't want that to be us someday," she whispered.

"It won't, Elle." Turning her chin, he leaned to see her eyes. "We'll promise right now never to let our problems pull us so far apart."

"Aren't we supposed to save those promises for our wedding?"

"Don't see how they'll mean any more then than now," Brooks said. His lips brushed hers lightly. "I promise you, Elle. I will always fight for you."

Until that time came. Don't listen to it. Don't trust it.

Ignoring the voice, Eloise kissed him back. "I promise I'll fight for you," she breathed.

***

The day of the wedding came quickly. The finishing touches on their home came only two days before. The eve of their wedding day was spent moving their belongings in, hanging curtains, and making beds.

Eloise's heart beat painfully as she tucked the sheets of what would be their bed. *Their bed.* The idea brought a mixture of excitement and fear that made her stomach roll.

Focus on truth, she reminded herself. But the prospect of what lay ahead was too big, too prominent to be ignored. Would she be able to give him what he deserved—well-cooked meals, a clean home, and children? And what of this bed? Would she be able to be a wife who fully gave her husband what he deserved?

An arm around her waist released the air stuck in her throat, and she took a deep breath. Resting her head against Brooks' chest, she focused on the peace of his presence. The comforting strength of his arm around her waist. "Don't let anything ruin this for you, Elle," he whispered. "It isn't just about me. I want you to experience everything with me."

Eloise laughed tearfully. "How do you always seem to know what I'm thinking?"

Brooks chuckled. "I love you, and I know you." He kissed her cheek. "And you will be more than enough for me, Eloise. I can only pray I'm enough for you."

She turned to face him. "Are you worrying too?"

"You aren't alone, Elle. You would know that if you didn't hide so much."

Wrapping her arms around his neck, she kissed him lightly.

Always aware, Brooks smiled against her lips. "Maybe we should go."

With the rest of the house ready, their families stood around the wagons, talking as Brooks and Eloise came out. Reluctant to separate, Brooks tried to convince Morgan to let him drive Eloise home.

Morgan laughed as he tossed Eloise into the wagon. "She's all yours tomorrow, Harper. Let us enjoy our last night with her." But he had the grace to look away as they said goodbye. Leaning against the wagon, Brooks caressed her cheek with his thumb. "I know it's going to be hard tonight, Elle. But try not to drown for me, huh?"

"I'll do my best." Eloise watched him with the sudden realization that it was the last time she would see him before she walked down the aisle. All of this man would forever be hers tomorrow, and she would focus on that for every moment the waves tried to pull her under that night.

Thirty-Five

May

Eloise kept her eyes closed when she felt herself pulled from sleep, certain that the moment she opened her eyes the dream that was yesterday would fade away. Eyes still closed, she rolled over, her fingers searching tentatively for Brooks. Finding his side of the bed cold, she rubbed the sleep from her eyes before looking around the room.

In the quiet, she heard him whistling through the door. Tossing the blankets aside, she grabbed a nightgown from her bag. In the kitchen, she found Brooks standing with his back to her in a pair of blue long johns. When he remained oblivious to her, she cleared her throat. "What are you doing?" Her lips twitched when he jumped.

"Geez, Elle. I thought you'd be sleeping a bit longer." Moving to her, he hesitated a moment before touching her waist. "Are you okay?"

Eloise laughed softly. "Yes, Brooks." It wasn't the first time he'd asked since last night. She looked over the small counter where two plates sat with eggs, toast, bacon, and potatoes. "You know how to cook?"

Brooks' face flushed red. "Well, I, uh, I know how to make breakfast. I asked Mama to teach me." Taking her by the waist, he brought her to him. "I was hoping to bring you breakfast in bed."

"Do you want me to go back in and act surprised?"

"If you wouldn't mind." Turning her around, he patted her backside. "I'll be in in a moment."

Brooks' cheeks were red as he carried in the plates. Taking the plate he offered, Eloise settled into his side. "I'm sure it will be good, love." And if it wasn't, she had no intention of telling him.

As they ate, Brooks spoke of the plans for the morning. "We don't have to stay up there if you don't want. But I thought we could spend the night up at the lake. Hike the mountain to watch the sunset."

"We can stay the night," Eloise said softly. "It will be fun."

"You sure?" Brooks asked. "I don't have a tent, and I know staying out in the open can be a bit unsettling for some. Mabel never got used to trips like that. We all liked sleeping under the stars, but my father always had to pitch a tent for her."

"I like camping, Brooks," Eloise insisted. "Daddy used to take me all the time, and we never used a tent."

Brooks smiled. "Good. Then we'll head out after breakfast."

Eloise took care of the dishes while Brooks readied the horses. Finding a basket, she packed enough food to last for days in the chance they chose to stay longer. Folding an extra dress and pair of shirts and pants for Brooks, she set them on the bed before adding blankets. Looking around the spare room, she tried to remember everything her mother had always packed for her trips with her father. She'd never been in charge of preparing for anything. She'd merely done whatever task was given to her.

She looked back over what she had. Nightgowns. Long johns. Coats. Trusting Brooks to take care of the lanterns and kerosene, she quickly packed everything into their bag and met him in the main room. "I hope I have everything."

"I'm sure you do, Elle, and it's not too far if you did forget something. I can always ride back." Taking what she'd gathered, he strapped the bag to a horse before helping her onto his own horse.

It was long after lunch by the time they reached the lake. Dismounting, Brooks unloaded supplies while Eloise laid out their lunch. Sitting next to her, Brooks took in the food. "You packed for a week, Elle."

She shrugged. "It's a honeymoon, is it not? And your birthday is tomorrow. I thought maybe we could stay a few days." Morgan had stopped taking her camping a few summers after Alma, and she missed it. She missed the stars.

"And head back when the food runs out?" Brooks smiled. Bringing her to him, he tipped her chin. "Sounds good to me."

The week passed in a blur of lazy mornings, afternoon swims in the lake, and nightly hikes to the clifftop, where they picnicked and watched the sunset.

On their last night, Brooks sat behind her and pulled her to him, a leg on either side as they watched the sun begin to dip below the mountains.

Settling against his chest, Eloise soaked in the final hours before their return to reality. "I'm not ready to go back," she said quietly.

Brooks chuckled in her ear. "Me either. But we can always come back, darlin'. Just say the word, and I'll whisk you away."

Eloise chewed her lip while Brooks toyed with a strand of her hair. She knew it was stupid to worry now. Nothing would change between them when they went home. But even still, it wouldn't be as it was now.

"What are you thinking about?" Brooks asked.

She was quiet a moment, her eyes closing when Brooks kissed her neck. "How afraid I am," she said.

"Afraid of what?"

"Of how happy I am and knowing it won't last." Eloise sighed as Brooks' lips stilled on her neck. "I'm sorry," she said quietly. "I don't mean to ruin this."

"You aren't ruining anything, my darlin'." Repositioning himself, he touched her face. "I have those fears for you. But Elle, this particular moment of happiness can't last. That's life. There will always be moments like this with hard moments in between. You have to change that mindset, honey. You're happy now. So enjoy the good while it's here instead of missing it by worrying about the bad that may or may not come."

"I'm trying."

"I know." Brooks kissed her nose. "I can see it, Elle, but I don't want you to be afraid of talking about it when you do struggle." His eyes went back to the view, where the sun was sinking below the horizon. "Do you want to go back to camp?"

"No." Resting back against him, she settled his arms over her shoulders. "Let's enjoy this a little longer."

Brooks set his chin on her head. "We can all night, darlin'."

***

311

Eloise felt the lingering sadness fall away as they neared their land. Their week by the lake had been a fairytale she didn't want to forget. But this was home—their home where they would start their life. Raise children, if they were so lucky.

By the time Brooks helped her down from the horse, she was excited to unpack. Letting Brooks tend to the horses, Eloise took their belongings inside, putting away their leftover food supplies before dropping their clothing and blankets at the bedroom door. Stripping their bed of its sheets, she tossed them in the pile of laundry and replaced them.

With that done, she took their used clothing and bedding and carried them outside to scrub clean.

Brooks found her as she hung the last sheet to dry. "They finished the barn while we were gone," he explained. "I was thinking I might go and pick up the rest of the horses. Did you want to come?"

Eloise glanced down at her dirt-soiled dress. There was dirt under her nails. Twigs were still caught up in her hair, and her skin was beginning to itch.

Looking himself over, Brooks laughed. "Maybe we should get cleaned up first?"

Eloise tossed the laundry water while Brooks fetched fresh water.

"You go first," Brooks insisted, tossing in the last bucket of warm water.

Eloise's heart pounded as she slid into the tub. It was larger than what she was used to. Brooks had withheld no expense where goods were concerned. He'd wanted her comfortable. But as she settled into the water, she was too aware of the space. The ease with which she could slip under the surface.

"No," she whispered.

Why? Why was that thought there? Why now, when she was happy and content?

But you know it won't last, that voice crooned. *Why wait for it to fall apart? Take what you've been given, and go before you get hurt.*

The waters were rising now, filling her throat. Clinging to the sides of the tub, she tried to focus on truth. She wouldn't sink beneath the surface, whether in her head or in that tub.

Call him, a small voice whispered.

Eloise shook her head. She couldn't let Brooks see her like this—wet and bedraggled and broken.

Call Brooks, beloved.

"Brooks." It was little more than a breath around the water choking her, and in the silence, she felt the panic within her rise. "Brooks," she shrieked.

Eloise heard the door crash open behind her. "Eloise?" Seeing her knuckles white with the force of which she gripped the tub, Brooks kneeled next to her and pried her fingers off the edge. Curling his fingers through hers, he spoke softly. "What is it, love?"

She shook her head. "Don't leave me alone," she whispered. "Please?"

Understanding, Brooks sat fully and crossed his legs. "I'm not going anywhere," he murmured. "Just breathe, darlin'."

"I don't know why," she cried. "I don't understand."

Brooks was silent a moment before speaking softly. "I'm afraid you have given Satan an all too easy route into your head, Elle." When she looked at him, he stroked her cheek. "That isn't me blaming you, honey. It's stating the fact that of all the ways you could have taken your life, you chose a bath. The one thing you have no choice but to face regularly."

"I didn't feel it at all when we were in the lake," she whispered.

"No. But you might have if you were alone. Or maybe it's just the tub. I don't know, Elle. But we'll keep fighting, and someday you'll beat this. Until then" —he gripped her hand tighter, bringing it to his lips— "I'll be right here with you."

Eloise was quiet for a moment. "Do you ever want to die?"

"Not-not now," Brooks said quietly. "But I used to."

Eloise nodded. "I was just six years old the first time I thought about it. Not like I wanted to die, but just that life seemed so long. But after a time, I did beg God to let me die. Every night when I went to bed, I would beg Him to end it so I wouldn't have to go to school or church. When I woke up, I would break because I was still here, and I knew I couldn't do it myself. So I started daydreaming about it—all the ways I could take my life. But I never did it." When she caught his eye, she blushed and apologized.

"Don't apologize, Elle. I want to know all of you. Not the just the good pieces."

"I wasn't planning to do it that day. I was just tired, and I wanted a bath. But ... I don't know why, but that's always been when the thoughts came the most. I was alone, and water seemed the easiest way to do it. The least scary." She shrugged. "My parents tried to keep it hidden. Called it an accident. But people found out anyway, or at least they suspected." Brooks watched Eloise's fingers move through the water. "I don't mean to hurt people. But I feel like I can't do anything right."

"Living is right, Eloise." Brooks considered his words. "I know it doesn't feel like it, and I know it's about more than me and your parents and everyone who would be affected, but if what is leading you to that decision is believing that your presence is hurting us? You need to understand that your death would be so much more, Elle." His eyes met hers. "My darlin', you have gone and made yourself a home in me, and sometimes that home feels like hell. But losing you wouldn't remove you from my heart, and I would rather face that hell with you by my side than without."

"I don't want to leave you," Eloise whispered. "But I'm afraid I could."

Brooks chewed his lips as he worked to staunch his own emotion. When he could trust himself, he spoke softly. "Maybe it's time to stop fighting them." When she glanced up at him, he laughed humorlessly. "I don't mean give up, darlin'." Encouraging her to relax, Brooks set his head on her shoulder. "Have you ever swam in a river, Elle?" When she shook her head, he continued. "Well, I have. My parents used to take us down to the river every Sunday during summer, and Dad would teach each of us how to swim in case we ever fell in the water. The thing about currents, Elle, is not to fight them. If you find yourself caught up in one, your safest way out is to stay calm and go with it." He squeezed her hand. "I know what you're feeling, darlin', and I know that fighting those feelings only makes it worse. It leads you to harm yourself. It led me to drink."

"I don't want to go with it, Brooks. I want it to stop."

"Is fighting it your way making it stop?" Brooks demanded.

"No." She sighed.

"Then would you please listen to me? I don't mean to accept it, Elle. I am simply saying don't fight against it. When you find yourself in that current, turn your eyes to God calmly. Don't beg Him. It's like a river, Elle. If you swim against the current, you could die. But if you let it carry you and swim to the side, slowly and calmly, you can make it.

"What if it's not a current?" she asked. "What if it's waves pummeling you? Dragging you under?"

"Swim with them. Not against them," he repeated. "No matter what the circumstance, fighting against something that strong is almost always a bad idea, Elle."

"So just stop fighting?"

Brooks was quiet a moment. "No, you're still fighting. You should always fight, Elle. But it's all about how you fight. Sometimes the best fight is refusing to acknowledge the opponent."

"Is that what you do?" Eloise whispered.

"It is. With my own head. With desire for drink. It took time, Elle, and I failed a hundred times over. But eventually, it got easier, and the easier it got, the less I found myself attacked or desiring a drink."

Eloise considered him a moment. "Fight my instincts. Not the waves?"

"Exactly," Brooks whispered. "Remember you're going to fail at first, but the key is not giving up. Come to your mother or me. It doesn't matter who, so long as you find someone when you sink."

Thirty-Six

Before Brooks could offer Eloise a hand down, Lily was out of the house and pulling Eloise from her wagon seat. "Oh, I missed you, sweet girl."

Eloise laughed softly. "I missed you too, Mama."

Brooks welcomed Lily's hug before stepping back. "Mama might be over in the next few minutes. My father and I are going to be transporting the horses back to my place, and I thought Elle would be less bored with the two of you."

"Of course," Lily said. "Tell your mother we'll be waiting for her and Maisie."

When Brooks was gone, Lily guided Eloise inside. "Is Daddy at the mill?"

Lily nodded as she got the water boiling on the stove. "He got a few boys in town to work for him. They've already got three different families making orders. It's why they went ahead and built your barn. Your daddy wanted to get to the others as soon as possible."

"I was wondering. Brooks said the barn wouldn't be done for a few more weeks."

Lily glanced back. "Did you two decide to go away after all? They were going to get your permission to build, but Merritt said there wasn't a sign of life at your place all week."

Eloise told her about their week at the lake. "It was originally only going to be one night, but it seemed silly not to stay as long as we could. We got back yesterday."

Lily smiled at the wistfulness in her daughter's voice. "I'm glad. You two would have been happy at home, but it's not the same as getting away."

"I already wish we could go back," Eloise said softly. "The world stayed away while we were gone."

"The world would have found you eventually, Ellie. But you will love your daily life with Brooks just as much as that dreamlike one."

Eloise was quiet a moment, considering whether to tell her mother what had happened the night before. "I thought that because I was happy—because I want to live for Brooks—that I would be ok now," she said quietly. "I thought that I could take a bath on my own and not struggle with those thoughts." Avoiding Lily's eyes, she told her of the previous night in the tub. "I don't want to die," she whispered. "But living like this? I'm tired, Mama. Even when I'm happy, when I have every reason to live, I still don't feel hopeful."

Because you know this joy is just temporary. There will always be more pain. Mama and Nanny struggled to have children. Even Elizabeth couldn't have children easily. Children get sick. Husbands die.

Swim with the waves.

The advice wasn't much different than Elizabeth's words. *When a thought plagues you, acknowledge it, let yourself feel it, and then move on.* It was all about staying calm. Something easier said than done. But still, she didn't know whether it was the fairytale week with Brooks or the comparison to the waters that filled her, but something in her had shifted, just as it had that night by the creek. "It can be scary, Mama."

Lily touched her daughter's face. "I know, baby. Just keep fighting. That's twice now that you've had the courage to say no. Hold onto that. Keep growing closer to God. It might not take these fears away, but it will make them easier. Trust me."

Eloise nodded. "I'm fighting, Mama, and I'll keep fighting."

When Elizabeth and Maisie arrived, Eloise was pulled into a tight hug by Elizabeth. "I've never seen Brooks so happy," she told her. "And to think he thought he'd never marry."

Eloise laughed with her as she pulled out a chair for her mother-in-law. "I don't know what he planned to do for food," she said. "The man makes a decent enough breakfast, but he's near useless with anything else."

"He gets it from his father. Merritt's been banned from the kitchen since our first week in our home. Near burned the place down."

Eloise watched her mother trace the rim of her mug, her eyes downcast. "Mama?"

"I never had much trouble in that area," Lily said quietly. "Morgan moved out of his mother's home at fourteen. Learned to fend for himself too young."

Eloise sank back in her chair, her hope for her parents' marriage crumbling with it. *God, please. Fix them. If not me, then them.* She couldn't stand to heal while her parents crumbled. Not when she played so large a part in it.

For now, Eloise clung to the small hope that rested in the simple protection her mother offered her father. Morgan hadn't moved out; his mother had kicked him out. Mama would never do that to him.

Sensing the change in both Eloise and Lily, Elizabeth cleared her throat. "Well, Ellie, I told Brooks we'll have to have you two for dinner one of these days. As well as you and Morgan, Lily."

"And Jeremy?" Maisie piped up, her cheeks red.

"And Jeremy." Elizabeth smiled. "So long as your papa's ok with it."

Eloise looked to Maisie, who pretended not to see her as she sipped her tea.

When they'd finished their tea, Eloise offered to clean and clear the dishes. "Mae, why don't you go and help?" Elizabeth told her.

When the door shut behind them, Maisie began to chatter. "Papa is putting away money for me to start at correspondence school in the fall." The girl was near bouncing on the balls of her feet.

"That's incredible, Mais." Eloise smiled. "You're going to do wonderfully."

"I'm sorry," Maisie said quietly. "I know it's hard for you to talk about school."

"Talk about it all you want, Maisie. It makes you happy." And if it made Maisie happy, it made her happy. Eloise focused on that to temper the nausea in her stomach. *Swim with the waves.* "But what I would really like to hear about is this sudden turn with Jeremy. What happened to wanting nothing to do with him?"

"I never said I wanted nothing to do with him," Maisie remarked. "We've always been friends."

"Mmm-hmm." As though she hadn't soothed the girl to sleep for weeks over the boy.

"Well, if you must know," the girl said, "I don't want to be afraid. Brooks was afraid, and it led him to drink. You were afraid, and it led you to—well, it doesn't matter," Maisie said. "I don't want to do that."

Eloise met the girl's eyes then. She really was stronger than her. "That's good, Maisie. That's something, to learn it now rather than later."

"Well, it's thanks to you," Maisie told her as though that were plainly obvious. "You said to find a friend who wanted me for me rather than convenience. That's always been Jeremy. No matter how annoying he might have been."

After a moment, Maisie took Eloise's hand. "I know you won't believe it, Ellie, but I was watching you. I could see how much you struggled. With me. With Brooks. With everyone, and yet you never gave up. You kept trusting God, and I figured if you could do that, I could."

Eloise almost snorted. "I gave up once, Maisie, and I almost did it again. I face the fear that I'm going to almost every day."

"Yes, but we all have moments, don't we? It may not all be in the permanent ways that yours could have been. But we do it in our own ways." Pulling her into a hug, Maisie whispered in her ear. "And I don't believe for a moment that you'll give up again. You're different, Ellie, and it's not because of Brooks or your marriage. I've seen it in you since that night." Maisie smiled. "That's when I decided I could be brave too."

Eloise laughed softly. She'd never imagined herself influencing someone's life, least of all in the positive way Maisie described. Maisie was the one who made a difference in someone's life for the better, like Elizabeth and Brooks, not her.

"Well," Eloise said quietly. "I'm glad to have been of service."

Thirty-Seven

June

Getting the ranch ready was proving to be more work than Eloise expected. Every morning Brooks met her with breakfast in bed before enlisting her help in clearing the land of rocks and toting them to the little section he had claimed as her garden. When they'd finished clearing the property, they would use the rocks to border the garden.

When they weren't pulling up rocks, they were mucking stables, downing trees, and stocking up on its wood and kindling.

Brooks had to admire her dedication. He'd never thought her lazy, but Huxley was anything but a farming town, and she was used to a different sort of work. She'd come to him thin and pale, her skin smooth and unblemished. As the weeks passed, he watched her arms and legs grow stronger, her skin darker. The blisters that had once been confined to the tips of her fingers now covered her palms.

She went to bed exhausted every night, and yet she never once complained. When they returned home, she made them dinner and reluctantly accepted his offer to help with the dishes at his reminder they were a team. After dinner, he massaged her tender muscles and carefully tried to work out the knots built from years of tension and stress.

"You're one big knot," Brooks teased.

Eloise laughed softly. "Mama used to try to work the knots out too. I think it's fairly pointless. I've almost forgotten what it's like not to hurt."

"We'll get you there, Elle. You're building muscle now, which will help, and you're doing good in your Bible reading. I know it doesn't seem like it now, but those things will help, darlin'."

Eloise's eyes fluttered shut as Brooks worked at a knot in the small of her back. He'd taken to working the tension from her muscles even before they'd begun the hard work on their land. Whether it would amount to anything, she wasn't entirely sure, but she loved him for it nonetheless. "You're helping, Brooks," she said softly. "Don't forget yourself."

He laughed in her ear. "Glad to be of service, ma'am." Taking his hand, Eloise settled against his chest. "Do you want me to read tonight?" When she nodded, he grabbed his Bible from the nightstand. "You're going to fall asleep again, aren't you?"

At her nod, Brooks' laugh reverberated through his chest. She loved drifting off every night to her husband's quiet voice and the love of the Father. "Then good night." He kissed her hair before beginning to read quietly.

Brooks played with her hair as he read, feeling the way her body relaxed and her breathing slowed and turned rhythmic. She was happier in the last few weeks. More relaxed than he had known her to be in the near year he had known her. But how much of that was exhaustion? How much was post-wedding bliss that was sure to end?

He wasn't sure he could take another night like her one in the tub. Throughout the day, they laughed as they worked, and he saw the joy in her, but the moment she grew quiet, his mind went to that night in his room when she admitted to the way she viewed herself. Did she still hate herself even now? When she laughed, he wanted to believe something was shifting in her, but then the nights came when he couldn't leave her alone to bathe, and he remembered her words.

I don't want to leave you. But I'm scared that I could. Losing her before would have been painful. If he were to lose her now, he wasn't sure he'd survive it. She was a part of him.

Papa, I need you to keep guiding me with her. Give me words. Give me patience. Give me what she needs to stay afloat. More than that. To get her out of the water.

Setting the Bible aside, Brooks eased her onto the bed before drawing her to him. He wasn't sure whether he'd ever see her healed. His mother had yet to be healed. He himself hadn't been healed. But they were happy. They didn't live on the line between joy and the desire to die. Even in his hardest moments, he no longer felt the desire to pick up a drink.

"Just get her there, Papa," he breathed.

That small voice bid him to trust.

The next morning, Brooks let her sleep later. Leaving her breakfast on the table, he went to start on the garden. If he worked quick enough, he might have a chance of getting somewhere before she woke. The woman liked her sleep.

He finished plowing before Eloise made her way out, a strip of bacon in her hand. "Mornin'."

"Why didn't you wake me?" she demanded.

Brooks nodded toward the field. "I think we're just about done there. Thought I'd give you a break and get your garden started. We're already running late in the season. A few more days, and we'll be waiting until next year."

"Well, what can I do?" she asked.

"Rest," he said. "I've been working you too hard."

"I can handle it, Brooks."

Brooks laughed at the scowl on Eloise's face. "I know, darlin'." Leaning on the plow, he wiped the sweat from his brow. "But it isn't your job to work the land. It's mine. All you've got to do is help me when it's needed, and I can handle it from there."

Shrugging, Eloise turned back toward the house. "I'll get caught up on laundry."

Even the laundry was proving to be too big a task. As she scrubbed at their dirt-crusted clothes, perspiration built on her face. Even still, she didn't give up until everything was washed and hung. When that was done, she helped Brooks plant seeds until lunchtime.

When they sat down to eat, Brooks watched the delicate way she lowered herself into her seat. "You need a few days' rest, Elle."

Her scowl was back. "I don't mind working, Brooks."

"Is that why you're a bit grouchy?" he teased. "Darlin', I will always have plenty of work for you. But you have to rest before you crash. Even God rested."

Eloise was quiet a moment as she considered him. "I'm sorry," she said softly. "It just feels good to be needed. I don't want you to think I'm not capable or ..." She shrugged. "I want to be useful."

"Elle, I know you are plenty capable. But even I need to rest some days, and I'm more used to this kind of work. I don't want you overdoing it." Turning her chin up, he met her eyes. "I need you, darlin'. I wouldn't want to do any of this without you, and a few days' rest won't change that."

Tears blurred Eloise's dark eyes. "I'm sorry."

"Don't be sorry, Elle. I just wish you could see yourself the way I do. You don't have to earn a place here. You don't have to earn my love or attention." Brooks kissed her softly. "I love you. Right here. Right now."

"I love you," she said quietly.

He loves you now, that old voice whispered. But what would happen when she couldn't work? When sickness or pregnancy or tiredness kept her from helping?

Swim with the waves, she reminded herself. *Counter it with truth.* Did she need him to help her with the dishes and dinner and laundry? Was that how he earned her love? She knew it wasn't so. The man could never touch a dish, and she would love him just the same. So why was it so hard to believe she didn't have to earn his? To earn anyone's?

Stupid. Selfish. Childish.

It had been weeks since she'd thought about those flaws. But now that they were there, Eloise let them sit, her mind turning as she remembered the words that had settled over her thirteen years before. She was bad. Selfish. Childish.

Grow up, Eloise. Do better. Be better.

Those words swirled in her mind, threatening to pull her under. *Swim with the waves.* She did. There was something to those words. Something almost comforting if she didn't let them pull her under.

***

The next morning, Eloise requested Brooks drive her to her parents'. The words were still circulating in her head. When had

327

those thoughts really started? Why had it been so easy for Alma to turn her mind into what it was now?

"Are you all right?" Brooks asked. "You've been quiet since lunch yesterday." When he touched her cheek, she leaned into it, the coolness of his fingers cooling her warm cheeks.

"I'm just thinking," she said.

"Is that a good idea?"

"I think so." She laughed. "I hope so. I just need to ask Mama something."

When they reached the Riley land, Brooks helped her down. "Well then, I'll pray you get what you need." He kissed her. "I'll come get you in an hour or so."

When he was gone, she hesitated before opening the door. She'd wondered in the beginning whether it was still within her right to simply walk into her parents' home. Lily looked up from the book she had resting on her lap.

Setting it aside, she moved to touch Eloise's cheek. "You look tired. Brooks is working you too hard over there."

"Brooks said the same thing yesterday." Eloise sighed. "I don't mind it." Taking her mother's hand, she pulled her back toward the table. "I was hoping we could talk. I've missed you." She'd never been away from her mother more than a day or two before marriage, and it had now been two weeks since she'd spoken with her.

Taking the seat next to Eloise, Lily let the girl rest her head on her shoulder. "I hope you've gotten a lot of work done over there."

"I think we're almost done. We cleared out all the rocks, and we plowed and planted for my garden yesterday."

They spoke about Brooks' future plans for the ranch. He had plans to make a trip out to Missoula in a few weeks to get supplies. He wanted to breed Era and Anthem. Juniper was coming along well in her training. Any day now, Brooks would start training the horse to ride.

When talk slowed, Lily curled her fingers through Eloise's. "Was there something more you wanted to talk about?" Though the girl seemed far happier than she'd known her to be, there was something quiet about her. Something was gnawing at her.

Eloise shrugged. "I just got to thinking about something last night." Sitting up, Eloise stared at their hands. "Do you think things would have been different? If I'd never gone to Alma? I don't mean to blame you and Daddy. There was no way of knowing, but ..."

"But it can't be denied that we made a mistake in sending you there," Lily finished. "It's ok to be upset about it, Ellie."

"I know that I would still struggle," Eloise whispered. "Because I always did but...I can't help but wonder what my life would be if there was no Alma. No school. No church. If I had grown up here." Maybe all of those thoughts had always been there. But maybe she'd have been able to fight them better if they hadn't been confirmed over and over.

"I think," Lily said softly, "that you would still struggle. But I do think you would be better off now if it wasn't for everything that happened in Huxley." Lily rubbed her eyes. "You've always been sensitive, Ellie. But after you stayed with Alma, your sensitivity changed into something else ... Instead of getting upset, you became inconsolable. As if, with one mistake, your father and I would stop loving you. It scared me sometimes—how fearful you were of making a mistake."

"I thought that if I messed up, that's all I would ever be—unloved," Eloise said quietly. The truth of those words released something in her. "I don't think I ever knew why until last night." She shrugged. "I had to be better than I was."

"You always wanted to be good at whatever you set your mind to. But you slowly started to expect perfection. In your attitude. Your work. When you couldn't do that, you went on a rant about yourself." It hadn't mattered that the girl was smart. Talented. Most of what she set out to do was done well, and what wasn't could be improved, but in Eloise's mind, she was stupid and refused to hear otherwise.

Bringing Eloise to her, Lily kissed her hair. "Maybe knowing all of that will help you in the future."

"Maybe," Eloise whispered.

But it didn't make it untrue. It didn't take the pain of it away.

But it doesn't make it true. Swim with the waves.

"I'm trying, Mama," she said quietly. "But it's hard." Every time she took a step toward progress, she remembered every step of progress before it. Each one always followed by three steps back.

Papa, don't let me fail again. Keep my eyes on you. Remind me of truth.

Thirty-Eight

Morgan heard the door of the house shut. Going to the barn door, he saw Eloise heading back toward her land. "Ellie," he hissed. She jumped and looked around before spotting him. "Can you help me a minute, Weasel?"

Glancing back toward the house a moment, Eloise turned her feet toward the barn. It took her only a moment to notice the bloody rag he held to his arm. "What did you do?" Even though her voice was filled with alarm, Morgan knew his daughter would be the lesser of two evils. "Mama's going to be hysterical," she said, confirming his own thoughts.

"I know it." He sighed. "I was hoping you would help me get it cleaned up so she doesn't have to."

Though Eloise looked slightly white, she agreed. Removing the soiled rag, she breathed deeply before placing a fresh, water-dampened rag on his skin. "What did you do?"

"My hand slipped while I was working." He nodded toward the tools on the bench. "They're all clean. There shouldn't be any worries of infection."

Eloise hmmed, knowing as well as Morgan did that Lily wouldn't accept that excuse. Her hands were shaking miserably as she dabbed at the wound. "It's good practice for you, Ellie. Husbands and babies can have a knack for getting hurt. At least you don't have your mama's fear of it." Morgan nudged her. "That was the one area I was always in charge of with you. Taking care of your wounds. Your mama couldn't do it, knowing she'd scare you with her worrying. After I'd finished and seen you were ok, I'd have to convince her it was nothing serious enough to warrant a trip to the doctor."

Eloise smiled. "I don't think I can make you laugh like you did me." Her breath was shallow as she wrapped the bandage around his arm.

"I think I'll survive." Morgan smiled.

When she finished, she stepped back and took a deep breath, eyes closed. "What do you plan to do with Mama?"

"I don't know." Morgan had watched Merritt handle Elizabeth with such patience and grace when her emotions ran high and each time he witnessed that, he grew more ashamed of himself and the way he handled his wife's hysteria. Merritt comforted his wife; Morgan snapped at his before he could think better of it.

"I don't know how to handle it, Weasel," Morgan said quietly, "when the two of you lose it like you do."

Eloise was quiet for a moment. "Why does it annoy you so much? I mean, I understand being frustrated. Brooks can get frustrated with me. But you just seem ..." She shrugged.

"It doesn't annoy me, Ellie." When she met his eyes, she looked unconvinced. "I know it's hard to believe, baby girl. But I promise I've never been annoyed by your struggles."

"Then what is it?"

Morgan was silent as he worked through the mess in his head. "It's no real excuse," he said quietly. "But you never met my mother, and there's a reason for that. She wasn't like your mama or nanny."

"She was abusive," Eloise said quietly.

"She wasn't always. It started after my pa left when I was about two or three. He left her with two children and a lot of hurt and shame. It didn't take long for her to realize she had the perfect little release for her anger." Morgan looked just like his father growing up, but that wasn't the reason his mother had beat him. His mother had loathed his very existence while adoring his sister's because she never wanted a boy—a boy that was bound to turn out just like his father.

"When your mama learned she was carrying you, I prayed you'd be a girl. I was afraid my anger would be more easily placed on a boy, seeing as that's all I knew. But then you went and started showing signs of struggling with something, and it became clear I didn't know how to handle anyone. I was angry, Ellie. But not at you."

After a moment's hesitation, Eloise leaned against the workbench, her head against his shoulder. "I'm sorry."

Morgan patted her cheek. "It is what it is, Ellie. I can't go back and change it. But the Lord was good when He gave me your mama. Even if she got the raw end of that deal."

Eloise laughed humorlessly. "Like Brooks."

"Brooks is good, Eloise. But I think he got a good deal." When she shrugged, Morgan sighed. "You did get a good one, though. I prayed your whole life the Lord would send someone like him." Someone patient. Someone he knew she was safe with. He'd never been certain she or his wife were safe with him.

He loved them more than life itself, but his anger scared him. He'd had more nightmares than he cared to admit at the beginning of their marriage. All of them filled with him losing his temper and going after Lily as his mother had gone after him. Seeing Brooks and Merritt with the women they loved made him feel inferior. In Huxley, he'd found it within himself to excuse his behavior. The men at the mill spoke illy of their wives daily. They spoke of visits to brothels when their wives thought they were on business. They reinforced the thoughts his mother had instilled in him that all men were trash.

But he was better than that. Wasn't he? He never cheated. He loved Lily. He loved his daughter. He wasn't perfect, but he was not the same kind of man his coworkers were. But Brooks and Merritt, and Matthew and Archer—all the men in this town were opening his eyes to the truth. He was wrong; his mother was wrong. He wasn't worthy of his wife as he was, but he might have been a better husband and father had his mother not only beat him physically but pummeled him with words that made him feel like the trash his mother said all men were.

After a moment, Eloise spoke. "Did you and Mama plan that trip to Tuffin?"

"No." Morgan sighed. "I don't think your mama's real interested at the moment." When the girl's eyes turned downcast, he stroked her cheek. "Don't you worry you on it, Weasel. Your mama and I will be fine." Kissing her hair, he urged her to head home before it got dark. "I can drive you if you want?"

"No, that's all right. I'm meeting Brooks at his parents'."

When she'd gone, Morgan started toward the house, rolling his sleeves down to cover the bandage.

In better times, Lily would notice. It wasn't like him to wear his sleeves down. But he wasn't entirely sure she'd notice the bandage if he didn't try and hide it. The distance between them was only growing the longer Eloise was gone. They had no distraction from the sorry state of their crumbled marriage. Eloise might have been the source of most of their fighting, but she was also the piece that held them together, if even in the simplest of ways.

Lily was reading when he came in, her back to him as she poured over the Word. Morgan took a seat next to her, too aware of the way she eased away from him. It was almost subconscious on her part, but it still hurt.

What right does she have to act that way? a dark voice purred. She was his wife. She was supposed to respect him. If she wanted nothing to do with him, she didn't deserve him.

The thought made him sick as he remembered his mother's words over men and the chatter at the mill. He didn't want to be those men. He didn't want to prove his mother right. His wife was hurting. She didn't mean to hurt him in return.

So love her, beloved.

"What are you reading?" he asked quietly.

"Hosea."

Her favorite. She read it when she was hurting. "No other book displays God's ability to work all things for good quite like Hosea."

Lily nodded. "That's what Daddy always said." Her voice was thick, and she kept her head turned.

Morgan sighed. "I'll leave you alone to finish."

Before he could stand, her hand took his arm. "Stay."

Doing as she requested, Morgan toyed with a loose thread on his sleeve. Even next to her, he didn't feel close to her.

When she'd finished, she started dinner. "You still going for tea with Elizabeth tomorrow?"

"Not if you needed me." She didn't meet his eyes as she set his plate in front of him.

It wasn't that Morgan needed her. He wanted her. Wanted her to look at him. To speak to him. He missed her blue eyes and the way they used to light up at the sight of him. "No," he said softly. "Enjoy your time with Elizabeth." His wife had never had much in the way of friends. Not with her father's reputation or her choice of husband. Eloise had been the nail in the coffin of any friendships Lily might have had. He wouldn't take what she had with Elizabeth from her. Not to cater to his own aching wounds.

Morgan wasted the hours before bed in the barn. With his arm throbbing, he couldn't work, so he paced. After several minutes, he began to pray.

"God, I can't do this anymore." He kicked at a hay bale. "God, I am trying with her. I've been patient. I've tried to make things right. She won't listen." Lily only drifted further the closer he tried to get. "She's stubborn is what she is." A sharp cry broke from his lips, and rather than fight it, he went to his knees. "I know I gave up on you a long time ago but don't give up on me. On Lily. God, I love her and Ellie. I can't lose them." Eloise was willing to try now, but what would happen if her mother gave up on him? "God, I can't lose them."

When he'd exhausted himself, he made his way inside just as Lily was preparing for bed. She kept her back to him as she undressed. Turning away, he went about getting ready himself. Forgetting the bandage on his arm, he didn't bother to hide it as he eased out of his shirt.

At the sharp intake of breath behind him, he turned to face Lily and found her eyes on his arm. "What hap-what—?"

Moving toward her, he spoke softly. "Lily. It's fine."

"What happened?" she whispered.

"It was an accident in the barn," he explained. "Ell—"

"Well, has it been cleaned? Your tools are filthy, Morgan." Her hands shook as she tried to undo the bandage. "It could get infected."

In her panic, her nails cut into his arm. "Lily." The word was sharper than he meant, and he closed his eyes.

Breathing through his own rising emotion, Morgan took hold of her hands, gently prying them away from the bandage. Holding both her hands in one of his, he took hold of her chin and turned her blue eyes to his. They were blurred by tears. "Easy," he breathed. "Eloise cleaned it, Lily, and I will let you tend to it again in the morning if that makes you feel better."

"But you could-if it gets infected, you could—" Her head fell against his chest. "Please, let's just go down to Archer's."

"Not tonight. It's been cleaned. My tools were clean. It won't kill me overnight."

"This isn't funny, Morgan," Lily hissed.

"I'm not laughing," Morgan said, working to control his temper. "But right now, you need to breathe, Lily. You'll clean it again in the morning, and we'll go from there."

"But infection—"

"Give it a day or so, and if you're still worried, I'll let you take me to see Archer."

Her eyes snapped to his. "You promise?"

"I promise, Lily Pad."

She watched him a moment before breaking down, her forehead falling back to his chest. "I'm sorry," she cried. "I don't mean to—but I can't …" She shook her head.

Morgan wrapped his arms around her. It had been months since he'd held her. It wasn't what it should be. She was limp against him, but she was there. He kissed her hair. "It's all right, Lily."

***

Lily messed with her fingers, wringing them tight with all the anxiety she felt, as she made the walk toward the Harper land. She'd thought with Eloise married, she'd be happier. Instead, Lily found herself facing an empty home. Missing her daughter and what had once been a happy marriage.

She had been grateful when Elizabeth requested that she visit for tea every afternoon. The woman offered a welcome distraction from the crumbled hope she'd put into what Eloise's marriage would bring. She and Morgan didn't fight anymore, but there was no longer any affection or desire between the two of them. At least she hadn't resorted to sleeping in separate beds. The idea had tempted her more than once with Eloise's empty room. But she wouldn't sink so low. She didn't want to sink so low.

Blinking back tears, she hurried forward, anxious for Elizabeth's distraction.

Elizabeth's soft laugh drifted through the open door as Lily neared the home. Unsure, Lily moved slowly to peer through the door and felt the knot in her chest tighten.

Merritt had Elizabeth on the counter, trapping her with an arm on either side of her waist. Elizabeth had her arms around her husband's neck as she spoke softly, too quiet to reach Lily.

Unwilling to disturb the intimate moment and unsure she could speak now around the lump in her throat, Lily slipped back quietly and paced the yard.

Wiping the tears from her cheeks, she tried not to think of her crumbling marriage. The previous night was the first night Morgan had touched her in any way outside of helping her in and out of the wagon or out of a stubborn corset, and it hadn't been in love. At least, not the sort of love she wanted.

She loathed to think of what her parents would have to say about the sorry state of their daughter's marriage. This wasn't what she had been raised to do. It wasn't how she was raised to behave. Forgiveness and humility were virtues taught at a young age, but neither existed in her marriage now.

"Mama, forgive me," she whispered. "I don't know how to fix it."

As another laugh drifted out the door, Lily bit down on her lip, forcing back an unwelcome sob. She couldn't remember the last time she'd had simple intimacies like that with her husband. They'd had them once when Eloise was just a girl, undamaged and happy. Back then, moments of such sweet intimacy came as often as Morgan's embittered boss would let him slip away for lunch. They were found when Eloise had been put to bed, and they'd read the Bible by firelight, Lily's legs crossed over Morgan's as he read in his deep, rich voice.

Eloise hadn't been the only one who changed after Alma. Lily and Morgan had ceased to be the same since.

God, I'll do anything. Just lead us back. Don't let me lose him.

Hearing Elizabeth and Merritt move toward the door, Lily wiped at her face and made her way to the house.

Seeing Lily, Elizabeth blushed deeply. "Lily," she said breathlessly. "I'm sorry, I completely forgot. I'll be with you in a minute." Turning back to Merritt, Elizabeth didn't resist as he pulled her to him, pressing his lips to her forehead in courtesy of their company. She laughed when he whispered in her ear. "I love you, you idiot," she said softly. "Now go."

When he was gone, she kept her head down as she quickened to make their tea, but it didn't hide the flush in her cheeks.

"You two are like newlyweds," Lily said quietly.

Elizabeth was quiet a moment before conceding to the conversation. The damage was done. "Sometimes." She laughed. "We have our stages, and you and Morgan will find your way back to that stage, Lily."

When Lily said nothing, Elizabeth sighed. "But anyway, I'm sorry. I should have been ready for you."

"It doesn't matter, Elizabeth. Enjoy your husband." As she wished she could enjoy hers. Lily wanted to be what they were before. But then, she wasn't sure they'd ever been as Elizabeth and Merritt were even now. They'd had their moments, as Elizabeth said, but that was all. Moments between arguments and tears.

Seeing Lily's tears, Elizabeth set a hand over hers. "Do you want to talk, Lily?"

"No," Lily whispered. "Not-not about that."

"Well then, we'll find something else."

Accepting her mug, Lily tapped the glass before speaking. "Ellie visited yesterday. She said Maisie was going to stay over tonight."

Elizabeth laughed. "She was so excited that she made Merritt take her over straight after breakfast. She's been missing having Brooks at her beck and call."

"I can imagine. It's still so strange not having Eloise there. Having her visit rather than just walk out her bedroom door."

"I know it. I thought it would be easier with Brooks. We'd been through it once, and we'd get through it again. But there are still as many tears."

"Just wait until Maisie goes." Lily laughed. "And you've got yourself an empty nest."

Elizabeth was quiet for a moment as she watched the other woman chew on her lip. "Did you, um, I mean, did you and Morgan ever try for more after Eloise?"

"Of course. We both wanted more, but it never happened." Lily let out a weak breath. "We conceived once about four years ago now, but we lost the baby almost immediately. We never even told Eloise."

Elizabeth squeezed the woman's hand again. "I'm sorry. Mabel lost her first child six months after she was married. It was the first time I ever saw Mabel struggle like that. She's normally so peaceful about everything, but that nearly broke her."

Lily shook her head. "I can only pray Ellie has better luck. I don't think she could handle that sort of pain, and it's not uncommon to struggle in my family. My parents struggled to conceive. They never lost any babies, but they had me late in life. My daddy was in his mid-fifties. Mama, her mid-forties. Don't even know how that happened."

"God knew the world needed you," Elizabeth said softly. "Brooks and Maisie each took time, Maisie especially, but I can't deny all my children came at their perfect time. Even if the wait did hurt."

"More would have been wonderful, but I'm grateful we at least got Ellie so easily, and she was the most perfect little baby."

Elizabeth smiled. "You know, you've heard about how Merritt and I met. But you have yet to tell me about you and Morgan." Perhaps getting the woman to remember would spark something in her. She knew how easy it was to forget those early moments when life hit you as it had hit them.

"He worked at the mill my father worked in. I met him when I was bringing my father his lunch." Lily laughed. "I was fourteen and intrigued at the very sight of him. I made a habit of bringing my father's lunch from then on." Her parents had been unhappy to find out she was catching feelings for the man who was well known for causing trouble. The angry son of the town drunk. A man who frequented brothels but had never set foot in a church.

"My parents hated it. But I felt something in me when I looked at him that day, and I was determined." At her plea, her parents had agreed with caution. "He wasn't as terrible as he was made out to be. He was angry alright, but he always treated me well enough." He'd stopped frequenting brothels, and after a few weeks, he'd agreed to go to her father's church as she steadily tamed the troubling parts of him. "My parents grew to love him quite easily. Mama adored him. His mother, on the other hand, never did like me. She used to taunt me for loving him. A girl like me couldn't stay happy for long with a boy like that." She'd regret it one day.

"Sounds like my mother if she'd been around to meet Merritt."

But was Etta wrong? Look at all the trouble he's caused you. Look at the way he treats your daughter. The way he treats you.

No. Whatever there might be, Lily had never regretted Morgan. Even in their darkest moments. His angriest. He'd given her Eloise, and angry as he might have been in their years, he'd always loved her.

"I know Morgan can be a difficult one to see the good in. He likes to look untouchable," she said quietly. "But he grew up different than I did. His mother was abusive toward him, and it left him bitter. He didn't come into our marriage the way I would have preferred, and he didn't take that thought lightly." She pursed her lips to hide their quiver. "On our wedding night, before anything else, he'd simply washed my feet. He said it was his way of humbling himself, his way of putting his past iniquities behind him."

When they had discovered themselves to be expecting only weeks after marriage, she'd watched a mixture of fear and joy pass over him despite the many expressed fears of becoming a father. When their daughter had been born, her hard and often unfeeling husband had dropped to his knees upon first sight of her.

"He's flawed, Elizabeth." He was broken and angry, and there were a dozen things Lily hated him for. But there would always be a hundred things that she loved him for. "I know he's trying so hard for me, but we can't seem to fall back together. Anger has vanished. We don't fight anymore, but we're more like roommates than anything else now." Lily let out a small cry. "I love him," she whispered. "But I don't feel in love anymore, and I don't think it's age, Elizabeth. Or time." Perhaps at one time, she had. But Merritt and Elizabeth were older, married longer, and she could see the love between the two of them as clear and fresh as what was between their children.

Unable to hold it back any longer, Lily's head dropped into her hands as she began to sob. As Elizabeth moved and put an arm around her shoulders, Lily choked out words. "I can't help but blame Eloise sometimes. I know it isn't fair. I know it isn't right. Morgan and I had our problems without Eloise's actions in the mix, and I know we might've torn regardless. But it was that one decision that pulled the final thread." Lily was quiet for a moment as she worked to calm herself. When she finally spoke, it was little more than a broken whisper. "She didn't die that day. But our marriage did."

When Lily had settled enough to listen, Elizabeth took her hand. "Your marriage isn't dead, Lily. It's simply been beaten down. What you see from Merritt and I is only a portion of our life together. When Brooks was going through his struggles, it carried a weight on all of us. Merritt and I fought constantly. The children were at each other's throats. Mabel has always been our easygoing one, and even she was giving us trouble throughout all of it."

"I can't imagine any of you behaving in those ways." Lily had never seen a family as close and peaceful as the Harpers.

"Sometimes it does seem like a dream," Elizabeth admitted. "It was out of character for all of us. But it was a difficult time. Watching your child suffer is hard, Lily. I don't think anything tests a marriage quite like it. But it isn't the end of a marriage. It isn't the end of love. Not if you don't let it become so."

"I don't know how to mend it anymore, Elizabeth."

"Stop treating him like he's nothing more than a friend you room with, Lily. Start looking at him as the man you fell in love with. The man you married. Not what he's become to you. Honey, you have to stop seeing those parts of him that you fell in love with as in the past. Because they aren't past. Not if you look beyond your pain."

Thirty-Nine

July

Swim with the waves. *God, I am trying.* Eloise stared at the pages of her Bible, trying to make sense of the jumble of words as the waves tried to pull her under.

Seeing her struggle, Brooks massaged her shoulders. "You're trying too hard, Elle. You're not always going to get something when you read it. But it's in there." Removing the Bible from her hands, he closed it. "Why don't you take a break? You've been reading it for over an hour, and if you keep forcing yourself to get something from the passage, you'll only end up discouraged the next time you read it." When she opened her mouth to argue, he hushed her. "You read it, Eloise. Now give Him time to use it."

"You always get something," she said quietly. "It's rare I understand anything."

"I don't always understand, Eloise. Sometimes I read it and wonder what purpose that scripture could possibly have. But I leave it to Him because I know that someday He'll reveal the meaning of it."

"I don't feel like I did anything today," Eloise snapped. "I haven't in days. I just need to try harder—"

"No," Brooks hissed. "No trying harder. You are trying to earn His favor, Eloise. That isn't how it works. The purpose of that" —he pointed toward the Bible— "is to grow in your relationship with the Lord. To provide a weapon against the

346

enemy. It isn't meant to shame or pressure or be used to gain favor."

"But I can't grow closer to Him if I can't feel Him. I feel like I didn't read it at all."

"But you did, Elle. That is what matters to Him. The desire. The heart." Brooks stroked her cheek. "How often have we had off nights together?" He watched her blush. The novelty of marriage had begun its slow fade as they argued more and spent many nights in silence as they learned to work through them. "They don't feel great in the moment. They aren't like nights when we talk and laugh and make love. But we're together. We're still learning about each other and growing closer in other ways. It's the same with the Lord, darlin'. You're going to have days of silence in His presence, and you'll have days of conversation and understanding. But neither is greater or lesser in His eyes when you've taken the time to spend even a few minutes in His presence."

But what happened when those off nights turned into months? When Eloise picked up the Bible a year from now and still gained nothing?

Brooks kissed her nose, silencing the thoughts. "Why don't we go work on riding?"

Eloise nodded. "When will I get to work with Juniper?"

"When she's gotten comfortable with me riding her. I'm not letting you on her until she's calm."

"What if she never does? She trusts me, doesn't she? So maybe she would do better with me?"

Brooks was quiet as he opened the barn door. "I can't take that risk, Elle. If you fell ..." He shook his head. "Horses can be dangerous, darlin'. I need you to trust me."

"What about you then?" Eloise whispered. She had watched him take several hard falls while training Juniper, many of which he'd come within inches of her feet crushing his legs or head. Watching him with Juniper had given her the very real taste of what she put him through. The constant fear of loss.

"I know what I'm doing, Elle. I've been riding since I was six. Been training since I was fourteen. I'm not saying there aren't risks, but there are less than if you were riding her." Seeing her anxiety, Brooks chucked her chin. "I know how to fall. Which is something I'd like to teach you before you get on Junie."

"So let's do that."

Brooks chuckled. "Are you sure about that? You've only just felt better from working. You're going to get beat up, and we still have to plan for Missoula next week."

Eloise shrugged. "That's ok. I want to learn, Brooks."

Brooks watched her a moment. "For who, Eloise? I don't want you getting hurt because you think it will earn you favor with me."

"It's for both of us." Eloise wrapped her arms around his neck. "This is my life, Brooks." Though tired and sore, most days she had never felt better than she did when helping Brooks ready their land. She loved working with the horses and learning his trade. She went to bed feeling accomplished and able to shut out the thoughts that told her she was useless. "I'm your wife, Brooks. I like being a part of what you do."

Brooks considered her. "I don't want to hear you complaining when you're sore and covered in bruises," he teased.

"I won't complain."

Eloise stared back at him with such determination in her eyes that Brooks sighed. The woman was stubborn when she wanted to be. "We'll start after lunch. But you are doing it on my terms. If I tell you you need to rest, I want you to listen."

"I'll listen, Brooks. I promise."

Brooks worked her until long after the sun had set, but she never once complained. Even when the breath was knocked out of her, she got back up and demanded to go again. The last time she hit the ground, he dropped down next to her. "Tomorrow you can try it without the mattress. If you think you're sore now, just wait." When she groaned, he laughed. "Is that a complaint?"

"Nope." When she tried to sit up, he grabbed her waist and pulled her back down. "I have to make dinner."

"We'll eat simple tonight. You need to rest." Relenting, Eloise settled against his chest. "You sure you still want to learn?"

When she said nothing, Brooks nudged her. "I was only joking, darlin'. You can admit if it's too much."

"It is a lot," she said quietly. "I feel like I could lay down and never move again, but …" Eloise drew circles against his bare chest. "Physical pain is better than mental or emotional pain. This pain is purposeful. It's making me stronger. It feels good, Brooks."

Brooks smiled. "Physical labor is good for you."

Eloise nodded. "It's got me thinking too. I wasn't entirely sure how to swim with the waves. I tried, but in the end, I felt like I was still panicking. But swimming with the waves must be a bit like learning to fall, right? Don't fight the waves. Don't fight the fall."

"Exactly," Brooks said. "It's all about fighting the instincts that tell you how to save yourself. Instincts can be good, Elle. God gave them for a reason. But they can also be deceiving when we have an enemy that wants to see you hurt."

"But where do I put God in that?" Eloise asked. "I don't know how to stay calm when I look to Him."

Brooks considered her a moment. "Well, when I started to train Charlie, I took a few hard falls. One of which broke my arm. I knew how to fall, but for some reason, when I started to go down, I panicked. I saw everything that could go wrong and, instead of leaning into the knowledge I had, I let those fears cloud it. I ended up paying the price for it. That's when it hit me that I was doing the same thing with God. Every time a thought got in there, instead of leaning into the knowledge of who I was to Him, I let the thoughts knock me down. That's when I taught myself how to fall mentally. The thoughts were the force that sent me falling, and like a real fall, you can't stop it, but you can control it."

"So God is the fall?"

"He's the knowledge. See, Elle, if I can trust myself in a fall, why couldn't I trust God in that same action? He's far more capable than I am." When Eloise said nothing, Brooks sighed. "For you, it's water. But you know how to swim, Elle. If you can trust yourself to stay afloat physically, why couldn't you trust the Lord to keep you afloat in here?" He tapped her head. "You know who you are in Him, darlin'. Nothing else matters outside of that. So lean into that knowledge when thoughts drag you under. It takes practice. But it works."

"Do I know?" she whispered. "Sometimes I read the Bible and all I see is confirmation that I'm not good."

"Well, I mean, you aren't good, Elle," Brooks said softly. "No one is. Not by godly standards. But you are still everything He says you are. You are still enough. If you weren't, He wouldn't have gone to the cross for you. You can't prevent the waves, Elle. God understands that."

"So long as I don't let them keep me under." Eloise sighed.

"Key word being *let*," Brooks said. "The Lord sees your fight, even beneath the waves."

Forty

It would take a week to reach Missoula. Ensuring Jeremy was comfortable in their home, Brooks lifted Eloise into the wagon and started off.

"You sure he can handle the horses?" Eloise asked.

"He's helped me a dozen times over the years, Elle, and Maisie promised to come by to help with Juniper." Seeing she was still concerned, Brooks smiled. "He's a good kid, and I promised him a job the moment I got things started. The kid wants to be a pastor. He has to make money to get to school."

"A pastor?" Eloise asked. Maisie, a teacher? Jeremy Tuft, a pastor? Fair or not, she couldn't imagine two people more mismatched for their dreams. They were too good for such things.

"Not all pastors are like the one in Huxley, Elle. Your own grandfather was a pastor."

Eloise shrugged. "I suppose."

Brooks considered her a moment. "What do you plan to do when Jeremy comes back to start a church?" he asked. "I'll want to go."

"I don't know," she whispered. "Can we really not just stay home and do what we've been doing?"

"I would rather not. A church would be nice, and it's only right to support Jeremy. Not to mention Maisie, with the direction those two are heading."

Eloise sighed. "Can we not talk about it now? We've got time between then and now."

"Don't you think it's better to have a plan before then?" Brooks asked. "We'll have children by then, Eloise. Do you not want them raised in church? And school? Will you not trust Maisie with them?"

"Of course I would trust Maisie." She glared back at him. "Why are you starting this now? Why can't we just enjoy our trip? It's not like we'd be able to attend the church anyway or send our children to school. The town is over an hour away."

"Which is why they would put the church halfway. Give everyone in Haven the chance to attend and educate their children."

"Wonderful." Crossing her arms, Eloise glared forward. "I wouldn't—" She bit down on her lip until she could trust herself.

"You wouldn't what, Elle?"

"I trust Maisie," she whispered. "But I don't want to send my children to school. I don't like the idea of them being gone that long. Not knowing what's happening." She met his eyes. "I can't."

"Eloise, they don't have to go if you don't want to send them. Maisie will understand. If that's one thing you can't feel comfortable with, you can teach them at home. But would you be up to a compromise? School at home, church with the community?"

"Can we just not talk about it now?" she breathed. "Please?"

Brooks watched her wrap her arms tightly around herself, rocking just slightly. "Later," he said quietly. "But it is something we need to talk about, Elle. We can't wait until we have children to decide how we want to raise them."

"I know."

When she didn't cease her light rock, Brooks slipped an arm around her waist. "Come here, darlin'." He kissed her forehead. "I'm sorry. You're right. Let's just enjoy the trip."

"I'm sorry," she whispered. "I don't mean to make everything difficult."

"I know. Let's just forget it now. We have plenty of time to make those decisions." Letting her slip her fingers through his, he squeezed her hand, trying to still its shakiness. "You don't make everything difficult. You have a past, Elle. You can't be expected to move forward all at once."

"I want to get better."

"You will," Brooks told her. "You've already been doing well. It's one step at a time. Swim with the waves. Remember?"

By the time they stopped for lunch, the tears had dried, the shaking had ceased, and though she didn't seem entirely settled, Eloise was trying.

The last night before reaching Missoula, she curled closer to him. "When we get back, we should camp by the lake. Before it gets cold."

"It's a plan," Brooks agreed. "I think that's just what we need." Anything to see his wife move forward rather than take the step back she was nearing.

When they rolled into Missoula, Eloise couldn't help but look all around her. She'd never been anywhere but Huxley and Rose Haven. Even the journey between the two hadn't taken them to anything but makeshift towns. Until then, Huxley was the busiest place she'd seen. It almost made her laugh now. Huxley was peaceful compared to Missoula.

Brooks slowed the wagon as they reached the busiest part of the city. People crossed the street, paying no mind to the wagons.

Children chased each other back and forth. "It's grown since the last time I was here." Brooks laughed.

Businesses ranging from mercantiles to saloons to establishments, such as banks and churches, lined the streets. Eloise prayed Brooks wouldn't notice that—the church. "Is that a hotel?" she asked, drawing his eyes opposite the church building.

"Looks to be." Pulling up outside, Brooks hopped down. "Let me get us checked in, and I'll come back for you."

Left alone, Eloise looked over the rest of the street. She could see the store Brooks would want to go to advertising horseshoes, saddles, and halters. Across the street was Tate's Mercantile. Maybe she'd be able to stock up on the supplies Annabelle didn't have.

When Brooks returned, he lifted her from the wagon. "They're going to take our stuff up to the room. Do you want to go and freshen up, or do you want to take a look around?"

Eloise shrugged. "We can look around."

Pressing close to his side, she let him lead her through the crowded streets. He nodded toward the mercantile. "Remind me to stop there before we head home. You and I are both in need of a few new pieces of clothing."

"Can we afford all of this?" she asked. "Paying Jeremy. New supplies. Fabrics." She wasn't sure she wanted to know how much the hotel was costing him. Though far from extravagant, the one he'd chosen looked far nicer than the three they'd passed since leaving the wagon.

"We have enough, Elle. Once we get home, I'll have what I need to be opening up the ranch." He nodded toward a restaurant. "One of these nights, we'll have a real dinner."

"We can eat our own food, Brooks. I packed enough."

"Eloise, I didn't get to spoil you with a honeymoon. Would you let me do so now?"

"I liked our honeymoon," she whispered. "Did you not?"

"Of course I did, Elle, and I wouldn't change it. But a man likes to spoil his girl, and I have yet to be able to do that." Slipping an arm around her waist, he whispered in her ear. "You telling me you don't want to get dressed up and eat a nice meal you don't have to prepare?"

"I'm just saying I wouldn't mind sleeping in our wagon and eating our own food." She didn't want him spending all his money on her. She didn't deserve that.

Seeing where her mind had gone, Brooks sighed. "Are you ever going to see yourself as more?"

"Are you? You don't see yourself very clear either." When he didn't argue, she shrugged. "If you want to spend all your money, go ahead."

Brooks ran a hand over his face. "Eloise, please."

"I'm sorry." She sighed. "This is why you shouldn't spend it all on me."

"Because you don't deserve it?" he demanded. "Do you think I deserved for my parents to get me Charlie? Or to find every odd job they could give me so I could earn the money to get us here? I didn't, Eloise. But they wanted to do it. I want to treat you." Taking a deep breath, he continued. "And being a bit difficult doesn't make you undeserving. It makes you a bit of a pain." At his smile, Eloise smiled back tremulously. "I've been planning this since we got engaged, Elle. I've put away what we need for it."

"All right," she whispered. "I would love a good dinner."

Brooks smiled. "I think we need it. We're a bit of a mess right now, aren't we?"

Eloise nodded. "I'm sorry."

"It doesn't all fall on you, Elle. This is all normal. If we weren't fighting over this, we'd be fighting over something else."

The next morning, they headed toward the shops. "Do you want to come with me?" Brooks asked. "Or do you feel comfortable going into the mercantile and getting what we need?"

Eloise glanced toward the mercantile. It was bigger than the one back home. Big enough that she might blend into the mess of people. "I can go," she said quietly.

He walked her to the door. First, pressing the money into her hand, Brooks kissed her cheek. "I'll come find you," he told her.

At that moment, a young woman reached for the handle of the door. Seeing her chance, Eloise hurried in behind her, avoiding the bell above the door.

Eloise took her time finding what she needed. She didn't know how long Brooks would be, and she didn't want to be left standing around. Finding the fabrics, she picked through them, quickly setting aside the extravagantly priced ones. She settled on four bolts of muted lilac, russet, olive, and one floral pattern she knew Brooks would like on her. For Brooks, she stacked three bolts of pale checkered blue, forest green, and a red flannel.

As she handed the bolts over to a clerk, she spotted a bolt of pale ivory. Digging it from the pile, she held it out, her fingers moving over the pale fabric.

"It would make a beautiful baby blanket, wouldn't it?" the woman asked. "I think it every time I see it. It's taking all I have in me not to get it."

Eloise looked at the woman's bulging stomach.

"I've already made one too many. My husband would kill me if I spent more now."

Eloise set the fabric aside. "Well, I'm not expecting," she said quietly. "It doesn't make sense to buy it now."

"It's never too early to make plans." The woman smiled. "How long have you been married?"

"Three months," Eloise breathed.

The woman laughed. "Well, I was married six months before I came to expect this one, and I had already made a few things for when the Lord blessed my husband and me." Taking the fabric back up, she set it in Eloise's hands. "I could see it in your eyes when you saw it. You saw yourself making the blanket to wrap your child in someday."

Eloise stared down at it, feeling that same tug in her chest as when she had first seen it. Taking back the lilac bolt, she set it back in the bin.

The woman smiled. "I'm Rosalie, by the way," she said. "Rosalie Tate."

"Eloise Harper."

"Well, it's nice to meet you, Eloise. I'll get your fabrics ready while you continue shopping."

Grabbing the last few things she needed, Eloise made her way to the counter. Rosalie beamed at her. "Is that all you need?"

Eloise nodded, unsure what to say. She glanced toward the door.

"Waiting for your husband?" When Eloise nodded, Rosalie smiled. "Well, I'm in need of a break. So why don't we set aside your purchases, and you and I can go for a cup of tea? Our living quarters are right upstairs."

Eloise blanched. "What?"

"Well, I'm sure you don't want to stand around all day waiting for him?" When a man walked out of the curtain behind her, she took his arm. "Michael, when a man named Harper comes in looking for his wife, would you send him upstairs?"

Michael looked at her. "Are you getting off your feet?" At her nod, her husband looked relieved. "Good. I'll keep my eye out for him."

When he went to help a customer, Rosalie led Eloise upstairs and into a small kitchen. Getting water boiling on the stove, Rosalie motioned for her to sit.

Eloise's heart pounded in her throat. What was she doing up here? She should have gone and looked for Brooks. She shouldn't have let herself be talked into buying fabric she didn't need. What would Brooks say when he learned she'd wasted the little money they had?

"You all right, hun?" Rosalie asked. "You looked a little lost there for a moment." Pouring her a mug, she slid it over to Eloise. "I hope you didn't feel too pressured to get anything. I just know how many things I wish I had gone ahead and made for this one. We have hope chests for marriage. Why not have a few things in hope for children?"

Eloise shook her head. "Brooks talks about children all the time. I don't think he'll mind it."

They were quiet a long moment, Rosalie glancing toward Eloise now and again. "How did you and your Brooks meet?" she asked quietly.

"Church," Eloise replied. "He came through my town while looking to start up his ranch. That was a year ago this month."

"Where is your town?"

"That was in Oregon—Huxley. My parents and I ended up following Brooks back to his hometown in Rose Haven."

Eloise spoke so softly that Rosalie only just made out each word. "Sounds romantic. My family wasn't so supportive of my marriage to Michael. They're very prominent in New York. They expected me to marry higher than a store clerk. But when you know you've found the right man, you know."

Eloise nodded along to the woman's conversation. Though Eloise didn't say much, the other woman seemed unbothered to guide the conversation. But rather than find herself comforted, Eloise's mind steadily pulled her under.

The woman would regret bringing her up here. She was bored. She'd be happy to see her leave when Brooks found her.

"Is this Rose Haven close?" Rosalie asked.

"It's about a four days' journey," Eloise said quietly.

"Oh." Rosalie sighed. "I'm still trying to find my people here. We've been here less than a year."

Eloise stared back at her. She was disappointed—that Eloise didn't live closer?

Before Eloise could respond, voices drifted up from the stairwell. A moment later, Brooks came through the door, deep in conversation with Michael.

Spotting her, Brooks smiled. "Hey, darlin'." Kissing her cheek, he brought his lips to her ear. "You've gone and made a friend."

Eloise stared back at him. A friend?

"Michael invited us to stay for lunch," Brooks told her.

Eloise helped Rosalie make a handful of sandwiches before going back to Brooks' side. Sitting next to him, she focused on his hand in hers to calm the waves.

Rosalie continued her easy conversation with Eloise while the men discussed everything from business to horses. By the end, Brooks squeezed Eloise's hand. "You ready?"

She nodded.

Pleading Rosalie to stay upstairs, Michael followed them down. "Well, it was nice meeting you two." He looked at Eloise. "You made my wife's day. Rose has been struggling to fit in since moving out here."

Eloise nodded and let Brooks finish with him. "Will we see you at church tomorrow?" Michael asked.

Brooks glanced toward Eloise. "I, uh, I think we could make that happen." Saying a final goodbye, Brooks ushered her outside.

Eloise kept quiet as he helped her into the wagon. If Brooks wasn't going to mention it, she wouldn't either. Back in their room, she showed him the fabrics she'd chosen, ignoring the ache in her chest.

When she showed him the folded ivory, he smiled. "Have you got something to tell me?"

"No." Eloise laughed. "But I loved it, and Rosalie convinced me to stow it away for when that time comes."

Brooks smiled. "Rosalie was sweet, Elle. She seemed to like you."

"She was," Eloise agreed. "But we're leaving on Monday."

"That's why I gave Michael some information. You two can write if you want." He wrapped an arm around her waist. "It's good for you to have someone outside of our family."

"She isn't going to write, Brooks. She'll forget about me soon enough."

"Why do you think that?"

"Because it's what people do," Eloise snapped. "It's what everyone does. Act like they care, and as soon as you choose to trust them, they get bored of you and leave."

"I didn't," Brooks said softly, unfazed by her anger. "Maisie and my mother didn't. Mabel didn't. Elle, there are people in this world who love you now, and there will always be a dozen more who will want to love you in the future. But they can't do that if you don't give them the chance to know you."

"And when she doesn't write?"

"Well, I can't promise she will, Elle. But you can't write her off without giving her a chance." Brooks tucked her hair back. "Don't let the people who have hurt you turn you into them. Even if she doesn't write right away, it doesn't mean she won't. People get busy. She's going to have a baby. But it doesn't mean she won't get to you."

"I don't need a friend, Brooks."

Sighing, Brooks held his hands up in surrender. "Just promise you'll write back if she does."

Giving him her word, Eloise packed up their purchases, her hands lingering on the ivory. It was too soon to start worrying. But it didn't stop an ache from forming.

When Brooks kissed her neck, Eloise sighed. "Our time will come, Elle."

That night, Brooks took her to dinner. When the topic of church didn't come up again, Eloise prayed the situation was forgotten.

As they readied for bed, Brooks watched her. "Eloise, we need to talk about tomorrow."

Sighing, Eloise kept her eyes down. "What about tomorrow?"

"Elle, this isn't Huxley. It's not the same church. It's not the same people."

"It doesn't matter. They're all the same."

"You say the same thing about people, Eloise, and you're wrong there. Why can't you see that you just might be wrong here?"

Like that, the calm they'd built shattered. "Why do you even want to go?" she demanded. "Look what happened to you when you went to church."

"It was one church, Eloise." Brooks sighed. "One. We can't hold them all accountable for what one church did."

"It was more than one pastor for me. I am not going."

"Yes, you are." Brooks glared back at her. "What's that going to look like, Eloise? Going into church while my wife stays back at the hotel?" When tears spilled over, he sighed. "Don't start crying."

"I'm not doing it on purpose." Eloise's lip quivered. "Is that what you think?"

"I know you're not doing it on purpose, but I do think you know how to use your tears." Brooks watched Eloise look away. "It would be rude not to go, Eloise."

"Just tell them I'm sick. Make something up."

"Am I supposed to do that every Sunday back home?" Brooks demanded. "Whether it's Jeremy or someone else, it's only a matter of time before Rose Haven gets a church."

"Why do we have to go?" she whispered. "Why can't we just do it at home? Like we always do."

"There's nothing wrong with doing it that way, Eloise. But why do it when we can come together as a family to serve Him? When we can have real teachings?"

"Real teachings mean nothing, Brooks. I grew up with real teachings, and look at me."

"Eloise, you cannot blame a whole people for what a few have done. I understand your hesitancy. I went to church once and felt a whole lot worse leaving it. But I don't want to blame all of God's church for what a few people have done." Brooks stroked her cheek. "This church might be different, Elle. Why wait until Rose Haven gets a church to face this fear?"

Eloise shook her head. "I'm not going."

Brooks sighed. "Do it for me?" he asked. "Just try, and if anything is wrong, I promise you we will leave. One word. One look. But just try, Elle."

She looked back at him. "I don't want to."

Brooks smiled wryly. "Sometimes we have to do things we don't want to do, darlin'."

Eloise chewed her lip. "You promise we'll leave?" she asked. "If I'm not comfortable?"

"I promise, Elle."

Forty-One

Lily's heart pounded in her ears as Morgan took her legs and crossed them over his own. It was only a moment's hesitation tonight before she settled against him, her cheek against his shoulder.

Resting the Bible against her knees, Morgan pressed his lips into her hair. "Where were we?"

"Songs," Lily breathed.

She sighed as her husband began to read, the small bit of uncertainty falling away as she melted into his chest, her arms going around his waist.

In their effort to fix what had been broken, they'd taken to reading any scripture they could find on love and marriage— from Ephesians to 1 Corinthians to the Songs of Solomon. They'd started at the kitchen table, not touching. Until one night, the man had reached across the table and gripped her hand in his, eyes never leaving the page.

Head against his chest now, she slipped her fingers between his. "Do you want me to read?"

He chuckled softly. "Is that how we do it?"

"No," Lily whispered, grateful for it. She loved the sound of his voice, most especially when he read from the Word.

As Elizabeth encouraged her to, Lily had worked to see the see pieces of the man she had married, not the man who was a stranger to her.

The moment she had returned home, she went in search of him, afraid that waiting to seek him out would leave room for doubt and insecurities to turn her mind.

Lily had found him in the barn, shoulders slumped as he sanded a rough piece of wood. Before she could speak, the man set the paper aside and slumped against the table, his head in his hands. "God," he breathed. "Bring us back. I don't know what else I can do."

Lily bit down on her lip as she watched him clutch the table, his knuckles white, before taking the paper up once more. "Morgan?" She watched him startle, a small smile pulling at her lips. "Sorry, honey."

Waving off her apology, Morgan gave her a smile. "Did you have a good time with Elizabeth?"

"Something like that." When tears filled her eyes, Morgan moved toward her.

"Are you all right?" he whispered. Taking her arm, he led her to a hay bale. "Is it the cut? Sweetheart, I went to see Archer while you were with Elizabeth. He said it's nothing to worry over."

Her eyes met his. "You saw Archer?" she whispered. "Why?"

"Well" —a slight red tinged Morgan's cheeks— "because I knew you were worried. I wanted you to feel better."

Lily chewed her lip. "So? My worrying has never bothered you before." As the words left her lips, Lily sighed. "I'm sorry. I don't mean to do that." She pressed her palms into her eyelids. Eloise was right—where they were now was by Lily's own doing.

"Lily, I have always cared. About you. About Ellie. I'm sorry if that wasn't always clear."

"It's not your fault. Not entirely. I know I'm not easy." Lily bit down on her lip. "I think I might be a bit more like our daughter than I realized." More than she wanted to admit. But one could only wash their hands raw so many times before they questioned their own sanity.

Morgan let out a small laugh. "I think you're the last one to see that, Lily Pad. Your parents and I saw it for years, but you coped so well with it most days."

"Lily Pad." It had been months since he'd called her Lily Pad. Her chin quivered. "I can't do this anymore," she breathed, not realizing how she sounded until she watched her husband's jaw set, unable to hide the way his lip trembled.

"You can't?"

"No." Desperate to fix the mistake, she took his hand in hers, pressing it tight to her chest. "Not that. Not us. This." Lily waved a hand. "Fighting. Not fighting." Her head dropped to his chest. "I can't lose you, Morgan."

In the silence that followed, Lily listened to the sound of Morgan's heartbeat slow. "I can't lose you," he whispered. "Not like this."

Morgan nudged her now, drawing her mind back to the feel of his arm around her waist and the cool night air flowing in from the open door. "You've been staring into space for a good five minutes, Lil. Where'd you go?"

Lily laughed softly. "Nowhere. Are you finished?"

"Read three chapters, though I don't suppose you heard any of it?"

Lily shook her head. "Sorry."

Setting the book aside, Morgan took her chin, the action as natural as it had been at the beginning of their marriage. "Are you feeling all right?"

"Just thinking." Her eyes closed as Morgan stroked her cheek. Though they still had a ways to go, they'd fallen together quicker than she'd allowed herself to hope for. "Thank you," she whispered. "For not giving up on me."

"You needed time, Lily, and I never made life easy for you."

"It wasn't about time, Morgan. I needed someone to call me out. I was stubborn. So much so, I snapped at Ellie all because she wanted to help." Tears burned Lily's eyes. "I'm sorry."

"I know, Lily Pad. There's no need to let it eat at you now." Lily met her husband's eyes. The man had been far more ready than she to move on from past pains. While she found herself struggling with each step, Morgan took each one in stride.

"How do you think the kids are liking their trip?" Morgan asked, hoping to pull her mind from the dark. "This was supposed to make up for their lack of a honeymoon, was it not?"

Lily laughed. "Maybe in Brooks' mind. Ellie was head over heels for their honeymoon. I'd guess she enjoyed the road more than the city. She always loved when you took her camping."

Morgan nodded. "I never should have stopped taking her. I saw the disappointment every year that we didn't go. But it just got harder talking to her every year."

"You can't keep blaming yourself, honey. Eloise forgave you a long time ago, and she understands she didn't make it easy."

Morgan smiled, having his words turned back on him. "No. But I'm her father. It's my job to put that effort in." He shrugged. "We've all got a ways to go on this road."

"That we do." Lily smiled as Morgan pulled her to her feet. "But we'll get there. So long we keep looking forward."

Forty-Two

Eloise slipped her hand into Brooks' as they neared the church. "It'll be all right, Elle." Spotting Michael, Brooks headed for him. "Michael said the people were good."

When they reached the Tates, Rosalie looped her arm through Eloise's. "Michael said you might be coming. But I wasn't sure with you leaving tomorrow." Leading her to an empty pew, Rosalie accepted her help as she lowered herself onto the wooden bench.

Eloise gripped Brooks' hand when he seated himself beside her. "Please, can we just go?" she whispered. "Please?"

"Elle." Brooks took her face between his hands. "Do you trust me?" She nodded. "Would I walk you into anything if I felt there was any chance of you getting hurt?"

"No," she whispered. "But Brooks—"

"Eloise, I felt it when I stepped foot in that church in Huxley that it wasn't right. I felt it about Huxley as a whole. I don't feel it here."

"You could be wrong."

"I could," he agreed. "But we'll never know if we leave now, will we?"

Seeing her unrest, Rosalie leaned over. "It's a good church, Eloise. I can promise you."

She doesn't know. The moment she learned anything about you, she would behave just as Huxley did.

Eloise took a deep breath. *Swim with the waves. Focus on truth.* But what was truth? She thought she knew until she set foot in a church or picked up a Bible. Then the thoughts and memories and words that had been spoken over her overwhelmed her. She wasn't enough. She wasn't loved. She couldn't be when the Lord hated what she was.

Turning her head into Brooks' shoulder, Eloise fought to stay above the water.

Papa, please. But the panic was rising, and when the pastor asked that they stand, she knew she would have fallen to her knees if Brooks didn't have an arm around her waist.

A few people glanced their way. No one in Huxley had dared touch their spouse during service, and she knew they wouldn't understand that she needed his arm. Not if they were anything like those in Huxley.

She felt Rosalie set a hand to her arm, and tears bit at her eyes.

What would the woman say if she knew that Eloise had tried to kill herself not once but twice? Or that she still struggled with the idea of it? The desire for it?

By the end of service, Eloise felt numb. When the pastor released them, Eloise urged Brooks to go.

"Why don't you go out with Rosalie?" he encouraged. "I'll be out in a minute."

Accepting Rosalie's arm, Eloise made her way to the door, nodding in greeting to those who offered it. Outside, she lowered herself onto the steps.

Sitting next to her, Rosalie was quiet, except to respond to the women that called out to her. Finally, she sighed. "You looked scared to death in there."

When Eloise couldn't respond, the other woman set a hand on her arm. "People can be rough. But they aren't all terrible, Eloise. I lost my friends and family when I chose to marry Michael, and it hurts. But I can't close my heart to other friends or creating my own family. If someone walks out of your life of their own volition, it speaks volumes about them, Eloise, not you. God knows you deserve better than what they had to give you." Rosalie chewed her lip. "I love my family, Eloise, and I miss them. But I choose to believe that I deserve more in my life than people who would abandon me because I didn't live up to their idea of what I should be."

"I've opened my heart a dozen times," Eloise said quietly. "And I've always gotten hurt."

"They were the wrong people, Eloise. You can't shut everyone out. Everyone needs a friend." Rosalie smiled. "Even when they think they don't."

Eloise felt a hand on her shoulder. Getting a hand under her elbow, Brooks helped her to her feet. "Are you all right?"

She nodded, knowing the moment they reached their room the tears would flow. "I'm tired," she whispered.

Brooks stroked her cheek. "We'll go back to the room," he promised.

Rosalie hugged Eloise before they left. "I probably won't see you again before you leave. But your husband told Michael where we can reach you, so I'll write when I can."

Squeezing her hand in response, Eloise let Brooks wrap an arm around her waist.

Back in their room, Brooks settled her on the bed. "Can I trust you to tell me the truth right now?" Though spoken softly, the words still stung. "Was it the church or the memories?

"I don't know," she whispered. "I don't know."

When she began to sob, Brooks pulled her into his lap.

"Darlin', they were good people," he said softly. "They were asking about you after you left. They thought it was sweet that I was holding onto you." He tucked her hair behind her ear. "The pastor wanted to be sure you were ok. He thought you looked a little sick."

"What did he say when you told him?"

"He said it's a shame when a church puts such fear and shame into one of God's children. Many of the Bible's greatest people suffered with matters of the mind and heart, and God never shamed them."

"Did you tell him about how I..."

"No. I don't think it would have changed his thinking, but that is something very personal to you, Elle. It isn't mine to share."

"I don't think I can do that again, Brooks." Her heart was still pounding painfully. "I felt like I was back in Huxley."

Brooks was quiet a moment. "Can we come back to it later, Elle? When you've calmed down?" When she didn't say anything, he sighed. "All right then. Can I ask you a question?"

Eloise was quiet for a moment before nodding.

"You love the Lord, don't you? You want to serve Him?"

"Yes."

"Eloise, whatever goes on in your head isn't a sin. But it does become sinful if you let it control you. If you let it keep you from making friends, from stepping foot in His home? You are letting the Devil win." When Eloise turned her face into his chest, he pressed his lips into her hair. "I don't say that to shame you, Elle. Those are words I have had to repeat to myself a hundred times. I had to repeat them when I stepped foot in Huxley. In that church. When I stayed with your family." He smiled at her. "Every time I looked at you in the beginning, my gut instinct was to run."

"Why?" she whispered.

"Because I had always imagined myself on my own. It was what I wanted, and then suddenly, there was this beautiful woman that I couldn't get off my mind. She had me thinking of marriage and children. With those thoughts came all the reasons as to why I imagined myself alone. I didn't want to get hurt. But I knew from that very first conversation with you that God had something else in mind."

"You deserve better, Brooks."

"I think I deserve less," Brooks countered. "It's a good thing the Lord views us better than we view ourselves."

***

Brooks watched Eloise in the days that followed. When they were in the wagon, she sat hunched and quiet, her hands nervously twisting the fabric of her skirt. In better circumstances, he would have teased her. But now wasn't the time.

Something was eating at her, and he wasn't sure what it was.

She wasn't good enough, was the thought plaguing Eloise's mind. No matter what Brooks told her, Eloise knew he deserved more. Better. Someone he could take to church and whose wounds he wouldn't have to nurse afterward. A man of God deserved a woman of God. Not one so riddled with demons that it was a wonder she still stood.

At night, Eloise let him hold her close, all the while knowing she was selfish. It shouldn't be her in his arms. He would have been better off alone than with her.

When he whispered words of love to her, she bit her tongue against the desire to rebuke them. She wouldn't hurt him further, and she didn't want to argue anymore. She was tired of countering the lies. Tired of seeing herself as worthless. Tired of hating herself. She wanted to believe the words he breathed.

He'll realize soon enough, Eloise. When the novelty has worn off.

When Brooks laid his head on her chest, she toyed with his hair.

The novelty has already worn off. He stays.

Eloise felt Brooks smile through the thin material of her gown. "I don't know how I thought I could do any of this alone," he said softly. "Life. These trips that go on forever. Thank the Lord He knew better than me." When Eloise said nothing, he propped himself on his elbow. "One way or another, I'm going to make you see your worth, Eloise Harper."

The name sent a thrill down her spine. She was his. He had chosen her. He wanted her forever. It all was there in the name, and she clung to that.

When they reached home, Brooks lifted her from the wagon, his hands lingering on her waist. "Swim with the waves, Elle. Please."

Letting her go, he led the horses toward the barn. Taking their bags, Eloise went inside. Leaving the washing for later, she dug out Elizabeth's Bible and held it against her chest. "Don't let me sink, Papa." Her fingers dug into the worn leather.

Was there ever any doubt you would? You were made to sink. You're weak.

Eloise bit down on her lip, fighting inward panic as she felt herself slip further. "No," she whispered. "I can do this. I can fight. Papa, please." She set her forehead to the pages, waiting for the ache to ease. When it didn't, she sighed.

Straightening up, she stood. She could do this. She would keep her head above the waves. With morning only a few hours away now, Eloise kept a prayer on her lips as she got breakfast on the stove before unpacking their bags.

By the time Brooks came in, she was setting his bowl on the table. "I'm going to take a walk," she said softly.

He watched her uncertainly. "I'll go with you."

"I just need a walk. That's all." Kissing him, she encouraged him to eat.

"It's two in the morning, Eloise, and you haven't said anything in four days. I'm not letting you out of my sight."

"Brooks, you asked me to trust you with church. I'm asking you, now, to trust me." When the man's lip trembled, Eloise almost caved. But she needed this. She needed out. She needed room to breathe and think. Eloise caressed his cheek. "I promise, my love. I just need to think." Promising she would be back, she took her Bible, and, once outside, she headed towards the trees.

"God, I need you," she whispered. "I don't want to go backward." But the waters were rising. She couldn't breathe. She knew she should go back to Brooks. He was her lifeline. The preserver that kept her head above the water and her eyes on things above. But she couldn't bring herself to turn back.

Quickening her steps, Eloise turned toward the lake.

The sky was showing the first signs of morning before she reached the lake, a battle waring in her mind all the while. She knew she should go back to Brooks. He would be looking for her now, desperate and afraid for her. But still, she couldn't turn back.

Stepping to the edge of the water, she breathed through the ache. Kneeling, she stared down at the Bible, the water wetting the skirts at her knees.

"Papa, I can't do this anymore."

Eloise was tired of the life she lived. Tired of the pain. Tired of the fear. Tired of endless doubt over who she was and what others expected of her. Brooks hadn't been wrong; everyone in that church had been pleasant, and she'd been unable to see any of it, too focused on her fear. Rosalie had been kind from the first word, and all Eloise saw was Kate and Emma, Edith and Grace, and everyone else who had grown tired of her.

"I'm not giving up," she breathed. "I'm not. But I need you. I need something. Anything."

She needed to let go of the pain. "I know it might always be harder for me. I know it. I can take it. Just take the pain, Papa. The old hurt. Let me see myself the way you see me." He had taken Brooks' hurt. Elizabeth and Maisie's. He had even taken her parents' pain. That last one gave her the most hope as she remembered the last time she'd seen her parents. After years of trial and months of healing, none of their old pain had remained between them as they spoke.

"Papa, do to me what you've done to them." As she spoke, a breeze blew through the trees, rippling the pages of the Bible. When the breeze died away, she stared at the book as a shaft of moonlight slanted down through the trees, illuminating a piece of paper wedged so tightly into the crease of the book that it was nearly grafted to the pages.

She recognized Elizabeth's handwriting, small and steady despite what Eloise knew she would have felt upon writing it. Like the rest of the Bible, the page was wrinkled in spots from long since shed tears. But this one was different; the page was so wrinkled with tears, it was almost illegible. But if she focused, she could just make out each word.

<u>Satan's Lies</u>
Satin grins as I cry yet again.
He whispers,
'Don't fight it; you know that I'll win.
Don't get too comfortable with the heart you're
About to share;
This one is no different; they, too, do not care.
You do this every time; you think that they're
Your friend
So you pour out your heart, but the
Friendship will surely end.
So take my advice and sit here all alone
Lock the door and pretend you're not home
Put down the Bible and blow out the light
Lay your head on your pillow and give up the
Fight.'

By the end, Eloise's own tears made it impossible to read as they blurred her vision and mingled with the old tears dried into the pages. Every word penetrated her heart like shrapnel. She'd never seen her own thoughts on paper before. Never seen them spoken so clearly. *Satan's Lies* was written in dark, thick ink as if Elizabeth had traced over the words a dozen times over. "Lies," Eloise whispered. "Lies." They were lies. Nothing but lies. "Believe it," she cried. "Believe it's a lie. Oh Papa, please help me." None of the words were true. They were lies.

Beneath the poem, Elizabeth had written a list of dozens of scriptures. Flipping to the first one, Eloise read slowly. "Fearfully and wonderfully made." Flipping to the next, she read again. "I have called thee by thy name; thou art mine." Scripture after scripture, Elizabeth had set herself a reminder of who she was in Christ, and in the silence of the meadow, Eloise felt that small voice whisper:

That is who you are, beloved.

Forty-Three

Brooks tapped the wood of the table, his food untouched. He couldn't have eaten if he wanted to. When he could no longer sit, he stood and paced. "Papa, where is she? What is she doing? Let me go after her."

The woman hadn't been gone thirty minutes, but those minutes had passed like hours, and Brooks wasn't sure how much longer he could stand them.

When that small voice bid him to trust, Brooks bit his tongue against his retort. When had the woman earned his trust? It hadn't been five months since he'd found her in that creek. He still sat with her through every bath.

Trust me, beloved.

Brooks dropped to his knees. "How can I trust you to keep her safe? Where were you when she was in that tub the first time? Where were you every other time?" He knew his questioning wasn't fair. He knew God had been there, fighting for Eloise every step. But all Brooks could see was his wife's pale face, blue lips, and chattering teeth as she stepped out of the creek. The fear in her eyes and voice when he found her in the tub that first night.

"Papa, forgive me. But I can't lose her." She was engrained in him in ways he'd never thought possible. Months of marriage —even their arguments—had opened the doors to an intimacy that went far beyond their physical relationship. She had begun to open herself up to him in newer, deeper ways. He knew the ins and outs of who she was. From the way she talked in her sleep, almost more than she did when awake, to the time she spent as a

379

child convinced that if she tried hard enough, she'd be able to see the angels her nanny said looked over her. He knew what she hoped and dreamed for and the fears that came with them. "Papa, don't let her take herself from me."

When that voice finally bid him to go after her, Brooks stuffed his feet into his boots and ran toward the barn. Taking the first horse he could reach, he started toward the trees. Somehow, he knew she wasn't at the creek, and he could think of only one other place he might find her.

Listening to the small voice within him, Brooks didn't push the horse but kept him steady. In his hurry, he hadn't paid any mind to which horse he was grabbing, and it wasn't until now he realized it was Juniper. "Junie," he whispered. It was the first time the horse had let him ride her without bucking him off, and something in that eased his mind. Juniper was going to be ok, and since the beginning, Eloise and Juniper had grown in step.

By the time he reached the lake, Brooks could hear the woods coming alive. Morning was almost here.

"Elle?" When she didn't respond, Brooks hopped down and walked the perimeter. "Elle?" Beating down the rising fear, Brooks searched his mind for any other place she could be. Leaving Juniper, he started on the path that led to the cliffside.

By the time Brooks reached the end of the trail, the sky was beginning to show hints of pink and purple. "Elle." The name came in a rush of relief at the sight of her, seated cross-legged ten feet from the edge.

Eloise startled and looked back. "Brooks." When she held out her hand to him, Brooks took hold of it and sank down beside her. "I'm sorry," she said softly. "I didn't mean to scare you."

"I knew you were all right, Elle." And as he said it, he knew it was true. Even through the fear, some deeper part of him knew his wife was strong enough to fight. Moving behind her, he pulled her back against his chest, just as they had done every night of their honeymoon, watching the sun set below the mountains. "I found you just in time," Brooks whispered, watching the sun break the horizon.

"I was praying you would." Eloise melted into him, her head against his chest. "It was never on my mind, Brooks. I need you to know that."

"I know, Elle. But it doesn't make it easier. Fair or not, it's going to take time to trust that I can leave you."

Eloise smiled. "Well, we have all the time in the world." With the sun risen, she turned to face Brooks. "I'm done living like that, Brooks. I'm done hating myself. I'm done believing everyone will leave." Eloise faltered, doubt digging its greedy fingers into the peace she had steadily built within her. "I'm not saying it's going to be easy. But I think I'm finally ready to let go of the old."

Brooks looked into his young wife's face. He had seen determination in her before. But what he saw in her now was different. There was still fear and uncertainty, but within it all was a peace he'd never seen in her dark eyes. And he knew, right as the sun rose into the sky, that the truth he had spoken over Eloise endless times had found her: she had an army behind her. A King and all His horses.

Epilogue

Eloise smiled as Brooks wrapped his arms around her waist. Setting his chin in the crook of her neck, they watched their boys play in the churchyard.

Their oldest two, Simon and Elijah, came a month after her and Brooks' first anniversary. In the years that followed, they had Isaac, then Levi.

Four miracles. Four more reasons to keep her eyes on things above. A reminder Brooks whispered in her ear now, as he often did, amazed even fourteen years later that these children had been entrusted to them. That she got to watch them run across the pastures of the family ranch and help their father train and nurture the horses that came through.

"To think I almost missed them," she said softly. "That I almost missed this." Her fingers interlocked with her husband's. She breathed a prayer of gratitude to the God who, on a star-filled night fifteen years ago, had freed her of the deepest, darkest desire that had almost taken her life.

The years that followed had not been easy as she worked to let light shine within the darkest crevices of her mind. There had been doubts to squash. Pain to release. Pasts not to forget, for she could never forget, but to forgive. There had been mountains to climb and valleys to endure. There were oceans to cross and waves to swim through. But slowly, she learned to keep her head above water—hour by hour, day by day, week by week—until those storms, though not gone, grew farther between, each one weaker than the one before it.

But when those storm-tossed seas did come, and come they did, she reminded herself of the army beside her: Her husband, who never turned away no matter how ugly it was. Their boys who, by the grace of God, radiated nothing but joy. Her parents, who remained an example of what the Lord could do in broken people. Maisie and her husband Jeremy, whose church had come to be the place Eloise left her mistrust of pastors behind her. Rosalie, who wrote every chance she could and visited every year with her husband and three daughters. Even a horse, given to her when she had nothing else to live for, was proof—proof that the Lord's hand was over her life.

Eloise picked up their family Bible, full of notes and prayers, and glanced toward her children. Inspired by Elizabeth's Bible, Brooks had brought this Bible home when their oldest boys were still infants—a book where the family could share the scriptures and prayers that comforted their hurting hearts. Inspired by that morning's sermons, Eloise flipped to Isaiah 43:2 —*When thou passest through the waters, I will be with thee; and through the rivers, they shall not overflow thee.* Pen in hand, she let her eyes find her children and watched their smiling faces widen as their father came to them.

To my sweet boys – Keep your eyes on Him and swim with the waves.

Afterword

All the King's Horses is a story that has been in my heart for over ten years. With mental health struggles being something that runs very heavily within my family I knew I wanted to write something that gave voice to the millions out there struggling—especially within the church.

This story is very personal to me. So much of Eloise's story is my story, and while it's a vulnerable thing to share, I know her story belongs to so many more than just me. It belongs to the millions out there who have struggled and continue to struggle with a mind intent on ruining them.

Depression and anxiety is something scary and often very isolating. It can be scary to open up about suicidal ideation and suicidal thoughts when you never know how someone will respond. That is why I chose to go in the direction I did with this story. Because though I may never have moved beyond the thoughts and fear of the possibility, I know there are so many others out there who have and I wanted to show a side that we often don't see within fiction—the after. The story of picking up the pieces. That second chance at life and what God can do within the individuals that so many people see as beyond help.

Because no one is beyond help, least of all with Christ. My hope and prayer for All the King's Horses are that, for those who don't struggle, you will come away with a better understanding of mental health and how to love those who struggle.

For those who do struggle, I hope they come away with a renewed sense of hope and the reassurance that their struggles are not their fault—whether that be depression, anxiety, selective mutism, or the countless other disorders that exist out there. Health is health whether it's mental or physical. It can be good or bad, regardless of faith or action.

Acknowledgments

I want to start by thanking my incredible mom. You have always been my rock, my best friend, and my biggest supporter. Without you, Lily and Elizabeth wouldn't be who they are.

Thank you to my dad. You may not be a reader but you have been one of my biggest cheerleaders since I first started writing!

Thank you to my Grandma Sally. You are always the first one to read my books and always have nothing but kind words and encouragement—reminding me, when I begin to doubt that the Lord gave me a purpose in writing.

Thank you to my brother and the rest of my family. Without your help and support, this book might never have made it out.

A special thank you to Caitlin Miller, my editor, and friend. You made the process of getting this book into the world so much easier! Thank you so much for your kind words and encouragement!

Thank you to my writer friends who have been so encouraging throughout this process.

Thank you to my sweet little dog-child, Oliver! I love your sweet snuggles when you sense my stress.

Finally and most importantly, thank you, Jesus! God, you have been there through everything, gently reminding me of Who I belonged to when the world tried to discourage me. Without you, I would have nothing. Thank you for being close to the broken-hearted!

About Author

Faith R. Mathewson grew up in Oregon and has been certifiably obsessed with stories for as long as she can remember. She tried her hand at writing at sixteen and hasn't stopped since. Faith loves Jesus and seeks to create stories and characters that glorify Him. Photography, coffee, and snuggling her dog-child Oliver, are just a few of her favorite things.

Made in the USA
Middletown, DE
06 December 2023

44864778R00234